John De Búrca

The Last Five Swords

First Published 2022 by PerchedCrowPress
An imprint of Philip Hughes Publishing

Source photos by Shutterstock. Alex_Maryna, artdock.

Special thanks to the sword artists:

Dwayne Moloney
Anthony O'Doherty (RIP)

For Fiona, Culann, Farra and Ísa,
and the Carragh Hill Burkes.

Thank you, Phil, for the belief.

Contents

Preamble

The Cast

Some characters you will encounter:

Cathal - *Kah hal* (Island inhabitant and nephew of Dathí Ó Madagáin)

Cónán -*koh-nawn* (Son of Morna. Fianna legend of infamy)

Caoilte - *cweeltia* (Fianna legend. Heroic and noble warrior)

Darragh - *dara* (Ruffian from the village of Ros Cam)

Dathí - *Doh hee* (Island inhabitant and uncle of Cathal Ó Madagáin)

Donnacha - *Don achah* (Travelling bowman and adventurer)

Eimear - *eemur* (Mysterious hermit. Past member of the Fianna)

Éine - *ayna* (File cú – Poet and coward. Past member of the Fianna)

Eoghan - *Owen* (from the village of Clochbeag)

Fergheal - *Fur gal* (Powerful Druid)

Laoise - *Lee shah* (Granddaughter of Caoilte and canny warrior)

Mac Áodh - *mock ae* (Legendary lucky person)

Mac Cumhal - *mock coo'al* (Son of Cumhal)

Moghrudh - *mou-er* (Ancient druid and General)

Ó Maolmhuaidh - *o may-leah* (Unattractive inn-keep)

Olfhainn - *ohllann* (More attractive and fair-minded inn-keep)

Rhíona -*reeona* (Mysterious young woman up a tree)

Rúadhan - *Roo-awn* (from the village of Clochbeag)

Uad - *Owad* * a mysterious villain

LANGUAGE

Here is a list of some of the words you will come across from the Irish language, Gaeilge:

Cailleach – *kay lee ak* * witch - an old woman or hag, known as The Queen of Winter or the Veiled One.

Clochbeag - *Clochbeug* (don't forget to clear the throat for ch) * a village in the west

Draíocht - *dree-ocht* * magic

Éireann - *air ahn* * archaic name for Ireland

Fae Rí - *Fae ree* * Fairy king

Geis - *gas* * a magical utterance of command – plural geasa

Gruagachs - *grooh a gak* * of the Fae, protectors of cattle

Léine - *lay na* * a soft linen shirt

Ros Cam - *ross cam* * a settlement in the west

Samhain - *sa win* * Celtic harvest festival

Scéalaí - *shkaylee* * a storyteller

Sciortáin - *skirt awn* * a tick

Seanchaí - *shan kwee* * a stroyteller

Taoíseach - *thee shuck* * a chieftain

Triús - *troos* * trousers

Túath - *thoo-ah* (the ú sound as in oo) * a district

Uisneach - *ush-neeach* * a town in the midlands

THE LAST FIVE SWORDS

CHANGE

***

Of Eoghan and Rúadhan, two boys who leave their home to make amends for causing trouble. They find themselves getting into more serious bother than they are accustomed to.

Bíonn cead cainte ag fear caillte na himeartha.

The man who has lost the match has permission to talk.

***

A group of braying and troublesome boys swaggered into the drinkery.

Those gathered in the darkened hut cast darker glances toward the noise. The young woman *scéalaí*, standing by the cosy firepit, had been lost in her telling of the deeds of Filí, Rúadh, and Aire, the three legs upon which the cauldron of the world stood.

The storyteller's voice strained to be heard over the din. Eoghan hadn't been listening anyway.

Many of the audience bristled visibly at such improper conduct under the roof of their host, yet none would quarrel in the house of another. Some were nearly unseated as the boys barged past. The young lady cut short her story and sat down, back straight and eyes brimming.

'It's the lads from the hurling match. If they see us, we're in bother,' Rúadhan whispered.

Eoghan sat and stared at them in the darkness. His friend was stating the obvious. Losing the match would have been a thing in itself, but the fact that the same lads had lost the fight after the match made it more of a thing.

Rúadhan scanned the drinking house, hands rubbing his thighs.

The hosteller moved to intercept the boys. Though he was a fine lump of a man with a stern eye and a serious brow, his awkward movements upon approaching the new arrivals told a story of unhappiness. Eoghan looked for an escape as the hosteller spoke to the rowdy intruders.

'Accept my pardon, my lads, but you are disrupting the entertainment and disturbing my guests this evening. If you wish to settle here, you are as welcome as spring after winter, but you cannot stay and continue behaving as you are.' The boys stopped what they were doing and looked at him.

Other patrons shifted in their seats and quickly started to finish drinks. One of the brightly garbed youngsters peeled away from the group and slowly moved towards the hosteller, squaring up so that their faces were close.

Eoghan counted seven boys. Two were dressed noticeably unlike their peers. They wore clothes of many bright colours, which showed wealth and status. They also wore the unmistakable sneer of entitlement. Even more worrisome, many of the boys bore signs of the earlier melee.

'I think you'll find it is you who is disturbing us, Olfhainn,' growled the leader 'And I want you to get us something to drink to make up for it.' One of his friends cast a challenging gaze across the room.

Eoghan met the boy's gaze with a defiant look. Though his eyes were a soft brown, he had long perfected the appearance of a mean-spirited soul. *Might as well give him a scare,* he thought, stretching out his broad shoulders.

The boy who scanned the room's mouth dropped open as he spotted Eoghan and Rúadhan. He moved to pat the chief troublemaker on the shoulder. 'Darragh...' he whispered.

Darragh's gaze was locked to Olfhainn's in a silent battle of wills. Custom and tradition aside, both obviously knew each other. For some reason, Olfhainn was not immediately clipping Darragh's ear as the onlookers might have expected.

Darragh rounded on his insistent companion. 'What?' he barked.

His companion just pointed at Eoghan and Rúadhan. Realisation dawning, Olfhainn was forgotten and the boys surrounded their new prey.

'Well, by the luck of Mac Áodh, look who came to visit. Two of the warrior hurlers of *Clochbeag*. But only two. What brings ye to these parts, warrior hurlers of *Clochbeag*? To conquer the men of *Ros Cam* and carry our women off with ye?' He gulped from a mug he had taken from a table. The slur of the boy's talk was more noticeable. 'They won the match, don't ye all know? But only through being cheating whoresons.'

It was not obvious who he was addressing.

'Not satisfied with just that, though. No. Not these lads. Them and their gang, they jumped us; attacked us as if they had planned it. Lucky that they caught us on the hop as they did, or we would have given them the same hiding they gave us.'

'Darragh. I'll not have you causing trouble like this. And I don't give a white owl's hoot who your father is,' growled Olfhainn.

This time Darragh would not be distracted. He pointed a finger at the hosteller without averting his gaze from Eoghan and Rúadhan. Two of the local boys intercepted Olfhainn and restrained him. Other guests began to leave.

'No bother from here, Olfhainn,' said Rúadhan. 'Here, boys, you can finish our drink and no harm caused. Now, Eoghan, it's time for us to go and—'

'Shut your face, you lanky son of an old bitch.' The room went deathly silent.

Olfhainn said in a hard voice, 'My lad, if you raise a hand to one of those boys by my firepit, I will kill you stone dead and let your father walk backways to the Underland.'

Olfhainn could not see it from where he stood, but Eoghan did not miss the spasm of rage that flashed across Darragh's face.

'Drag them outside,' Darragh said, turning to face the drinkery's keeper. They exchanged growled words as the six other *Ros Cam* boys dragged Eoghan and Rúadhan outside.

They were quickly surrounded, preventing them from an easy escape. Darragh emerged, red-faced, surveying the situation with a sneer made more ominous by the lengthening shadows.

'Ye made a great job taking us by surprise at the match,' said Darragh, rubbing his swollen jaw.

A growing sense of anger crept over Eoghan.

'You yapping little bitch,' he said as calmly as he could manage, despite his temper rising. He stood at his tallest, though still shorter than most of the lads his age. His broad shoulders and thick arms would surely give them second thoughts. 'You spoiled, frightened fool. Without this titsucking rabble around you, I would make you cry. Bawl and weep and snivel like the child you are. Do you know I had a tooth stuck in my hand after the fight?' He held it up to show them the fresh scar. 'Was it yours I wonder?'

Rúadhan smiled a politely deflecting smile as if the boys might not have heard Eoghan's jibes. His pale, freckled face was a picture of innocence.

'Right,' he said, moving a little in front of Eoghan. 'So—'

'Silence,' Darragh roared.

With little chance of things improving, Eoghan threw his head back and laughed bitterly.

'We came all this way to apologise for giving ye're skins a tanning after we won the hurling match. And now you're pissy? When ye ran off home to your mothers' legs, you weren't roaring at anyone. I hardly heard any of ye speak as it so happens.'

'Look,' said Rúadhan quickly, hands raised as if Eoghan hadn't spoken.

'Things have gone sour, there's no doubt. We've been sent by our own elders to apologise for the match and what happened after. It wasn't your first match and it wasn't your first bit of a row either. This is not the right way, lads. We were going to go to see the chieftain after a quick drink. We've already been in trouble with our own elders.

'We'll leave now and stay in the sparehouse tonight with whatever travellers are passing. We can fix things with the chieftain in the morning. Or even, let's go to your chieftain now altogether. You can join us and we'll set this straight,' continued Rúadhan. 'And you may not be aware of Eoghan's recent loss of his father.'

He shook his head slowly, making a near comical attempt at a saddened face, before adding, 'A blow far worse than any you might be tempted to land.'

Growling suddenly, one of the rival lads who sported two blackened eyes marched towards Rúadhan with his fist raised. Eoghan cut his progress short with a punch. The boy was unconscious before he started his fall to the ground.

'So, that's probably not going to settle things,' Rúadhan said to himself with a nervous laugh. Eoghan scanned the faces of the circle around him to identify any empathetic souls. There were none. That's when things became unpleasant.

TWO BOYS GO ON A JOURNEY

***

The two youngsters have no choice but to flee into the countryside. It is the beginning of a great adventure.

Go n-éirí an bóthar leat is do chosán cóngair.

May the road rise to meet you and your path be short.

***

The *Ros Cam* boys rushed in all at once, throwing punches and kicks, pulling hair and arms. Eoghan did his best to defend himself and even be the cause of an injury or two, but the numbers were against them, and he started to take damage. A punch to his temple and a blow to his stomach saw him fall in a heap. He noticed Rúadhan curled up in a ball beside him. Kicks started landing on both of them.

Olfhainn came to their aid once again. Eoghan was becoming a great admirer of the hosteller, who had a hurl with him and used the flat to redden a few of the local boys' arses and move them clear. Face red from exertion, he reached to remove Darragh from the fray, grabbing the boy by the scruff of his neck and throwing him to the ground. A few more swings of the hurl re-established the same broad circle as before – only the initial offender was still down, stirring limply. Both Eoghan and Rúadhan were lying on the ground. Olfhainn stood over them as their protector.

Eoghan's face felt like it had borne most of the ill will meted out by the *Ros Cam* boys. He stood, holding his father's hunting knife in front of him, sure his father would not have approved. Eoghan no longer cared. His father had died four days before.

He reached out a hand to his friend. Rúadhan took it and managed to stand; tall and gangly; looking indignant. He was blinking back tears from his pale blue eyes.

It was Olfhainn's turn to growl. 'That's that. It's time for you all to go home. Now.

'If there is any further violence done, I will match it equally and do worse. That goes for each and every one of you. And that means you will need to put the knife away, young man. You will not need it, and you've made a mistake drawing it.'

No one moved. Eoghan was unsure how to proceed. Rúadhan tugged once at his arm and moved, walking directly past Darragh, almost close enough to brush shoulders.

Eoghan followed but was less inclined towards a quiet end. His brush of shoulders ended up more like a shoulder charge that landed the *Ros Cam* boy on the flat of his back. Eoghan's fist crashed down before Olfhainn's hurl could fly. The first punch snapped the boy's head back; the second punch caused the boy's nose to break; the third released an eruption of bloody spluttering.

'Bitch,' Eoghan spat.

By the time the droplets of blood landed, Eoghan and Rúadhan were already mid-sprint, heading through the gate for the outer edge of the settlement. Eoghan followed Rúadhan as his friend ducked between two houses, not bothering to check whether they were being pursued. They leapt over two fences, ran through a fallow field, over another fence and through a field of curious sheep. The last wall they hurdled delivered them into an orchard. They stopped, hands on their knees, breathing heavily.

'Is this the direction home?' Eoghan finally asked as he peeked over the wall.

'Is this the direction...? How would I know that any more than you would know that, you angry prick?'

'Shh with your moaning.' Eoghan listened and could make out raised voices close by, with activity to match. Several fired brands became visible through some of the buildings. They were being hunted.

'What do we do?' asked Rúadhan

'Hide here until either later this evening or tomorrow morning and go home fast. Did I just feel...'

Tiny droplets of misty drizzle started to land on their skin. Rúadhan sighed loudly.

'I am delighted that it is raining,' he said, voice flat. 'That will really add to the charm of the whole evening perfectly.' He held out a very healthy-looking apple to Eoghan. 'However, there are these.'

Eoghan was pleased. *It's about time for our luck to improve.* The boys grabbed what they could from the low-hanging branches.

'Look,' shouted a voice a little bit too close for comfort. 'They went through the grain field there. They're in the grain fields. Hey. They're in the orchard.'

The two boys took off running again.

They walked or ran in silence for the most part, as well as they could. Sounds of pursuit faded to none after a time, but they kept moving for fear.

Eoghan squinted into the night, then back to his friend.

Rúadhan's tall, thin figure was cloaked almost entirely in shadow as they walked; a picture of contemplation. A sheen of drizzle was visible on his shaved head. A bout of head lice in his house had resulted in Rúadhan's near scalping at the hands of his well-meaning father and an overly sharpened blade. Several picked scabs still dotted his wet and cold-looking head. His handsome face, which was so quick to smile, was hidden.

Rúadhan turned to look at him.

'All things considered. This is a pain in the hole.'

Eoghan grumbled. It was. They had gone on long enough and were well lost. Going back to *Ros Cam* was out of the question. They would just have to go home and report their failure and accept the punishment. Finding their way back on track in the morning would be a job. For now, however, that track was getting no closer.

'Better find somewhere to sleep.'

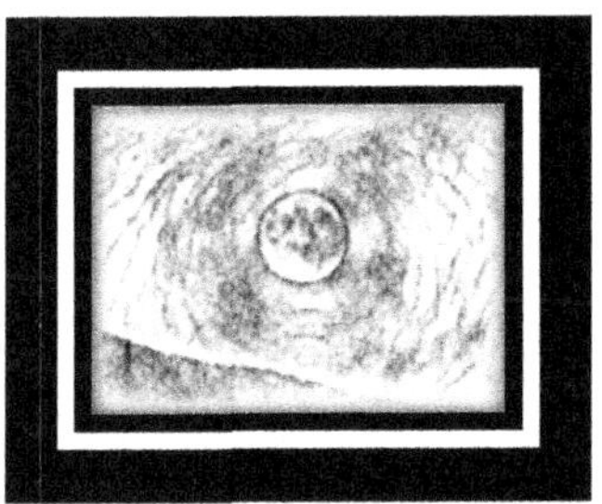

A NIGHT UNDER THE MOON

***

The boys witness a terrible deed. They meet an unexpected person in an unexpected place.

Is ait an mac an saol.

Life is a strange son.

***

The thick drizzle was incessant. Though the scant shelter the boys had found under an ancient solitary oak had been close to comfortable, to begin with, the damp chill began to creep through Eoghan's bones.

'I suppose we had better not chance a fire,' Rúadhan said.

Eoghan grunted. He wondered where they were. *Maybe if we just go back to Ros Cam, those lads will surely be asleep by now.* That said, he had recently come across a relatively comfortable spot of ground and was afraid to move. A thought niggled at him. *Anywhere but home.*

'Do you think they're still looking for us in this pissy weather?' Rúadhan asked, his voice hollow. 'No, they're gone home to play with their white pudding in their warm beds,' he answered himself.

He sat upright. 'I'm lighting a fire.'

Eoghan grunted again. *If I don't move, maybe he'll just make it.* Rúadhan's boot lashed out at his arse. 'Help me, would you, you useless, grumpy, self-absorbed shite?'

Eoghan sat up and surveyed his surroundings. The night sky had begun to change: thick clouds were backlit by silvery light. The hilly wooded terrain around them seemed ominous as shadows played their slow, silent games. Still, it would protect them from any nasty winds the night might send their way.

The boys worked together to light a fire. Neither was a noted woodsman, but years of working on the edges of the forests of the west had left them with some basic skills.

As they worked, Eoghan heard noises that caused him to freeze and look up at his friend, panic-stricken. Horses. Which meant riders. Perhaps the village boys were not yet abed. Access to horses at their age was unheard of, however. Eoghan felt like lying down. *Who is this father of Darragh's? The King of all the world?*

'What do we do?' asked Rúadhan.

'Shh,' urged Eoghan. He looked around him, eyes wide.

'Get up the tree,' he whispered.

'We'll be trapped,' Rúadhan whispered back.

They scattered the evidence of their labour and climbed the tree to the middle branches – no mean feat under the circumstances.

They let the shadows and shelter of the trees cover them like a blanket.

The sounds remained. The riders were not moving quickly and seemed to have come no closer. The boys strained their necks without disturbing the branches, trying to see through the leaves, drizzle and darkness. They spotted the torches just as they heard someone shouting.

'Ho there, young men. It is a strange evening to be gallivanting, is it not?' spoke a voice, still a long way off. Eoghan froze. *How were we seen?*

'And armed to the teeth, I see. Are you invading somewhere?'

There was an unpleasant harshness to the laugh that the riders let out, but it was becoming clear that the voice wasn't addressing Eoghan or Rúadhan.

'It's a strange time of the evening to be out hunting, too,' replied a familiar, defiant voice. Darragh. He and his friends must have been close and surprisingly good at tracking.

There was a singular hearty laugh; no more laughter from the others.

'Indeed, young sir. It is that. If I might ask, however, have you crossed paths with a young woman around your own age this soft evening? She is lost and very dear to us, and any assistance would be greatly appreciated.'

Eoghan adjusted himself slowly to better make out some of what was happening.

'We saw no woman. For a few rings, we can help you find her.' It was one of the other boys who spoke. 'We know the area and all the nooks and crannies. It's too late to be out trotting without putting the horses' legs and your necks in danger. You don't want her to be out at night all by herself, do you?'

The horsemen, numbering ten, were spreading out in a circle. 'I would not be so concerned for her safety if I were in your place, my poor boy.' An ominous cackle from his fellow riders followed the man's words. 'And what's this you say about rings?'

Another rider spoke. 'Ungus. We were told not to be seen by anyone in *Ros Cam*. We cannot risk the wrath of Uad. We saw what happened to Cearbradh and his men.'

'Well…' said Darragh, quieter. 'We'll go home now and leave you to your work in peace. Goodnight to you all.'

'No, my young friend,' said Ungus. 'You most certainly will not. My friend here is most correct. We don't want people to know we are here. Ongoing politics and such. Life can be hardest on the young.'

Eoghan watched through the branches in utter disbelief as the slaughter began. Spears stabbed, and swords swung. Each swing dragged eruptions of blood and innards away from young bodies. With difficulty, the boys craned to watch the strange scene unfold. The drizzle came down in murky waves, trying to gently wash away the evidence. The turmoil quieted when only one village boy remained.

'The girl,' asked Ungus. 'Have you seen her or not? Speak honestly, and I will let you home. If I feel you are spilling lies, I will chop your head off.'

‘P-p-pleasssee s-s-sir… we s-s-saaww nooo g-g-g-girl.’

There was a moment of quiet before Ungus’s sword swung cleanly through the boy’s neck, causing his head to fly and hit off one of the horses’ flanks. The horse whinnied in apparent disgust but made no move.

‘I believe him,’ Ungus muttered. ‘This poxy evening is starting to make me irritated.’

‘Let’s go back to the camp. We’ll find nothing now, Ungus, and I badly need to mount someone,’ pleaded one of the others.

‘Mount yourself,’ came the angry retort. There was a long pause.

‘The Ros of Cam is too large to be drawing attention to ourselves for now. And we don’t need any more ill favour or punishment like Cearbradh and the lads,’ said Ungus. ‘That said, I have no interest in lying out this night, and the bitch’s trail is gone cold. To camp. We’ll search around this area in the morning or until we hear something from himself.’

The efficiency with which the warriors retreated into the night was cold and indifferent. Neither Eoghan nor Rúadhan spoke nor moved for some time.

‘What do we do?’ Eoghan eventually whispered, shaking uncontrollably. ‘What is happening, Rúadhan? Rúadhan?’

‘It’s you Ungus is looking for, isn’t it?’ said Rúadhan in a strange voice.

‘What?’ said Eoghan, in complete confusion.

Rúadhan was looking further up into the branches of the tree. Eoghan’s eyes followed upward. There was a bundle of rags above them. Eoghan saw teary eyes looking down. He almost fell from the tree in shock and amazement. His hand shot out to grab onto Rúadhan's arm. Rúadhan let out a hiss with the effort but ensured Eoghan slipped no further.

'P-p-perhaps you could light your f-f-fire after all,' said the bundle, a girl. 'I am very c-c-cold.'

The two looked at each other in the pale light. A kestrel in a nest somewhere nearby tittered at the boys' unfolding situation.

Once down from the tree, getting comfortable was as difficult as before, compounded by the addition of a filthy girl wearing tattered dresses, who was more miserable than the two combined. She sat solemnly with her back to the tree. Every now and then, the sound of her teeth chattering jarred him, but Eoghan would not allow the fire to be lit. Rúadhan made no argument, sitting silently, looking out into the evening.

Eoghan used his knife to core the apples, handing her most of what was left.

'Who are you?'

'My name is Rhíona.'

'They were looking for you?'

She cradled her knees to her chest and nodded.

'Why?'

The darkness and shadows were playing tricks, but she seemed to be regarding him from behind her knees. She glanced at Rúadhan and then back again.

Eoghan could not make out the colour of her hair nor the colour of her eyes. The eyes, however, seemed enormous, alien. Something about her face, though shrouded by the night, made his heart beat quicker.

'It is a difficult thing to explain,' she continued, 'and probably not something you two need to know about. Whoever you are.'

Rúadhan cleared his throat, and spoke softly, not looking directly at her.

'I am Rúadhan. He's Eoghan. We're from around here. There's not much else to tell. You?' When he turned to look at her, her face was shadowed.

She bowed her head into her knees for a moment.

'My father has sent them after me,' she said. 'He is… not from around here. They are men of the mercenary leader, Uad, who is in my father's service.'

'Why? Why did you leave your father? Why has he sent killers after you?' Eoghan's voice sounded harsh in his own ears.

'He seeks to stop me from doing what I have been sent to do.'

'Why speak in riddles? Why not tell us?'

'I have no reason to trust you. Either of you,' she said harshly. 'Why are you here? Up the same tree as I am?' She nodded her head towards Rúadhan. 'I can believe he is from these parts, but you? With dark eyes and sallow skin? That I find less easy to believe. Who are you really, and what are you both doing out here?'

Rúadhan snorted. 'We all wonder about his dark eyes and sallow skin. We used to joke about his father wondering about…' He stopped with a click of his tongue, and looked at Eoghan, teeth bared in an awkward smile.

Eoghan sighed, far too tired to care. *What are we doing here?*

'We started a fight after a hurling match with boys from *Ros Cam*,' said Eoghan and went on to tell her about the hurling match. He told her about the fight he had started and Rúadhan had joined. He told her they were sent to *Ros Cam* because the *Taoíseach* thought it fit that Eoghan and Rúadhan should travel and apologise to the *Taoíseach* and team from the *Túath.* Though the boys would normally have been delighted with an excuse to make the half-day-long journey to the fort, this particular visit had filled them with a sense of dread.

The match had been proceeding as normal until Eoghan's bad-tempered use of his shoulder to knock a player off the ball before he scored the winning goal. After the match Eoghan was informed that because of his foul play, many noses were out of joint, both figuratively and literally.

When he finished speaking, he looked across at the girl who was asleep against the tree.

Eoghan found himself staring at her. *She is beautiful.*

Without much talk, the boys took it in turns to stand watch while the other two slept. No one mentioned the bodies lying across the way.

During his watch, Eoghan searched the bodies. He didn't think Rúadhan would be up to the task and had far more experience with death. His grandparents. His baby brothers. His Father. It was a grim task. Eoghan thought it justice to relieve the *Ros Cam* boys of their three best cloaks and a few copper rings. There was little else of worth. He saw no reason to take their knives or hurls.

When he returned to the camp, he covered himself and the others with cloaks. Because the girl was still shivering, he gave her his cloak and tried to shield her from the night. As he settled down for the rest of his watch, Eoghan arranged himself so that he could wake the others in a hurry.

He drew his father's knife to examine it. In his home the evening before he left, his mother had called to him as the fire burned low. She gave him a small bundle during an increasingly rare moment of clarity on her slow journey into madness. Eoghan had opened it to find the hunting knife. The hilt was plain wood that was grip-ridged. The sheath was plain, with no ornate markings but good quality leather. Eoghan's knowledge of metalwork was rudimentary, but there was a gleam of something that made him instantly value the thing. She had said a few short words before falling into sleep, 'It was your father's and now it's yours.'

Sheathing it, Eoghan sighed. He would never lead an army or defeat a mighty foe with it, but it had already proved useful and would surely do so in the future.

Eoghan grimaced in the dark as he thought of his mother. How her face had changed over the years. He had spent a long time hoping for things to go back to the way they had been before the death of his brothers. She had faded, dying slowly, while his father was away more and more often. For a long time, Eoghan had hoped his da would come to help her, to become more than a distant adventurer. Eoghan's grimace turned to a frown. Frowning, his eyes closed and he went to sleep.

THE ARRIVAL OF DAWN

***

Without any way of knowing where they are, the three seek cover in the forest. They meet a herd of giant deer which is not a common occurrence.

Is maol gualainn gan bhráthair.

A shoulder without a friend is undefended.

***

Stiff bodies, curled around softly glowing embers, started to stir as the nearby birds sang to welcome the sun's arrival. It took some time for Eoghan to shake off the night. Not a word was uttered until the three stood, looking at one another.

Rúadhan spoke first, his tone sombre. 'We need to move, leaving as little mark of our passing as we can. It makes sense to assume that they will start where they left off, which is here, and that they are already on their way. Any arguments against leaving this place right away?'

‘I can leave by a different route than you mean to take. They will not hunt you, and you have a chance to get away.’ The girl spoke slowly. Her enormous eyes were blue, and her soft lips were distracting. She was caked in dirt. Her long brown hair showed evidence of hard travel.

Eoghan watched her. She was as grim as the morning sky.

There is likely to be more in store for her.

He was about to speak when Rúadhan chimed in. ‘They will, won’t they? We all know it. They will hunt us and kill us. I also suspect they are not the only ones looking for you?’ He paused to allow for argument. None was forthcoming.

‘Hmm,’ Rúadhan nodded. ‘We will have to leave you go, I’m afraid. None of us wants to be found, but those boys were... killed for nothing, and we will be killed the same if they come upon us out here… especially if we are with you. It may sound heartless, but perhaps then there is a way for us to walk away from this, Rhíona. Do you know someone who can help you?’

Eoghan continued watching the girl as his friend spoke. She stood looking at the ground, but he could tell her mind was working frantically.

‘I need to get to *Uisneach*,’ she said, ‘past Midlakes and the Great River and there find a man called Éine Mac Éine. Perhaps… Perhaps if you help me get there, I will get you silver so that you may make your way home safe and wealthy. Consider it gainful employment.’

‘Silver?’ said Rúadhan.

‘Silver rings.’

'Silver rings.' Rúadhan repeated the words as if saying them for the first time. Looking at his friend, his lips pursed for a moment.

'Silver rings do change things a bit. Eoghan, how far away is that *Uisneach* place?'

Eoghan stood looking at him in disbelief. 'How in the name of Fionn Mac Cumhal should I know that, you complete arse?'

Rhíona's head snapped up to look at him.

'Oh, eh, I am very... eh ... apologetic for being the user of such coarse language in front... in the eh, presence of… a... young lady...'

'It is east of us. I am sure of that,' said Rúadhan, before shaking his head. 'Wait. What am I going on about? Sorry, Rhíona. I am. It's just that we have to get back. We have to let them know what happened here. If those killers ride into our home or even *Ros Cam*, they could destroy either or both. Thank you for the offer of silver, but we're in danger here. Proper actual danger.'

'Could you not just come with us?' Eoghan asked. 'Even if we went back to *Ros Cam*? They should surely be told what happened. Someone should know.'

'Let's just get home and let the chieftains deal with it. You can come with us even, Rhíona. Let's just go.' Rúadhan turned to walk away. He moved in the opposite direction from where the bodies lay.

'We can track back the way the boys came, Rúadhan. We can do that. We saw what they did, and we certainly can't let this girl be found. We have to do the right thing here. We'll be safe in *Ros Cam,*' Eoghan's voice was raw.

Rúadhan turned. 'I just want to go home,' he said softly.

I don't, Eoghan wanted to reply. He stopped himself and turned to face Rhíona, but she was walking towards the forest cover. He and Rúadhan exchanged glances. Eoghan's unease was increasing rapidly.

'Hey girl,' he called. He trudged off after her, frustration mounting. 'Wait, would you?'

Rhíona spun on her heel. Her cheeks were flushed. 'I made you an offer. You said no. Your friend is correct. You are in danger and should go home. Fare well.'

'Come with us,' Eoghan implored. 'What's wrong with that? You can go towards *Uisneach* from *Ros Cam*.'

Her blue eyes were cold, making him feel very alive.

'The safest thing for anyone here, anyone you know or love, is for me to be gone. I am the singular cause of danger. Once I leave, they will follow me.'

'How much silver then?' Eoghan said. He wanted to go with her. Anywhere. Anywhere but home.

'What?' asked Rhíona.

'What?' cried Rúadhan.

Turning to his friend, Eoghan spoke frankly. 'Maybe I should help her get away.'

Rúadhan clearly couldn't believe what he was hearing. 'Eoghan. What are you doing? We have to go home. We're not warriors. We're not guides. We're young lads. That's all.'

Eoghan looked at the girl. 'How much silver?'

Rúadhan raised his voice. 'Eoghan.'

Eoghan rounded on him. 'I'm not going home,' he snarled. 'Not now. I'm going to leave. There's a world out there, and I can make a living and come back when I'm someone proper. Head off if you like.' He turned towards Rhíona. 'You heard me. How many rings?'

'Ten silver rings,' she said, back straightening.

'Ten?' the boys asked together. It was a fortune.

'It will only take a few days walking,' said Rhíona softly. 'I think. I'm not so sure. I'm not sure…' Her lip started quivering, and she covered her face.

'Let's go anyway. We'll come across somewhere or someone and get help then. I don't think you will need me all the way, maybe, but you said ten. So, you'd better give me ten,' said Eoghan and set out in the direction of where the sun had risen not long before.

The girl stared at his back, mouth agape.

'We need to find cover,' said Eoghan as he marched, focused. 'They'll be looking for... you… us… well, you but me as well, until the rings are in my hand.'

Rhíona was about to speak when Rúadhan suddenly stomped past her, muttering. '...thick-headed arsehole. If his da wasn't just in the ground, I would knock him over and…'

'I can hear you,' growled Eoghan.

'We live in a land almost entirely covered in forest. Let's walk fast, get under cover and keep walking fast,' said Rhíona.

Eoghan turned to Rhíona. 'Look. If you've managed to evade people like that, you can guide us to safety.' He glanced at Rúadhan, who was trailing them tight-lipped and frowning. Eoghan was relieved his friend had decided to come but did not mention it.

'Let's go together and have it done,' Eoghan said. 'I'm sure you want to get home, and so does Rúadhan, so the sooner that's done, the better.'

Rhíona's lips twitched downward. 'I do want to go home,' she sighed.

Rúadhan shrugged. 'I don't know how I'm standing here. Or why I'm saying this, but,' he looked at Eoghan for a moment, 'let's go if we're going."

Eoghan felt the tension in his shoulders ease a little.

They set off at as quick a pace as they could manage. As Rhíona promised, it wasn't long before they were swallowed by the protection of the forest. Their passage was slower, but they all felt far more at ease to be out of the open meadows.

Drizzle returned as the day went on. As soon as the apples were finished, the walk was punctuated by long bouts of silence.

Eoghan's heart was heavy. The same drizzle had sent the boys on their way the morning before. The elders watched Eoghan leave with pity in their eyes. He knew they felt the trip would take his mind off his father's death, and perhaps lighten his sadness.

Eoghan had left, wanting never to return.

As the morning wore on, they came upon a large herd of giant deer, and the boys were cowed by their size. It was a humbling experience to stand before the great gathering of enormous animals. Graceful and strong, the deer made no move to retreat. It was likely that they rarely came upon people in their forest.

'It's a shame I don't have a bow. We could eat well this evening,' said Rúadhan.

Eoghan rolled his eyes. Even if Rúadhan were standing up to his waist in the middle of the herd, he was unlikely to hit a single thing with a bow and arrow, only his own arse.

He looked at Rhíona, who appeared deeply aggrieved at the thought of shooting the deer. She said something he couldn't make out and altered her course to head for the herd. The boys stopped to look on. Rúadhan barked a laugh, and Eoghan called out to stop her.

'Have a think before you traipse over there. You may scare them.' Nothing. 'Hey there, come back with us, please. Rhíona.'

Rhíona continued walking towards the deer, and Eoghan grew nervous. There must have been close to one hundred deer spread out amongst the trees, many larger than carthorses with vicious-looking antlers.

Scores turned to face the filth-covered girl as she approached. None moved, though a few that were lying down stood. One notable exception was the sliver-streaked buck whose antlers had thirty points if they had two. He was at least twenty hands tall and looked like he must weigh the same as ten hardy men. And he was walking out to meet Rhíona.

The boys stood in open-mouthed amazement as she moved to within paces of the animal and knelt, eyes cast downwards in a servile display. Eoghan heard her say something. That is to say, noises came from her, though he couldn't make them out or make sense of what they meant.

The buck circled Rhíona once and stopped in front of her. His nose ruffled through her hair and snuffled noisily and wetly from the sounds of it. She continued making strange noises, and the buck appeared to listen. When she stopped, she bowed her head further.

The buck roared in response, a long bellow that commanded attention. The boys were startled by the noise and leapt in fright. Another head ruffle, and the buck turned and walked away. He roared again, this one loud and barked. The herd disappeared into the trees. Moments later, there was nothing left of them except dung and the echoes of their exchanging roars.

Eoghan stared at Rhíona as she walked, almost skipping, back to them with a beaming smile.

Rúadhan seemed like he might erupt into cheers. Eoghan, on the other hand, was entirely incredulous.

'What... was... that?' he asked. 'What did you... do? How did... you... Have you lost your mind?'

'Eoghan, we are travelling in their domain. It is only right to honour them and ask for permission to pass through, do you not think?' She wore a mischievous smile. 'I am sure that if they came to visit your home, they would do the same.'

'Ask for permission? Ask a deer for permission?' Eoghan stopped himself short of shouting. 'He could have crushed you. Or gored you. Or trampled you. It was a deer. How can you ask a deer for anything?'

'Just like that,' she smiled and started walking. Eoghan turned to face Rúadhan.

'Aren't you going to say anything instead of standing there in such open admiration? You look like a plant.'

'I think it was an excellent idea.'

'What?'

'Well, I think it is a very important thing to have in this world, you know, Eoghan.'

'What is a very important thing to have?'

'Dear, deer friends.' Rúadhan walked past his friend with a smirk and winked at Rhíona, who was writhing with laughter.

Eoghan's stomach started to make curious noises at him, not unlike the roars of the deer. He knew they would need to find water soon too. As they walked, they started foraging. Goose grass was plentiful this time of year but might lead to loose bowels, so they avoided the temptation to take too much. They took some young dandelions, with leaves for eating raw and roots for roasting. Wood sorrel and a haul of oyster mushrooms were a great find by Rhíona. Her face turned cold when Rúadhan noted how well they would go with some tasty venison.

They amassed a respectable number of edible leaves combined with enough mushrooms and dandelion roots to make a nutritious, if not filling meal, for all of them. The next job was to find water. As they walked, Eoghan and Rúadhan asked her questions that she did not answer.

Rhíona stopped regularly to smell a leaf or a flower or observe an insect or a bird. Eoghan caught himself staring at her more than once as she scrutinised the world. One thing he knew that she didn't was there were few as stubborn as he. So, he kept badgering her.

Stopping suddenly, she said, 'Fine. I will tell you both about me. I fear my story will sound very strange to your ears, but I ask that you let me speak. If you wish to ask me questions, then I will answer them as best I can. What I told you about my father was true, but not the full truth. What I wish to tell you… well, you will find extremely difficult to believe.'

Rhíona was clearly uncomfortable and waited for the boys to interject with a comment or a question. She wore the look of a troubled soul carrying a weighty burden alone.

Eoghan glanced at Rúadhan, who was nodding furiously at her. Eoghan felt his own eyebrows rise. *What is she going to say?*

Rhíona was just about to start when the riders arrived.

They came in a single line, horses walking slowly. They spotted the three, who stood helplessly amongst the trees. They were quickly surrounded by the warriors. All manner of weapons were produced; swords, for the most part, some spears and a vicious-looking axe.

There were three women amongst the ten warriors. The boys had not noticed any women in the group they had watched from the tree the previous night. Though they were dressed in similar black leather armour and clothing, this was not the same band. Gael warriors usually dressed colourfully with armour to match. There was something deeply unsettling about warriors dressed all in black. The boys were suddenly more curious than ever to find out more about Rhíona.

'What have we here?' asked one of the women of no one in particular. A jagged scar left a ridge across her brown skin. Her accent was foreign. 'Could this be the one we are looking for? Maybe Uad is not without skill after all.' She raised a stump of a missing hand to signal her band forward. Rúadhan cleared his throat.

'I am Rúadhan and this is my sister Sinéad and our friend Eoghan. We are making our way to *Uisneach* and have strayed from the trail. Is there some reason for ye to be surrounding us and drawing arms against us as if we were foreign invaders? We have done nothing amiss.' His voice trembled.

'Nothing amiss? I am not saying you have, my boy. Still, we have been searching through these trees for a long many days now, and you are the only ones we have encountered with a girl this age, so your sister is going to be coming with us.'

'Going with you?' said Eoghan, bile rising up his throat. 'To what end? She is nothing to you.'

'You do not need to be alive for the rest of this boy. The girl comes. You,' she nodded to one of her men, 'you carry her.'

She held a long sword in her good hand, which she levelled at Eoghan. 'Do not speak any more, or I will put a hole in you.'

One of the warriors dismounted and walked towards Rhíona. The memory of the slaughter was very fresh in Eoghan's mind. He stood and watched. *What can we do?*

Rhíona spoke softly as the warrior neared. 'I am sorry. I cannot go with you.' Her fingers started to dance gently midair as if spinning yarn, expertly delicate.

Cupping her hands around her mouth, she let out a roar similar in sound to the buck they had met earlier.

The warrior woman's eyes narrowed.

'*Draíocht*,' she hissed. 'She's the witch.'

The circle of warriors froze for a moment, observing. Eoghan shoulder-charged a warrior, who was caught unawares, knocking him square in the chest. The warrior pitched to one side, dropping his sword as he did so. Rúadhan was quick to react with a vicious kick, which knocked the man out cold. He scooped up the sword, and the boys backed closer to Rhíona.

'Drop the sword, boy, or you are dead.'

Rúadhan held the sword out in front of him, smiling a smile that would fool nobody.

The mounted warriors clicked their horses forward. Rúadhan was not a swordsman, but his skills with a hurl were significant. When he twirled the sword as if he was getting ready for a game, some of the warriors paused. Even Eoghan was surprised at how convincing it was.

The warriors moved forward, and one of the spears licked out at Rúadhan. He was too late to block it, but a jerk of his head meant that it missed his face by a hairsbreadth. Swinging the sword in broad circles, he tried to keep the warriors at bay. As if to answer, two spears darted towards him. He blocked and was forced backwards.

Some of the warriors watching laughed appreciatively. They could see how the spearmen were backing the three together and would soon trap them.

Suddenly, from somewhere in the forest came a roar. Everyone stopped. Another followed, booming and raw. The second was answered by many from all directions. Twelve heads snapped to look at Rhíona when she suddenly threw back her head and answered with a roar of her own. A strange silence was followed by a rumbling sound like thunder.

And then, from the belly of the ancient forest, came the herd of deer.

They swept out of the trees like a flood, leaping, bounding and running at speed. The cacophony that accompanied them was louder than a storm. They ran through the clearing where the bemused warriors sat astride their horses, streaming past, around and in between. A young buck leapt over one of the horses and knocked the rider off his mount. A large doe butted him as he tried to rise, and he was trampled by passing hooves.

Panic washed over the warriors. They tried to steer their unnerved horses in the direction of the stampede, but the task was near impossible. Another rider was unsaddled as a leaping deer slammed into her. She landed amongst the hooves and died screaming. One by one, the riders were knocked out of their saddles. Though they swung their weapons in a vain effort to protect themselves, the deer were too many. Rhíona and the boys backed away as much as they could but were being given a wide berth by the deer. The horses were being spared as much as possible, even though their own panicked wheeling caused some of them to be trampled. The forest was filled with the terrified screams of the warriors and their mounts.

Just as quickly as it had begun, it was over. The deer were gone, and all that remained standing were four white-eyed horses, two wide-eyed boys and one blue-eyed girl.

THE CATCHING OF BREATH

***

The flight of the two boys and their new friend Rhíona continues as desperation builds. They reach a village but do not arrive alone.

Ní mhealltar an sionnach faoi dhó.

You won't fool the fox twice.

***

Rhíona moved to one of the horses and started rummaging. Hanging from the saddle horn was a recently filled water skin. She turned to the other two, offering them a turn. Both accepted wordlessly. Rúadhan's shaking hands made opening the stopper a challenge. When he finally opened it, he took a long drink to wet his dry mouth.

Who is this girl? How did she do, whatever she did, to save us? He wanted to ask Eoghan but wasn't sure he could speak.

She continued to rummage and found a wrapped cloth containing scallions and a heel of hard brown bread.

'Check the other horses,' she said, avoiding Rúadhan's questioning gaze. Eoghan and he stood watching her for a moment before she repeated herself.

The search yielded more scallions, one more piece of chewed bread, an ageing chunk of cheese and a few pieces of dried fish. Combined with three more filled waterskins and their forest foraging bounty, they had enough to eat a decent meal. There was no celebration. Rúadhan found himself replaying what had happened with the deer.

'We can take the horses now and get away from this place. Perhaps we can sell them as time goes on, or you can use them to get home when we find our bearings.' Rhíona was matter-of-fact.

'Boys,' she said when neither moved to action.

Rúadhan shook his head suddenly. 'What do you mean take the horses?' he asked, a sickly feeling in his stomach. *Horses*.

Rhíona frowned. 'I mean, we take them. They have nothing better to do for the day, so we take them.'

Eoghan walked over to the nearest horse to offer his hand. The horse became tense, so he stepped back, hands raised, with a smile. 'Neither of us can ride. I just never learned, and Rúadhan is afraid of horses, though he pretends he is not.'

Rúadhan scowled, looking from one to the other. *Prick.* 'I am afraid of nothing, you donkey. We just never learned. Our village has two carts and very few horses, so they were always hitched.'

Rhíona stood, lips pursed, regarding the boys. 'Oh.'

Rúadhan's wan smile broke out again. 'We aren't that much help to you, are we?'

'You have helped me more than you can know. I thought I would die up in that tree. I thought I would die from the hunger until you fed me and thought I would die from the cold until Eoghan covered me with the extra cloak.' Eoghan's face was flushed when Rúadhan looked at him. 'I know I would have been caught if you two had not stood as my protectors while the deer travelled to our aid. I can never repay you both.'

Rúadhan could see Eoghan did not know what to say. He felt the same way. She seemed sincere, and suddenly she looked very delicate, fragile. Rúadhan shook his head. She had just summoned the deer to her aid, as if… using *draíocht*. The warrior woman had said it herself.

Draíocht. There is no such thing as draíocht.

Rúadhan looked down at his shaking hands to find the sword still there. He dropped it and looked at Eoghan, standing like a child, staring at her. He could see why Eoghan had taken to staring at Rhíona. She was mysterious and exciting and needed help. Just what his friend craved.

What do I crave?

Rúadhan walked towards the shortest black horse, who was skittish. The horse backed away, and Rúadhan froze, hand outstretched.

Not this, anyway.

He felt the audience of two people and three other horses watching him. There was nothing else for him to do except keep going. The horse seemed to feel the same, and a brief, moving standoff took place. The horse pinned its ears back, and Rúadhan feared it might try to bite his grasping hand. *Don't do it, you shite.*

'Rúadhan.'

Rúadhan stopped and turned. 'What?'

'Maybe this one might be more willing to carry you,' said Eoghan.

Rúadhan looked at them. Rhíona seemed to be looking off into the trees as if searching for something that clearly did not exist, and Eoghan stood offering the reins of a larger sable brown.

If he opens his mouth...

Rúadhan trooped over and grabbed the reins. He put his foot into the stirrup and surprisingly deftly swung his leg over to mount the beast. He sat looking down at them defiantly. 'Now.'

Eoghan was obviously quite impressed with the display, nodding in pale-faced approval. 'Maybe I'll go behind you, Rhíona,' he said wearily, 'I am not the horseman my friend seems to be.'

'I would like that, Eoghan,' Rhíona smiled, and Eoghan's face lit up. 'You can hold the reins of one of the horses. Perhaps the gallant Rúadhan might hold the other?'

Rúadhan was concentrating on his horse, which seemed to be walking sideways away from the group. The reins were too loose in his hands, so drawing them back had no effect. The frightened horse became bothered by the strange jerking and swaying. A bad-tempered snort aimed at Rúadhan caused him to jerk his hands back, letting go of the reins.

The horse had had enough and took off at a canter, bucking angrily as he did so. Rúadhan whipped around like a straw doll, only managing to cling on by squeezing his legs and grabbing the horse's mane with his hands. 'Eoghan. Help. Take the horse. Stop horse. Stop, you donkey,' he squealed again as the horse cantered through the trees.

The other two, however, were struggling to catch their breath as they laughed at the sight. The laughter had a nervous, maniacal edge after the day's events.

After that they decided to lead the horses behind them and walk regardless of any blistered feet or how long extra it would take. Rúadhan walked quietly with his head down, rethinking this new course his life had taken. He noticed Rhíona whisper something to Eoghan, who whispered something back. *Prick.*

Against all their instincts to avoid people until they reached *Uisneach*, they decided to follow a narrow trail that they came upon. Rúadhan was tired and filthy, hungry and afraid.

This is Eoghan's fault. All of it. Always. Always Eoghan's fault.

He looked at his friend. The broad-shouldered, dark-featured, trouble-making friend. He shook his head. He was the bigger fool for always having to follow. He thought back to his mother's chat before he and Eoghan had set out. 'He'll get himself in trouble if we let him. It's your job to keep him out of it. Stick with him. He needs help, Rúadhan, and you've always been a kind-hearted soul. Mind him.'

She was right. Trouble was right. And Rúadhan followed as he always did. Like a gobshite.

'Looking for help. That's what we should be doing. Not skulking,' Rúadhan said.

'I have tried to stay away from people until now,' said Rhíona, 'But I am too tired to go much further on my own. I can still hear those boys screaming.'

All were silent for a moment as if the memories gnawed at them. Finally, Rúadhan spoke to keep the memories away.

'We will get you the help you need, Rhíona. We cannot get caught, though. We will not last long against those fighters. Once we get to the next village, we will be able to get you the help you need; for whatever it is you're doing.'

He looked at her but made no attempt to find out more. It was not the time.

The trail ended as they came to the edge of the forest. They could see a fort in the distance. A crown-like wooden stockade stood atop a hill, which rose from the middle of a small village. Evidence of a belt of an older fort was visible from where they stood. The hill and surrounding fold were carpeted in blooming *Fraoch mór* heather, so the hill seemed to be floating on a sea of purple.

The pointed wooden buildings, numbering around twenty, stood in a lazy circle around the rickety wooden fort. Each one stout and compact and humble as if to represent the villagers they housed. Acquisitive heather had taken root on the roofs of some.

There was very little activity, nor would they have expected there to be. At this time of day, the villagers were likely hunting, gathering, fishing, farming or felling. A few could be seen going about their daily routines.

The companions stayed in the forest for a long time, looking for any signs of the warriors hunting for Rhíona.

'We need to go to the village,' said Rhíona quietly. 'Without supplies, any passage to *Uisneach* will be too difficult.'

Leaving the sanctuary of the tree line was difficult. Fear caged them until Eoghan turned to scratch his horse behind its ear and then walked wordlessly away from the trees. The others followed.

They weren't out of the forest very long when riders appeared from the tree line behind them. They galloped from cover and surrounded them. Five warriors dismounted, armed and ready for trouble. Reins were snatched from their grasp, and their wrists were bound with leather straps. Weapons were pointed at their necks.

When the leader spoke, Eoghan's blood froze. He recognised the voice from when he was up the tree.

'Get them into the village. The villagers will have seen us now, so move quick, before they all manage to get into that poxy fort.'

It was Ungus.

Oldfort and a Timely Introduction

***

It all seems very grim, until the arrival of a newcomer changes things.

Fileann an feall ar an bhfeallaire.

The evil deed returns to the person who did it.

***

While some villagers made it to the fort, others did not. The warriors herded them onto the village commons. Rhíona, Eoghan and Rúadhan were tied securely and made to kneel in front of Ungus, who was in jubilant humour.

'So, you allowed yourself to believe you were heroes saving the girl. Walked like the clueless wretches ye clearly are. In one fell swoop managed not only to get caught like minks in a trap, but you've also made things far, far worse for the people in this village. You see, Uad bid us to break the will of the Gael population who might think to stand before us. A chance to cow these sheep furthermore. A great thing has begun. A great change will happen. We will lead the way.' He nodded to the small group of villagers who had not made the sanctuary of the fort. He pointed to two women among the prisoners who were forced away from the others.

'Do you hear?' Ungus shouted so those cowering inside the hillfort could hear. 'I will show you all what happens should our... undertakings be interfered with in any way by anyone. Now, or in the future, when you worms are going to see far more people like me.'

He grabbed one of the women by her hair and threw her down, where she landed on her knees.

'Keallach,' he called, 'it's been at least a week since you've known the pleasures of a fine woman such as this, has it not?'

A swarthy bearded man carrying a club smiled in the most unsettling way one can smile. He threw his weapon down and started to unbuckle his greaves.

The other prisoners started to scream; obscenities, threats, pleas and begging all falling on deaf ears.

'Donal,' called Ungus. 'You go too, I think. Keallach has a habit of finishing quickly, and we don't want this to be forgettable.' Keallach turned crimson but kept unbuckling. The other warriors laughed as Donal started to remove his armour, more eagerly than Keallach. The young woman looked around her, weeping silently.

One of the warriors guarding them spoke up. 'I could do with a release too, you know, Ungus.' The remaining warriors signalled similar intent.

'Keep silent, or I'll break your teeth,' shouted Ungus. 'When the lads are done here, ye can all drink and ride for the day. We have our prize, and it's too late to travel anyway.'

At this, two women broke from the villagers and raced for the questionable security of the old fort. Three warriors in front of it waited for the women to reach spear-throwing distance and made a short but noisy game of trying to hit them as they ran. Cries and screams came from inside the fort. They were both dead quickly enough. Ungus smiled.

'Good practice for them,' he said, turning to the other prisoners. 'If any of the rest of you wish to try, I will be indebted.'

Keallach and Donal had their armour off and were taking off their leggings. The woman started screaming. An old man among the prisoners tried to get to her. One of the warriors knocked him down by bashing his head with the hilt of his longsword.

In all the commotion, no one noticed a stranger walking into the village at a steady pace whilst working with his bow and arrows. Neither did anyone see the arrow protruding from the neck of a warrior at the edge of the fracas.

The warrior himself was unable to tell anyone. He dropped, hands working at his wound until he died.

Another warrior guarding the prisoners suddenly dropped, with an arrow lodged in his chest. This, however, was noticed. The warriors all turned and saw the stranger striding up the path at the edge of the village. He was carrying a bow in one hand and an arrow in the other. Over his shoulder sat a quiver full of arrows. As he nocked the arrow, he shouted to them. 'Three of your men half a league away with no spears left… Two of them wear their trousers around their ankles and ...' he paused, righted himself, and let fly. This arrow passed through the unprotected shoulder of, a third warrior bringing quite a lot of tissue and blood with it. '...now three of them dead or dying?'

He nocked an arrow in the blink of an eye. 'By dad, all things considered,' he said to Ungus, 'you really are a fairly questionable strategist and worse commander of men, aren't you, really and truly?'

Ungus issued a guttural bellow of pure rage. His sword flashed into the air. He and the remaining guard both ran at the archer. The three men beside the fort ran to find their spears. Keallach and Donal started to dress and arm themselves. As Ungus and his comrade ran, the archer let loose another arrow, which caught the guard in the eye. He fell limply to the ground, twitching. The prisoners ran towards the wooden fort. The temptation for Eoghan to join them made him grit his teeth. Neither Rúadhan nor Rhíona moved but just watched the archer.

Ungus kept running at the attacker. At twenty paces an arrow bit deeply into his thigh, and he collapsed.

Next to drop was Keallach. An arrow pierced his groin, and he died slowly. Donal stopped running when Keallach fell. He looked around for options and realised that his only hope for survival was to get to cover in one of the little cottages. He did not make it after being shot in his back.

The three spearmen had also stopped. Though they had re-armed themselves with their spears, none of them seemed willing to engage with the stranger. All three turned and ran through the heather into a nearby field. Their heads could be seen bobbing through the fields until they finally disappeared.

The stranger unstrung his bow and put the string in a leather pouch, which he tied to his belt. He put the bow into a long unadorned leather satchel that he slung over his shoulder before walking towards Ungus, who was propping himself up with one hand, sword in the other.

'Don't come near me,' he screamed. Twisted strands of spittle flew from his lips.

The archer walked past Ungus, who swung his sword at his legs as he did. The man did not flinch as the sword arced within two hands of his calf. Instead, he placed his foot against the body of the nearest warrior and pulled the arrow out of his head. A horrific noise accompanied the action, and the three bound onlookers turned away as the archer removed the eyeball from the bloody arrow.

He went to the bodies one by one, taking the arrows that weren't broken or stuck fast. Finally, he arrived in front of the captives and inspected them. A broad smile full of good humour lit up his face.

'I would have to say, well done, me,' he said. 'You must admit, that was a fine bit of work, was it not? Wasn't it perfectly fitting that I stuck the big one in his groin? Sure, of course it was. He was a lout and a thug to be sure and we can't have such men around our women, can we?'

He surveyed the area again, drew in a long breath with his eyes closed and released it. 'Quite an adventure today all in all,' he mumbled to no one in particular.

'Can you just release us?' asked Rhíona quietly.

'Release you? Oh, I'm not sure about that, pretty girl. My listening and watching have gleaned a few little snippets of interesting information, haven't they?' The good humour never left his face. 'I've come to understand that you might be worth quite a sum of rings if one was partial to such things and in a position to claim it.'

He ran his hand back over his balding, weather-worn head. His face was tanned and leathery, with a full brown beard threatening to conceal his cracked lips. Lines covered his face and seemed to gather beside his meadow-green eyes. It was difficult to assess his age, but he must have seen his fair share of winters. Though he was suitably attired in a tanned leather traveller's cloak, the sun, wind and rain had shown his head no clemency. Long boots resembling the top of that head added to the wizened look. His motives were far too unclear for Eoghan's liking.

The bald man looked over towards Ungus, who was trying to escape in a mixture of a crawl and a three-limbed shuffle.

'Now,' stated the archer, 'if you don't rest yourself down as quick as could be, I will put an arrow in your arse, and none of us want that, do we? The smell off you is bad enough as things stand, I would say.'

Ungus stopped. There was a lot of blood around him.

'Now, again,' the archer said, turning back to the three captives. 'Where were we?'

‘Let us go,’ said Eoghan. His lips were dry. ‘The girl too. You see what’s going to happen to us if they catch us. You are most certainly not one of those, are you? You would not have interjected if you had not the mind of a decent man. A good man even. There could be more of them here any moment. You will then be a party to them murdering us two and worse to her. That is not something you want. We all know that. Let us go.’

The archer’s face lit up with a delighted smile.

‘Ahh, don’t worry about my silly talk. I’m only codding ye and being a dose. I’m not one of these stinking badgers, sure I’m not? You’ve spotted that in me, young friend, and that is right and true. Fair play to you, mighty man,’ he chuckled as he started undoing the leather bands from around their hands and feet.

‘What would I, of all the people you met, do with rings anyway, to be fair?’ he muttered. When they were standing in front of him, he placed his hands on his hips and looked at them one by one.

‘However,’ he said, ‘I am going to have to ask you to explain what’s going on here as we eat together shortly if it’s not too much to ask of ye. And it would want to be believable.’ The smile suddenly had an edge to it. In a flash, it was gone again. ‘My name is Donnacha. After I kill that man over there, probably; then help the villagers bury them all; talk to the chief about improvements to the fort; find some damn thing to eat and, more importantly, drink. After all that, then maybe we can sit and talk for a long time, can’t we, my young cubs?’

His question was met with nodding heads and nervous glances.

‘All is well, all is well, come out, come out, one and all, for we must decide what to do with this man here,’ shouted Donnacha. ‘Come back from the fort and come out from your hiding.’

Whether he felt his invitation would be accepted or not, he started back towards Ungus and stopped just short of a sword’s distance. Ungus held his sword up between them.

Eoghan and Rúadhan went to find swords and scabbards for themselves from the dead warriors. Rhíona walked to stand beside Donnacha.

‘I’m going to tell you once only,’ said Donnacha to Ungus. His eyes suddenly ice cold, and his voice distant. ‘Throw that sword away.’

Grimacing, Ungus did as directed.

Donnacha sat cross-legged in front of him and began inspecting his reclaimed arrows. He scrutinised them as a mother would a child after a fall, each arrow in the same way, with the same attention to detail and almost loving caress.

‘You aren’t very nice, nor are you good in any way,’ he said to Ungus. ‘I hardly know you at all but know you for a black-hearted man.’ Turning to the three freed prisoners, he asked, ‘Am I right? I am, aren’t I? Sure, I know I am.’

Turning back, he spoke matter-of-factly. ‘So, I think I should kill you here and now. Or I could torture you and then kill you. Slowly. It would take an age, and then you’d realise that I’m not very nice, though I might look like a lovely and very pleasant young man.’

He turned and winked melodramatically. ‘I am really, though. A little lamb, but don’t tell him that.’ He chuckled heartily and turned back to Ungus. ‘Or I could find the father of the woman you were offering to your friends.' He examined the arrows again. 'I'd think he might bring you to a smithy and brand your sack. Or that's what I'd be shouting for anyway, and I think fair enough really,' he said over his shoulder, winking and nodding his head sideways towards his captive, as if they were sharing a joke with Ungus at the butt.

Ungus's eyes darted nervously. He was sweating and bleeding profusely.

'There must be a way that...' Ungus was unable to finish his statement because Donnacha plunged an arrow into the soft part of his ankle. The mercenary screamed in agony.

Donnacha's face turned a purple shade of fury as he hissed through bared teeth, 'You will never, ever speak in this world again, unless I tell you what to say and when to say it.'

Donnacha plunged another arrow into the other ankle, rousing another shriek, sitting back on his heels, closing his eyes, and resting his chin on his chest.

He drew in a long, noisy breath and said, 'You are not very nice at all. You have lived a life that makes you think you can go on the way you have been going on. That life is over now. Tell me a story, Ungus. And make it very interesting, or I will empty your insides on the ground in front of you as you watch and go for a meal and a chat with my new friends.' This time he did not look over his shoulder. His eyes were still closed. 'Speak now. Who do you serve, and why are you here? Only the truth and succinctly put...'

Ungus was staring in horror at Donnacha. His voice was filled with barely controlled pain.

'Uad,' he spluttered. 'That's his name. A mercenary leader who has risen to power in the East. Many chieftains have succumbed to his way of thinking. He is powerful in... *draíocht*.' He shifted gingerly.

Eoghan absorbed every word: it was like a story from a madman. He looked at the others. Rúadhan's face was a picture, and Rhíona shifted impatiently from one foot to another, fingers worrying, looking anywhere but at Ungus.

'He has a sharp mind and a swift tongue and is… driven. There are those who suggest that he is a madman and others who suggest he holds affiliations with...' his voice changed to a whisper, 'the Fae folk.'

A large pool of blood was developing around him. 'He was once just a mercenary. A nobody. Something happened... to change him.' A short grunt escaped his lips, and his eyes rolled slightly. 'A pact with them... Fae and some of them came. Ambassadors. They came to him, and he changed. Three of them are among us now. They live in our world. They gave him some kind of *draíocht*: an amulet that gives him great power.' He grunted again.

Eoghan heard Donnacha mumble.

'...have naught to do with a madman or a wicked one.'

He saw Rhíona's mouth fall open when she heard him. She seemed to look upon Donnacha anew. Ungus, who was failing badly, continued as he sank into delirium.

'I took or take no notice except to the silver rings he gives me. We were told to find the girl. Not just us. A hundred experienced men are looking for her, most from across the Bloody Sea. There are more coming...

They are building… an army of mercenaries.' His voice became faint. His breathing more and more ragged. 'They are looking for her, and we are told where to look. We don't know why, but she is to be brought alive and not harmed or touched under pain of torture.'

As if they all had the same thought at the same time, all eyes turned to look at the young girl who, in turn, chose to avert her own.

Donnacha's voice was distant as he regarded Rhíona thoughtfully, almost fondly. 'Any mention of what this man wanted with her? Betrothed scorned? Enraged silver lender? Any of that kind of thing, if you understand my meaning?'

'It was... never... spoken outright. We were told... a witch.' Ungus lay back on the ground. 'I have a... fierce thirst.' Eoghan looked around for a waterskin but saw none nearby.

'Keep talking. One of you boys get water if you wouldn't mind, please and thank you.' Rúadhan rushed off. Eoghan shook his head slightly and stayed where he was. He did not want to leave Rhíona alone with the strange newcomer.

'We... have to meet... again. At *Uisneach* in a month. We have to ruin the places we visit… Break people down. We have to report news... and...' The pain was no longer showing in his face; his eyes were distant. His speech was starting to slur. 'Maeve. You don't... know her. I should... Maeve. Maeve... I never...'

Ungus died.

Donnacha turned and sat cross-legged in front of Rhíona. His face welled up with emotion and seemed like he might suddenly weep. 'Maeve, Maeve, I never learned to dance a jig,' he wailed. 'Maeve, I never wore warm enough clothes in the winter...'

His face changed again, full of expectation. When he saw that Rhíona, Eoghan or Rúadhan – who had returned with a waterskin – were not in hysterics as he may have hoped, he shook his head as though annoyed with himself. He looked down at his crossed ankles for a moment. When his head came up again, his eyes were clear and full of intensity.

'Rhíona is it? Rhíona. First thing is a movement, Rhíona. Food then; calm the people; long interesting chat, hah? I'm thinking we'll knock a bit of conversation out of each other this evening, indeed. And I don't mind telling you that much.'

Then he was up. He looked around as if slightly disoriented and then strode off towards a nearby ditch. Eoghan wondered if they were being tested or if the bowman was as eccentric as he appeared.

'We need to get out of here now,' said Rúadhan, almost pressing himself against Eoghan to convey his sense of urgency. 'And I don't mean her. She needs to stay. We need to go. Now.'

Eoghan looked at Rhíona, who was watching Donnacha with a deeply furrowed brow.

'No. I want to hear that conversation too,' said Eoghan. Rhíona's story was more important. 'Let's listen and take stock. We're not just going to leave with one arm longer than the other.'

'Where are we going to get this stock, Eoghan?' asked Rúadhan.

'Rhíona,' said Eoghan. 'I think if we approach the fort, we will not be welcomed. You might. Just tell them we need food and maybe new clothing.'

‘And some blankets,’ piped in Rúadhan, suddenly uplifted by the thought of something warm and meaty to bury his teeth in.

‘Just say that we mean no harm and will be no trouble.’

Rhíona smiled suddenly and rose from the ground gracefully. ‘Am I to do your bidding now, Eoghan?’

‘I don’t know if that tone is fair considering what we’ve been through since we met you, princess,’ growled Eoghan. *Ungrateful bitch.*

‘Fair is not really something I am accustomed to of late. What I would be more appreciative of is some respect from my hired boys. Please do not think to give me orders.’

Rúadhan shook himself out of his shock. ‘Rhíona. He wasn’t ordering you. He only suggested.’

‘You need to stand up for yourself, Rúadhan. I am not as happy to take commands from him as you are.’

‘Perhaps you would like to pay us now, and we’ll be on our way,’ said Eoghan.

‘Really?’ Rúadhan asked before looking at Rhíona and saying, ‘Actually, that would be ideal.’

Rhíona’s eyes widened and narrowed in the blink of an eye. Her head shot around her as if scanning for other listeners and then back to Eoghan.

‘I told you. I don’t have your rings until we reach our destination.’

The two locked eyes. Eoghan had neither the will nor the energy for conflict, but she was as stubborn as an ass, and he was right, so a staring match ensued.

‘Eh,’ interjected Rúadhan, ‘in that case, if truth be told, I could do with a movement myself. Then I reckon I would like to refill the soon-to-be empty stomach, so could we get the turnips out of the ground rather than pulling leaves off the stems?'

Rhíona turned and marched up the hill, muttering about men and their short list of uses. The gate seemed to anticipate her arrival and swung open as she marched. A woman walked out slowly, as if trying to determine whether the danger had passed. As she left, the gate was slammed behind her. The woman straightened and strode out to meet the oncoming Rhíona.

Eoghan admired such courage considering what happened on the path in front of her not so long ago.

The two women met face to face, and after a brief but earnest conversation, the villager strode past Rhíona in the direction of the two boys. Walking between them, she barked, 'Follow me,' and continued towards one of the larger wooden huts.

The woman did not pause as she called, 'You in the ditch who killed those others, we're in here. We need to have a quick talk before we attend to my people,' and disappeared inside.

Just as the three were lining up to enter, they heard Donnacha's voice.

'I see ye. Don't worry. I'm moving while sitting and watching unmoving.' This was followed by a self-congratulatory snort and chuckle. The three youngsters stopped to look at where the voice had come from but could see only undergrowth and brush.

A Meal to Make Strangers no Longer

***

Truth comes into the light as Rhíona speaks of her background. It is difficult for the others to believe and rightly so.

An rud is annamh, is iontach.

What is rare is amazing.

***

The five unlikely fellows busied themselves preparing food. Eoghan worked quietly, though all he wanted to do was drink a barrel of water and then sleep for a month.

Some of the bravest souls who had ventured from the fort, when they saw that danger had seemingly passed removed the fallen.

Donnacha was quieter with others around as if cowed by the presence of numbers. Eoghan could see that he watched the three of them very closely. He made no effort to hide it. That said, he had worked to help restore order, and sweat was dripping from his chin when they were done.

'Hard work is good currency,' he noted to a terrified-looking youth who passed.

Nora, the village chieftain, had been the one to come out of the fort to speak to Rhíona. Quickly enough, it became apparent to Eoghan that she was as able a person as any he might meet. She was wise beyond her summers and a sound thinker.

'You will have your men leave down whatever weapons they have collected, and all of you will follow me.' She raised a hand to a young man, who ran to her. 'Gather all of the weapons and hide them in the lowbarn. He nodded and went about his business. Eoghan did not resist his newly acquired sword being taken.

Donnacha would not hear of it but discussed it calmly enough. 'I am in absolute agreement with Nora, a hardy lady, and right she is. But my bow will stay with me. Lest more of those louts come by. I'm sure you can all see the sense there.'

Nora nodded once, and the young man moved on.

She looked at Rhíona with a finger pointing to Eoghan and Rúadhan. 'You will control them?'

There was something about Nora's manner that left him happy enough for Rhíona to answer.

'They are not like the others,' said Rhíona. 'They are good… men.'

Eoghan and Rúadhan exchanged a glance. Eoghan smiled a little as his fair eyebrows raised at the mention of them being men.

Everyone was hungry by the time food was right and ready. The villagers whispered of the great victory that

Donnacha had won for them. More than one used the word hero, and by the time a mug or two of mead had been drunk before dinner, a song or two was being sung. The hero in question was starting to wince as if every tuneless note pierced him as an arrow might. The crying somewhere in the distance over those who had died by the warriors' spears, made it awkward.

Nora suggested that the five of them take their dinner and go somewhere quiet to discuss what had happened, and what might happen next. Donnacha was first out the door, with enough relief on his face and speed in his step that Eoghan allowed himself a half-smile.

The lone cabin in the corner of the village where they went had a roaring fire; smoky, warm and heartening. Nora had planned this meeting well before dinner.

'Sit,' she bade, and they did so. Eoghan was fascinated by her. Her manner was efficient, bordering on being cold. Still, the smiling lines that creased around her eyes showed her to be a woman who was more accustomed to warmth. Around her neck was a silver torc, possibly a wedding gift, as the ornate silver was excellent quality and was the only item of such quality on her. Her humble village skirt and blouse were functional and had been stitched and scrubbed many times. Her face was plain, and her eyebrows thick. Her eyes were almost yellow and piercing. Her full lips and weather-bronzed skin made clear a subtle beauty. Her most remarkable feature, however, was her hair. It was long, thick and shining. Of the rarest tawny, the two streaks of white that sprang from her temples pronounced its uniqueness further. Her capable manner; her strong character; both made her more attractive, withering any argument that the torc did not match its recipient well.

'I have a few things to say before I leave you four to your meals and whatever conversations you wish to have...' Nora paused. She took a long breath before continuing, 'Those warriors who came here were looking for you.' Her astute gaze fixed upon Rhíona. 'Are there others?'

Rhíona nodded, rubbing the bridge of her nose.

'Will they be coming here?'

'It's difficult to say.'

'So it is. We will conceal any evidence of their passing and will keep their horses as payment for the trouble that has been caused here. They will be sent to our furthest pastures, so as not to be noticed until we are safe again. We don't know when that might be, but your presence here puts us in danger.

'I have sent our returned hunters to find the three wretches who ran from the bowman. We need to know what adventures befell them. Had the hunters been here, we could have defended ourselves, but they were gone. They will not be allowed to report the happenings here. We cannot have that. We will keep the weapons to defend ourselves, all of them. If such a need does not arise, we will use the metal for other purposes. You three will leave here in the morning, washed and fed, clothed and fully provisioned and with our blessing. You,' she looked at Donnacha, 'are welcome to do what you please. You are a hero to us... all of us. You could find a wife and a home here without much effort and you will see that it is a wonderful place to live with the land.'

She stood abruptly. ‘I don’t know why they want you, girl, nor what you boys are playing at, but you are all meddling with danger indeed. I would like it if we could offer you more, but you have brought terrible evil upon us. We need to protect our own. I am sorry for you, and what troubles lie on the roads you will travel, but you will not be welcome here again. We... I have... plans for the people here; ambitions to improve and make our lives better. War and aggression will ruin everything. I have seen war...’ She paused, eyes fixed, looking at nothing. A shadow passed over her face, and it was chilling to behold. ‘I have seen all the terrible truths and what’s left. I will not become a part of it again, and it will not happen to my people. I will do anything I can to ensure this. Even if I have to go and fight the war myself. Please do not return here.’

Nora turned and left.

There was silence for a time.

‘So, Rhíona,’ said Donnacha softly. ‘Why are those horrible people and their mean-arse friends that have been galloping around the place chasing you? And just before you begin, let’s keep this friendly and honest. There is no need for trickery or that kind of thing here. It will be ill-received, if not worse if you understand me. I, and – I suspect by the heads on them – these young lads, need to hear the truth. Those men who took ye, there are more, and that’s the size of it. I have come across their like before today and have a feeling I might be seeing more of them, so I do, and that’s not a word of a lie.’

Rhíona looked at each of them for a moment. ‘I am sorry that you have been put in danger on my account. I am sorry and thankful too. The three of you have saved me and protected me, and I cannot ever repay you or show my gratitude as I would wish. I will tell you the truth, though I fear you may look on me badly after. It is going to sound... strange. It is strange, but it is going to sound far-fetched. I will still tell you the truth, but I want to thank you first. And I want to apologise.' Her gaze flickered to Eoghan and then away again.

Eoghan spoke in response. 'Rhíona. You are beginning to sound like him with the long-winded talk streaming out of you.' He gestured his head towards Donnacha. 'You can trust us by now. Spit it out.'

Smiles broke out, and Donnacha wagged his finger. 'Ah, I tell you, this boy is a sharpened tool, indeed, so he is. I see what you did there, and I'd say to be fair, you might not be too far off on this matter at all, at all.'

Rhíona was blushing but kept going. 'As I told Eoghan and Rúadhan already, I am not from here,' she said and paused. Her audience glanced at each other and then back to Rhíona.

Eoghan asked the obvious. 'You're not from here, then where?'

'I am not from your world.' She sat taller, and a slight look of defiance shaded her features. 'I am Fae.'

Smiles broke out again. 'Greetings, Fae woman. I,' said Rúadhan, 'am actually Fintán Mac Bóchra, the salmon of knowledge himself. Pleased to meet you, indeed.'

Donnacha chortled. Eoghan was about to but stopped himself when he realised that Rhíona's face remained solemn. Holding his hands up for silence, Eoghan became bothered. She had not made a jest. 'Ah, no, Rhíona, you're not because there are no Fae, and you are very much not a bedtime story, so that's a bad start if you're saying you're going to be honest.'

'I am inclined to agree with the sharp one,' said Donnacha as he looked closer at Rhíona.

'Listen to me. Just ... listen.' Rhíona was looking down at her feet now, head shaking slowly. 'I am the seventh child of the Fane and Fand of the Fae. The King and Queen, as you might say.'

'A Fae princess no less,' mocked Rúadhan. 'Eoghan. We have to get home away from this nonsense fast.'

'I am the seventh of eight children of the Fane and Fand. As a result, I have been enmeshed in the Struggle since I was born. My parents have fought for control of our world throughout the ages. We, their children, have been dragged into their fight. My brothers have sided with my father, the Fane, and wish for chaos, decadence and conquest. My sisters and I side with my mother, the Fand, who longs for peace and harmony in our world: a place for everyone and their ways.' She started to pace slowly as she spoke.

'The war ebbs and flows like a river. At times, our world is violent and fearsome, other times tranquil and beautiful. In all things, there can be balance. Indeed, there has been balance. Until now. Our race is old; of that, there is no doubt. Our numbers, too, have diminished greatly. A terrible event there killed many of the Fae on both sides. Our offspring are not born in numbers like yours. Newlings are very rare. But as we have aged, we have become stronger in other ways. The *draíocht,* which we draw from our world and welcome within us seemingly, gets stronger as time passes. There are few of us there to share it. And this is why I have come.'

She drew a long breath and looked each of those listening in the eye.

'My father is powerful. His *draíocht* is strong enough now that he can set and achieve goals that he would not have considered in the past. And so, he means to do something no one thought possible. He plans to bring the Fae horde to your world and take it for his own. He has acquired an ally here: someone building an army to pave the way for the Fae horde. I do not know who it is, but they have been given gifts by my father. Gifts that will make them strong. I now also believe that I am not the only member of my family who is here. If I am correct, then the danger we face is…'

'Stop,' said Eoghan. He found himself irritated that she continued to talk nonsense. He rubbed his face and found some bruising caused by *Ros Cam* fists, which fuelled his rising frustration.

'Stop, stop, stop. Rhíona, you are not speaking sense. You are... you cannot believe that you are a Fae because there are no Fae. It's a story for children. You sound like someone who hurt their head.' He was almost pleading, begging her to come out of her apparent madness.

'Listen to me, Eoghan,' she pleaded in return. 'If you do not like what I have to say, then we will part company in the morning, and you never need to worry about me again. From here you should be able to find your way home, but for now, just sit and listen.

'The link between our worlds is tenuous. The worlds are becoming so dissimilar that they have begun to reject one another. The link is brittle and should already have broken. Something is stopping that from happening. Heritage?

'As the *draíocht* grows stronger, so do the links with the Fae legacy here. Over time there have been a small number of mixes where a Fae and human have a child together. Many of them were quickly killed by the agents of the Fane. He views them as an unacceptable besmirching of our peoples. Few have lived past infancy. As far as we know, only two children of the races mixing now remain. One came to my world and changed things. That one's *draíocht* is… unique.' She passed a hand through her matted hair.

'The other one grew into a legend. This one sired a son who has since left this world and gone to mine. His *draíocht* is the same as the rest of us.'

Eoghan noticed Donnacha's face turn deathly pale and his mouth open as Rhíona spoke.

'You all know of whom I speak. You have all heard his name. Heard of his deeds, and the legends surrounding him. While others become exposed to – and affected by – our *draíocht*, he is the link that holds the gateway between our worlds open. *Draíocht* loves him and will not leave him.'

'I don't know of whom you speak,' said Eoghan, rubbing his eye with the heel of his hand. 'Am I expected to know at this juncture? Because I do not.'

Rúadhan squinted and spoke slowly, 'I don't know who you are talking about either, but I'm fairly sure you've lost your mind entirely…'

Rhíona looked into Donnacha's eyes. 'You know. You spoke his teachings when you sat with Ungus.'

Donnacha stared back at her. He seemed fixed in thought, unsure of what to say. 'He is dead, Rhíona,' he whispered. 'He died in a battle that took place a lifetime ago.'

'He is not dead. I have been sent here to find him. I have been looking for two seasons, and I have finally found a clue, a possible guide who may have knowledge of his whereabouts.'

'Do we have so little bearing on this that you both continue to ignore us entirely?' asked Eoghan quietly. 'Should we leave, or are you going to tell us what in the name of Fionn Mac Cumhal you are talking about?'

Both heads turned to face him, and Rhíona wore a thin smile that made Eoghan feel like a child about to be praised.

'Him,' she said. 'Fionn Mac Cumhal. He is the link, and I must find him. The future of this land and the land of the Fae depend on it.

A QUEST OR NONE

***

A plan is formed, an end in sight, and four leave the village together in the direction of Uisneach.

Tús maith leath na hoibre.

A good start is half the work.

***

Donnacha sat back. His mind reeled: questions rattling around the inside of his head.

The other three were arguing. All trying to make points, while not listening to others, their points getting lost in the ether around them as new ones were raised. Questions and answers but not a lick of it made sense. Things were much easier yesterday when he fished on the bank of a stream, cooked a trout and ate it with greens. Today there had been bloodshed and terror, captives freed and a siege lifted, all before the girl told her story and her contrivances became clear.

Unlike the boys, Donnacha was more inclined to believe in the Fae. He had travelled for many years, never laying his head in one spot for long. He had seen things the boys would not have dreamed about. His experience was similar to many who wander, cruel realities around one corner, and yet the most beautiful magnificence around the next enticing and taunting him. His search, which he had never seen as a search until today, was starting to become realised. He might have found what he was looking for, hoping for with every fibre of his being. A chance at living the old ways; a chance to become the ideal; one of the Fianna.

Fionn Mac Cumhal was the island's great hero of legend and countless stories. To Donnacha, he was more. He represented the best that the land ever had to offer. His cunning and sharp wit had been his most important weapons, and his warband was responsible for keeping *Éireann*'s borders secure for decades. Their service to the land ended more than two generations before with a crushing defeat in battle after treachery and betrayal by the brothers Mac Morna. Donnacha's long-held hope was that he could find a way to resurrect such a group. A way to restore the old ways: the honour among warriors, the selflessness of their deeds, the sacrifices made for those who needed protection.

He looked upon the girl as she made her arguments. She was filthy and half-starved, but there was strength in her manner, chin upright defiantly and eyes intent with passion and belief. There was a wisdom about her that belied her years. She was speaking the truth, and he knew it. There was more talking to be done about this.

'Yes,' he said aloud, standing up with arms raised for peace. 'There is more talking to be done about this, indeed, and there is, and I'm sure of it. But not tonight.'

They quieted.

'We're all tired, and the village hunters should give us at least one night of peaceful sleep with a roof over our heads. With the new day, we will bathe and break our fast here, then make our way to *Uisneach*. I will join you on your quest, Rhíona, if I'd not be too much of a burden, all the same? I can offer my talents in return. I would very much like to meet this man that all the talk is about if the opportunity arises. You boys should probably get home from here, but should you wish to come along, so be it. That's enough nattering about it anyway, I reckon. I will go to sleep now.'

And with that, he did, almost immediately, almost exactly where he stood.

Eoghan sat upright in the near pitch-dark room, thinking he had heard something. He looked around and didn't know where he was for a few moments. As he listened, he heard what sounded like a racking sob outside. He looked over and saw Rúadhan on the other side of the firepit. He could not see Rhíona; could hardly see anything; head still heavy from sleep. He got up from the pallet and went to peek outside, anxiety rising. Something was wrong.

'Don't,' came Rhíona's whispering voice as he reached for the door latch. She was sitting away from the fire and bathed in shadow.

'Wha?' said Eoghan.

'It's Donnacha. He has wild dreams. Buried memories that must eat at him. He is pacing outside as if to relieve himself of them. He is … upset.'

'Oh.'

'I'm sorry.' She whispered.

'Oh. Wha?'

'I was quick to anger today. I am afraid and worried and … I am sorry.'

'Ah.'

'I am going to go and see can I help him, Eoghan. You should get some sleep. It should not have an audience.'

'Yeh,' said Eoghan

'Sleep well, Eoghan.'

'I'm sorry too, Rhíona. I'm not much help. Sleep well.'

He heard the latch of the door opening. Rhíona paused there and spoke a word that Eoghan did not know. Then he went to sleep.

They were woken by Nora, who brought them food and provisions as promised. The packages were generous, overly so considering the short journey they were to provide for. She was apologetic for the most part but insistent that they would leave after eating and changing into the clean clothes that she had brought for them. As she left, Donnacha noticed that she motioned for Rhíona to follow her.

'She's in need of a more serious scrubbing,' Nora said to Donnacha when she saw his curious glance.

Rhíona rejoined the three at the edge of Oldfort markedly changed. Nora accompanied her. She was the only villager who came to see them off.

Rhíona was breathtaking. There was no other way to describe it. Her hair and skin had clearly been scrubbed down to near bone, and tattered rags exchanged for a hunter's clothes of shirts, *triús* on her long legs and hide shoes. They were all given good quality cloaks to replace the ones they had taken from the fallen *Ros Cam* boys, but where the boys looked well wrapped in theirs, Rhíona managed to make it look almost regal. The boys and Donnacha had been getting to know her ragged look and had seen her as hardy. Now she was all softness. Her skin, her sad eyes and her sudden smile as she observed their openly amazed reaction, her small stature in the clothes that were too big for her frame. Her long brown tousled hair had been scoured and combed, so it shone. She was as beautiful a person as Donnacha had laid eyes on. He had seen her soul's beauty first-hand as she talked to him under the moonlight. His eyes closed for a moment as he remembered the soft, soothing words that had helped him to sleep so soundly.

Donnacha gauged the reaction of the two boys. The taller with the sheared scalp, Rúadhan, was impressed, but his smile had something else to it. His blue eyes twinkled. Was it pride? *This one has a protective streak? Unwise to be so full of trust even if he is a nice lad.*

The gruffer one, Eoghan – with the brown eyes – was clearly smitten and on the verge of floating away to the land of the Fae, judging by his battered-looking, awestruck face. Donnacha's smile turned sad. The poor boy didn't realise that this girl, though just that in their eyes, could be as old as the hills around them if she was a true Fae.

Their time is not our time.

At this rate, the lad would be deeply in love with her by around lunchtime. He would learn heartbreak over the coming days. *The one lesson life never tires of teaching.*

They left for *Uisneach*. Donnacha had many questions, as did the two youngsters, who continued to ask about the Fae world. Donnacha noted that the boys were both sceptical about her tale and curious. The girl gave them little. Questions about the Fae were sidestepped. Questions about Fionn Mac Cumhal were evaded. She stood by her promise that Éine Mac Éine would be the man to ask of such things. She was merely a piece on the board in a game between two larger players.

They decided that if warriors appeared again, they would put up Rhíona's hood and ignore them: the warriors were not looking for four hunters. It was a simple plan, but it would work if no one looked under her hood.

Later, when Donnacha asked the boys about their plans to go home, they went quiet, their differing views unresolved. They sat looking at each other, their battered faces telling a tale of their shared discomfort and put the decision on the long finger.

A day and a half after setting off from Oldfort they approached *Uisneach*. The four were wary about entering the town's fortifications. Donnacha noted that the two youngsters were overawed by the place. As they neared, the girl seemed worried about the potential presence of the warriors chasing her. It was unlikely, however, that such mercenaries could work openly here without incurring the wrath of the King of *Uisneach* and his sizeable warband. Donnacha was apprehensive for the same old reason: people. Lots and lots of them in one place. People to offend and disappoint him. People to be let down and hurt by. People to fight and kill.

The bowman closed his eyes, taking a long, deep breath. Rhíona's calming words were fading, replaced by the ever-present, shifting knot in the pit of his stomach.

That darkest memory made a go of bursting into his thoughts. His black deed. He battled it back and drew another slower breath.

As always, his thoughts returned to what he had done that night. Had he not been with his new friends, he would have drawn his cloak over his head to hide from the crowd. Years ago, he would not have passed within twenty leagues of such a place. He shook his head and tried to think of something else.

Uisneach was like a nightmare born of the groups' fears combined. The inner fort was walled but awash with coloured flags and streamers. It was as if the inhabitants were trying to hide a rock with flowers. The large foreboding fort was not well concealed. The strong breeze shifting the flags made it almost comical. A settlement spread out around the fort. It skirted the walls closely and was considered one of the largest in the land. A second palisade wall surrounded this settlement and was manned by armed men and women. Flags decorated them. A strange counterpoint to the hardened soldiers standing among them.

The buildings were less humble than those of Oldfort. Slanted thatched and wooden roofs on squat wattle and daub buildings created a brown bed with coloured flags frolicking above. It was akin to the Ó Hehir flower garden that Donnacha would visit often.

Despite the impressive look of the place, the air around the settlement was dank. The smell of human filth greeted them as they arrived. Vast and bustling, it was alien to the boys. Such an array of people in one place, with the accompanying smells and sounds, the stink and the braying, was an overwhelming assault on their senses. Many trade stands had been set up in just about any free space available. Horses, cattle, sheep, goats and even pigeons were being traded feverishly. Buildings and stands closed around them, offering only narrow pathways winding throughout.

Rhíona looked on edge, walking nervously and seemingly in danger of faltering. The two boys walked on either side of her; as if mindful of her vulnerability in this strange place.

Donnacha just saw the people. All shape, size and manner of them. It was not that he hated them; he felt afraid; anxious around them. Always treading lightly but never putting his feet in the right places. There was one thing different about this rare visit to a settlement: he could not be so quick to violence with the three youngsters at his side. This was going to end badly, as it so often did.

They moved inside the outer gate into the market. A sprawling square was filled with stalls and carts that held all manner of things for trade. No one seemed to notice their passing. Even those hawkers showing their wares saw not faces but the possibility of ring pouches. In the case of the four guests to *Uisneach*, most of the hawkers just looked past them.

'What do you know about this Mac Éine?' asked Donnacha, speaking loudly over the din.

'He was the *scéalaí* and a poet whose talent was beyond compare. If you have heard tales of the deeds of the Fianna, the chances are that they originated from this man's mouth. I was told that he could be found telling stories in drinking houses here. I do not know what to do if I cannot find him.'

'You need to find an erstwhile member of the Fianna,' said Eoghan. 'He is one. If there is one, there are probably others. Or their children. Someone knows other than this man. We just find the one who does. They will be able to set the story straight.' He hawked and spat. 'One way or the other.'

A logical way to begin, in Donnacha's opinion, and as good a way to start as any. The boy had ideas that made some sense, at least.

'When there's nothing else left to do except the job being avoided,' Donnacha said. 'Have one quick look around for something else to do and then eventually do the job you've been avoiding. Hah?'

He searched for a reaction. Rúadhan gave him a limp smile, and Rhíona looked at him with sad eyes. Eoghan's eyes narrowed for a moment. Donnacha sighed. *Logical but not so trusting*. He looked down at Rúadhan's heels and followed them quietly.

Éine Scéalaí

***

The four find their man, a past member of the famed Fianna, the greatest warband of them all.

Beatha teanga í a labhairt.

It's the life of a language to speak it.

***

They entered the largest of the drinking houses with as little fuss as they could manage. Stout wooden chairs and tables littered the sawdust-covered floors. The darkened interior gave them cause to hesitate at the front door. Donnacha felt vulnerable and tried to shuffle forward towards a less conspicuous spot before his eyes had fully adjusted. The others followed him. The smoky heat was stifling, which added to the difficulty of seeing their surroundings. A singular sound in the place became apparent as Donnacha reoriented. It was the voice that belonged to the storyteller standing by the blazing fire. Low and filled with dramatic tension, the man who owned it prepared the audience for something fantastic that was taking place in a world of his creation.

Though small in number, the audience was seemingly enthralled by the man and the story he delivered. No one seemed to notice the group trying to navigate their way to a bench in the darkest corner. Donnacha searched for the hosteller.

The man was standing at the doorway into the back room, keeping the door ajar with his arse, his eyes glued to the storyteller, jaw agape. Donnacha became openly curious. It was as if the hosteller and the audience were under the storyteller's *geis*.

Donnacha took another chance to look at the *scéalaí*. Dressed in baggy, colourful woollens of greens and yellows, he had pure white hair that grew down to his shoulders. There was not enough of it to be impressive, and what was there was greasy and knotted, further lessening the grandeur. He was neither lean nor fat; neither handsome nor ugly. His blue eyes peeking out from under bushy white eyebrows were rheumy and caked with yellow discharge. His voice was glorious, though, full of character, which he used like an instrument. When he lowered his voice to a whisper, the gentle curve at the top of his back gave him a conspiratorial look.

'They battled for four days and four nights, stopping only to take water. The ground shook below them. The animals of the land and air went silent with fear. It was a costly duel for Fionn. On the morning of the third day, the Fae prince Aill'en broke his shield into pieces. On the evening of the same day, the Fae prince broke the legendary great sword of Fionn, *Mac an Lúin*. Though Fionn despaired at the sight of the great weapon destroyed, he had no choice but to drop the remains and fight on. Fionn had to use *Birga*, the enchanted spear that had helped him resist the *draíocht* of the Fae and stay awake. They danced together until Aill'en began to falter.' The *scéalaí's* voice swelled as he stood to his full height, spreading his arms wide.

'Balls of fire came from his eyes and mouth then; the flames almost engulfed the hero Fionn. He touched his spear to his forehead again, and the flames disappeared around him. Aill'en took fright and made to escape. A black door appeared in the air before him, and he leapt through. Fionn had no choice but to cast his precious spear into the black shape as it closed. He cast it with venom and with the hope of finally killing the dark Fae prince, the only way to be sure of saving Tara from future peril. No sound reported, no sight recorded, no word relayed ever confirmed success or failure. Of *Birga*, the spear that did not miss, none of this land heard tell of it. Nor of the Fae prince. Has Tara stood unmolested for many *Samhains* past? Yay, I swear to you that I laid mine own ageing eyes upon its walls, not two seasons past. Will it stand two seasons from the next?' His hands moved behind his back, and he shrugged.

'That, my great friends, is something to which I cannot attest now nor wail prophecies regarding any day soon. However, I will speak this truth to you. The dark Fae prince, Aill'en the Burner, will not be the one to cause its demise, for if it's not dead he is, then it's afraid he is, knowing that Fionn lies in a cave somewhere beneath this very land, ready to come to our aid when the need grows anew...'

He dropped his head into his chest for a moment, turned to take a deep thirsty draught of his ale, and bowed with a flourish. The audience sat quietly as if waking from a joyous dream, they shook off their distant gazes and all burst into applause. Some of them took out metal rings and, after tapping them loudly three times on the table, tossed them into the cloak of the storyteller, which was bundled near his feet.

Donnacha was impressed. The audience was small, but their show of appreciation was large indeed. Moments later, they got back to themselves, some going out the door about their business and some returning to a drink. Donnacha watched as the storyteller sat down, looking thoughtfully into the fire with his ale in one fist and the collected rings jingling in the other. His hunched posture seemed less conspiratorial now. It became more like a badge of passing years.

The man was eclipsed by the pockmarked hosteller, who appeared before them with a toothless grin. 'How can I please you people today?'

Donnacha mirrored the behaviour. 'My good fellow, the mere offer of your hospitality is nourishment enough, though perhaps the thirsty necks of my friends and myself could be rinsed wet by your finest thirst-quencher.'

The man's face changed. The smile faltered. 'What cac are you selling, man?' he growled. 'You sound like the poxy storyteller. What do ye want and be quick or be off.'

Donnacha felt a wash of mixed emotions as always. The wave of disappointment, followed by the cynical, knowing disgust. *There is little kindness left, and I will find none here. Not kindness, nor even civility.*

Eoghan was the one who spoke up. 'Bring us drinks, you grumpy old shitbag, and send someone more attractive to serve it, so none of us has to suffer your ugly face any further.

The toothless grin appeared once again. 'At once, *Taoiseach*.' He made to leave when Rhíona, seated on a stool close to him, reached out to touch the man's arm.

'Wait a moment, if you will? Perhaps you can help us with a small query?' she said with an open smile. 'You seem to be a man of some standing, and not by accident, I suspect. We are in need of such a fellow.'

He looked down at her hand pointedly until she removed it. 'You are very pretty, like a clay doll, *girlín*, but spare me the batting eyelids. Much as I would delight in such things, it is just a little too unlikely a situation whereby you might open up for me. So, keep your hands and simpering sweetness to yourself and speak plain.'

A chuckle suggested that Rúadhan was warming to the man. Eoghan's face had set into an angry glare, but for some reason, he did not speak to the hosteller. Donnacha remained gutted like a mackerel during early autumn shoals. *Why are people the way they are?*

Rhíona's eyes narrowed. 'I did not bat my eyelids.'

Rúadhan spoke up. 'Someone named Mac Éine. Have you any notion of where he might be? We were led to believe he is or was here.'

The hosteller's eyes narrowed. 'Couldn't possibly say m'*ladín*. Wouldn't have a great memory for names at my age.' He held out an open palm.

Donnacha noticed a rheumy gaze flit towards the group as the conversation continued. They were being spied on by the storyteller.

'Let us pay you for some of your finest mead, and you can tell us where the man we seek is,' said Eoghan, a growl in his voice. He tossed a copper ring on the table in front of him.

The ring was snatched up before it had fully settled. As the man turned and walked away, his other hand shot out to point at the storyteller, who was smiling broadly while looking at them.

The storyteller stood and bowed extravagantly. 'Lest my fine employer has left any lingering doubt with his hand cast wide in my direction, then allow me to introduce myself to those who would enquire about me so assiduously. It is I whom you seek. I, Éine Mac Éine, most humbly at your service.'

Rúadhan could not help but feel disappointed. This strange storyteller who now sat beside them at the table, instantly fawning over Eoghan, was not what he was expecting. His fine story had offered a glimmer of past grandiosity. Yet his look, manner and delivery suggested a tired old man. His story had enraptured the room. Sitting at their table, he was less out of a folktale and more out of a darkened drinking house during the day.

Eoghan narrowed his eyes, seemingly unconvinced. 'Are you really the man we're looking for?'

'I hope to my core that I am, young sir, for a steady thump from the weary, dusty chambers of my heart suggests that you might be the young man I've been looking for. And it grows for you. Like a swelling honeybag…' He slid his stool closer to lean into Eoghan, and a gnarled, arthritic finger brushed up his arm towards his shoulder.

'You are Éine Mac Éine?' said Eoghan as he leaned back, grimacing. Rúadhan found his obvious discomfort amusing.

'I swear to same and hold the title proudly. Should you seek a *scéalaí*, ye shall cross paths with none superior. Indeed, let me tell you this, there was a man once who I met in the pig fort, Ros Muc...'

'I do not have time for a story,' snapped Eoghan. 'We have a need to discuss business with you of a different nature.' Rúadhan looked around to see if they could be overheard.

'The lad speaks the truth, and that's one thing I can testify to in no uncertain terms,' chimed Donnacha, his face a picture of urgency.

Rúadhan bit back a smile. He enjoyed the company of the travelling bowman. At times he was positively childlike.

'Well, by the hounds of Fionn himself, this sounds like there are mysterious and inscrutable goings-on that I am not yet privy to. Enlighten me if you please, my young sir, and I will try not to stumble and fall into the pools of brown intrigue that you look at me so solemnly with. Even if they do look somewhat worse for wear. It sends despair through my brittle soul that someone, anyone, would wish to lay a hand on such a sweet visage.'

'How do we know you are to be trusted? You might give us up if we put faith in you,' challenged Eoghan.

'Oh, my fine young boy. Put your faith or anything else you might desire in me. Trust me most deeply. I would sooner walk into the wailing arms of *Ban na Sí* than to give up such a pristine presence as yourself.'

Donnacha shifted. 'Take it easy, man,' he said, with a creased brow.

The storyteller's eyes never left Eoghan's. 'If that is what he yearns, then I could take it easy, indeed. To begin with, at least.'

Rhíona sat watching the old man before saying, 'I found and spoke with the *Caoránach*. She said you would be here and that you would be the only one who might offer assistance to me proper. I am looking for a great man. A man you knew and served under. I have a great need to find him or sound *Dord Fionn*, his hunting horn, three times to summon him. I would not be here were the need not great. I have travelled from... far-off lands.' She leaned towards him, mouth tightened. 'Many suggest that he has perished. I know this to be a falsehood. I was told you might also be able to get help from *Síor Feargach*; such are the grave necessities of the dark times ahead. You can help me. I know this to be true. And so, here we are.'

Éine neither moved nor made a sound as if stopped in shock. He turned and his blue eyes bore into Rhíona's blue eyes. Then, as if nothing had been said, he was suddenly jovial and eruptive.

'Oh, my lady, you are fair and full of mischief. Were I to know of such things, I would lay the knowledge at your feet like my cloak over a puddle. Alas, my sweet, I can offer only darkness and not illumination in such matters.' He looked around the room.

'Ó Maolmhuaidh,' he called when the hosteller appeared. 'My friends have decided to stay in the room next to mine and will be pleased to pay the outlandish price you are sure to quote them as I depart.'

He bowed with a flourish once again. 'My words cannot express my dismay at being impotent in this matter of your need. All I can hope is that if there *were* anyone who can offer assistance, they might visit that room this very evening. Or if not this evening, then the next. Or indeed, quite possibly the one after that.' He turned and disappeared up the stairs.

The group exchanged glances. Donnacha spoke, nodding slowly. 'I think he wants us to wait in that room until he comes to us in priv–'

Rhíona laid a hand upon his. 'We are aware, Donnacha, thank you.' Her lips were tight.

The arrival of Ó Maolmhuaidh with four drinking mugs did not allow them to discuss it further.

Éine's suddenly secretive manner had made Rúadhan feel ill at ease. He could tell from the other's silence that they were similarly confused. They downed their drinks and went to their room. Donnacha told them he had enjoyed the drink so much that he might stay for another and to send for him if anything happened. The thought that Donnacha might not feel the tension plaguing him caused Rúadhan to stop and stare at the man. The archer merely sat there with an apologetic grin and then a slow, mysterious wink that caused Rúadhan to shake his head in disbelief. Strange man.

The sleeping loft, up a sturdy ladder, was sparsely furnished. Hay pallets scattered around served as bedding. The wooden floor had started to give in areas. There was a hole in one corner where they could have easily climbed into the storeroom below had anyone felt the urge. The smell was rank as if past tenants had not bothered to go to the midden pit and half-hearted efforts to clean up had begun to add a permanent feature to the otherwise featureless room. Rúadhan inspected his bedding. The hay at least was recently changed and, on first inspection, appeared to hide no unseemly guests. Lying down, Rúadhan expected to toss and turn. However, he drifted into a deep sleep despite the loft being uncomfortable.

Donnacha huffed up the ladder to them as the sun rose. Rúadhan was quickest to his feet, and he woke Rhíona and Eoghan, while trying not to wake the other guests. Even in the candlelit loft, he noticed that Donnacha had a sheen of sweat on his brow and was breathing heavily.

'It seems that, as is becoming the norm, further adventure lies ahead of us today, my young companions. It is best that ye come away from that shaky-looking floor to this sturdier-looking bit until you hear of our nimble-footed storyteller.'

'What do you mean?' asked Rhíona.

'Éine is gone. I sat down there having my drink for more than the one reason and meant no harm, but was right in my thinking. My observations of the house chief – a sneak if there was one before him – led me to thinking that something was up. I took a walk to where he did not want me to and found Éine in the business of escaping. I kept myself to myself to see what he would do. And sure enough, off he's gone like a hare from a dog. Had his bag on his back and his staff in his fist.'

'Do you know which way he went?' asked Rúadhan.

'That I do, my young friend. I followed him for a time. I think we'll need to go after him...'

The three youngsters made to move when Donnacha held up his hands. '...but... if I may make a suggestion before we trample out the gates?' He took a deep breath.

'The man we seek has left the place we do not want to be in. It is a chance for us to be free of these walls, with no need to return. I have followed long enough to track his intended passage. He will be easy to catch up to for a sprightly bunch such as ourselves. If we push any bit of pace, we'll catch the old goose.' He looked down into the storeroom below and nodded.

'Let us leave only after we have provisioned ourselves for the wider world. We can get supplies and food and have the road rise for us rightly. We'll have found his trail, and we can keep going after. Those warriors are here, as you know. We are drinking water by the wolves' lair, and the opportunity has arisen to walk free without disturbing the beasts. I'd say I'm making sense were I to be listening to myself.'

Rúadhan nodded slowly, as did the other two. Eoghan spoke.

'Rhíona and one of us could stay here to avoid her being spotted. There's no point in dragging her around when the things we require can be gathered and brought back here. Rhíona, you might be able to drop into that storeroom and see if there is anything that we could lift with us? Seeing as we won't be using the room after all, and we did pay a bit for it.'

Rhíona smiled at him. 'Your thieving ways reveal themselves, at last, Eoghan,' she said as she moved to the hole in the floor to look into the darkened room below. 'And asking a lady to do your work for you? I am shocked.' She suddenly leapt forward and disappeared soundlessly into the dark. The three left behind smiled at each other in admiration. Rúadhan saw Eoghan's smile was particularly wide. *She is an interesting soul, to be sure, especially for him.*

'Donnacha and I will go,' offered Rúadhan with a grin to his friend. 'You stay here and act as protector and hero to the lady.'

Donnacha smiled too. 'Oh, I think that sounds like a good idea if there ever was one. Do stay and sweep her off her feet with your charm and wit.'

Eoghan closed his hands into fists, and his brows furrowed.

'Maybe you should jump down there with her just in case she's in danger,' said Rúadhan. Donnacha chuckled.

'Oh, but what if ye got stuck down there together with naught to keep yourselves warm... except each other,' said Donnacha. The two were laughing now as Eoghan's face grew darker again.

He opened his mouth to speak but was interrupted by Rhíona's voice from the room below. 'I can hear you two and would suggest that ye get gone lest I come up to you both.'

Rúadhan and the bowman shared a look and then made themselves scarce.

A CAUSE FOR AVOIDANCE

***

Rúadhan and Donnacha become embroiled in a dispute that lands them in peril. Deadly violence ensues.

Múineann gá seift.

Necessity is the mother of invention.

***

Donnacha, though good company for his part, was obviously not enjoying the number of people bustling around them. Hawkers and sellers, traders and tricksters all populated the multitude of small marts and markets that opened up before them as they walked. The vigorous sights, sounds and smells accompanying these trading pits were almost overwhelming. They also served to mask the less pleasant sights, sounds and smells of this many people in one place. There were squat round huts visible along the rows of stalls, but most had become one with the stall fronts.

Rúadhan and Donnacha went about the place stocking up, making as little fuss as they could. Satchels, blankets, food, water skins, arrowheads and bowstring, whetting stone, rope and a slew of other items to fill up the bags and renew their ability to remain independent for the foreseeable future. A number of the same traders were delightedly under-haggled by the pair, who were eager to get done and be gone.

As they walked, Rúadhan noticed that Donnacha was giving him sidelong glances as if about to say something.

'Donnacha, what is it?'

'Nothing. Nothing at all, my young friend.'

Another glance.

'Donnacha. Spit it out.'

'Well …'

'Well, what Donnacha?'

'Why are you here?'

'Are you asking me to tell you about how my parents made me? I'm not sure either of us wants to have that thought in our heads.'

'You are a witty young fellow, indeed, but that's not what I'm talking about, and you know that entirely. Rúadhan, why are you not gone home?'

'Are you so eager to be rid of us?'

'Do you know, I am not at all. I find you both to be fine young men, and that's the plain truth of things. However, I'm not referring to the two of you. I'm referring only to your good self. I might be prying, and tell me if I am. I wonder, why is it that you follow

Eoghan around the way you do? He seems to be far less interested in heading towards home. Yet you stay with him throughout the mess that has been unfolding. I suppose it just makes me curious. If you get me.'

Rúadhan paused, thoughts straying back to long months on the sleeping pallet where he drifted in and out of the feverish horrors of the pox. Of crying out in anguish and hearing his friend whispering soothing words of support. The stories he told. The treats he would bring. Even as Rúadhan's mother sat with him, Eoghan would be nestled in behind her, that worried look in his grave eyes.

In the long months of recovery, as he learned to walk and run again, Eoghan would be the one standing beside him for each step, urging him on. Eoghan would help him practise hurling and wrestling. Rúadhan recalled clearly how, over time, Eoghan would lose wrestling matches on purpose and swear blind that he had tried his damndest. Both knew the lie, but Eoghan's face would grow dark at the suggestion that he had let Rúadhan win. As he got stronger, Eoghan would knock down any lad who challenged Rúadhan. Rúadhan almost smiled as he recalled Eoghan trouncing those three lads who would not let Rúadhan pass.

'We're friends,' said Rúadhan matter-of-factly. Donnacha regarded him for a moment.

'I see. You're a good friend, I think.'

'So is he.'

The two came upon a drinking house where some customers had congregated outside to enjoy the fresh air as they drank. Amongst their number was a group of seven mercenary warriors wearing black. Uad's men had ventured into the town, after all.

The warriors were enjoying the spectacle of a merchant who had caught a young boy trying to pick his ring purse.

'This rat tried to steal from me. Me.' The merchant said. 'He needs a lesson. Who among you wishes for rings in exchange for cutting the boy's fingers off as punishment for his effrontery?' He was speaking to the group of mercenaries. The boy was slack-jawed. The bulk of the onlookers were appalled at the notion.

'What kind of rings and how many?' asked one of the warriors.

The youth tried to wriggle free from the merchant's grip, crying, shaking. Cuffing him across the face, the merchant opened a cut over the boy's eye.

'One silver ring,' exclaimed the merchant, a smug smile creeping across his face.

A few voices in the crowd urged the man to let the boy go because no harm had been done. They were ignored in favour of the ongoing conversation concerning the future of the boy's fingers. Some of the onlookers ran off looking for warriors of *Uisneach* to come and set things straight.

A large-bellied, redheaded mercenary who had lost a hand himself spoke up.

'You are right to feel aggrieved. The little ass deserves to be punished. You must consider my long-term view, however. What if this boy becomes a great warrior in years to come, despite his missing fingers, and hunts me down, bent on revenge? What of my life? What of the lives of my children?'

'You don't have any children,' said one of the other warriors.

'Well, none that you have claimed anyway,' said another. This drew raucous laughter from a number of them. They were enjoying themselves. 'I fear that one silver ring will not suffice,' said the red-headed one.

Rúadhan almost jumped when Donnacha took a pointed step forward, hands balled into fists. Rúadhan's hand shot out to arrest his march, and he whispered. 'You are unarmed, outnumbered, supposed to be avoiding that type of attention and about to make a terrible mistake. Turn around with me. Éine is on the move, and you have given yourself the task of catching up to him. Getting us killed will surely end in Eoghan and Rhíona failing, or worse. Let's go. Turn around with me. Donnacha. Now.'

The merchant spoke again. 'Fine. Two silver rings. Just do it now and be done with it.'

At this, several warriors nodded in approval as if pleased with their associate's toil.

The redhead drained his mug and stood, belching noisily and drawing a sword as he did so. 'So be it,' he cried dramatically. 'I will reap justice in your good name. Whatever that name might be.'

Donnacha shook free from Rúadhan's grip and broke into the circle that had formed around the unfolding commotion.

He walked out to stand in front of the boy, and the redheaded warrior stopped with a look of genuine surprise on his bearded face.

Rúadhan was unsure what to do next. How well did he know Donnacha? Did he care that the man was about to be chopped up into tiny pieces? Surely getting back to the other two was his concern now, to make sure that they were not drawn into this mess? He had spent years sorting out messes that Eoghan had landed him in. He was increasingly tired of it. Why would he sort out anything for this strange man? Many passers-by sensed the increasing tension and moved to get clear before trouble erupted.

Donnacha said, 'I think, really, you should sit back down and enjoy your drink on a grand day such as this. This young man has surely learned his lesson and has been bloodied to match. There is no need for cutting or trimming or any kind of swordplay, I would say.'

Rúadhan's mind raced, and he scanned around him. Three of the other warriors had risen, though their expressions were mainly amused. They seemed to think that Donnacha was simple-minded. Rúadhan agreed.

Rúadhan looked at a bench to his right. A thick earthen jug lay amid several empty mugs. Unfortunately for him, he had just had an idea that might provide a chance for Donnacha and the boy. Even worse, he had decided to give it a try. What he needed was time to put his plan into action. *Happily enough*, he thought, *Donnacha has most definitely captured their attention.* He moved as quickly as he could.

The redheaded warrior spoke first. 'You make a lot of sense, friend, and I was very much enjoying my drink and the company along with it.' He turned to nod and wink at the other warriors. One or two raised a mug in his direction.

'I feel the same,' one replied.

'All you have to do is provide me with two silver rings for my trouble. I will obey your directions in their entirety and wish the fellow well in his future endeavours.'

Rúadhan grabbed the jug and moved towards the nearest mercenary. He tapped the brutish-looking man on the shoulder.

'Wha's happenin'?' Rúadhan rasped as drunk sounding as he could manage.

'Piss off, boy,' said the warrior, still watching the scene before him.

Donnacha's smile was apologetic, but his eyes were iron. 'Well, I am filled with dismay, for a wealthy sum like that is not in my possession, and I would have to say that it's unlikely to be in the future ahead of me. That said, would you afford me the opportunity to make you an offer that you might find equally attractive?'

The warrior bowed slightly. 'By all means, bald man, but be quick, for I am thirsty, and this is not drinking.'

Rúadhan tapped the shoulder again. 'Can I have a ring or two for my sick mother?' he said.

The warrior shrugged him away, watching Donnacha as the bowless bowman spoke.

'Well, my offer is plain in nature but precious in spirit. I offer you your life; in return, all you have to do is sit down, and that's that, really and truly. Should you not sit down and let the boy go, you are nothing but dead meat, and that's something to avoid, I think, in the main,' Donnacha said, his tone unchanged. The onlooking warriors howled with laughter. This bald man was clearly simple but provided great sport nonetheless.

The redhead held up his stump without looking behind.

Rúadhan took a step back and braced himself. He would be very pleased with himself if this worked;

quite possibly butchered where he stood if it did not. He found it interesting that he felt no fear. Only the urgent need to act and to win.

'As you wish, bald man. It seems bloodshed is inevitable at this point, so let's be on with it.'

As Rúadhan glanced over, the redhead launched a vicious swing at Donnacha's head. Donnacha dropped to a squatting crouch to avoid the blow. He launched himself at the warrior's fore-knee while his hands grabbed the man's heel. A loud crack signalled the warrior's knee joint capitulating as he landed on his back. Before he could do anything other than grimace, Donnacha leapt forward and plunged a previously concealed hunting knife into the warrior's neck, below the ear, which killed him instantly.

As the rest of the warriors sprang to arms, Rúadhan shoulder charged the nearest one, pushing him into two others, which knocked all three onto a bench in a heap. He lashed out with the jug, striking another in the face, knocking the warrior out cold.

Donnacha came among them with the redhead's sword. He was no expert swordsman but had the initiative. He started swinging wildly around him, causing massive damage.

Rúadhan used an opportunity to deliver a knee to the face of a kneeling warrior, which seemed to do little more than enrage the warrior. Praying for a better result, Rúadhan kneed the man again, and he fell senseless beside the bench. Rúadhan picked up the warrior's sword, just in time to block an axe swing. The swing was followed by another, and another. The warrior continued hacking at Rúadhan's guard. Rúadhan was not a swordsman either. Though he was accustomed to wielding a hurl with skill, the weight of the sword, combined with the focused assault by the warrior, meant his arm started to tire. Rúadhan's adroit deflection began to slow, but the warrior had started to flag too. A combination of afternoon drinking, being snared in a trap, and a near-frenzied attack meant his aggression was spent quickly. His years as a veteran showed as he changed his style of attack to a more sporadic and prying assault. Rúadhan could sense that it was designed to highlight the obvious weaknesses in Rúadhan's guard.

A second warrior appeared from behind the first, and Rúadhan started to panic. No ancient rule of combat ensured Rúadhan would not be attacked by both at once. Those rules lived only in stories. The only course of action left to Rúadhan was to embrace his rising panic, attack them both and hope that Donnacha would appear sooner rather than later.

He waited for the second attacker to swing, and when he did, Rúadhan took a large stride, following the sword ark, aiming his hips to meet the warrior's two-handed grip. He thrust his own sword up against the first warrior's swing.

He came much closer to the second warrior than anticipated. The warrior head-butted Rúadhan on the ear, sending him stumbling backwards.

The two warriors sidestepped away from each other as they approached, increasing their angle of attack. Rúadhan's panic began to overwhelm him. He was going to die.

One of the warriors made a hupping sound and they attacked in unison. Rúadhan could only block one sword and put his arm up in a futile effort to try and slow the killing blow from the second.

No killing blow arrived, and he backed away, confused. The second warrior had stopped mid-attack and was standing with both hands scrabbling to reach something protruding from his back. He jerked once, then twice more and fell forward onto the muddy ground. Four darts were jutting, a hand's length, out of his back. They were thin, weighted iron stakes, which must have been thrown by a skilled caster.

The first warrior raised his guard and crouched, surveying as much as possible while protecting against Rúadhan's attack. He retreated towards the wall of a nearby building removing any chance of an attack from behind. Rúadhan could see that Donnacha was still fighting with a very able warrior woman amidst her fallen peers. There was a large cut on the crown of his head that was streaming blood into his eyes and making it difficult for him to see. He needed help.

'Drop it and run,' Rúadhan said, trying to distract the man. He leaned his body back to prepare for a leaping attack. A dart struck the warrior's thigh, and he gasped in shock. His sword remained in place, however, and his eyes locked on Rúadhan as if reading his mind. Another dart struck his cuirass but was deflected. This was Rúadhan's chance. He attacked using the sword as if it were a hurl, swinging it wide and downwards to bring up the warrior's defences. He flicked his wrist while stepping in, changing the trajectory mid-swing. The warrior parried some of the swing, but the blow had enough force to bite into his arm, leaving little of it attached.

The warrior threw down his sword, grabbed his arm and ran. Rúadhan made no move to stop him but turned instead to Donnacha. The archer's face was covered in blood like a butcher's block. The woman was dead. There was a dart jutting from her back too. Rúadhan's eyes scanned around them. The crowd had almost entirely dissipated except for the bravest or nosiest few.

It was her eyes that caught his attention. Pale green and full of fire, she stood between two huts, beckoning him urgently. He motioned for Donnacha to follow as he went towards her, picking up and buckling on a sword belt. Donnacha followed, though his legs looked shaky.

Seven blooded warriors. All had fallen at the hands of Donnacha and him. He felt strong. It was a deed worthy of poetry.

He looked at the girl who stood watching him. She was close in age to Rúadhan. She had smooth, soft skin; long brown hair was braided to one side, making her look a picture of innocence. She wore a saffron *léine* that hung down to her knees and tied leather *triús* beneath. She held three darts in her hand and had several more on a bandolier around her waist.

'Follow me fast. There will be more of them looking for you. We need to leave this place.'

'They were already looking for us. And they found us,' said Rúadhan.

The girl rolled her eyes skyward. 'Follow me and, more importantly, be silent. Especially if you are going to talk like that.'

'Who are you?' asked Rúadhan.

'Not now. We go.'

'Your name, at least.'

‘My name is Laoise. Now be silent, and let me think.’

Donnacha wiped the blood from his eyes. ‘We need to get to Ó Maolmhuaidh’s place,’ he said, voice distant, fresh blood dripping into his eyes.

‘I know. You are also cut badly.’ She stooped to pick up a cloak and took off running. ‘Follow,’ she said over her shoulder.

THE WALLED ISLE

***

After being rescued from Uisneach by the mysterious Laoise, the four are brought to the safety of a Crannóg.

Dá fhada an lá tagann an tráthnóna.

However long the day, the evening will come.

***

Eoghan stood outside the settlement boundary out of breath, his heart beating fast. He looked at the others, who stood panting beside him. They had, for now, evaded further altercations with the warriors. After he and Rhíona were collected from Ó Maolmhuaidh's, the girl had guided them outside of the walls. Donnacha had been quiet as they left. Though Rúadhan offered him an arm, it was clear the archer was wilting.

'Let me look at your wound,' Rhíona said. Donnacha frowned, but after a quick inspection and a light clean seemed noticeably better, though still weak.

The girl with the darts stood, regarding them with a glare. She carried darts in each of her hands. 'We will rest here briefly, and then you will follow me. No discussion on this matter is required. If any of you reach for weapons, I will knock you dead.'

'Who are you?' asked Rhíona.

'And why are you helping us?' added Eoghan.

'And where are you bringing us?' asked Rúadhan.

'And thank you, I might add, for saving us back there,' chimed Donnacha.

She looked at them, one after another then shook her head slightly. 'Not now. Not until we are away from here. You two,' she looked at Donnacha and Rúadhan, 'are some right pair of fools with your heroics. Madness.'

She looked back towards *Uisneach*, checking for pursuit. 'We need to get past the hill, and then we go to the island. We'll be safe there for a time.' She looked at them all again, angry glare reset. 'These are fast becoming dangerous times. Go that way.' She gestured to them.

As they started walking, Donnacha spoke to no one in particular. 'This is the way our other friend went. Quite an interesting turn of events, I think, so I do.'

Over the day, they skirted the hill of *Uisneach* and continued northeast. It was slow going as Donnacha's energy waned. The sun started to take its leave as they arrived at the edge of a calm lake. The fading saffron-lit scene mirrored on the tranquil water made it difficult to judge the lake's size. However, they could make out a *crannóg* on the tiny island. It would be more accurate to say that the wooden walled fort was itself the island. Sharpened stakes had been lashed together to form a ringed palisade. There was a large round wooden building in the middle of the isle. It had a raised crows-perch to observe the goings-on on the banks of the lake. A footbridge extended from the palisade to where the girl led them.

As they approached, a bowman appeared on the wall with an arrow trained on them. Another appeared on the walkway. 'Are you happy enough, Laoise?' he called.

'I am,' said the girl. 'Let us in.'

'We will,' said the man, 'but we'll take the swords and put them away for safe keeping.'

The two guards put up their bows, and the group crossed the bridge. The bowmen were an elderly man and a young boy. They embraced the girl.

'We will eat if there's food for us,' she said.

The old man nodded. 'I'm sure we might manage something. Go and speak with your grandfather. Éine is with him.' He turned to the group and gestured for their sword belts. 'I hope you people will behave yourselves here. It will be a problem for you if you find you cannot. For now, in there, if it's your will.' He motioned to a small wooden house near the front gate.

'I gave you the sword. Don't ask me for the bow,' said Donnacha quietly. The old man stood up straight and looked in his eyes without speaking. 'I give you my word, I will not break the peace,' Donnacha said. He was pale and seemed hardly able to stand, never mind raise a bow. The man glanced at Laoise, who nodded. Shrugging, the man put the two swords under his arm and turned.

The boy was pulling the foot bridge onto the *crannóg* as best he could. The old man went to help him, as did Rúadhan. Together, the three dragged it in with no difficulty.

After lighting a fire in the hut, the old man said, 'You will come and join us in the main house shortly, once we have had a chance to talk and take stock. Until then, please remain here. You will be summoned when it's time. There's water there if you want to wash. I would if I were you. I might clean out that cut too.' He nodded at Donnacha's scalp.

There they waited and washed, enjoying the security of the place. For the three youngsters, it was the first time they had felt safe in days. Rhíona tended to Donnacha's wound. By the time she had finished, there was hardly any evidence of the cut, which impressed the group enough to raise eyebrows.

'Sometimes those small head cuts can really bleed,' Rhíona remarked off-handedly. Eoghan found it strange, because it had seemed to be a much more significant cut, made more unusual by Donnacha's energy levels picking up.

Rúadhan moved to sit beside Eoghan, face serious. Eoghan sighed. A face like that meant only one thing. Talk.

'You're gone very cross all the time, Eoghan,' he said. 'I know you're sad about your da and that. You're so angry, though, with everyone. You can tell me about how you're feeling if you want.'

Eoghan squeezed his soft brown eyes shut in frustration.

'I'm not sad. Or Angry,' he snapped.

Rúadhan sighed.

'I mean… I am…' he started. 'My home and yours are not the same; were not. It's not a happy place. It wasn't up until now, and it will be worse now that…'

'I know,' said Rúadhan softly.

'Maybe there'll be changes off the back of your da going to meet the gods?'

Eoghan sat staring at nothing.

'It will all be fine Eoghan,' said Rúadhan. 'I'll look after you. Sure, I've been rearing you since you grew into those bullock shoulders of yours anyway.'

Eoghan smiled ruefully. 'You couldn't rear a shite,' he said.

'Whatever about that; whatever about anything, this is not where we should be.' He looked around at the strange room.

Eoghan knew what Rúadhan was going to say and said it first, loud enough for the other two to hear.

'It's time for us to go home. They will be worried to sickness because of us. Rúadhan is here because of me, and I have not treated him fairly. We have done what we said we would do and helped in whatever way we were able. I... am sorry, Rhíona. It will be a hard thing to leave you when you are still in danger.'

'We are sorry, Rhíona,' said Rúadhan. 'We have jumped into a lake, and the water is over our heads. We are no warriors. We are afraid and sinking more and more out of our depth. It does not seem right to leave you, but I cannot see what use we might be the way things are going.'

Rhíona sat looking at them, herself looking dejected, exhausted and malnourished.

'But... now? After everything? Why now? The two of you have been invaluable.'

'Don't you see? We have nothing to offer,' said Eoghan, picking a scab on his face.

Rhíona walked to him. 'Everything we have faced; you have matched, and we are here. I was so tired of searching alone. You are both…'

'My lads,' said Donnacha. 'I think what Rhíona was about to say was, you are both entirely correct, and I'd say she might not mind me saying so. You have shown yourselves to be brave and worthy, a pair not to be taken lightly, and that's naught but true. You are both correct, I would reckon, in your assessment, though. It is time for you to be clear of these goings on for, as Rúadhan so astutely put it, the water is rising.' He moved beside her and placed a gentle hand on her shoulder.

'I have a vested interest in Rhíona's success. I long to lay eyes on Fionn Mac Cumhal more than anything I have ever done or might yet do in the future, and I am willing to brave the obvious risks. I am not suggesting that you are both unworthy of being here. Indeed, ye have all been through a lot, so ye have. A fine little story has been carved out in the world. I do think, if I might say, I have some skills that might be of use for what's ahead.'

He looked at Rhíona, half smiling.

'If you'll have me, I'll help you find him. Through whatever hairy places we might end up.'

Rhíona smiled back and threw her arms around Donnacha.

'I was hoping you might help me,' she said. He wrapped his arms around her like a protective father.

Next, she threw her arms around Rúadhan. 'And I would not have got this far without you.'

Rúadhan stood with arms held out. Looking awkward he wrapped them around her in a similar protective embrace.

Rhíona turned to Eoghan, whose face was suddenly scorching and his body rigid. She stood for a moment as if unsure how to proceed before something strange passed between them. They looked into each other's eyes for an intense moment. Her arms extended, and she started towards him.

The moment was lost when the door opened, and Laoise appeared. She had changed into a different *léine*, pleated and dyed navy and green, and the leather *triús* had been changed for skirts. Her soft skin glowed in the firelight.

She looked to Rhíona and said, 'Firstly, I have taken a risk bringing you here without knowing you or your history. It was my mistake, and it should not have been done. Since I played a large part in prolonging the lives of two of your group, I would ask that you would see fit to keep the peace while you are among us. My grandfather, the master of this place, wishes to speak with you.'

Rhíona stood and spoke softly.

'I will speak with your grandfather, and I thank you for the part you have played in our safe passage. You are brave and fierce. We bring only peace to this place.'

'It remains to be seen what you have brought.' The girl stared at Rhíona for several moments.

Rhíona nodded her head slowly. 'I was told we would be offered aid freely by the *scealaí*, Éine. Had he not left, we would have had no need to follow.'

'Had you not asked for his assistance in such a manner, he would not have left. In light of the growing number of armed mercenaries in these parts every day and talk of their foul deeds spreading, you are a cause of anxiety here. Should you be the cause of more, you will see fierce up close.'

Rhíona pursed her lips for a moment before she continued.

'I understand, Laoise.'

The two locked eyes.

'You don't fully. Don't do anything that makes me illustrate it clearly for you.'

Rúadhan spoke from the back of the room before Rhíona could respond.

'Who is your grandfather, lady?' His voice seemed higher than usual, causing both Eoghan and Donnacha to turn and look at him.

'My grandfather is Caoilte Mac Rónán.' Her voice was thick with pride.

There was a palpable sense of shock. They had all heard stories about the deeds of Mac Rónán, thought to be one of the greatest Fianna of them all and one of the only ones to walk away from the battle at *Gamhra*. Yet the battle had taken place two generations ago. No one was affected by this revelation more than Donnacha.

'What is that now? Your grandfather is Caoilte Mac Rónán, and he is here, and we are going to speak with him?' He had become very excited, and *his* voice bordered on a squeal.

'You have heard tell of him. Good. It will save the storyteller from stinking the place out with his despoiled tales about heroic deeds and past glories that might or might not have happened.'

Donnacha was standing open-mouthed.

‘Caoilte Mac Rónán is here,’ he muttered, shaking his head slowly with his hands open wide. Rúadhan clapped him on the back. ‘Grab a hold of yourself, man, and let’s go and meet him.’

DIMINISHING GREATNESS

***

Excitement mounts as they are brought to the table of the renowned warrior Caoilte Mac Rónán. The weight of expectation is a heavy burden for anyone to bear, or to have placed upon them.

Ní bhíonn in aon rud ach seal.

Nothing lasts forever.

***

Laoise led them into the island's main house, a large round wooden building of one room set around a large fire, spit and hanging cauldron in the centre. It was well-lit by small hanging braziers. There were low tables, a few stools scattered around, and hide rugs carpeting the floor. Herbs had been left in small bowls, suspended over the flames to create the aroma that greeted them as they entered.

Two tables were together on the far side of the fire. Three men sat cross-legged on the floor. Éine Mac Éine was one, and the old man they met at the gate was another. They were waiting with empty wooden plates in front of them. As hearty a meal as they could have hoped for covered the table. Trout and pike from the lake, salted beef from the fields, pigeon from the woods. Bread, butter, cheese and honey, beans and roots. Eoghan suddenly felt lonely for home.

What home? A home from my memory. Nothing more. That home is gone.

The old man beckoned, and the guests knelt and ate their fill before a word was spoken. Donnacha spent a lot of the meal looking over at the person they had not met before.

Caoilte Mac Rónán.

He looked somewhat frail, though a near giant, with broad shoulders and scarred hands the size of axe heads. He had cold blue eyes and a face that must have been handsome in his youth. Now it looked gaunt under the long, peppered beard. His clothes were plain and worn down in places. He seemed only mildly interested in the guests and ate little, instead busy drinking plenty.

After eating, Éine spoke, his tone awkward. 'It is past time for introductions. Our most gracious host on this island is Dathí Ó Madagáin. I have been told you are acquainted with his nephew Seán, who visits the island and provides assistance. He learns skills in return. Laoise, whom you have all met, is the most capable and obliging granddaughter of this man. For him, no introductory preamble would do him justice. He is Caoilte Mac Rónán. The greatest of all the Fianna outside of Fionn himself.'

The storyteller seemed to want to give them an opportunity to revere the man for a moment. Eoghan found that they were not given much to revere. The man sat and drank and made no move to suggest that he was even paying attention to the goings on around him. After his words, Éine sat down and crossed his legs, looking at them expectantly.

Eoghan caught on the quickest and said, ‘I am Eoghan.’

Rúadhan, Rhíona and Donnacha did the same. Donnacha’s pained expression suggested he longed to make more of a first impression on someone who was one of his heroes.

Éine too seemed underwhelmed but saw it as another opportunity to take the floor with a dramatic gesture.

‘My new friends, I wish firstly to right a grave ill; a slight of the most heinous nature or at least travel towards the place where amends may be made. When first we met, I took both fright and flight and am nearly overcome with ignominy. The young lady presented me with information that shook me to my deepest recesses. I felt it prudent then to seek assistance and counsel from an old friend. I had Ó Maolmhuaidh dispatch a runner seeking Laoise, who I knew to be in *Uisneach* trading fish. I met her shortly thereafter and beseeched her to keep track of you until I had the chance to discuss the matter with Caoilte. We have long speculated as to the identity of the girl they seek, those black-hearted brutes. It is apparent that we need speculate no longer. You said you have need of me. You may speak to us of this need and how it has arisen. So, if you please... enlighten us, young lady.’

Rhíona looked at those around the table. They sat watching her, and both Rúadhan and Donnacha nodded in support. Her eyes met Eoghan's for a moment.

She cleared her throat and began her story. Again, she provided little detail of her homeland, suggesting that it would not have made sense to them even if she were to try. She spoke about her trip through one of the three portals to this land. She told them of her efforts to find Fionn Mac Cumhal and the reasoning; the journey he must make to the Fae world, closing the gateway forever. She told of a trip to the island where a mysterious witch, the *Caoránach*, told her the futures that might yet be. She told of her struggle to find food and shelter as her search took her far and wide. She told of constant pursuit by the warriors who seemed to be able to divine areas in which she was travelling. She suspected the use of *draíocht* from those gifts that her father had presented to Uad.

Then she told of her chance meeting with the two boys from *Clochbeag* when she was at her lowest and on the brink of capture. She told how they rescued and aided her in ways that allowed her to continue to evade discovery and whatever black ends awaited her.

She told of Donnacha's arrival in Oldfort. As she spoke of his deeds, they seemed larger than life and gave everyone a chance to reflect on the heroic manner in which he saved them. She told them of their attempts to find Éine and of their trip to the *crannóg*.

'And now here we sit, and it seems I have been blessed. I came looking for one of the last living Fianna and instead found you two. I need to find Fionn Mac Cumhal. I know he yet lives, or the gateway would be closed. His *draíocht* came from our world. The gateway cannot closed while it, while he, remains here. I think one or both of you know how I can find him. You have heard my story, but now I must ask you to consider something.'

She knelt forward and made eye contact with each of them.

'Those warriors are not just looking for me. They are also looking for Fionn. They are led by the man Uad, but he is a pawn in this tale. My father: The Fae *Rí*, the Fane himself, wishes to conquer this land and the world around it and his strength in *draíocht* might allow it sooner than many would imagine. Your people will become nothing but slaves if this happens. The Fae horde will come here; your world will change. Eventually, your people will die out. Only two Fae worlds will remain.'

Éine shifted as if to speak but said nothing. As if answering his unspoken question, Rhíona continued, 'I do not know where Fionn is, but he has a decision to make, one which will change many things. I will ask him to come back through with me and save this land one last time. Once his *draíocht* blends into our world, it will know the way home. If Uad's men capture him, they will imprison him. Hold him. Until the Fane's powers allow him to control the gate. Perhaps even open other gates to this world; or other worlds. It is impossible to know how close he is to accomplishing this feat.' Her eyes grew moon-round as she seemed to consider the situation.

'You have both served your land and done more than most could dream. Yet I need your help this one last time, to protect what you fought so long and hard over, *Éire* and its sovereignty. These... friends you see with me have been dragged into this through no actions of their own. They have been doing what is right.' She looked at Eoghan. 'They want to go home, and I think they have done enough for me; put themselves in enough peril. I had hoped that you could perhaps compensate them for their troubles and then aid them in their passage home.'

There was silence. Caoilte's hand slowly reached out for his mug and drained its contents in one go, before reaching for the jug and refilling it. He wiped his mouth roughly with his sleeve and then spoke in a rasping whisper like a sword dragged across a stone floor.

'Is that all? That is nothing for such heroes as us. Is there anything else, Fae princess, that you might require?'

His voice was thick with sarcastic venom, eyes searching for her though they did not seem to focus on her, and his speech slurred.

'I... I'm sorry?' she asked, head shaking slowly. Eoghan felt his stomach shrink. The man was as drunk as an ass.

Éine interjected, allowing Caoilte to descend back into sodden silence. 'Caoilte is alluding to several grim practicalities that must be addressed at this juncture, my lady. Regrettably, our assistance might not amass to your expectations of such. I can recompense your fine friends, and there are few roads we three have not travelled. So, rest easy that they will walk the most desirable after they depart.' He turned to his friend to regard him for a moment and then looked pointedly back at Rhíona.

'Alas, a scathing truth must pass among us now, new friends as we are. Fionn Mac Cumhal left consumed and embittered after the battle. His utmost desire upon departure was future solitude, an absence of responsibility or duties of conscience. He was betrayed, Rhíona. He may never have recovered. We do not know where he is and would not know where to look.' He paused to stretch theatrically and run fingers through his thin white hair. 'My youthful friends, we are three men devoid of youthful notions. We are devoid of interest in things that do not engross us unequivocally. Things in the here and now and for the near thereafter. Unless you four construct plans to bring us fine foods or finer potables, you have come to the wrong place. That is not to say we cannot aid in bestowing information, lending direction to your quest. Wisdom to guide, rather than a blood-chilling charge of the *Síor Feargach*.'

Donnacha slammed his hand on the table, and stood, his face awash with emotion.

'I cannot listen to this talk.' Looking at Caoilte, he continued, 'I've searched for… what you were. I would give my all to have such men again, so that perhaps, someday, I might be named among them. You... you are lost.'

After speaking, Donnacha turned and stormed out of the hall.

Caoilte smiled a hard smile as he watched Donnacha leave but kept his thoughts to himself.

'Your friend is filled with fire, and yearnings and rightly so,' said Éine. 'The epoch of the Fianna has long since ended. We are not now who we were then.'

'If I may say, at this point?' Rúadhan interjected. 'You? Fianna? I do not know about that. I have no great knowledge of the chronicles of the Fianna, but I do remember a certain number of maxims? Mottos? Tests too, I recall; and a certain warrior persuasion of those who joined the band?'

'My lad,' said Éine. 'It is a brave thing indeed for you to confess your ignorance so unambiguously. It displays a desire to join the less ignorant; perhaps someday, you might take your first newborn steps towards your lofty goals. Those trials of the Fianna of which you speak were for those untested warriors, those who wished to prove themselves of due worth. The maxims were rules to govern. For some such as myself, however, there were no trials nor assessments of value. There was only Fionn Mac Cumhal himself, requesting that I might adhere mine talents to those swelling talents of his band of heroes.

'Perhaps he heard tell of the satire I made of *Críoch Kois* that caused the *Túath* to destroy itself and rebuild anew, strengthened and upright. Perhaps he had heard tell of the poetry I spoke to the Gaul Prince whose bed I shared as he lay dying. Some say the poetry I whispered in his perfect ears kept him alive for longer than he should have lived and that his death was a blissful passing...'

Dathí cleared his throat pointedly.

Éine, whose cheeks reddened as he spoke, nodded graciously. 'I stray like a thirsting lamb. Pardon my digression, my young friends. I am prone to occasional outbursts of nostalgic meanderings. Please forgive this, my most irresolute dithering.'

'What are we doing here if you cannot help us?' asked Eoghan. 'This gets us nothing.' He looked at Rúadhan and Rhíona in turn. 'Perhaps we need to thank our hosts, accept their hospitality over the night and be gone once the night is. These men are not what we are looking for.'

'Young lord, pause and embrace wisdom.' Éine said, kneeling and placing his hands on the table. 'Among we three, there might be the answer you seek. Fail to take heed of our counsel, and you might fail wholly.'

Dathí spoke at the table for the first time. 'He is right in what he says, whatever way he says it. There is a lot that ye can learn from us and many ways we can aid ye if ye let us. He just means that gadding around the place on adventures or quests is not something these spring chicks would look forward to in their autumn years.'

Rhíona spoke, brow knitted. 'Now is not the time for words. Fionn will need you both before the end when we find him. He is the focal point of everything. The futures of two lands, two worlds, rest on a decision he does not know he has to make. He will need strength and support. The time is now. My father, the Fane, will not rest. He will not dither. I know this.'

None of the three older men responded. They sat and drank.

'There is no strength here, Rhíona,' said Eoghan. 'These men can offer us little more than food and shelter.'

Rúadhan turned to Rhíona. 'You ask them what you need, and let's see if they have any information that might be useful. I ate too quickly and am left feeling sick to my core.' He stood and walked to the door, stopping to turn and look at her. 'When I was sick, Eoghan or my father told me stories of *their* deeds.'

Rúadhan nodded at the old men. 'I dreamed of someday becoming one of the Fianna as Donnacha has. As many children have. But not like them. They are then, Rhíona. We are now. I will help you, and so will Eoghan and Donnacha. We will do it. We will leave first thing in the morning and find whatever path needs to be walked.'

He left, head bowed.

Eoghan glared at the three men who were looking at him. 'There are no Fianna here. Just aging hutkeepers.' He lifted his drink and poured it on the table. 'Apologies hutkeepers, I seem to have spilled my drink. Perhaps one of you should clean that up. Thank you for your hospitality. The meal was both delicious and... enlightening.'

To Navigate a Lake

***

The walled isle proves a false security, and the chase is reconvened after a bloody morning encounter.

An té nach mbeireann ar an ngnó beireann an gnó air.

He who does not get a grip on the job, the job gets a grip on him.

***

The four guests awoke to the sound of Dathí screaming and cursing. Eoghan rushed outside, Rúadhan close behind him, to find an intruder holding Laoise with a knife at her throat. Laoise and her captor stood over the body of young Seán, whose throat was cut. The warrior was dressed in black, was missing an ear and was baring his teeth. He was dripping wet and breathing heavily.

They are here, Eoghan realised. He looked around. *Only one invader for now.* He watched Donnacha disappear back inside.

'You son of a whore. I will rip your life from you, you pitiless animal,' Dathí screamed.

Caoilte and Éine appeared, looking for where the man scaled the walls and whether others followed.

The warrior crouched shouting to warn his comrades. His words were made difficult to understand by a thick accent from abroad.

'I will cut her throat. Don't tempt me. Extend the footbridge. Do you hear me?'

He opened his mouth to repeat the demand, just as an arrow punctured his face above the jaw and he fell back lifeless.

Eoghan turned to find Donnacha standing drawing another arrow. 'I think we might need to have a little think about how we can get out of this place with our lives, and that's the truth of it,' he said.

Eoghan, who felt a burning urge to piss, turned to Dathí. 'Is there a tunnel?'

The old man's eyes were watering as he moved to kneel by the body of his nephew. 'Boat,' and a pointing gesture were all he could manage.

Laoise moved to her grandfather. 'We will get our things and meet you at the back building by the hens. If you have anything to get, get it. Move fast. Where is the poet?' she growled.

Éine, who had vanished in the confusion, appeared from the main hall. 'I felt concealment might serve me best in that exchange.' His voice was distant as he stared down at Seán's limp body, lip trembling.

Rhíona knelt beside Dathí. She neither spoke nor moved to comfort nor console but just bowed her head.

Rúadhan and Eoghan stood looking at her. Donnacha moved to stand in between them and said, 'They will not let us row away, I am thinking.'

'I will not leave here for them or for any. I will give you the time you need. Éine, fetch my bow,' Dathí said, giving them a glimmer of hope.

Perhaps there is a way. 'Rúadhan and I will row, and we'll move that boat as fast as it can move, but we will need a chance to get going.'

Donnacha smiled, saying to Dathí, 'I might join you for some shooting if that is all right with you. I have an urge to balance the scales a little.'

Eoghan's face registered his dismay.

'Don't worry, don't worry, Eoghan, my old trout. I'll join ye as ye set off.'

Rúadhan took off running towards the gatehouse where they had been staying. 'I'll get our things.'

Éine arrived with a bow and quiver and his pack over his shoulder. He dropped the weapons beside Dathí and walked quickly towards the boat.

Rhíona leant over and whispered in Dathí's ear. The man sat back on his haunches and straightened his bent shoulders. He embraced the princess, both their faces wet with tears.

'It's time to do some damage, Dathí,' Donnacha said. 'I want to see what skills you possess with that fine bow of yours.'

When Laoise and her grandfather reappeared, the group moved towards the boat. She looked at Eoghan and Rúadhan.

'You need to lower the boat onto the hidden waterway under the palisade. You two can row, I hope,' she said, before striding off with her grandfather.

Eoghan and Rúadhan each took Rhíona by an arm and followed them, Rúadhan nodding as he passed Donnacha.

'Where do we shoot from?' asked Donnacha. He needed the old man to focus.

With dried tears, and a face of stone, Dathí, who was stringing his bow, nodded at two small platforms either side of the gate.

Donnacha was about to speak but stopped himself. He walked over to the quiver Dathí had hung over his shoulder. Reaching out, he pulled an arrow with awed deference.

'Dathí, these arrows,' he gasped. 'Where did you get them? The fletching, the cut... they are masterful.'

'I made them,' Dathí replied as he nocked one.

'What? Where did you learn. Who taught you to make arrows like this? I have never seen finer.'

'I learned on this very island when I was a little boy,' he said, going to the steps jutting out from the wall. 'You can have them when I die.'

'Who taught you? I must know, or I'll fall over.'

Dathí stopped for a moment and looked back at the others busying themselves on the other side of the *crannóg*. 'The greatest warrior of them all,' he said sadly.

Donnacha followed his gaze. Caoilte was standing looking over at them, ragged and worn.

'Come and let's see how they fly,' said Dathí as he began his ascent.

'Hold your head down now for a bit and let me have a look first,' said Donnacha before leaping up the steps and kneeling out of sight. He peeked over the wall for three heartbeats and grimaced.

'Right mess here now and cac beside it,' he said turning to Dathí, who was waiting with his head tilted. 'Seventeen of them out there. Six with bows standing, the rest bar one mounted and armed, ready for the gate to open. There's one lighting a fire down there, so it looks as though they might be thinking of shooting in some fire if the first plan is not going well. Shower of poxy badgers, I think, and that's the truth of it.'

'What do we do?' asked Dathí.

'I'm thinking we should kill a few of them. I'll start first, working from the left. After I shoot twice, you start on the right. One arrow per archer and then move on to the next man. Even if you miss wildly, we need to get their heads down. If we knock them down, the others will go running, so hit their horses, and then we'll go back for them. Don't be worrying; no need for worry here. Just hitting bodies with arrows.'

Dathí nodded and gulped down a breath.

'This will be an exciting little tussle, and that's no lie,' said Donnacha.

He stood with his bowstring drawn, nocked with the arrow he had taken from Dathí, and loosed it. The arrow flew into a warrior's chest with a thud. The other bowmen reacted as Donnacha released his second they let fly with their own. Donnacha's arrow hit a woman in the arm, and he tutted with frustration. The sudden appearance of Dathí caused the warriors' arrows to miss, although their skill was apparent. Many of them came close to their mark.

Donnacha was happier with his next shot, which took his target square in his chest as he reached for his quiver.

Dathí was a fine shot and hit his first target in the stomach, causing the man to crumple forward, screaming in agony. He nocked again in a flash. Pausing for a moment, he picked out one of the more vocal commanders and took aim. As he released, an arrow hit him in the shoulder, causing his arrow to land harmlessly in the lake. He righted himself and nocked another his face grim with a pained edge. The arrow had almost passed through his shoulder, but the pain did not stop nor slow him.

When an arrow lodged in the palisade wall beside Donnacha, he tutted again, watching it vibrate to a halt. Returning his attention to the mounted warriors he was in time to see them begin a retreat and Dathí's shot kill the warrior he thought to be the commander. He turned to congratulate Dathí, just as he was struck in the neck and fell off the platform.

Donnacha resisted the urge to go to his aid. He wounded one and killed the last of the bowmen as arrows hissed by him, one grazing his bald head.

'My poor shagging head again,' he murmured as he watched his enemy. They were retreating well. No panic or despair. Just a tactical decision that Donnacha agreed with. He drew back on the bowstring and aimed high. It would prove difficult to pinpoint a target. However, sometimes all it took was a shot in the right direction.

The riders were almost out of range as he let fly into the middle of them. He nodded in satisfaction when he saw a horse go down, throwing its rider, and bringing down the horse behind, rolling over its rider in the process. Some of the riders looked down impassively but did not slow.

Without checking the result, he scooped up his bow and jumped down from the platform. Dathí was dead. He took the old man's quiver and ran towards the others.

The fishing boat was on the water, with Eoghan and Rúadhan sitting in the centre, each with an oar. Éine and Caoilte were sitting on the deck in front. Laoise and Rhíona were behind them. The boat was around fifteen strides. The boys had taken the nets and pots out to give everyone space.

As Donnacha approached, they lifted the wooden panel that allowed the boat to pass under the palisade. As soon as he was aboard, they cast off.

Laoise looked around. 'Where is Dathí?' she cried.

'We showed them a thing or two, so we did,' said Donnacha. 'Put them in their place, he and I.'

'Will you tell me where he is?'

'He's dead back there, with two arrows sticking out of him.'

Laoise opened her mouth. They looked at Caoilte, but hint of emotion registered on his face as he looked off into the distance. Looking at nothing, tears in his eyes, Éine made a long, groaning noise. He turned to the others before covering his face with shaking hands.

'We need to be gone from here,' said Rhíona quietly. 'They will be coming.'

'She is right in fairness,' said Donnacha as he took one of his own arrows and nocked it, eyes scanning the shore. 'You boys need to get us moving somewhere fast, or we could end up looking very silly out here on the water.'

Rúadhan and Eoghan started to row but moving the boat with the weight it carried was no mean feat. Moving it quickly would be a near impossible task.

Through gritted teeth, Rúadhan said, 'Where exactly are we supposed to be going?'

Laoise pointed towards the middle of the lake and off into the distance. 'We keep as far from the banks as we can. If we move straight north, the lake will take us where their horses cannot travel quickly, if they pass at all. It will give us a day or two on them, and then we will have to decide what happens next.'

Slow Passage

***

To escape from the warriors in pursuit, the group must put themselves directly in their pursuers' path.

Breithnigh an abhainn sara dtéir ina cuilithe.

Study the river before you go into the middle of it.

***

The boys were sweating, though they had built up a fair speed. They were hard workers if naught else, and Laoise was impressed by their quiet ardour.

She could see the warriors to the east, galloping along the bank to try and find a way to slow or stop the boat. As helpless as the rest of them, fear clutched her stomach.

Donnacha watched them closely. Laoise found herself holding her breath for at least a dozen heartbeats as he assessed the danger.

‘They’re heading for that headland,’ he pointed. ‘It’s the closest they will get to us. They will be able to snare us with ropes and use the horses to bring us to shore. Not a bad plan in fairness to them. Might work too, so it might.’

Éine’s tear-reddened eyes bulged. ‘I am sure a man of your great talents can find a way to ensure it does not?’

Donnacha did not seem to be listening. ‘My young oarsmen, we will need to move as far away from the headland on that side as we can manage.’

‘...and we need to go faster,’ said Laoise, cursing the rising sound of panic in her voice.

‘They’re doing their best,’ Rhíona responded.

Laoise could not decide how she felt about the girl. There was a haughtiness to her. As if she was better than Laoise and her family. She seemed to offer little in the exchanges. For now, Laoise decided to dislike her and review the decision later. She was not wrong about the boys, though. Instead of complaining or giving up, they exchanged a glance, and in unison started to wrench the oars through the water, necks straining.

‘I have no doubt the boys are at full capacity,’ Éine said, another feeble attempt at encouragement. ‘They are well aware, I am most sure, that laziness will get us all quite killed.’

Laoise’s admiration for the boys grew, just as her fear of the warriors grew. She knew the boys’ lungs would be burning, their backs aching. They could not maintain such a level of exertion for long.

Donnacha stood at the back of the boat, bow at the ready, but did not shoot. Though she knew the answer, Laoise felt compelled to ask the obvious.

'Are they very far out of your range?'

Donnacha looked at her. 'Perhaps. Maybe I might hit something if I was to have a try,' he held up the bow, 'but this can be a tiresome thing to shoot. The more I use it without a rest, the less control I have over the arrow's flight, and the more arrows get wasted. I think I might just hold off until we are in the mire a little deeper if you get me. You can believe me when I say, I'm interested in getting away from this as much as you, young lady,' he said with a grin.

It was impossible not to like the bowman; he was far too affable. She had no interest in letting him know that, however, so she scowled at him and turned to check on her grandfather. He, too, was watching Donnacha, in his own way at least. Anyone else looking at him then would have thought him detached and bored. Laoise caught a look in his eye, suggesting he was enjoying himself immensely. He was an impossible man. One of many.

'Look,' cried Rhíona. One of the horses went down, possibly into a bog hole or on a loose stone. At such a gallop, it was unlikely the rider would walk away unscathed. No one went back to check on him but continued towards the headland as fast as the horses would take them. Laoise could hear them shouting instructions to one another, forming a plan as they went. She could not hear the words, but as some of them started preparing ropes, their intent was clear.

When the boys started faltering, and the boat slowing, Laoise removed her cloak and checked her darts. She would not be able to use them for a while but having them to hand was a comfort.

Rúadhan gasped aloud and Laoise could see blood dripping from his hands onto the oar handles. Eoghan's mouth was downturned at the edges, and his pale face trembled.

She was about to tell them to stop, when Rhíona knelt between them and set a hand on each of their shoulders. Looking at them, she started to speak quietly.

No, not speaking, Laoise amended, *more like a chant.*

She watched as Rhíona continued with the words; words Laoise could not understand, though they were comforting. And as the chant continued, so the demeanour of the boys changed. Their faces calmed and relaxed, pain no longer etched in their features. Their breathing was ragged no more. The boat started to pick up speed. Éine and Caoilte looked away as if they knew what they might see and wanted no part of it.

Laoise was filled with wonder. Rhíona had done *draíocht*. She turned to see if Donnacha realised, but her breath caught when she saw the look on his face. Turning to see what he was looking at, she gasped and held a hand over her mouth. A new band of mercenary warriors were sitting astride horses on the opposite shore, watching things unfold. With both sides of the lake covered, the chances of escape were dwindling.

'What do we do?' Laoise asked.

How can I save them?

'Fie and Fae fire. All is lost, by the black hand of Goll,' cried Éine.

'I suspect it might be time to start shooting,' said Donnacha. He looked at Rhíona, green eyes clear. 'Can you do that for me when my strength falters? I hate wasting good arrows, you see.'

He managed a thin smile. Laoise judged the distance to the nearest rider to be three hundred paces if it were ten. She looked in amazement from Donnacha to Rhíona.

Rhíona looked up, her face pale and weary. Nodding, she returned a thinner smile. She suddenly looked wretched. Laoise decided she no longer disliked the princess.

'You'll do it for him when the time comes?' she asked.

Rhíona looked at her and their eyes met. They shared a moment; something familiar in the fear and weariness.

As the boat and the riders converged on the headland, Laoise turned to watch the bowman in fascination. Donnacha took a long deep breath; eyes narrowed; bow rising. He continued raising the bow until he seemed to be pointing his arrow into the cloudy sky. Then he moved to aim slightly into the light breeze, before sucking in his gut and pushing out his chest as if to widen his body. He drew back the bowstring until it met his pursed lips. Happy, his fingers slid away, releasing the tension and the arrow flew. Everyone in the little vessel except for Donnacha watched it take flight, soar through the sky and arc down to earth. It buried itself in a horse's flank. Both horse and rider went down, causing two following to leap over or become entangled themselves.

Donnacha set himself for a second shot but stopped when an unlikely sound arose from the warriors. Laoise's mouth fell open. Clapping and calls of "fine shot" and "impressive" from the waiting warriors showed their appreciation for the display of skill. Laoise shook her head. *Men and their madness.*

The boat and riders were fast approaching the point of confrontation, one group far quicker than the other, when Donnacha's second arrow flew. It sailed and landed wide of riders. He cursed quietly and went again. When the distance had halved, the arc of the arrow was lower and the accuracy much improved. The first rider was knocked clear off his horse, arrow almost passing through both his leather armour and chest. Already dead, the warrior got caught in the hooves of a following horse, which also fell, causing four others to stumble.

The audience of warriors roared and clapped enthusiastically. Donnacha even went as far as giving them a wink and a nod for the encouragement.

Madness, thought Laoise. *Nothing more and nothing less.*

She looked at Rhíona, who sat there with similar incredulity.

The riders slowed as they approached the stony headland. It was both a finger pointing the way to escape and the point where they would succeed or fail. Five warriors dismounted, each carrying a coiled and noosed rope.

As Donnacha changed his bows, he spoke to Eoghan and Rúadhan. 'My fine young men, ye must not stop rowing, and that's that. We must not lose forward momentum. They will surely come close to boarding us or dragging us in or some such rigmarole. Laoise and I will give them a scare if they come too close and that I can tell you.'

Donnacha suddenly nocked his arrow on the other side of the bow. Using his thumb to draw, he released tension quickly and moved to repeat the action. Laoise found the bowman's speed breathtaking. The two arrows seemed to converge as they struck one of the ropers, but one glanced off the leather breastplate and hit the warrior behind.

Donnacha quickly fired another arrow, which struck the chest of a roper, who screamed and fell to his knees cradling it.

As the remaining ropers and the floundering boat came within thirty paces of each other, Laoise was tempted to start throwing darts. She resisted. She needed a cool head and patience, not wasted darts.

On the bank, riders ran to collect the ropes and take the place of the fallen. Donnacha shot and the warriors fell, but his arrows were running out at an alarming rate. The roars and orders of the warriors was like the sound of fighting dogs. They seemed to be making noise and doing little else. However, it wasn't long before they were casting ropes and the boat was snared. Eoghan and Rúadhan were starting to flag again, whatever *draíocht* Rhíona put on them was wearing off. Éine and Laoise tried their best to rid the boat of the ties but their hands were getting slippery from the water splashing over the gunwale.

The remaining riders dismounted and ran to heave on the ropes. The boat started to move towards the shore. Warriors who were not pulling the boat in, armed themselves and began to wade out to greet the vessel with weapons raised. One who held a spear made to throw it. Laoise was about to scream for Donnacha to shoot him, when she realised that he had stopped shooting. The arrows were spent.

With a warning cry, she lashed out a dart with all her might. It grazed the warrior's wrist as he was throwing the spear and caused a deflection. Only just. Her second dart bounced off his armour. The third buried itself in his shoulder, and he fell back into the water, writhing. Laoise watched helplessly as hands reached for the oars. Donnacha jabbed with his bow, trying to fend them off.

Laoise threw her darts as fast as she could with any accuracy. She was running out of them, but she could not save or scrimp at this point.

Laoise stood and threw two darts simultaneously. One stabbed into his neck and the other into his left eye. He fell back, rocking the boat. A warrior grabbed the front of the boat and the craft rocked alarmingly as he tried to board.

Laoise felt herself falling.

She heard someone cry out, 'Laoise, no!'

Her head struck an oar as she fell, and she felt cold darkness engulfing her. She wanted to scream as the water rushed to silence her. Hands grasped at her as she began to lose sense in the cold.

The darkness called her.

Suddenly, someone pulled her, and her head broke the surface. Another body went into the water beside her, and she reached out numbly to help. She felt strange armour and realised it was one of her enemies. Splashing, frantic, Laoise somehow managed to grab the gunwale and cling there. She retched loudly as she was pulled into the boat, coughing. Lying down on the wet deck, Laoise retched again. She could see the boys were rowing. Donnacha and Rhíona, and even Éine were pushing away invaders.

The sound of applause faded to silence and memory. Beating hearts and heavy breathing mixed with the gentle lapping of waves and trembling; slow-moving oars became the only sounds accompanying them. Eoghan moved. Hoping the rhythm of the splashes might keep him going.

Éine sat glaring at the shivering Laoise.

'Do you ever even think at all? Do you ever consider any such thing as consequence? To stand like you did near cost us all our...'

'Be silent,' said Rúadhan, eyes narrowed as he rowed.

'Whine less and use some of your baggage to dry her or warm her up or do something of use. But do it silently.' He looked down at Laoise. 'She was incredible.'

Éine's shoulders slumped and he sighed dramatically, before searching his belongings for something warm. Caoilte had roosted beside him and, having unstopped a wineskin, was attempting to empty its contents in as expedient a manner as his open mouth would allow.

Eoghan and Rúadhan attempted to remove the splinters from trembling hands using shaking fingers. Both had capitulated and the splinters now bedded down for the night. Eoghan's only goal was to keep the boat moving. Only just, but moving it was.

'What now?' whispered Rúadhan, sounding weary. 'I can't imagine they are far behind us. We'll soon be on foot and directionless.'

Eoghan nodded. His friend had identified their problem. 'They seem to know where we are and where we are headed even before we do.' His gaze drifted to Rhíona. 'How can they know that?'

Rhíona's eyes were closed, and her breathing was shallow as she slept; her face looked sunken and wan. Éine was staring at her.

'She is not one of us,' Éine said 'Not in the least. There are many more things that we don't know about the Fae than things that we do. What we do know is there are powers at work here beyond our ken. It is becoming apparent that your cunning adversaries are employing ways to keep an eye on her general whereabouts. It must be inaccurate enough, I am thinking, for you not to have been captured yet. Perhaps this represents something you might turn to your advantage.'

'Your?' said Eoghan, with bile in his mouth. 'That's twice you have said your.'

Rúadhan turned towards the *scealaí* wearing a sour look.

'I think he means that the three of them plan to part company at their earliest convenience.' He turned to look at Caoilte. 'Would I be right, great hero? Champion of the people?'

Laoise sat up, still shivering. 'Why should we do anything but exactly that? You have brought death and ruination to our home and turned our lives upside down.'

'We have, have we?' growled Eoghan. 'Because I was sure we've been doing our best to keep this girl we found alive. Perhaps you would prefer to cut her throat while she sleeps to save you from further danger?'

‘You do seem to have a taste for violence,’ said Rúadhan. ‘You might be taking after your grandfather in that regard’.

Laoise lashed out with her fist, which struck his nose. Rúadhan tried to pretend he was not hurt, but his watery blinking eyes gave him away.

Eoghan smirked as he said, ‘By all means, hit him as often as you wish. It will never cease to be hilarious. You telling us how unfair all of this is is funny, too, Laoise. We came to look for help from the last surviving heroes of the Fianna, and look what has been presented to us.’

He spread his hands in front of the two older men and shook his head in amazement. ‘How could the stories have been so wrong?’

Éine, who was midway through a chunk of discovered cheese, stopped eating when he realised the conversation was directed at him. He put the cheese down and slowly wiped his hands together, swallowing the remainder of his mouthful.

‘I am not quite sure I understand what you mean by that, my lovely lad.’

‘Is that so?’ said Eoghan. ‘You may be the last of the Fianna, bar Fionn himself, and here you sit. When the land for which you fought and bled is most in need, you eat and get fatter and drink and get drunker and try to let the world pass you by. What will he say when we stand before him and tell him what you have become? Will it be a source of pain for him to hear that you were so quick to turn us away? Ye are nought but doughy, soft, afraid and of no use to anyone. I know I’m hardly any help and can’t do much, but that doesn’t mean I don’t need to try.’

Éine raised his eyebrows, and became cold. 'If it is that you are trying to rouse us with an uplifting speech, I feel that you may need work in that field. Recall, if you will, my pretty, tight-arsed little boy, we have been walking these lands since your grandfather was a child and before. We have seen all manner of threats to these shores and each more dangerous and urgent than the last. Each battle and war, each skirmish and adventure, each rescue and homecoming, lessens the attraction a little at a time. Errant thoughts of restoring former glories under a new banner do not become men of our advanced years. It would take a fool to suggest otherwise. The galling notion for me, however, is that a little starling like yourself would stand there before us, challenging us, knowing nothing of true and constant peril. Not one thing. We have nothing left to give. I have explained to the girl what she needs to do. I can do no more.'

'Lies, it sounds like to me,' said Rúadhan, still holding his nose. 'You could do more, but you choose not to. He,' he said, pointing at Caoilte, 'can do very little but drink, and there's no need to strike me again, lady. I am quite positive disagreeing with me would only be for the sake of it.'

'He is sick from drinking too much,' Laoise said, scowling. 'I know his greatness is there. It has been concealed over time by his love for mead.'

'What did you tell Rhíona?' asked Eoghan.

Éine's eyes narrowed. 'If I recall accurately, my dear sweet fawn, it was my understanding that you two boys were also planning your departure. Why suddenly feign interest in her future, if you are no longer a part of that future?' Though his tone was pleasant, the question stung.

'Things change.' Eoghan looked at his friend. His face still bore marks from the scrap at *Ros Cam*. There was blood on his clothes from his splinter-ruined hands. There were dark circles on his pale face and the now ever-present troubled look in his eyes. 'We never meant to be here but here we are.'

Rúadhan looked into the distance and stretched his neck. 'We are not going too far for now, I'm thinking.'

LANDING

***

A review is in order and the future membership of the group is decided.

Ní neart go cur le chéile

There is no strength without co-operation.

***

A weary crew drifted towards their destination, a shoreline bearded by reeds and rushes. The small vessel slid into the apparent sanctity of thousands of upright protectors. The thick silt slowed the boat and the pebbled shoreline halted it noisily. Everyone sat, drooped, as lapping waves busied around them and pike that had lain patiently in the reeds waiting for passing supper, swam away in disgust.

Éine returned to his monologue, still stewing, 'I have been in the company of the great men and women of our day and many upon either side. I can recount to you all first-hand stories of their greatest deeds and of the noble, honest, and just causes that they fought for. I have quested and ranged far and wide, seeing things that would set wonder in the eyes of the most jaded cynic. Many, many days in this world I have witnessed. And alas, where now I should be bathing my tired feet and supping fine ales and finer mead in the company of a tall dark southerner, I sit here in this leaking apple crate with two bullocks from the edge of the gods know where and a mysterious other-world creature from legends of old and I can safely say this: you people are a pox and naught but trouble and no good will come from a company such as—'

'We have a braying ass that wanders the low hills alone, for not one farmer nor family can bear its constant wailing,' Eoghan interjected, looking at Laoise. 'Is that why you keep this old ass on that isle in the middle of a remote lake?'

Donnacha snorted laughter, and nodded approval at the young man's quip. Laoise did not know how to react and went red to the ears.

'Braying ass?' Éine growled. 'You insolent little pup. I will have you know this—'

Rhíona sat up straight and addressed Caoilte, looking him square in the eye. 'I have asked only your aid. Not your sword arm necessarily, only whatever assistance you might provide. You deem it unreasonable? So be it. Take your boat and go back to your isle.'

Rúadhan held up a hand to interrupt, and said, 'Perhaps we should have a little chat about this before—'

But Rhíona would not be distracted.

‘I am truly sorry I have brought such terrible acts upon you all. I am sure they have no interest in you. It seems that they have a way to keep a track of my whereabouts, or near enough to it, so I am confident they will bother you no more after you leave me.’

Her head tilted slightly as she turned to Caoilte.

‘Among my kin you are regarded as a hero without equal in skill and standing. The *Gruagachs* speak to their young about your cunning. I have seen nothing to support that thinking being anything other than legend, nostalgia, or just false memory. I have, however, had many disappointments before and will have them again.’

She looked at Eoghan, Rúadhan, and Donnacha. ‘I am also learning that there are heroes in this place. Perhaps they were all I needed all along.’

As she stood and disembarked from the unsteady vessel, Donnacha looked directly at Caoilte; disappointment was etched in his features. He shook his head and walked away.

Éine watched him go. He had been impressed with the bowman, and he felt a growing disappointment in himself.

Laoise’s head hung low, but Éine managed to meet his gaze when Eoghan looked at them. Smiling a smile that did not reach his eyes, the youngster followed the others.

Before he followed, Rúadhan turned back and looked at Laoise. Frowning slightly, he shrugged, slowly holding out a bloody hand to her.

Her mouth opened; her conflict was apparent on her face. She slowly lifted her hand towards his but stopped and dropped it into her lap, along with her gaze.

Rúadhan shrugged again, then turned and stalked away.

Éine could scarcely believe what was happening when Caoilte stood, as awkward and unstable as a new foal. His hands grasped out for anything to hold onto as he made his way off the boat. He stood, eyes closed and took a great breath into his lungs; then another which he held for a moment, then noisily expelled.

Laoise's face was a picture that Éine could understand. The journey from stern to bow and ashore represented as much voluntary independent activity as Caoilte had done in years.

Éine felt nervous energy wash through him making his stomach flutter wildly.

Will he finally come back to himself?

'You mean to do this thing?' he asked.

Caoilte nodded slowly. He cleared his throat and hawked up something foul. 'Best find him,' he said no more than a whisper, then sighed. 'Need to die anyway. May as well, now that I'm up.'

He reached out his hand, shaking almost comically as it did.

'Give it here.'

Éine grabbed the bag he brought from the island and rifled through it as quickly as he could, heart beating fast. He pulled out a scabbarded sword as theatrically as his weary bones would allow. Long and thin, the curved scabbard whispered much like its owner. It whispered of one-time speed and deft skill. It whispered of history and actions over words. It was smooth, black leather, with an ornate daffodil etched expertly into the leather. The top of the hilt was a golden daffodil. The strapping around the long curving hilt grip was like new, because Laoise had cared for it as though it were her newborn child.

Éine grimaced as he recalled the last time it was drawn in anger; that cold autumn morning where Caoilte stood before the one warrior who might have claimed to be his equal: *Síor Feargach*. Éine had heard the Fae girl when they first met, asking about not only finding Fionn, but also finding and enlisting the help of *Síor Feargach*. Without finding one to calm the rage of the other, as Fionn had, the world might face a danger equal to the king of the Fae.

He shook the thought out of his head as the tendrils of recollection reached back to the scenes of chaos in those dark days. Caoilte had drawn his sword to face a skilled foe. Were it not for Fionn finding a way to stop the duel… Éine glanced at Laoise. There were tears in her eyes as the sword exchanged hands.

'*Lus an Chrom Cinn*, the Daffodil Blade,' said Éine, with suitable reverence. 'I had thought the day truly passed, unlike some,' he glanced towards Laoise, 'but it seems that the hardy bulb was just planted deeper in the soil than we knew.'

Laoise leapt from the boat to the shore in one bound and threw her arms around her grandfather. She was weeping and wore a fierce look of pride. Éine smiled grimly. She had longed to see this day. He was surprised by her incredible leap; a leap more than the length of three tall men lying down. Had anyone else but Éine seen such a thing they may well have fallen out of the boat in shock. Lips pursing in thought was his only reaction. Her grandfather's remarkable talents had not disappeared with lineage. Nor, perhaps, had the *draíocht*. Time would tell if she had inherited his gifts.

'In the interests of realistic appraisal,' he said, 'it must be noted that Mac Cumhal has not been seen in these lands since the Battle. It is likely he is dead. Furthermore, it is likely we will never find the body. It is most likely that we will find only discomfort or perhaps even our death by the hand of violence or some harsh lesson the world wishes to teach us.

'If Fionn is indeed alive and well as she suggests, who is to say that he is not rich and fat and sitting among two score grandchildren in the southern parts of Gaul? I am pleased to see your sudden lust for living.' He clambered from the boat.

'There is madness and then utter madness. Why not choose a different path? The appearance of these mysterious warriors is a concern, yes. The fight against tyranny is a cause that is just and true. It is not ethereal and speculative in its very nature and will lead you to the glory you deserve. Let us go and weed out the heart of their strength. The search for Fionn is madness. That girl is lost. Lost, I say to you, and her companions are still showing downy fluff.'

'Not the bowman,' corrected Laoise. Éine shook his head in irritation.

'I will come where you lead, Caoilte Mac Rónán, and though I could never tell a saga of your impulsive nature, I suggest that you pause towards reflection ere you set a foot forward on this path.'

Caoilte did not seem to be listening to a word Éine said, but Éine knew better. The man missed very little when his mind was not wandering from drink.

Caoilte took the hilt of the sword as if to draw it. Looking at his two companions, Caoilte let his sword hand fall to his side and walked after the Fae girl and her unusual troop.

Éine, stood and stretched, before throwing the bags onto the shore, and climbing out of the boat, set off after them.

Éine groaned loudly when he reached the clearing to find the party being robbed.

Why is there always another kick? he thought, rubbing his eyes.

Archers poked, leaned, and jutted from behind bark, brush, and bough, aiming bows at them. Éine considered a timely quip about the cowardice of having too many bough-men but wondered if he might have to then explain to those gathered.

Oh, for a cup of mead and shelter from the world of fools.

There was a sickly-looking middle-aged man speaking. He was gaunt, pale, and it was apparent that his efforts to speak loudly were causing him pain. He was the only one of the robbers without a weapon.

'Here they are now after all,' he said. 'We have been expecting you, and I was just about to send escorts to liven up your pace. I hate to repeat myself, for obvious reasons. We mean to rob you of anything we wish. Your friends have pointed out that ye have nothing of value but I will make that judgment in due course. This whole business can be done with ye alive or dead. I am not going to—'

Caoilte's scabbarded sword landed at the speaker's feet, making no sound. The robber looked down at the blade and back to its thrower. Caoilte did not speak but stood there, half watching.

During the robber's words, Éine had counted the robbers he could see. Nine were visible and threatening, most of them partly hidden behind trees. All bark and then bite. There was likely to be one more still hidden as a safety precaution; maybe two. None reacted to the sword. He looked at the sickly robber. The man was of an age where he knew something of the world. There was no need for words. Not until the man reacted.

'*Lus an Chrom Cinn*,' the sickly man said quietly, looking back down at the sword. 'As sure as I'm standing here, that's the daffodil blade. Are you he?' he asked looking at Caoilte.

'He is,' answered Éine. Caoilte's air of mystery was usually an advantage with newcomers. This situation would be decided on the name more than the man. Against a weaker foe, legend could be a weighty ally.

'Who is he, Seán Seosamh?' asked one of the bowmen. Seán Seosamh raised a finger to silence him.

'Will you let us go?' asked Seán Seosamh. Silence greeted his question, and he started babbling. 'We watched... were watching that ye were coming up the lake. In a boat. And we need to make a living and feed our own. I mean... we have mouths to feed... and—'

'He is hungry, too,' Éine interrupted, having enough now to work with. 'Indeed, we are all hungry. This is a way in which you could help yourselves out of this and help us out; as neighbours, as friends.'

'Why is he not talking to you himself, Seán Seosamh?' asked another robber.

'Exactly. And who is he anyway and what's the fuss about the flowery sword?' asked another.

Éine fumed at their ignorance. A lifetime ago they would be dead or dying. The trees they hid behind would provide no shelter; they would have been cut down as effortlessly as the bowmen. Arrows would have been released in vain. Robbers would have been dead some moments before they realised it. Others would be sitting in the other world before their heads landed.

They were asking ridiculous questions. Éine kept his voice low and menacing.

'Two of you have a decision to make in the next moment or two. Seán Seosamh here understands...' he raised his voice for the benefit of those listening, 'the nature of respect and honour. You have threatened our safety. Seán Seosamh here comprehends the symbolism involved with casting a great sword at the feet of an enemy. There is no further time for discussion on the matter I'm afraid. Choose, Seán Seosamh.'

There was no symbolism, of course, but it was clear that the remainder of Éine's adopted band were completely oblivious to the ruse, and they stood like grazing farm animals. Éine felt like casting his hands towards the sun gods and going back to the boat.

Why is the world so totally devoid of the sharp-minded?

Seán Seosamh, through great effort, knelt to pick up the sword and brought it back to Caoilte. He, at least, was engaging in the ruse, even if it was unintentionally. It was madness. Why would anyone in their right mind throw away their sword? Éine was appalled and shocked that Caoilte had done it. Stern words would be required at a later juncture.

Seán Seosamh presented the sword with two hands raised and head bowed. Éine reckoned he would have knelt down but it seemed like Seán Seosamh was doubtful he would be able to get up again. Caoilte took the sword.

'I offer you whatever hospitality we have to offer you, and a thousand welcomes in exchange for a single pardon. We did not know it was you.'

The surrounding men lowered weapons in frustration. It was clear that the robbing part of this afternoon was over and that they, in fact, would have to share out some of their lunch with their erstwhile victims. The world was a strange place, to be sure.

'A wise choice by a wiser leader. Now, Seán Seosamh my fine man, what did you say about hospitality and when is the earliest that we might eat? I feel a ravenous need, as do we all. None more keenly of course than your newest ally, Caoilte Mac Rónán.'

None of the bough-men, brush-men, or bark-men were left unaffected by the final words. Mouths opened, they exchanged glances, gasps escaped and one of the more knowledgeable scoundrels dropped his bow in despair and covered his face with both hands.

A Call to Arms

***

In the camp of the thieves, Eoghan raises his voice and speaks sense to those who are seemingly without.

Ní féidir an dubh a chur ina gheal, ach seal

You can only deny the truth, for a while.

***

They ate together around a roaring campfire. The quiet clearing came alive as shadows began to dance among the trees surrounding them. Many of the group weren't quite sure what they had just witnessed but welcomed the warmth of the fire. Eoghan was impressed by Éine's deft handling of a dangerous situation. He had taken Éine for a dose of something foul. Now it seemed he was not without uses.

The robbers were well provisioned and had only recently been back to visit their homes, so they were almost overladen with delights. The robbers gave them, wild boar, peas, trout, oats and lastly, a honeycomb was shared around so that everyone could take a chunk in their fingers. The lake water tasted slightly of silt but was cooling. Though Seán Seosamh appeared a welcoming host, Eoghan could feel a brimming hostility towards his guests. The bandit hid it from Caoilte and Éine, but less so from the others.

Talk turned to the world and the goings-on of its people. The guests spoke little and listened lots. They heard of worrying happenings to the east, where an army of mercenaries was being recruited by a man named Uad, and those who presented themselves were well rewarded. Numbers were swelling even though Uad's purpose remained a mystery. The recruiters were foreigners; killers and rapists and were seemingly free from obstruction. The High King and other kings in the East were remaining frustratingly slow to react. Many of the warriors shook their heads at the thought of the inaction; more than a few suggestions were made as to how the situation could be rectified. One or two know-it-alls told anecdotes of how someone they knew was aware of corruption and bribery at the highest levels. Some said that even the High King had been bought. Others suggested that the High King was afraid of an all-out invasion and was bolstering coastal and tactical fortifications in preparation. All present found the situation unacceptable. Eoghan found it frightening.

Rhíona listened to every word impassively.

After the meal, many of them sat around the fireside to talk of what had happened. The boating party was exhausted, so the old men and Laoise found somewhere to sleep shortly after finishing their fine meal.

Eoghan, Rúadhan, and Rhíona stayed to talk with Seán Seosamh and his men.

Eoghan knew he should feel more tired than he did, but he was alert. Rhíona was pale. Eoghan had urged her to retire several times, but something about the thought of sleeping made her resistant. She had whispered of the kind of sleep she experienced after using *draíocht*, but when he pressed her, would not say anything more on the matter. She had performed *draíocht* on them. Healed them. He wanted to ask her about it, to catch her when she could speak in private and ask the thousand questions that had come up since it happened.

Could she have saved my father's life? My mother's mind?

It became apparent that Seán Seosamh wanted more than just a fireside chat. He began to ask them about their journey and their destination. His questions were directed mainly at Rhíona who dodged them admirably.

'We are a group thrown together by chance and unclear of our choices and our next port of call,' she said, or 'Caoilte will ultimately decide on our next course of action.'

It clearly grated on the Seán Seosamh's nerves and he persisted with his interrogation, his eyes fever-bright. Fire-lit faces seated around them were no longer hospitable.

'You say these things because you are a conniving young thing are you not? We have given you a fine welcome and our finest fare and yet you play games.'

'I think it is time for us to retire,' said Rhíona with a frosty look. 'I am not used to being addressed in such a way.'

'You will sit, and we will talk more. I want you to consider this. Your two young friends here are sitting around a fire with a group that will quite happily hurt them if I wish it. Your older friends are asleep and will not be able to help you in time. So, for the sake of this pair's continued robust health, I ask you again: where are you going and to what end?'

Eoghan felt anger building.

Rhíona's eye narrowed and cheeks reddened. 'You talk of welcome, yet you threaten and insult. You call me conniving, yet here you sit surrounded by men trying to intimidate an answer out of us? I am beginning to find your company most unwelcome.'

Rúadhan spoke with a sneer. 'Your threats are no more than a sham. You would not dream of harming us because you know who is lying over there and what he would do to you if you did. Indeed, I might wake him now and ask him what he would do to you.'

'You are all so eager to hear what has Caoilte Mac Rónán walking the land once more?' shouted Eoghan, standing suddenly. His face was a picture of rage to match the feelings welling up inside him. 'I will tell you.'

Rhíona looked stiff, leaning forward as if about to speak. Others who were not around the fire, started to arrive to see what the commotion was about.

'There are forces at work that threaten the safety of our lands and our people,' said Eoghan. 'I have seen a small group of them slaughter children. An army of mercenaries amassing unhindered not that far from here? You people talk about little else. Why has Caoilte Mac Rónán emerged after decades unaccounted for? Because it seems that the men and women of Ireland are hiding in trees robbing honest folk. Because those two men, the last two Fianna, and their friends are the only ones who have answered the call. Are ye blind to it? Or have you all made yourselves blind to it? Save your answers and think on what you might say. I do not care, nor do any of us. We are going anyway. You go back to robbing people and eating your fine meals out here away from your families and any responsibility. Or you there, who's aiming the bow at me. Why not shoot and be done with it? Why? Because you are afraid of him.' Eoghan pointed at Caoilte who was standing in the shadows. 'Instead of trying to be like him. Instead of being better than this, or at least working at it.' He walked around them, looking into their eyes.

'We have seen first-hand the kind of black-hearted demons that roam our land. We have seen what they will do to achieve their aim. And they'll be here. I'm just letting ye know now, they'll be here. On horseback, wearing armour and carrying spears with very sharp points. What will ye do? Hide, is it? Hide and hope that they simply ride past? Or is it time for something else now?' He pointed to his elder companions again. 'When these great men turn around looking for strength in the coming dark days, will they find strength after all? Which of you will be there standing ready?'

He glanced at those watching. 'I will be there. Me. I might not be able to help very much, for I am neither bowman nor swordsman, but I will be there.' He stalked away from the fire. Past Rhíona who looked full of pride. Past Rúadhan who looked full of doubt. Past Caoilte and Laoise who looked surprised. Past Donnacha who was watching everyone else; eyes reflecting the flames of the firepit. As Eoghan passed, Donnacha turned and followed him.

As Eoghan walked past Éine in the deepening night, he could just make out a huge grin; a smile that seemed to match the oncoming darkness.

THE LAY OF THE LAND

***

Rhíona delivers further truths. The swelling band is subject to the position of its individual members, some of whom have business to attend to elsewhere.

An té nach bhfuil láidir, ní mór dó a bheith glic

He who is not strong ought to be clever.

***

They decided to leave the camp at sunrise. There was a strange mood around the fading embers after Eoghan's rousing speech. The only one of the boat's crew who stayed beside the fire was Éine, who was coy about what happened. Laoise asked him had he been up to no good, to which he guffawed heartily.

‘They say that idle hands are the tools of the Fa...’ he started to say, then cringed and looked in the direction of the only Fae within earshot. Rhíona was looking at him with a thin smile.

‘They also say that it is often a mouth broke a nose, master poet,’ she said, the smile never leaving her face.

‘So they do, my young princess, so they do,’ he smirked. ‘I assure you both that I was not so careless with my words in days of old. Nor was I last night. Not in the least.’

Laoise watched Éine turn to look at Eoghan, who was just back from relieving himself, and washing. His wet hair was still dripping so he was leaning over, shaking his head like a wolfhound. Laoise did not miss Éine’s eyes rolling to the Sun Gods. Eoghan was also receiving strange looks from the robbers who were whispering and poking each other, before sneaking glances at him.

Éine, it seemed, had been developing a back story with Eoghan as the hero. He certainly was up to no good, and likely planned to use the boy to some end. It was Laoise’s understanding that the boys intended going home as soon as chance allowed. Éine would do everything he could to ensure it did not happen. She had seen his work before. He was a devious soul; more so when handsome young men were involved. But this time she felt there were bigger cogs turning in his wizened old head. The darker of the boys had shown a side of him that was surprising.

Laoise looked over to see what Rúadhan was doing. He was sitting with his back to a tree eating some dried fish, staring directly at her and blushed furiously, pretending he had been looking at something else in the middle distance.

She prepared her smuggest grin for when he sneaked a glance again. He did. This time pretending to pick a bone from his teeth. When he saw her grin, she heard him choke a little, before retreating to less awkward climes.

Laoise smiled at Rúadhan's back as he left. He handled himself well beside the fire, and had impressed her on the boat. In fact, both of the boys were impressive at the oars. Although gangly, Rúadhan had a smooth flow to his movements. Not as awkward as he thought himself to be.

Thinking about it, Laoise realised she was not unhappy at the thought of Éine causing them to stay. Rúadhan was still a boy perhaps, but a man in the making. Maybe even a good man.

Turning back to her breakfast, Laoise found she was the subject of Rhíona's scrutiny. Unlike the last observer, the princess did not turn away.

'He is an interesting person,' Rhíona said.

'The two of them are. And Donnacha even more-so. He has an incredible talent.'

'You must be of similar age, you and Rúadhan,' Rhíona continued.

'I suppose we might be. You and Eoghan could be said to be of similar age too, could you not?'

Rhíona laughed. 'It could be said, yes. It would not be correct, however. Do you find him attractive?'

'What? Who?'

'Rúadhan. Do you find him attractive?' Rhíona asked.

'Who do you think you are asking me that? We don't even know each other.'

Rhíona grimaced a little. 'I am sorry, Laoise. I meant no offence.'

Laoise felt herself blush, regretting her sharp tone. 'No. Forgive me, Rhíona. I did not intend to be so cross sounding.'

There was silence for a moment. Laoise wondered how to proceed.

'I'm not going to apologise to him,' she said.

'He has definitely suffered worse of late,' said Rhíona, still staring at Laoise.

'All to help you, Rhíona. All of this. Daithí's death. Young Seán,' she hated the tears welling up as she spoke, but was pleased when Rhíona broke her gaze, tears forming in her eyes.

'It was never my intention for people to get hurt… or killed.'

Laoise hawked and spat. 'What is your intention? What price are you willing to pay to find Fionn Mac Cumhal?'

Rhíona wiped a tear from the tip of her nose. 'I do not know. I wish I could make you understand what's coming if I do not find him. The danger for everyone. I would not risk anyone unless I knew that most certainly.'

'Perhaps it's something you should consider. There are no Fianna left,' Laoise said, looking around the camp. 'Just us.'

As a silence descended, Laoise could feel her heart beating in her ears.

‘I wish there was some way you could trust me, Laoise. You saved us all on the boat. I would take you over the Fianna any day, after seeing you fight.’

Laoise sighed, feeling a sadness growing in her. She wanted to cry but would not let the Fae girl see her do it. Not if her head fell off.

‘Would it be so terrible if we did get to know each other?’ asked Rhíona. ‘Perhaps you would allow me to prove I am trustworthy. That I am a friend?’

Laoise looked at Rhíona, eyes narrowed. As she looked, she had to admit she didn’t see a Fae princess or a *draíocht* user. Just a girl who had seen her share of horror.

‘I would like to get to know you better, Rhíona.’ It was true. She realised that she longed for friendship; especially that of a girl. She was lonely. She suspected that Rhíona was too.

‘So, do you have an interest in him?’ Rhíona asked, her face a picture of steadfastness and companionship. ‘You can tell me things like that. We can share interests.’

Laoise relaxed and the two girls laughed openly. She had very little interaction with girls her own age, or seemingly her own age.

‘I think you should mind your business,’ she said. Rhíona’s jaw dropped again. ‘That said, in a general sense, he has a pretty little arse and nice long legs.’ She laughed and Rhíona did too. ‘It’s a bit soon to be telling you about my romances. You want me to trust you? Tell me about yours. Do you have a... well, an interest in someone where you are from? Or will you be forced to marry someone? I hardly know a thing about you.’

'I will not wed because of my standing. Marriage would complicate things. I am not the eldest. So, I am effectively able to do as I please in matters of the heart.'

'And who does your heart want?'

Rhíona looked a little stunned for a moment. She looked in the direction of Eoghan. Laoise saw that he was trying to force water out of his ear by using far too much of one of his fingers.

Rhíona smiled sadly. 'I am not well liked among my people. There are a few reasons why, many of which I have brought upon myself. There is no one in my world who holds very much of my heart. There exists considerable complexity in such things there. Perhaps in a simpler world… with someone…' Her gaze flicked towards Eoghan again for the briefest moment before she fell silent.

Laoise felt strange with the princess so unsteady sounding.

Rhíona patted her legs. 'Let's just say that I will do as I please when it comes to my heart. It's less mysterious sounding.'

'Well, you are a Fae Princess. If you can't have a little mystery around you as a Fae princess, who else can?'

'That is the truth of it indeed, Laoise,' she nodded, smiling. 'I will try not to be mysterious around you, though. We can be open with each other.' Rhíona's eyes searched Laoise's. 'Perhaps we might even become friends?'

'Friends?'

'Yes. Friends. You and I. In these times, friends are badly needed I think.'

'I will be your friend, Rhíona. No matter what surprises you might have left in store.' Laoise meant what she said.

'Most of the Fae I know are mysterious, I suppose. A conservative lot, though, and few, if any, enjoy surprises. I, on the other hand, love surprises.'

'Well then let's go see what happens if I pinch Rúadhan's little bum,' said Laoise and the two girls folded over laughing.

The morning was busy. The group took stock of belongings, and gathered supplies from the robbers, paid for by Éine's rings. Little was said to mark the event. Seán Seosamh was lying down, and no one else felt the desire to represent his band. As they left, much of the talk behind them was about the young man who had spoken so passionately at the fire. Laoise overheard one of the younger robbers say a name. Eoghan *Canteóir* – Eoghan the speaker – Laoise shook her head; it seemed Éine *was* up to his tricks.

As they left the camp heading south and east, they exchanged nods with the robbers. Donnacha led them in a direction that would avoid the hills to the north and the bogs to the west. Their pace was slow, and their mood tense. At midday they came upon a clear stream and stopped to eat. Rhíona spoke to them as they found somewhere to sit.

'I have a duty that must be fulfilled. It simply must. I have come from a land that is so very different in many ways. It is similar in other ways, but subtly so. My people have seemed very strange to yours in the past because the *draíocht* distorts and perverts. It is open to our kind here and we may use it more freely than at home. I cannot understand why. Yet using it here comes at a cost.

'It is similar for those few of your people who have walked among us there. They invariably become changed. Ruined. We know this all too well after *Síor Feargach* came to our lands and changed our world forever...' She paused, her eyes unfocused. When she spoke again, it was almost a whisper.

'The *draíocht*, however, seems to be retreating from this world; moving more towards my own, as if it never really held sway. It has now lost interest here. There is a mundanity in this world. The truly great deeds of individuals are lessened for the deeds of the people; the *draíocht* is leaving this world and without my father's machinations it will be gone within a few generations. As it becomes stronger there my father will soon have an opportunity to change things entirely.

'The day fast approaches where my father plans to send an army here. An army of conquest made powerful by the same *draíocht* that is leaving this place. It can only happen, however, if the gate between our worlds still exists.'

'There is a gate? Where?' asked Rúadhan with a worried look.

Rhíona tutted a little and shook her head.

'No. No, I have oversimplified it. Forgive me. A gate is not an accurate description. If I were to analogise badly, it is more akin to the way that ants find their food and bring it back to the anthill. The first ant finds the food and marks the way for the other ants. They are attracted and follow the same route as set by the first. Without the first to mark the way, they will not find it.

'When the first of us built a portal to this world, many followed to search, and explore, to do good, and evil, to create and destroy. Whereas once there were many of us amongst you, now there are almost none. The Fianna destroyed our foothold here and most of my kind have no further interest in this place. There is nothing for us here, only anger and hatred. My father wishes to bring a greater and more focused source of anger and hatred. If he does so and establishes a strong presence, the *draíocht* will surely follow him back. Now that the Fianna are no more, now the destructive rage of *Síor Feargach* has been forgotten; there will be none to stop him. Your land will be the first to fall but he will not stop at that. My father will come instead in never-ending waves until this world is washed clean of men and becomes his.'

'What do you mean never-ending waves?' asked Laoise, brow furrowed. She was suddenly very worried. A hand strayed to one of her darts and she drew it without knowing why.

'And this *Síor Feargach* that no one has ever heard of?' said Donnacha.

Rhíona shook her head slightly in irritation. 'It is as I tell it, Laoise. There are far more immediate concerns. And as for how you have never heard of *Síor Feargach*, I think perhaps because the Fianna did not want their name blackened for evermore.' She looked at Éine. He was pale, mouth drawn into a line. He held her gaze for a moment, then turned away.

Rhíona said, 'The cruel acts of *Síor Feargach* haunt my people. Better to speak no more of those days or deeds. That is not for now. This island as it is now will have no happy future. Its greatest days may well be in the past. It will be desecrated and will fall. All but memory will remain of what it means to be one with this ancient land and of its people and its ways. Then the memories will fade, and there will be none here but those who no longer care. All these things considered, the imminent threat that my father represents must be dealt with because if we do not, your entire world will be forfeit. My father will wipe your kind from existence.'

Rhíona started to pace over and back.

'We must also fight him because we must always fight against what is born of hatred. Change will happen and will bear all kinds of fruit. Hatred brings only destruction. We must cling to the things that are good and just and protect them as if they were nursing babes. Such babes grow to do the greatest deeds, but they need constant protection.'

'What about today? I mean, right now? What do we do to fix this starting from here?' Eoghan stood and asked.

Éine spoke, quietly at first, as if he had just been roused from sleep.

'We must find out more. We need to find out about this Uad and what he's about. We are foully ill-prepared, clearly ill-equipped and lack neither bark nor bite. We will need to find the horn, *Dord Fionn* or some clue Fionn left behind; if he left one. We need to go to the High King. It is unlikely that any of you young delightfuls will attract his attention. To lend credence, one of us Fianna must do it. Someone who has the talents required to help us change the course of things.'

'So that must mean you?' said Donnacha. 'Without casting aspersions on the other member of the Fianna here, he cannot be described as a good choice of representative. I think ye'll agree?'

Éine's eyes locked onto Caoilte's. 'No. Neither of us. Someone is going to have to go and get Eimear.'

Caoilte's eyes opened wide, and opening his mouth as if to speak, he said nothing.

Éine paused, as if considering what to say next. 'It cannot be us. There is a considerable history that would make things difficult.'

'Who is Eimear, if I'm not out of line asking?' asked Donnacha.

'She was one of us back then. Not many survived the final battle, but Eimear was not there.'

'Where was she?' asked Eoghan.

Éine paused again. 'She left the Fianna some years before. The violence… became too much. We will need her involvement in this. She has cunning and will find a way to convince the King.'

'And I'm thinking by the way that you're talking that you know where she is but have no intention of going to see her yourself?'

Éine turned to Donnacha. 'As a matter of fact, my fine talented fellow, you are correct. *You* will go to see her. She will have no interest in talking to me, and it is unlikely that she will join us on our quest. She has turned away from that life. However, I do believe that you might convince her to do what is right and speak to the King on our behalf. Once he agrees to aid us, you can make the arrangements from then on. Eimear can go back to whatever she has been doing all these years.'

Donnacha was studying the ground.

Rúadhan's face turned dark and he said, 'You don't answer to him and certainly don't have to obey his commands. We owe them nothing.'

Donnacha waved a hand. 'I'm afraid the thought of a little solitude does appeal to me, my young friend, and that's just the truth of it. I have a lot to think about and would welcome the chance to walk alone. I do not mean to suggest for one moment that the company you all provide is anything less than a pleasure and that I don't mind telling you.' His gaze flicked to Caoilte. 'I have a lot to ponder as I wander. That's what I say sometimes. To myself usually. A lot to ponder as I wander.'

'Then,' said Éine, 'that is our first course of action. Caoilte and I will go to visit an old *seanchaí* friend, to discover what we can about our adversaries. You youngsters will go search for a clue or a guide to the whereabouts of our erstwhile leader. I have knowledge of a *cailleach*, a witch, who lives on *Cuilcagh* Mountain to the north. She has powers of sight and will help you if you can motivate her to do so. She is an odd character but retains formidable talents. Find a way to do so, please and thank you. If you choose to leave now, fare well.'

Rhíona faced the poet. 'Why so helpful now?'

Éine raised his eyebrows. 'Why, my lady, our assistance was offered from the outset. It was a question of youthful exuberance wanting more than we could offer at that juncture. Alas, the times and the situation have changed. This thing must be done, you say. Then let us do this very thing. Donnacha will travel south to the valley at *Uí Garrchon* to Eimear and then back to the King at Tara. The four youngsters will go to *Cuilcagh* and seek clues to the whereabouts of Fionn

Mac Cumhal. Caoilte and I will go to see our friend who knows of politics and such matters of the day.

'So, I suggest that when we meet in twelve evenings from now, we shall do it west of here. We will meet at the ringfort at *Uí Failge Túath*. Prudence dictates that we do not stall for long, however. Those not accounted for in twelve evenings can meet with the group at the river *Gailleamh* where it meets the great lake in fifteen. It is a well-worn path and will bring us away from Uad's army. Let us keep together until the morning lights the paths we walk tomorrow. We can keep moving south to stay ahead of pursuit.' He opened his palms to the boys. 'It will also bring us quite close to your home, young men. Perhaps you both might consider an exit then?'

Eoghan looked at Rúadhan and Rúadhan looked at Eoghan. 'Have we not proved our worth? Why do you wish to be rid of us now?' Eoghan asked, voice rising.

Éine's eyes closed for a moment as he took a long breath. 'Eoghan. Rúadhan. You have been more like men of the Fianna than any I can remember for a long time. But you are both too young, and there are too many dangers ahead. It is not right that you follow Rhíona blindly into what will likely be the demise of us all.'

'That man gives me a pain in my neck', said Rúadhan. 'And he'd give you a pain in your arse. You're probably right Éine. You probably are. But there are no Fianna left. Only us. And we will go where we are needed. Both of us.'

Eoghan glanced at Rhíona and nodded. 'Both of us,' he echoed.

Éine patted his stomach. 'Now. Let us eat and I will tell Donnacha to where he must travel. I feel that I am fading away to nothing. What will my stomach think if I keep it from food much longer? It will be horrified.'

STORYTELLING

***

Éine stands before them and tells stories of the Fianna. The others soon find that the stories he tells are not the same stories they are familiar with.

Tarraingíonn scéal scéal eile

Stories beget stories.

***

The members of the band conducted themselves in relative silence that evening. A bitter wind blew across the camp, cutting through the trees as if they were only a memory. It swirled around the group, respecting no attempts to create a barrier against its chilled tendrils.

Against good sense, they lit two fires, and were soon cocooned by huddled bodies. Wrapped in hide and wool, they were contented with taciturn grimaces. Caoilte and Laoise set themselves apart from the others. Caoilte sat, abjectly staring at nothing, his mood plainly sour; the shake in his hands obvious. His granddaughter glared at anyone who so much as glanced in their direction, which for Rúadhan, was often.

Eoghan prodded the ground with a twig. Hunched over, being stung by the cold, he began to think of home. The stout wooden half doors that kept the wind shut out; the firepit that would surely be fed and stoked, and the smells of stewing meat and vegetables that would emanate from it; his mother's kindly smile, rare as it had become. Even the gaudy oversized tapestries seemed less absurd. Despair began to cover him like a sodden blanket. His breathing started to become ragged.

What am I doing here? Rúadhan has been right all along. Who are these people? They are nothing to me.

His anger rose.

As did Éine's voice. 'I will tell you, if you will listen, of the days of Fionn Mac Cumhal and *Fianna na h-Éireann*. For there are things you need to reflect upon and take heed of. I can offer you words, if you would receive them, of the type of men and women that we are dealing with'.

All eyes were focused upon him, and the chill seemed to lessen.

Éine's voice rose once more; not the sometimes-snide voice they had become accustomed to, but the sonorous, intoxicating voice, which had greeted them in the drinking house.

'There are many things I could speak of, were we to navigate through the Fianna's history and of Fionn himself. It is only right, however that some facts are set before you. The stories told are just that: stories; some based on the truth and others not at all. Some characters have been depicted as something they were not, and others have been forgotten and their names will be lost before too long.

'In the glory days, the Fianna were described as a heroic band who heeded neither hot nor cold and who could walk from one end of the island and back without the need for food or drink. The truth, as it can be, was nothing so romantic nor charming. The Fianna's members were a mixed lot and lived and died like anyone they marched past on their travels. All manner of women and men could be found among their ranks; with them came troubled pasts, human uncertainty, and most of all an aptitude for violence.

'There were ways for Fionn to weed out the less worthy. The tests of entry, the maxims and mottoes of the Fianna and his own constant, lofty expectation. All of these, you see, were not just ideals for the common man to strive for. No, they were equally an effort to keep the band in check, to control the group who had, with some regularity, *draíocht* running over them or surely would do as time went on. *Draíocht* was drawn to the members of the band. I now understand that Fionn's presence was a cause of that or at least in part.'

'You think that Fionn knew about this *draíocht* as Rhíona does?' asked Eoghan.

Rhíona looked at him in the dark.

'It is impossible to know,' answered Éine. 'Fionn himself was like no other person that has walked in this world. Fionn's supreme gift was his ability to read people and bring out a greatness in them that might have been buried too deep for anyone else to see. It was an unenviable task at times, for there were some of the

Fianna who were as black-hearted as any they fought against.

'Tricksters and snakes like Goll Mac Morna and his brothers who played at being friends of Fionn for long years, only to betray him and ultimately assist in the downfall of the Fianna. Fionn knew it would happen at some point, yet never said a word against them and always sought ways to earn their respect; nurture their limited honour. Even towards the end, when they presented him with the Adopted Blades – Bran and Sceolan – named after his most beloved hounds, he knew they plotted against him.

'Mercenaries and runaway soldiers, thieves and pirates routinely petitioned for membership of the band. Many sought glory and profit. There were some who longed only for battle and to mete out death and who lusted after it and revelled in the spilling of blood.

'Indeed, there was one amongst the Fianna who was beyond a killer; beyond those who lose themselves in the slaughter of war; more a merciless butcher. One for whom anything except battle was naught but wearisome and tedious. The one you asked about, Donnacha. The one who became known only as *Síor Feargach* - Always raging. For *Síor Feargach*, the maxims of the Fianna would never have been enough to quell the murderous intent, but Fionn knew a way to calm the rage and spent many long years bringing about change. In those years, however, *Síor Feargach's* sword *Sciobtha* slaughtered many with such skill and malevolence that many of the Fianna themselves were filled with dread when *Sciobtha* was drawn into sunlight.' The poet's voice cracked a little as if the memory tormented him.

'A blade that was bathed in blood so often that it turned crimson up to its hilt and would drip with blood even after it had been cleaned. You will not hear tell of the deeds of *Síor Feargach* as Fionn ordered none to ever speak of them. Deeds of such wanton destruction and fury could not be at peace with his vision. Indeed, those of us who witnessed the drawing of *Sciobtha* into daylight have been ever since shadowed by it. Many fled from the ranks of the Fianna in despair as a result.'

Éine stopped speaking and stared into the fire. His words had washed over those listening as if they could see the sword dripping blood.

When Éine continued, it was quieter, 'You will not hear of the deeds of *Síor Feargach* by the fire sides. No saga could describe such horror… such…'

Caoilte shifted as if uncomfortable.

'Evil', he whispered pointedly.

He looked at Éine, and the two men stared at each other, reliving some kind of shared memory. Both faces hardened. After a long moment, Éine continued.

'Another of the most loyal members ran away with Fionn's love Gráinne sometime after the death of Fionn's wife. It shook the foundations of the Fianna and caused a rend on the man's heart from which he never really recovered. The flight of Diarmaid and Gráinne is only known to the world because of their own telling of their tale during their evading of Fionn's pursuit. It came to light then that Gráinne had put a *geis* upon Diarmaid so that he would follow her, but Fionn never came to terms with what had happened.

'This was Fionn's lot. To manage the unmanageable and create a fighting force the likes of which had never been seen. All this while trying to protect and teach his son Oisín and later his grandsons. Against all barriers in his way, he succeeded in his goal and the acts of the Fianna were acts to protect our land and its people. There are none who could do the same. There will not be again. And there are many stories about his own great deeds.

'For now, instead, let me tell you of the tasks that were set before those who petitioned to become a member of their ranks. Any man or any woman, whether highborn or tinker or ploughman or the *Ammaitán* himself, could present themselves. Each was given seven tests. Everyone who passed those tests would later learn that they were just the beginning. Life in the Fianna was about learning and growing. Testing your own courage, or your knowledge, or testing your kindness or your loyalty, or testing your wrestling or your fishing. Life in the Fianna meant a life of testing yourself. Putting aside the regrets of the past or worries of the future and doing.

'That, however, was not for the applicants to know. Because to be truly able to look inside and test oneself, you must first be tested by others.

'The first test was the easiest. It showed patience and self-control. The applicant would be presented with a hunting spear. The spear would be stuck into the ground and the applicant would have to leap atop unaided and stay atop for seven days and seven nights.

'The tests grew in difficulty thereafter, and many fell short and were asked to walk away, never to look back nor speak of what they saw for fear of retribution.

'While standing in a hole as deep as their waist, those petitioning had to be able to defend themselves using only a shield and a branch from a hazel tree against nine attacking warriors with nine spears. Wounded applicants were not accepted.

'They would next have to attempt escape from warriors in pursuit by sprinting through the forest without snapping a twig or making a sound. Applicants who were caught or who returned with disturbed hair or torn clothing were not accepted.

'While running as fast as their legs would allow, they had to remove a thorn from their foot without stopping nor slowing.

'The next test was to leap over a branch level with their brow and run under a branch that was placed at their knee without missing a step nor making contact with either.

'There were demands upon the knowledge of the candidate. They had to recite twelve books of poetry and also know many of the old legends and stories whether of Setanta, the hound of Culann or Balor the one-eyed. They had to be able to compose verse in rhyme and meter that bathed the listeners in eloquence and grace.

'Those men in the band who had an interest in women were not permitted to take a dowry with a wife. Fionn believed that two lovers should become one, firstly in respect.

'Their capacity for accumulating knowledge was tested. They would learn a wealth of skills to include all forms of combat and martial arts: sword-mastery, fencing, wrestling, fighting, archery and marksmanship with all forms of weapons. As well as many other skills: fishing, riding, and woodsmanship. Over time they would become specialists in one area or more, for of all the things the Fianna were not, we were a band. We relied on one another and worked hand in hand on all things. We would explore our own skills with a mind toward improvement, and we would pass on what we knew with a mind toward the ideal. The ideal would never be ideal enough. During peace times, we would hunt and help build, fish and help farm. And in the main, it was good.'

He stopped and tutted loudly. Taking a twig, he rooted dirt from under his nail.

'Perhaps I was overly harsh earlier. The feelings of bitterness are oft the ones that present themselves the quickest. Legends of acts of bravery and heroism in the defence of these shores are indeed based upon truth, for there were many such deeds. Great men and women gathered in that group and protected the land around us. But they were not all great, even though the Fianna was.

'It was him. All of it rested in his hands, on his shoulders. And he was different. He had no warrior nature, nor lust for battle. Indeed, after many battles he would spend time wandering the field, assisting with the bodies of the fallen. Even mourning the passing of his enemies. His love was for this land and its integrity. His goals were improvement and respect. His ability to get the best traits of his band to surface and shine were an incredible gift.

'It was the same gift that made him less aware of the more devious few around him. And that made him open to betrayal for the right price or when lust commanded.

'If we do find him, I do not know what we will find. The Fianna are gone, his son remains in the otherworld, and he has long outlived most of his kin. He has the soul of a poet and has lost everything. Tomorrow we will part company and our groups will go about the task of locating some clue of his possible whereabouts...' Hesitating, he looked frail. 'I do not know what we will find.'

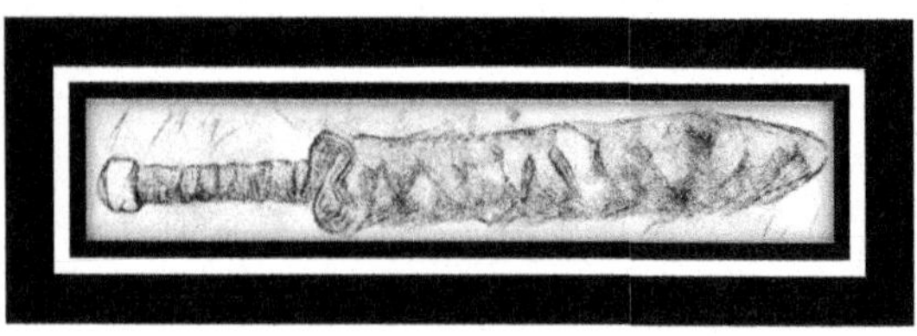

The Rocky Grey Path to Acquaintance

***

Laoise and Eoghan reach out hands of friendship.

Aithnítear cara i gcruatan

You recognise friends in hard times.

***

Laoise approached Donnacha as Rúadhan watched. There was something about the way she moved that oozed confidence. She was quite an intriguing person.

Strong all the way through, he thought. *Even the soft bits*.

She was no one he had met before. Able, fiercely independent, intelligent. He felt ill at ease at the thoughts of walking away from her. Rúadhan was extremely interested to see what she might want, however. They were all used to her maintaining a distance.

Standing in front of Donnacha, she watched him inspecting his bowstrings.

'I want to ask you something, and I will not feel aggrieved should you refuse straight out.'

'Fine, I refuse,' said Donnacha.

Laoise's mouth fell open. 'Eh. Ah, I see. Erm...'

An apologetic smile crept across the bowman's face. 'Ah, my lady, I am only having a little jig with you. Just acting the maggot for a bit of fun. I could not refuse such a fair face as your own, and that's no lie. And the granddaughter of Caoilte Mac Rónán. I would never sleep again with regret if I was not able to help in any way I could.'

Rips of snorted laughter from Rúadhan were short-lived when Laoise turned with a withering look. Donnacha sat, his face a picture of innocence. 'How can I be of service, Laoise?'

'I have noted your skill with the bows. I have been most impressed and hoped you might teach me to become more proficient. I have my darts and some rudimentary skill with a bow myself. I long to improve, and I think you could be the man to help me.'

Donnacha's face became thoughtful. He replaced the bowstrings into the pouch and put it back on his belt as he stood.

Cracked lips pursed, he said, 'I have long wondered how I would react if someone was to ask for my tutelage. What can I offer an apprentice? I always asked myself, so I have. Would it be the right thing to do, considering that I taught myself the intricacies of the bow and the arrow over many long years with no such instruction?

'I am not unhappy with your request and the answer is yes. Yes, I can help you to the point where I can tell you exactly what to do and the exact process required to becoming, quite possibly, the greatest bow-wielder the world has ever known. Indeed, I was younger than you when I started teaching myself, but I did not have advice to guide me, and I did not have the patience and drive that I have today. It took a number of different things to happen before I really put my mind to it. I mean, to actually set about achieving perfection. It would obviously be fair of you to say that I am a long way off reaching my aims, but the road to perfection is a great and high road to travel; a road upon which one can truly be content and learn wisdom.'

Rúadhan sat up now. He had never heard Donnacha speaking like this. He noticed that Éine and Caoilte were listening as they ate. His passion was intoxicating.

'There is a price you will have to pay, however, which may prove an issue for one as young as yourself, wet behind the ears and eager to know everything yesterday so you can tell everyone about it later today.'

'You will not find me impetuous. I learn quickly but will remain focused and patient,' said Laoise, head bowing.

'Well therein, you see, Laoise, lies the issue in question. You will not learn quickly. You must abandon expectation; give up notions of immediate or short-term reward and prepare for a long journey. You must start in the morning and practise with the bow. You must examine your form, first, against an easy target. You must observe, scrutinise, and reflect on the way your body moves each and every time. Then you must see how each minuscule action affects the flight of the arrow and see what difference is made when the fletch is adjusted and then when the target is further away or smaller or larger or moving. Then you must re-examine your form and begin again because bad habits creep in like a coughing sickness. Action, review, reflection, improvement.' He stood and started pacing. Laoise looked to the others as if trying to gauge their reactions.

'You must move to a place where the wind changes and practise there for a year. All the time reflecting and readjusting and compensating and checking them against each other to ensure the basics are done correctly and consistently. Another year must go to loosing arrows in very bright or very dim conditions; another to hot and cold and the effects on the flights of the arrow and on the wood of the bow. The bad habits will act like a tide turning hill to cliff and back to stony beach. The only way to combat them is to practise the ideal and accept nothing else, learning from each and every arrow released. And for every new thing you try, an improvement will become apparent and for every improvement you make, a difficulty will present itself – the increasing strength of your drawing arm and fingers creating a slight pull to one side, adjustments made to allow for a strong breeze, the sudden onset of rain unaccounted for. All the time the form must remain correct, and during practice you must give your best. Never, never anything less than your best. Then you might even consider a start on your weaker shooting side to ensure your muscles are balanced.'

Rúadhan noticed Laoise's frown becoming a grimace.

'If I were you, I would start now and not delay a single heartbeat longer. I would use all of the daylight of all of the days for the next year to analyse your form and address the basic issues. The following year we can start making initial fine adjustments and all of that fiddly business. Therein lies the real crux for the would-be master.

'I must confess that I am nothing but excited for there is lots to do and, together, with time as both our ally and our enemy, we can discover wonderful things together; travel the road to perfection together. Who knows, Laoise, if you are indeed a fast learner, then who's to say that we won't reach the moment together as our arrows pierce the sky to land on the spot that we have chosen, whether it be the side of a distant hill or the eye of a pigeon?'

Laoise's mouth was open. A flash of something passed across her face and she snapped it shut. 'I preferred the first answer. At least you were trying to be funny.' She turned on her heel and stalked away.

Donnacha stood palms outstretched, lips downturned. Caoilte went back to his meal with a look of sudden disinterest. Rúadhan found that Éine was looking at him with a grin.

Rúadhan kept thinking about Laoise long after she had stormed away. She had barely so much as looked in his direction, which filled him with a strange disquiet. A need grew inside him to impress her or give her cause to notice him; better yet, acknowledge his existence in some way.

But how do you impress a granddaughter of one of the greatest warriors who ever lived?

As they resumed their journey, Eoghan went to walk beside Rhíona who welcomed him with a smile.

'How are you getting on?' It was a silly question, he knew well. He wanted to ask her about the healing. It gnawed at him. There was so much more that he wanted too; her respect, to see her smile, to feel less lightheaded around her.

Her smile widened. 'I am getting on well enough. How about you?'

'How about me?'

'How are you getting on, Eoghan?'

'Oh. Yes. I'm grand now.'

'You are preoccupied with something and have come to talk to me about it,' she ventured, looking ahead.

'Yes. Yes. I am... that is, I want to know about your world. What it's like there. And you. Tell me about your life as a princess there. Do you live in a great house? With slaves and servants? We have been in each other's company for a while now. I think there might be no harm for us to get to know more about each other?'

Rhíona's smile faltered and faded as he spoke.

'This is going to sound terrible, and I hope you can understand that I do not mean it to, but I can tell you very little because…'

She looked at him for a moment. Her arms folded and she took a deep breath.

'It would be difficult to explain. Well, I could tell you, but I do not think it would be a very good idea.' Eoghan felt himself blush and searched for a way to retreat. Rhíona blushed too.

'I have overstepped my mark, I think. I am sor...' he mumbled as he backed away.

'Wait,' Rhíona said. She tutted and continued. 'I mostly live in a place by myself. As do all my sisters and brothers. We are charged with the protection of a group... a settlement, you could call it. Our lives in our own places are interesting and comfortable. To leave them means difficulty. There are other places that are unruled and unruly. Trading happens between those settlements not at war. The divide means that my mother and father war constantly because that is the way, but the crease keeps them apart. The crease is a chasm. A bottomless, endless void. My sisters and I fight alongside our mother, but on occasion we fight amongst each other. It is the same with my brothers who fight alongside my father.

'Some of my brothers and sisters look like me, and others are very different. We of the Fae are far more varied in our appearance depending on what settlement we come from. My place and my appearance are the least like my mother's and most like the people here. As such, it made the most sense for me to come to this world. On the rare occasion that one of my brothers or sisters is killed or perishes, my parents choose another to replace them.

'It is incredibly beautiful there. Yet the dangers are far more numerous. We live for longer but give birth to few. Many of my people are killed by the wars and the other dangers.'

She fell into silence.

Eoghan backed away, mouth agape, trying to process what he had heard. 'Oh,' he half whispered. He found his head was shaking slowly.

'I suspect you are beginning to understand why I didn't want to tell you too much. I think I have done so already,' she said with an apologetic smile.

'I think... I wish I hadn't asked,' he said. He looked at her confused; his face and neck felt warm. He felt his shoulders slump. She was an enigma. Her speaking to him about this alien place just showed how mundane his existence must be to her. ‘I shouldn’t have asked.’

CAILLEACH

***

The group splits. Donnacha goes South. Éine and Caoilte go East. The others head North to visit a witch. They discover that she does not live alone and they face an unexpected danger.

Briseann an dúchas trí shúile an chait

True nature breaks out of the cat's eyes.

***

The wind was biting and cut through Eoghan as they trudged. The house on the side of the mountain had seemed closer from the bottom and they were becoming despondent at the slow passage and failing conditions.

'Four of us approaching might be a cause of alarm. Perhaps two of us should stay here and watch proceedings from a distance,' said Eoghan.

'Perhaps Laoise and I can wait here, and you two can go ahead.' Rúadhan proposed, his voice high-pitched.

There was a moment of silence. Rúadhan looked at Rhíona, eyebrows raised.

'You and Eoghan can approach in the open, in plain sight.'

Eoghan noticed him shooting a sidelong glance at Laoise.

'Or I could go with you and Eoghan can stay with Laoise. I don't know. What say you all?' asked Rúadhan, grimacing slightly.

Eoghan thought that something unspoken passed between the two girls.

'That sounds like a fair plan,' said Rhíona.

'Some plan indeed,' said Laoise with a small smirk. Rúadhan's face changed colour.

'Come Eoghan and let's see about this *cailleach*,' nodded Rhíona. Eoghan was not about to argue, and they headed for the cottage.

The mild dread that he faced at the thought of meeting a *cailleach* was quickly forgotten, because the walk was proving difficult. Unlike Eoghan, Rhíona was nimble on her feet, and made light work of navigating the path. Eoghan was wet to his knees, and his shoes were covered in muck. He lumbered forward grumbling to himself.

At one point, Rhíona skidded on a slick mound of sodden turf, and her feet seemed to go from under her. Resigned to a most unpleasant landing, she did not try to stop herself from falling backwards. She gasped when his hands caught under her arms, halting her descent. It took them a moment to re-establish their footing. Eoghan helped her to stand, and they looked into each other's eyes.

'This whole thing that I brought upon Rúadhan and you,' said Rhíona, eyes wide. 'I can never apologise enough for it. You have been at my side since we met, and I am not sure I deserve it.'

Her hands were open at her side.

Eoghan spoke softly over the scything breeze. 'I... we are here because we could not have turned away. I want you to know that...' He smiled. 'Though I may not look it, or act it a lot, or feel it in this bog... I am happy, Rhíona. Happy with you.'

Rhíona's sudden concern was apparent. 'Eoghan, I...'

'I know. I know. You are Fae and a princess and are being hunted by the worst folk to walk anywhere and would have no interest in a nobody like me, only that we climbed the same tree. I know all that. And I know we seem to be collecting a group of extremely unhappy people to bring them on our difficult road to make it more difficult. And as we meet more of these people, I will become more and more a nobody without a use or a reason for being amongst the group. I don't care. You are a girl, whatever age you might be in your world. When I am with you, I am happy. That is that. Why do you think I am here?' He searched her eyes, looking for something. Rhíona's face was unreadable when she spoke.

'I was not going to say what you think. I am not who you think I am, however. I am not like you. I come from a place where the rules are so different, and I am here in accordance with those rules. In truth, I have precious few choices of my own to make in this place, Eoghan. Being with you... being with you is something I would choose. Even if you are a nobody.' They smiled at each other. 'And you caught me before I fell into a bog, which means you are very useful entirely.'

She stopped, face serious again. The wind rose. 'I am happy too,' she said, just audible over the breeze. She turned and started walking, shaking her head slightly. Eoghan spoke and found that his voice had changed in tone.

'Princess,' he called, removing his cloak, and throwing it to her. 'A lady such as yourself should not be subjected to such red-raw, pig-filth travelling. I will not stand for it any longer.' In one sudden movement, he took her hand and drew her towards him, picking her up and swinging her atop his back, where he grabbed her legs. She put her arms around his neck. 'My lady, if you would be so kind as to drape my kingly gown over us so that we can travel in style and comfort.'

She giggled as she unbundled his cloak and attempted the near impossible task of covering them both from the increasingly resistant wind.

'On we go,' roared Eoghan before they took off at a steady squelching march. As her arms drew tight around his neck and her head came to rest on his shoulder underneath the cloak, he decided there was nowhere else in the world he would rather be. He also regretted lifting her onto his back. His knees started to wobble, and within three or four steps, he struggled to walk in the boggy mud. Rhíona snorted back a laugh and slid down to stand beside him.

'I was wondering how long it would take you to realise that that was a really terrible idea.'

Eoghan wanted to feel indignant, but a laugh burst out of him before he got the chance.

'I am quite talented at having terrible ideas, I think.'

He broke into laughter again.

His laugh choked to a stop and his heart missed a beat when he saw a pair of gleaming yellow eyes regarding him. Across the mire, a large wolf sat studying them. No, there were two, the second lying a short distance from the first. Both staring at them in a very sobering manner.

'Do you want to try and talk to them or whatever it is you do?' whispered Eoghan.

'There is something about them,' she said. 'I do not get a sense of them. They are under a *geis* and will not listen to me. There is a *draíocht* around them that is not so strong, I think, but strong enough to keep them under control.'

She looked at the tiny house.

'We are expected in that place. We are being watched as they watch us. There is nothing to do but keep going. This *cailleach* is not without teeth, it seems.' Even whispering, there was admiration in her voice.

'And they look worryingly well fed,' she added.

Eoghan looked straight ahead and started to walk as fast as he could, barriers to expedience notwithstanding. It wasn't long before some of his body parts were burning from the exertion. His realisation that there were far more than two wolves motivated him to keep going through the increasing pain until they arrived at the witch's house.

The dull, dreary day made the featureless square cabin seem more eerie and mysterious than it probably was. The foreboding, however, was further supported by a large she-wolf standing outside the front door.

The wolves, who had been following, surrounded them. They stood at a respectable distance. Some wolf cubs played in a marshy field nearby.

Eoghan waited for Rhíona to call out or make their presence known in some way. He looked at her and noticed she was standing upright with her chin out, beautiful and defiant. He realised someone had watched their arrival, and now it seemed their mettle was being tested. He turned to face the she-wolf.

There the wolf sat, huge yellow eyes watching and there they stood, tense and fearful. A voice from behind them caused Eoghan to leap clear off the ground from the fright.

'You are interesting, you two.'

They whirled around to see a woman with a young wolf cub in her arms. She was hefty with a shock of red curls. A covering of freckles framed her bright grey eyes. Her face lit up with a pretty smile. 'But you would have a beautiful litter the very same two of you.'

Moving between the two visitors, she went to the she-wolf, who greeted her with a nudge. The woman put the cub beside its mother, gave them both a loving caress and walked to the cottage. The wolves walked away.

The woman turned to them as she opened the door.

'I am Únagh. You may enter, but I must extend a warning. This place is neither an inn nor a haven from the cold. You have questions as do I, so we will exchange information and then you will go. We will not delay, for if you remain too long then you will become a part of the night. The protection I have extended to you will be no more. My babies are always hungry.'

Her smile was kindly. 'Come in but ask for no hospitality. We will talk and you will leave.'

She disappeared inside.

Eoghan looked at Rhíona. She was still looking at the door, clearly anxious. 'Are we really going in there?' he asked.

Rhíona pursed her lips. 'Nothing about this is right, but we have to see if she can help us. Be wary, Eoghan.'

He looked again at the door. 'I'll go first so,' he said.

'Eoghan,' Rhíona whispered. 'Go inside.'

'Just doing that now,' he whispered back.

He straightened and opened the door.

The inside of the house was unexpectedly pleasant. It was homely, well-lit, and the earthy smell of a root vegetable soup filled the place. There was cloth lining on the inside of the walls, with each panel dyed a different colour. Except for a low table and a rush-covered cot in the corner, the only other piece of furniture was a loom in the centre of the room.

Únagh was tidying up dyed clothing and wool spindles from the table. She looked up apologetically. 'My home is in no fit state for visitors. It is not often people will brave the sight of my babies and progress forward. Your need must be keen.'

After arranging the various items into smaller, neater bundles on the floor of the house, she moved to the head of the table. Rhíona and Eoghan sat on either side.

'So, I suspect you are not here to trade for clothing so urgently that you could not have waited until I visited the market next month.' She turned towards Rhíona. 'That said, I am sure you of the Fae have far finer pieces of clothing to dress in.'

The two youngsters exchanged a dismayed glance.

'How did I know, you ask? Well, I don't think you would have been told to come and visit me if I could not spot something so plain. Speaking of plain,' she turned to Eoghan, her grey eyes piercing. 'What in the world is she doing with you, my young friend?'

Eoghan looked at Rhíona. 'We were in the same tree,' he said.

Únagh smiled, though clearly confused. 'That sounds like an interesting story to be sure. I would very much like to hear it, except your time here is running out if you plan to be out of the valley before my hungry babies eat you.

'So, perhaps it might be wise to press forward to two things that I need to know. Who sent you and what do you want of me?'

Rhíona straightened her back and cleared her throat.

'We were sent here by Éine Mac Éine and Caoilte Mac Rónán. We are looking for Fionn Mac Cumhal and need your help in finding him.'

Únagh's eye fluttered downwards towards the table.

'I thought this day was turning out a bit strange. Just had a bit of a feeling. That was before the Fae, and her simple friend arrived to tell me two deceased legends told her to come for help in locating the greatest legend of them all, who is also dead and dust. A bit strange indeed.'

She looked at Rhíona. 'The trade will be this. In exchange for my assistance, I wish to know a piece of information and you will tell me. He can wait outside. That is my offer.'

Rhíona nodded. 'The offer is accepted, though I think perhaps Eoghan should stay to hear whatever it is you wish to ask me and the answer I provide. I would worry about his safety were he to venture outside the front door.'

'Thoughtful indeed, Fae girl. I promise you he will be safe. Though I cannot promise my babies won't admire him and consider which part of his lovely body they might eat first.'

'I would like to make a suggestion on that matter,' said Eoghan, feeling decidedly irked. 'I have always thought my buttocks would be remarkably tasty.'

'Be quiet, good lad,' said Únagh patting his hand in a motherly way. 'So be it. I will assist ye. Take his hand if he is going to stay,' she said to Rhíona. The two blushed as their fingers met and danced a little to find a good hold.

'And mine,' said the witch, extending her hands. 'Think of your need and your need alone,' she said, and then looking over at Eoghan, she added, 'that does not include your need to be around the Fae girl or any such romantic notions. Concentrate as best a boy of your years can manage.'

Eoghan's blushing made his entire head warm.

'Attend,' she said and closed her eyes.

Eoghan waited for something to happen; some kind of *draíocht* or what-have-you. Except for the other two having their eyes closed and looks of complete concentration etched on their faces, everything else was as it had been. Closing his eyes, he thought about what they were looking for. A man born of legend whose name was known to every man, woman, and child on the island. *And further again*, he surmised. Every one of them thinking Fionn dead made trying to think about him difficult. *Where could he be? Lying in wait for a horn to sound?* It would have sounded farfetched only a few days ago. Now? His shoulders shrugged and he set his mind on the need to find Mac Cumhal.

Just as he did so, Únagh released his hand. He opened his eyes to find the two staring at each other. The look of concentration was still etched into their faces.

'How did that go?' he asked.

Neither spoke. There was a sheen of perspiration on Rhíona's brow and Eoghan felt a sense of unease.

'Is everything—'

'You need to find the last two who might act as your guides, one of whom will know the way,' said the witch through gritted teeth. 'Look for one at the waterfall at *Droma Cliab* to the north and west. It is beautiful beyond words, and holds a great secret wrapped in a chest. It remains to be seen if the secret will be revealed to you. The chest will not open for just anyone. Once it opens, the guide will come to you.' Her eyes were not moving from Rhíona's. Rhíona's teeth were also gritted.

Eoghan's unease grew as Únagh continued to speak. 'The other can be found in the broad valley at *Uí Garrchon* to the south and west. This one may prove uninterested in worldly affairs and will require a subtle approach.'

Eoghan listened intently but watched Rhíona as his heart thumped louder in his chest. 'Well, there is no point leaving things longer than need leaving, so Rhíona, should we head off?'

A twitch in the corner of her was eye her only response.

‘Boy, she is still helping me search for my answers. You would not understand, but my question is not one that can be answered by words. Perhaps you should wait outside the front door. We will be...’ she grimaced slightly, all the time staring into Rhíona’s eyes. ‘... finished here in just a few moments.’

‘I am sorry,’ said Eoghan.

‘There is... no need to be sorry. Just wait out...’

His fist lashed across Únagh’s face, and she crumpled into a heap. Rhíona’s eyes rolled into her head, and she proceeded to do the same.

Outside the house several wolves started to howl.

IN NEED OF ASSISTANCE

***

Things spiral out of control for the two at the witch's house.
Rúadhan and Laoise decide to try and save them.

Is fada an bóthar nach bhfuil casadh ann.

It's a long road that has no turning.

***

Rúadhan and Laoise had been sitting in silence for what seemed like a month. This was not at all as he had planned their first time alone to be. He had practised conversations and imagined himself being charming, humorous, and all-around good company. Now he sat on a very wet and uncomfortable rock, and worried that he was the cause of the rock's sodden discomfort. She was surely aware of the awkward silence between them. It practically pulled at her skirts. The longer that silence roared, the more difficult it would be for him to do his charming best. Or perhaps he hadn't woken up yet, and this was a nightmare. He looked at her as the silence jeered at him and decided that it could not be going worse.

And then the howling began.

The two sat up in alarm as the eerie chorus of a dozen wolves echoed through the hills and mountains. The source of the noise seemed to come from the same direction in which Eoghan and Rhíona had gone. Rúadhan leapt to his feet.

'They need our help,' he cried.

Laoise stood ready with her dart bandolier around her waist. There were only three darts in it. Rúadhan's thoughts darkened. He looked at her.

'You don't need to come with me. This is not your fight, Laoise. Wait here.'

Despite Rúadhan having no way to be anything other than an irritation to wolves, he could not let his friends face them alone. He started running as fast as he could. As he passed a stone the size of a child's head, he stopped to pick it up. It was heavy and would slow him but would cause damage were he to lash out with it. As he lifted it, and started off again, he felt something brush past him.

Looking on, he could see Laoise running in front of him. He felt a huge relief, tinged with exuberance. The two of them might be able to create more sport, especially with her darts as a limited resource.

'I mean it, Laoise,' he said to her back. 'There is no need for you to come. Go and find your grandfather.'

'Now? Now you decide to talk to me?' she called to him.

He smiled and upped his pace to run alongside her. 'What exactly are we going to do about the wolves?' he asked.

'We will just make them very fat, I think,' she answered as she leapt over a large rock.

'We will, won't we? At least we'll have had a conversation'

'Well, be quiet now and start watching out for the...' She stopped speaking suddenly. The howling had stopped and, in the distance, Laoise and Rúadhan could make out a fire. A house was burning.

Eoghan knelt beside Rhíona and pushed her damp hair back from her face. 'Rhíona? Can you talk to me?' he asked.

'Eoghan?' she responded, eyes still closed. 'Eoghan, she was trying to control my mind like she does the wolves.'

She took a long breath trying to regain control of herself. 'She is not what she seems. She is from the old world and has a powerful *draíocht* on her.' Her eyes shot open, and she looked directly at him. 'She means for us to die here at the hands of the wolves. She wants to take what information she can from me about *draíocht* to make herself even more powerful. We are in danger, Eoghan.' She sat up and looked around, still somewhat dazed.

'Where... where is she?'

'Over there, in a heap. I was unkind to her face.'

'The wolves are outside. They will attack us the second we leave,' said Rhíona.

'I have an idea. But I need to know she will not hurt you or do... whatever *draíocht* thing she was going to do to you again.'

'No, she took me by surprise. I was a fool to be so open with her, but my thoughts were...' She looked into his eyes and blushed. 'I was not concentrating on what I was doing. She will not be able to reach into my mind so easily again. She would not dare to try now that I am guarded.'

'Fine. Then we bind her a bit, push her out in front of us, and use her as a shield. We will set this place on fire and bring torches for ourselves to scare the animals outside.'

'Confuse them? I think they will probably want to eat us regardless of what we carry,' said Rhíona.

'Can you think of any other way of going back the way we came?'

'We could wait and hope they leave,' she suggested.

'The others will come looking for us and inherit our danger. You know they will. And even if they didn't, waiting anywhere for any length of time generally attracts other animals who want to kill us.'

Rhíona looked around. 'It seems a shame to burn down such a lovely little place.'

Eoghan levelled a gaze at her to suggest he would not consider that a viable argument. He made sure the witch woman was tied and gagged before he threw some water over her face. She woke up with a muffled shriek, focusing a baleful glare at him.

'We are in a bit of a difficult situation, as I'm sure you can understand. I have a knife here and if you become too difficult to manage, I will stick it in you and leave you for the wolves. Regardless of their loyalty to you, I cannot imagine they will resist you tied and bloody for too long. Nod if you understand.' She did.

He started to pull her up and stopped. 'No *draíocht* either. I might not know but Rhíona is ready for your tricks now and if she tells me you're at something, then it's this for you.' Eoghan brandished the knife and presented his most threatening face. He pulled her up and he walked to the table. He lifted his foot and brought it crashing down several times until the wooden legs started to loosen and come away. He and Rhíona prepared makeshift torches wrapping the wall covering materials tightly around the wood. Before he went to the door, he lit the witch's bedding. She moaned loudly at the sight, her shoulders slumping.

'Well,' said Eoghan. 'We only have one option.'

Rhíona looked back at the fire spreading quickly. 'It might have been nice to have somewhere safe to come back to if your plan doesn't work,' she said.

Eoghan looked at her, suddenly full of doubt. 'I thought you agreed with the plan.'

'I do, so far, but I haven't been outside among the wolves yet.'

'Well, I hope their teeth don't cut as deep as you doubting my perfectly reasonable plan does.' It was not the time for humour. Yet again, and much to his delight, their eyes fixed on each other.

The way was difficult underfoot and hampered Rúadhan and Laoise's progress. While the howls had gone silent, the fire had grown large in the distance. On occasion, Rúadhan could make out movement somewhere in front and then it would be gone.

Straining his eyes, he peered into the gloom, searching for any sign of their friends, until Laoise pointed at two torches moving in their direction. The torches were swinging in wide arcs.

'Lots of wolves,' said Rúadhan. With his arm burning from carrying the stone, he changed hands.

Laoise nearly tripped but did not stop. 'What are we going to do when we get there?' she gasped.

'Make noise and lash out and keep moving,' he answered between breaths. 'They might run away. Wolves are afraid of fire. Maybe noise too.'

The sudden sound of snarls and screams pierced the evening, echoing through the hills. The torches were waving frantically as if beckoning for help to come quicker. Rúadhan was filled with dread and the instinct to turn and flee. Laoise must have felt it too. Neither did.

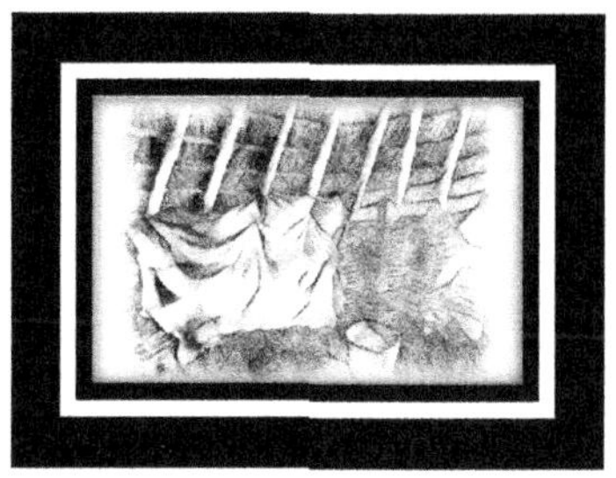

EIMEAR

***

Donnacha finds who he is looking for.

Trí ní is deacair a thuiscint: intleacht na mban, obair na mbeach, teach agus imeacht na taoide.

Three things hardest to understand: the intellect of women, the work of the bees, the coming and going of the tide.

***

Donnacha could no longer be said to be walking. It was more like a confused ambling. He had been on a trail since the forest ended, but his progress had recently taken a curious turn. Or, more accurately, dozens of curious turns. Donnacha found himself perplexed by the haphazard way the trail proceeded. It was almost directionless, seeming at times to turn back on itself. Though it would have been nearly impossible for most to recognise a path existed, Donnacha could see that it was used regularly by someone. It was causing several exasperated sighs, head shakes and scene surveys.

It was when he allowed himself to mark the terrain through which he was travelling, combined with his pauses for head shaking and scene surveying, that a possible reason for these strange movements started to emerge.

This is not a trail. This is a tour.

Noting the sights the path's course brought him to, he smiled. An ageing cherry blossom with all its branches reaching out in the same direction, as if trying to grow away from the wind. Without its swaying pink jewellery, the tree was elegant, if somewhat bothered looking. Donnacha could imagine the beautiful sight it would be when the flowers bloomed.

A lazy curve in the trail brought him to where the long grasses parted, revealing a slow-running stream brimming with small perch. The pebbled bottom marked the water's clarity. Donnacha could not resist kneeling on the bank and plunging his head in for a spluttering, gasping drink.

He could not make sense of the next diversion until he noted smudged tracks around an earthen rise thirty paces off. Another smile; badger watching at night.

Rare flowers, common herbs, wild mushrooms, berry, and honey gathering, cultivated fruit bushes, an enormous web with an average sized, yet wonderfully optimistic spider and more. The path even passed an area that seemed to be used for exercising. Flattened muddy grass told of the toil. The tracks around that area were even more captivating. The exercise was not always alone. There were deer and fawn tracks, a large wildcat and several different birds had all come to spectate or participate.

As he walked, he found himself… no, not jealous, as such; more filled with admiration; growing respect.

He took off his bow and quiver, removed his knife belt and cast them aside on the long grass. They were impeding his enjoyment and he would recover them later.

Donnacha hoped it would be a while before he would have to meet the person who visited these little islands of Nature. He was so full of respect and admiration, that they would surely only spoil it by being themselves. He found it hard to imagine that the Fianna woman had wandered this trail. It was a routine exuding energy and youthful curiosity; not one of an old female recluse.

A child or a grandchild perhaps?

Hearing the sound of his knife sliding out of its sheath, Donnacha froze; surprised, and more than a little frustrated that someone dared ruin this experience for him.

Turning slowly, he saw a woman discard the knife and belt and pick up the unstringed bow. She examined them offhandedly, then cast them aside too.

She looked up at him. She was a woman of around two score summers who was brown in appearance. She wore a tanned blouse tucked into torn brown skirts. Her brown sandaled feet were caked in mud and dirt as if she had been trudging through bogland. Blouse sleeves were turned up to reveal brown freckled arms.

Her face, while not as caked as her feet, had still been visited by muddy fingers several times today. Her freckles seemed to bunch together under her brown eyes, which were almost being covered by her long brown hair. Donnacha was delighted that when she suddenly smiled at him, her teeth were a beautiful white.

'I really enjoyed looking at your arse when you took a drink,' she said.

'Well by dad, and my granduncle Tavish from across the Leaking Sea, I think I'm in love, to be honest about things, in all fairness.' He bowed with a flourish.

The brown lady threw her head back and laughed a musical laugh. She held up a bushel of carefully wrapped stinging nettles.

'I think we need to make hot steamy... nettle soup and have a delightful chat as to why you might have come to visit me.'

'How long, might I ask, if I'm not being too ignorant in doing so, have you been following me?'

'Since before you entered the forest at the valley-mouth.'

'By the stout trees of *Kinbeg*, you are some woman. I am yours to do with as you please, but just remember, I've been hurt before... by nettles... and ask you to be gentle with me.'

'You'll have to leave the weapons.'

'Well, indeed, any of them that can become detached are at your feet, if ya get me.' He threw in a wink.

Her eyebrows raised and she put a hand to her mouth in mock surprise. 'And I thought I was the dirty one of the two of us.'

'Ah, sure, you are right, and I was trying to be the wit and ended being the aberrant lout altogether. May a pox land upon me so I might curl up in a ball, in a hole in the ground somewhere cold and distant, and die.'

'What is your name, vile debaser?'

‘I am Donnacha, and though I don’t understand how, I think that it is you I have been looking for, lovely woman.’

‘I am Eimear, and I feel like making soup.’

Donnacha looked out the window of the modest hut. Eimear was still bathing in the stream. He dressed and stirred the nettles at the same time. The warm metallic smell reminded him of his hunger. They had spoken very little since his arrival some time ago. He could not shake the utter contentment that being in this place made him feel. It wrapped around him like a blanket. The place existed entirely a part of the lands and could have been visited by any manner of God, and Donnacha was sure they would feel the same warm blanket. He stirred.

‘You seem to be enjoying your custodial role as chieftain soup stirrer.’

He did not look up. His head did not fill with the noise that was always present when he had to talk to other people. It was quiet and calm.

‘I am indeed.’ Stir. Stir.

‘I don’t know why you’re here. I don’t know who sent you. I’m not going to go with you no matter who you think I am, or how you think I can be of service or what revenge people seek upon me. If you were to point two bows at me, I would still not go with you. You are welcome to stay with us here, though. For as long as you want. It calms your spirit here, and your presence adds more than you can know.’ Stir. Stir.

He smiled again. Calm and warm, stirring slowly. ‘I doubt I would leave either, were I you. And you saying that, to be sure and true, makes me feel a great honour and longing. That said, Eimear, I will have to go back along your path and back through the forest and back to... my adopted quest, if that's what you might call it, I suppose.' Stir. Stir.

'A quest? Oh my, that does sound very exciting. Who exactly are you, Donnacha, and why might I have an interest in a quest?'

'Any of the Fianna would.' Stir. Stir.

For the first time since the valley-mouth, he felt a tinge of something other than peace. Stir. Tap.

He dropped the wooden spoon against the side of the pot and turned. Her face had become wary with a look of growing concern. 'Fianna? Who? Me?'

Raising his open hands, he moved towards her. 'You will never need fear me or my hand or my action and that's as true as your smile is beautiful. I will never tell another person in all the land, or even at sea for that matter. We are to gather the remaining Fianna who still survive, even though they are few in number. Most were at the battle at *Gamhra.*'

'I was not,' said Eimear, suddenly cold.

'I was told you would not come with me at first but that if I told you my part in recent goings-on, you would come. Well. More so that you might come.'

His gaze dropped to the floor. It was hard to look at her discomfort.

'In fairness, really, I feel bad that I might end up bringing you away from here. I would promise to protect you but reckon you are well able for the world and all its challenges. Eimear, I think you should sit down and listen to me.'

'Who have you been talking to about me, Donnacha?'

‘Éine File Cú Mac Éine.’

Her eyes glazed over somewhat. ‘It pleases me to hear he lives. A great poet from another age.’ Her pleasure was not apparent.

Moving to the pot, she said, ‘Well, if we’re going to hear this story then let’s do so with a full belly. You sit down and I’ll bring you something to eat as you talk.’

Donnacha absently picked at his fingernails. ‘He told me to tell you something before we start because you might be upset if I leave it for a length, and it’s safe to say, really, that I intend nothing...’ The bowl and its bubbling contents landed roughly in front of him, soup spilling over the side onto the table.

‘Tell me what, Donnacha?’

‘Fionn Mac Cumhal, Eimear. He lives and we must find him.’

There was a long pause, before Eimear buried her face in her hands and started weeping silently. Donnacha’s carefree blanket slipped from his shoulders. He sat, red-faced, looking around him and continued to not know exactly what he should do, until long after the soup had gone cold.

THE ELDEST OF FRIENDS

***

Caoilte and Éine travel to meet an old friend, who they think might have knowledge that could help them.

An té a bhíonn thuas, óltar deoch air. An té a bhíonn thíos, buailtear cos air

When you're up, they drink to you. When you're down, they kick you.

***

As their journey approached more populated localities, it wasn't long before a passing slave trader's cart stopped. Two old men walking was not something the self-proclaimed honourable driver could pass. Éine had anticipated and hoped for as much. They knew that after reaching a main thoroughfare, the chances were, they would find passage to the town at *Átha Cliath*.

The settlement had grown around a great ring fort. The agricultural demands of such a place were evident for many miles before the town began. It had become a centre for slave trading, from raids into Wales and up and down their coastline. It was aptly named The Slave Fort by many. It sat on the land like many broken pieces of pottery placed in a circle around a large black fort. As a blooming port of commerce and trading, it represented the opposite mindset of the small settlements scattered across the island, which were almost entirely agricultural and self-sufficient. Most never used metal rings. Nor did they trade other than to share and exist as part of the local community. Éine smiled. The world, it seemed, had other plans for this sleepy island.

As they rode, the slave trader, Gos, prattled. He seemed to be a wise man in his own mind, speaking of goings-on, troubles and threats; of the mercenary army being gathered, and about himself. Mostly about himself. His plans for his own gain were significant, even though he had come from a sleepy hamlet and was relatively new in the slave market. Self-affirming nods as he spoke suggested he was impressed by his own progress in life, even if others were not.

The notion of slaves was not new to Éine. Indeed, it was part of how the highborn and noble world worked across Europe. Still. Éine never enjoyed his time in *Átha Cliath*. The settlement was grey and tainted, a grim place.

Fortunately, their destination lay on the outskirts of the settlement, well away from the ringfort and the cunning queen Líadain. As one of the wealthiest people on the Island, it was widely said that there was no corner of it where her influence wasn't felt, directly or indirectly. Éine was aware that this was not even slightly true. These rumours were the work of the queen's *scealaí*, Cassius. A testament to his notorious skills of story weaving.

Cassius the Roman had wandered far before he found his voice. Éine had heard him ply his trade several times, and his skill could not be doubted. His motives, Éine had discovered, were not so pure. He was even more interested in wealth and stature than the queen he served. A man of questionable integrity was a moderately kind view of Cassius.

Though a more beautiful man has never walked the world, Éine thought glumly.

'Here,' said Caoilte. Indeed, he was correct. Éine's daydreaming had distracted him from proceedings. Naturally, Gos had not heard Caoilte's near whisper so Éine passed on the message.

'My fine man, you have done a grand thing today in helping two old donkeys arrive safely at our chosen destination. I can only hope your action has been noted by gods who will ensure you are repaid by fortune.'

He made ready to descend from the cart when a hiss from Caoilte made him pause. He looked back at his friend, who was staring past him at the dilapidated hut towards which they were bound. When he saw what had given Caoilte cause for concern, he was immediately filled with alarm and froze.

There was a kindly looking old lady standing at the doorway, waving at them both with a welcoming smile.

Éine's heart filled with dread. He made a show of slowly getting off the cart and while he did, he spoke quickly and quietly. 'Gos, I have two gold rings in my purse that I will give you. One now and one at this place in two days but you need to do two things for me in return.'

Gos sensed the change in mood and tone and looked up at the smiling woman curiously. Two gold rings made him very obliging, all the same, and he spoke in hushed tones from the side of his mouth. 'What?'

'Get off the cart and help my friend down. My friend is going to put on a show of being utterly decrepit; not in control of his own body. Once he is down, I want you to take the cart back down the track from where we just came. There was an old hay shed not too far back. It was in worse condition than the hut we now sit in front of.'

'I know it. It was old Hernon's, but he died three seasons back.' Gos climbed down from the cart and went to where Caoilte was sitting.

'Put our baggage there, and mark it discreetly with my purse. We will be back to collect it later, but we may not be staying here for too long. Let no one know what you have done or see you do it, and the second ring is yours. The ring will be in the purse where our baggage was left when we collect it. Come back in two days to claim the ring. I give you my word that there is no deception here. Are we happy enough with that?'

Gos started to lift Caoilte down. 'Very happy indeed.'

'Good man. Good man.'

By now Éine was around to Caoilte and took him under the arm steering him away from the cart towards the kindly old lady. He left a gold ring where he had been sitting.

Her name was Neala Uí Cárthaigh, and Éine and Caoilte knew her as they had known her mother.

Neither woman was kindly or smiling, and neither would have bothered their arse to get up and wave at unexpected guests. It was far more likely they would have roared at them to begone with the door firmly shut. There were others in the cottage. Her acting in this way was as clear as if she were to cup her hands around her mouth and roar it at them.

A swift extrication from such a situation was unlikely for now, but at least they had a warning and could downplay their own value. It had also ensured that Caoilte's sword remain uncaptured. For such a sword to fall into the wrong hands would be a travesty. Éine had taken a risk leaving the sword with Gos. Should Gos decide to take the sword instead of the ring, it would mean Caoilte would have to go and find it and likely kill people. Yet for Caoilte to use it blindly would put Neala's life in danger, which was not an option for either of the two men. The draw of the second gold ring would surely keep Gos straight.

They walked slowly towards the woman. Éine's mind raced. Who was inside and how had they foreseen their arrival? Neala's face was fixed in a grin, but she looked worn and gaunt. It was possible that whoever was inside had been there for quite some time. Éine decided to put it out of his head for now. He was tired.

'Welcome, my two old friends,' said Neala.

At another time it would have been comical to see her act this way. She was delightfully happy looking. Éine had never seen her even break a smile.

'By the gods, Neala, I've missed that infectious grin of yours,' he said heartily. 'Indeed, were old Deaglán here able to speak, I am quite positive he would echo the same sentiment.'

‘I only wish that my home was more of a welcoming sight. It is not the house it was once. At the current rate of decay, it will soon need to be knocked down and rebuilt.’

‘I am sad to hear it. Has it been this way long?’ Éine asked as they neared the doorway.

‘Longer than you would think,’ Neala said, as she went to embrace him. With arms around him, she whispered, ‘Eight of them. Well-armed and talk of business. As I put out the fire inside, we make our move.’

She turned and pushed the door open, speaking loudly. ‘I think you should find the old place comfortable enough. I have some mutton stew, only three days in the pot. I’m sure you two are hungry.’

As the two guests moved inside the trap was sprung. The eight warriors emerged from the darkness as Éine and Caoilte’s eyes adjusted. Someone closed the door behind them.

‘Remember our agreement,’ Neala snapped. Her smile was gone, replaced with the comfortable frown with which she was most associated.

‘I seem to have forgotten what the old lady is talking about,’ jeered one of the warriors as he slid a sword into her side.

Her face came alive with dismay. The warrior took out the sword and pushed it through her again, this time his face mimicking hers in a contorted mask of pain and surprise. He pulled out the sword, and with the third thrust he killed her.

Éine could feel Caoilte’s arm tense. He felt like screaming in anguish at the death of his friend; he felt like screaming even louder at the thought of the same end befalling him but tried to hide his rage and fear as he asked, 'What is happening here? Who are you and how can you have done such a thing?'

The warrior fixed Éine with a wild-eyed stare. Éine was filled with the urge to throw Caoilte at him and run. Hands grabbed him from behind and the opportunity was lost.

'Check them for weapons,' said the leader.

'Weapons? Exactly who or what do you take us for?'

'No weapons chief,' stated one of the warriors.

'Bind them and let's go.'

'Bind us? What manner of men are you? My friend Deaglán can barely stand, not to mention being trussed like a hog. If you plan to bind him, then I would suggest that you kill him first. He will not survive being tied up and dragged.'

There was a moment's indecision as the men looked at each other.

'So be it,' said the leader. 'Bind the mouthy one and take hold of the dotty one.'

Éine nodded to himself. 'You are considerate after all, sir. We will co-operate and cause no bother, until whatever misunderstanding we face is behind us.'

The one who had murdered Neala, was already at the doorway.

'Let's go. The smell of the old woman in this little rathole has made me sick for long enough. Having two more of them around will drive me to drink.' He stalked away with a bark. 'Move. Fast.'

Éine and Caoilte were unceremoniously dragged out of the cottage. Éine had been correct in two assumptions. They were likely being brought to the ring fort, and the way there had not changed. They turned back up the track that would pass the tumbledown hayshed.

Éine would have been pleased but kept picturing the death of his old friend at the hands of a dog. He would be pleased soon enough. If Caoilte could do what was required.

Caoilte did not disappoint. As they drew level with the old hay shed a loud and lengthy fart ripped from him. One of the guards let go of the old man in disgust.

'Take hold of him,' said Neala's murderer.

'We've been on the road since after noon. He will likely wet and soil himself if he does not go soon, and then you will know about smells,' Éine said in foreboding tones.

The warriors exchanged looks. It was apparent that none of the eight were pleased at the prospect. Éine surveyed the setting around them.

'There,' he pointed at the haybarn. 'Bring him in there and let him do what he needs to.'

Neala's murderer was unimpressed. 'Make it fast or I will stomp his face open with my boot.'

The two holding him, led Caoilte towards the shed. Two more followed behind, clearly disinterested by the events of the afternoon. As they disappeared into the hayshed, Éine turned to the murderer.

'She was an incredible person, you know. She was both a midwife and a *seanchaí* for twice the length you have lived. She knew everyone and their mothers, and all they were up to. She was wise and brave and brought countless lives into the light of this world.'

The murderer was about to speak when *Lus an Chrom Cinn* passed through his chest from behind, Caoilte's hand upon his shoulder.

'Look in my eyes as you feel what she felt,' said Éine. Again, the sword passed through the wretch, this time lower. The murderer's eyes were wild no longer. Only afraid now.

Éine's other three guards stared in disbelief as Caoilte's sword went through the murderer a third time, who stood looking into Éine's eyes, until his head was chopped. The guards reached for their swords, but it was too late. A blur moved among them, a yellow beam of death. They were in pieces before the swords were unsheathed. Caoilte stood and stretched his back as the last body parts fell. Though his body was old and haggard, the *draíocht* that made him great was never too far away from his sword arm.

'To the fort to see the queen?' Éine asked.

Caoilte nodded and wiped the blood from his sword. As always, when Caoilte held it, it gleamed brightly as if catching a ray of sunshine, even though the skies above were grey, clouds laden with eager rain.

Grey, it seemed, was to be the colour of the day until Caoilte Mac Rónán changed it to yellow and crimson.

A BITING EVENING

***

The wolves attack and the four youngsters come face to face with their most dangerous situation yet.

Is leor ó Mhór a dícheall

All anyone can do is their best.

***

Eoghan and Rhíona pushed the witch in front of them, making little headway. The night and the wolves were closing in around them. Eoghan was beginning to panic. He had his torch held high and had taken out his father's knife. The terrain seemed harsher than it had; the ground was less soft and more chilled. Jagged stones seemed to have appeared as if to add danger. Brambles, nettles, and thistles were eager for the attention of passers-by.

‘Stand behind me if they attack. At least I have this knife. Don’t run away. They can run faster,’ Eoghan said to Rhíona.

They were in trouble. There was no way out of this except through wolves’ innards. There was nowhere to hide and no way to move much quicker.

‘What do you plan to do with that?’ she asked.

‘I mean to try and defend us,’ Eoghan said, not credibly.

‘There is a way we could put it to better use,’ she said, strangely calm.

‘I don’t know what you mean,’ he said, panic bubbling just under the surface.

Despite the movement all around them, he couldn’t seem to see anything moving. It always took place at the edge of his vision, behind the harsh torchlight.

Without warning, Rhíona grabbed the knife and plunged it into the witch woman’s stomach, who fell on her face moaning. When Rhíona kicked her over, Eoghan found his hand come up over his mouth. He had seen it happen in front of him but couldn’t believe his eyes. The matter-of-fact way Rhíona attacked the woman jarred him to his core.

As she signalled their retreat, Rhíona said in a cool unwavering voice, ‘She will not be able to maintain her spell on the animals. And they will be unable to resist the smell of blood.’

As Rhíona and Eoghan retreated and swung their torches, the wolves seemed confused as to who they should be surrounding. Large shaggy heads swung from the two moving away to the bloody one. They knew her, but her command on them had now disappeared. Wild snarls signalled their intent. The first wolf moved to the screaming woman. A second followed, and the rest joined the lead pair. Eoghan turned away as they attacked hungrily. His eyes were wide as the screams became shrieks and then roars. More and more of them arrived to feed, and the screaming soon stopped.

Eoghan's mind reeled. There was absolutely no doubt that Rhíona had saved them from a similar fate, but he could not believe her actions. He shook his head. He had pushed Únagh in front. Had he not considered the same?

What do I know about Rhíona? Who is she?

'We need to move, Eoghan. We will not run but we will walk with haste,' Rhíona said as she handed back the knife.

Eoghan nodded, looking at the bloody blade. They backed off until reaching what they considered a safe distance, when they turned and started walking, checking every step or two for signs of lupine pursuit.

They started to move quicker and quicker as the sounds of the wolves feeding became distant. Eventually, they were moving so quickly that neither noticed a large wolf stalk past them, teeth bared. When Eoghan finally noticed it, he opened his mouth to alert Rhíona, but he was too late. The wolf had crossed the distance and leapt at him. Mid-air, it squealed in pain, and its body writhed. It landed on top of him, and even though he had the torch in one hand and the knife in the other, his arms flailed about uselessly in alarm.

The wolf continued to writhe and make a sad whining sound. Eventually, it became still. Its rasped breathing stopped and Eoghan could see a dart sticking out of its neck.

It was then that Rúadhan arrived and bashed the deceased wolf's head in with a large rock. Some of the head's contents, including brains, bone chips and blood, ended up on Eoghan's face. For a moment he couldn't breathe and started to panic when he realised he couldn't move the heavy beast. Rúadhan pushed it away, and someone he couldn't make out helped him sit up to wipe the gore from his face.

'Laoise,' he realised. 'Thank you.'

She smiled an odd smile at him and turned to take her three darts from the wolf.

Eoghan turned to Rhíona. 'And you,' he said. 'You saved us both with quick thinking. I thank you too Rhíona.' Then he turned to Rúadhan who wore an altogether smug grin.

'You. The wolf was dead when you almost drowned me in horribleness, you absolute plant,' he growled and did his best to remove more of the horror from his clothing and neck.

'How do you know it was dead? More importantly, how could I know it was dead?' Rúadhan growled. 'I was trying to help you, you ungrateful ass.'

'You didn't let me finish.' Eoghan was annoyed too, but Rúadhan was right. 'I was going to say that I know you weren't actually trying to half drown me, or even bathe me in brains. Thank you for coming to help me. All of you. And I'm sorry, Rúadhan. I'm sorry that I haven't been the friend you have been to me. I have wandered off around the country and you have been there to keep an eye on me.'

Rúadhan seemed content enough that the smug smile made a reappearance. 'Red hair suits the two of us it seems. And you look a good bit brainier than when

I saw you last.' He looked over at Rhíona. 'Love is obviously having a very positive effect on my friend.'

Rhíona's jaw dropped, shocked.

'Rúadhan,' growled Laoise, recognising his effort to land his friend in manure.

Eoghan smiled through clenched teeth. 'I will take that rock Rúadhan, and I will stick it...'

'Enough,' said Rhíona, looking back the way they came. The house was still burning brightly.

'She was large enough to keep them busy, but it's time for us to be getting away from here. Childish nonsense won't help us in that regard. Be wary.'

She stormed past the three. Laoise's eyes were hidden by the falling night, but her look to Rúadhan burned like the cottage.

Rúadhan looked at Eoghan. Eoghan gave him a similar look, and it was his turn to smile. The two chuckled in spite of the world as they followed the girls into the darkness.

Seán Seosamh, the robber, woke in the same darkness. His band had set up a tent for him in the rain, and it was extra dark inside. It was strange that he would wake during the night. He spent so long sleeping in this type of weather. He wasn't sure but he thought he had heard what sounded like a... there... he heard it again. If he could have sat up in alarm, now was the time to do so. A scream. And another. Bloodcurdling and full of despair. His men were in trouble. He rolled onto one side grimacing and grunting. His heart pumped and fear raced through his body. The sounds were horrific. Screams and cries, impacts and something else... a growling sound. Snarls unlike Seán Seosamh had ever heard before. He made it to his knees and crawled out from the tent, desperately trying to see what was happening. It took so long for him to get out, however, that most of the screaming and noise had stopped. There were still one or two crying and wailing.

He looked around and tried to make something out. Anything. The embers in the firepit were low. A heavy drizzle was falling to compound poor visibility. He heard something close beside him and turned abruptly.

When he saw the thing, he was far too frightened to scream. Piss streamed down his leg. The last sound Seán Seosamh ever made was when his ruined head landed on the ground, with a thump, some thirty paces distant.

Átha Cliath

***

Caoilte and Éine become aware of the long reach of their enemies as they are brought before queen Líadain and her storyteller, Cassius. This is when they meet the first of the three ambassadors sent by the Fae *Rí*.

Is í an chiall cheannaigh an chiall is fear

Sense that is costly is the best sense.

***

Éine was more than half tempted to let Caoilte go about his own business in the fort. It was a depressing place at the best of times. Large towers of blackened wood and sections of wooden parapets were set around a great fort. The walls were manned with armed soldiers and dotted with mighty ballistae. Huge wooden gates with a large volume of traffic in and out, were monitored by dozens of Uad's warrior folk. Many had weapons in hand, intentions clear. The fort was like something from a story of olden times in far-off lands of war and armies and great keeps, stout and intimidating, prepared for a war not seen in long years. Its very presence was a methodology to cow those who lived around it and was an instrument of control in its own right.

This place would infect the rest of the land as sure as the traders and their currency would. Éine was sure of it. Irish innocence would be lost and replaced with the wariness and weariness of the wide world from which they had been nestled away.

It was not a place to walk idly into, especially when Caoilte had sour intentions. Indeed, in days of old, it was quite probable that Éine would have let Caoilte go. He would have been better off without the hindrance, anyway. Éine was most certainly going in this time, however. *He* was inside those walls. Cassius. To look upon him once again would be enough. To be in his arms again; was too much to dare to dream. The possibility of his presence in the fort gave Éine the courage to keep in step with Caoilte. The memory of Cassius' deep brown eyes motivated him to keep his head high and his eyes clear and focused. His utter hatred for the pompous swine kept his lips hitched in a look of disdain for those around him. How could such a man be the cause of such confused feelings so many long years since?

Love. That's what it was. Love.

He looked to Caoilte. They would do what needed to be done in this place and then go and find Fionn Mac Cumhal to whatever end the gods saw fit. He hoped that the daffodil blade would bring its light into the dark halls before him. The world was going to change at their feet as it had in the old days.

A hand came out to halt their progress. 'Where might you two old goats be heading?' asked the warrior, surely younger than Laoise.

Caoilte was disinterested. Éine gazed sternly at the hand before him and spoke. 'Well now. All honour to you and power to your sword arm, strong it looks indeed. We are going to see the queen, my young wolf. Should there be a cause for question, tell her that Caoilte Mac Rónán and Éine Mac Éine of the *Féinnid* have come to speak to her. We come in with naught in our hands and peace in our hearts. We will be hereabouts anticipating your speedy return. We are not men to be kept waiting, young wolf.' As the warrior backed away to speak to his superior with a smirk, Éine shook his head. 'The youth of today, Caoilte. They lack the basic respect that was once a prerequisite. I despair.'

Caoilte stood impassively. Éine took that for complete agreement.

As runners were sent to notify the queen, Caoilte and Éine were quickly surrounded by warriors armed and on guard, as expected. There was no smirking, and it was apparent that things were becoming a modicum more respectful now.

One of the warriors, twice the first's age spoke.

'You will not set a foot inside the queen's hall wearing that sword. Even if it is a sword the queen might find fetching to look at.' His accent marked him as hailing from Gaul or further east.

A ripple of gruff laughter amongst the guards sent Éine's head shaking once again. 'Can you not see why I despair, Caoilte?'

Caoilte stood impassively. Éine took it as further resounding agreement. More guards started to appear. At least they were being taken seriously.

'I'm speaking to you, old man,' said the warrior. 'Take the sword from your belt and throw it away.'

Caoilte stood impassively. Éine took it as non-compliance.

'It seems that my friend has decided not to do as you have suggested,' said Éine.'

He spoke loudly so those passing in and out of the gate might take note. 'I suspect that should you wish to remove his sword, you will have to take it from him yourself. Or perhaps killing us both where we stand might be prudent, but one would wonder how your queen, swathed in beauty as she is, might react to the news of such.'

'Be silent, worm.' The warrior extended his own sword toward Caoilte's neck and spoke slowly. 'Take off the sword or I take off your head. Decide right now.'

Caoilte turned his gaze to look into the eyes of the warrior. The warrior's face dropped, followed quickly by his sword. One by one Caoilte looked into the eyes of the guards who had encircled them; his ice-cold stare whispering promises. One by one they followed the first, lowering their weapons and standing as if reconsidering their position.

Éine felt eyes upon him and looked up at the walls of the fort. Cassius was watching. The two saw each other. A confusing mix of love and hate rattled through Éine.

Cassius was the first to look away, but he said for all to hear, 'Adopted soldiers of this fine fort, these men are friends and should be welcomed as such. If the great son of Rónán wishes to keep his sword and says that he comes in peace, then so be it for it is true. Mark my words: there will be no barriers to their entry or exit, and they will receive our most robust hospitality. Come men, enter.' He disappeared into the parapet, and Éine breathed once again.

The queen's long-hall was a spartan place of muted colours and hushed tones, shaded and stark. Tapestries depicting slave trading and military strength were outnumbered only by the tapestries depicting the queen. She was in various dresses, sitting in similar poses, and wearing the identical frosty façade. There were no benches or pews for petitioners to rest or sit down on. No tables to leave belongings while conducting business. No glass on the windows to keep the weather outside. The very environment was a tool to keep heads bent low and voices quiet.

The queen sat on what had come to be known as the Long Chair. Her stern oaken throne was more impressive in appearance than any others in the land, including that of the High King. It was set upon a tall oaken dais, with steps at the rear so that petitioners and guests alike were assured to be looking up at her without the means to climb and stand as her equal.

Her beauty could not have been held in question. She had seen fifty winters or more, but her skin was smooth and youthful. Dark green eyes were framed by arched questioning eyebrows with purple paint on her eyelids and below her eyes. White powder had been applied to her long, elegant face. Her thick lips were also painted purple. Golden hair sat tall on her head, and braids fell like streams of a waterfall down over her shoulders. A golden crown sat atop her head, and a matching golden torc rested around her neck.

At her right hand was another lower wooden dais with a plain three-legged stool. This was the place of her *scéalaí* and advisor, Cassius, who sat, coolly observing the two men who had just entered. He only wore his roman toga. He thought it added to his reputation for being exotic. When any asked him, he just said that he never felt the cold. Éine knew well of the thick woollen undergarments and the balms that he applied to his skin over the day to keep himself warm.

Éine and Caoilte were brought before them. They were still surrounded by guards; thirty of them. All had weapons drawn and were standing on edge.

Since Éine had last been in the hall, there had been a notable addition. A third dais to the left of the queen. It had a three-legged stool, on which sat no-one. Éine had no time to consider it further. The queen spoke.

'I find it both strange and amusing that you are here. A little bird told me you two might appear and appear you have. I did not even have to send for you.' A knowing glance passed between the queen and her *scealaí*.

'So, when you sent men to capture us at the home of Neala, did you not consider that to be sending for us?' asked Éine. Despite the queen's frosty demeanour becoming even frostier, he continued, 'Indeed, it makes me wonder if there were other houses that you sent your warriors to? Casting out the net as it were? Those very same warriors are doing something similar over the length and breadth of the land, but I suspect you have very little influence over them. It begs the question...'

Cassius threw his head back and laughed.

'My apologies, my queen,' he said. 'An outburst like that is unforgivable; it seems like my erstwhile mentor has learned courage since he and I last spoke. *File Cú* some called him. The hound poet. None could match him for speed of escape. It would be far more common for him to turn and flee from confrontation and bold talk. Something must be motivating him.'

'Cassius,' said Éine. 'You show wisdom beyond your advancing years. As someone who has presented his back to many warriors over those long years, I know you have some neck and can be valiant in intimidating groups with men's spears pointing at you.'

'Enough,' roared the queen. 'I have an interest in your recent activities, old man, and you would both be best served by enlightening us about the company you have been keeping, and the nature of the relationships you have been forming.'

'He is incapable of telling the truth, my queen. He speaks only lies and half-truths. Best ask the other one,' Cassius spat.

'My dear, wishfully enigmatic, Roman, that in itself is a half-truth. I am capable of deceit, as are we all, yet my truths can be as sharp as spears when the need arises. As to our whereabouts, I'm afraid my dotage has left me quite forgetful. I remember being chased from my home by warriors like yours after they killed two of my greatest friends. After that, the memory fades.'

'You are over-evaluating your importance in these matters, I think,' said the queen. 'I am very aware of what happened at the lake. I am just curious as to what is going to happen next. Your friends being alive or dead matters to me, not a jig.'

Fishing, thought Éine.

She was trying to make him angry, so he would lose his calm and give something away. He was angry, for sure. He knew well enough that she was both over-evaluating her own position and the likelihood of her own survival if she was to make Caoilte angry.

'I wish, if I may be so bold, to know one thing before I tell you our tales,' said Éine. 'How many rings has Uad promised you that you would become his whore and let your hall be filled by his men with their weapons in their hands?'

The queen's jaw dropped. Cassius did not hesitate. 'You and your friend here are a spent force representing an era that no longer exists. We are the future and will help to make the land grow anew. None will stop us, so why not be the coward you have always been and join our cause. It will be safer for you, and we know well enough that your life is worth more to you than any cause or rings or... association.'

'None who will stop you?' smirked Éine. 'I think you will find that is also a half-truth. We and others like us will stop you and your mysterious leader. I am quite sure you don't realise who your mysterious leader actually is, and that is what is both galling and amusing.'

'A rabble of less than ten is hardly cause for our alarm,' said the queen.

'Well, then we will need to get more than ten. Far more. And I know of a way to do just that,' said Éine. 'Indeed, such realities may be closer than you know.'

When Caoilte spoke, he stood like a poised snake.

‘Did you tell them to kill her or was it by their own hand?’

Éine suddenly scanned the room for a place to hide. There was a space in between the daises that he might be able to squeeze into. He would need to be quick.

‘How dare you ask such a thing of me, regardless of who you may have been in the time of my great grandmother,’ the queen hissed, her frost melting as her temper rose.

‘Did you tell them to kill her?’

‘I grow weary of this company. Put them down,’ she said, turning her head as if eager to move onto the next business of the day.

One of the warriors raised his sword as if testing it out. With no warning, Caoilte moved. None present had ever seen anything like it except Éine. The Daffodil blade flashed and took the warrior’s hand off, caught the falling sword on its own shining blade and flicked the sword so it flew upwards towards the queen. It pinned her to the throne through her chest with a crack and a crunch. She looked down at it and died. Before any could react, Éine darted towards the gap and squeezed himself in.

His head was facing the rear, and he could not turn it to see what was happening because there wasn’t room. He closed his eyes and listened to the sounds he had heard on many occasions. Caoilte’s sword cutting and stabbing, blocking and bashing, killing and more bloody killing. Éine had wondered whether Caoilte’s drink-ruined body would be able for the violence that had made him a legend. The *draíocht* must have been waiting for his return to allow him to work.

There were a few grunts and swears but little or no screaming. Caoilte was not in the mood to show off his swordsmanship. He was killing them quickly.

'You can come out,' said Caoilte when the noise had abated. 'Your friend is still here.'

Éine's eye's shot open. *Still here?* He pushed himself back out of the small space and looked up with a panicked expression. Cassius should be gone, would be gone, unless...

'Forgive me, Éine. I was afraid. We were given no alternative,' said the Roman. Panic went through the poet, and he thought of escape. Something was utterly wrong. 'I regret what happened between us. I know you do too.'

A long thin spear passed through Cassius' neck from behind. Éine ran over behind Caoilte as a hooded figure alighted on the dais where the gasping, clutching Cassius was dying. Both men watching, recognised the spear though they had not seen it in many long years: Birga. The famous spear of Fionn Mac Cumhal. Even Caoilte's granite face spoke of his shock upon seeing it.

A ghostly voice spoke, alien and playful in tone.

'I have been thinking about your choice of language, *File Cú*. "We will need to get more" was what you said. We will need to get more, you said, as if the plan was already in place.'

The speaker lifted their hood, and the two old men gasped in astonishment as long flowing crimson hair spilt from underneath.

It was Aill'en, the dark Fae prince.

LATERAL THINKING

***

Rhíona speaks more of her people and the situation. They decide upon a change of tack.

Éist le fuaim na habhann agus gheobhaidh tú breac

Listen to the sound of the river and you will get a trout.

***

Four sat huddled, surrounded by prickling branches, damp leaves, and misty chill. The delicate-looking fire struggled for its existence, offering no heat. The gently swirling mist seemed noncommittal in its presence but effective in its wetting. Their conversation was in hushed tones because they had seen too many dangerous days of late. Quiet and concealed, they ate the diminishing provisions from the robber's camp.

'She must have been talking about this Eimear lady. That's who the second guide is. It suggests that she was speaking the truth. Donnacha is heading there as we speak, so we are the ones meant to find the chest she spoke of. We need to go to the waterfall,' said Rhíona as she chewed. 'We can do it, just us and make up time that we lost elsewhere. We might even find Fionn there, and no one else will be in danger because of me.'

Laoise shook her head slowly. 'No. No, I have been wholly unprepared for any of this since we first met. Rhíona, now is not the time for making up lost time. Our time has never been our own.'

'What then? Just give up, Laoise?' Rhíona's face was a mix of emotions.

'Of course not. That's not what I mean.' said Laoise, standing and picking a thorn from a twig. 'In my view, it is time to take stock of things, and get ourselves right and organised. We have been haring from one danger to another. There must be a better way.'

'I am sorry I have brought this upon—'

'No, Rhíona. That's not what I mean either. I'm not blaming you.'

'Laoise is right,' said Eoghan. 'We have been hunted non-stop without a chance to prepare or even take time to figure things out a bit. They seem to know how to find us or are tracking us in some way. Maybe we can confuse them; give ourselves a chance to escape pursuit. That way, the mystery of where Fionn can be our main focus.'

'We have been too lucky for too long.' Rúadhan was nodding slowly. 'There might be a way like they said.'

'They are using *draíocht* to track me. Had I some way to conceal myself from it, do you not think that I would have by now?' Rhíona was exasperated.

'Then we must be like the hare. We must confound them as best we can. We can go the opposite direction to reach our objective. We can walk slowly for half a day and steal horses to ride like the wind for a day and a night. We can move among people first, then among the trees in the wilds. They can track you, yes. They haven't been able to catch you yet. They haven't got the accuracy.'

'Or else they are rushing you along so that they can arrive at the last to claim the prize from under your nose,' said Laoise as she flicked away the thorn. There was a pause as the notion was considered. Faces darkened.

Laoise looked up, her face flushed. 'I'm sure that's not the case. I was only being sombre of thought. I apologise. That said, they need to find him too, do they not?'

Rhíona's face flushed now. 'They do. They also have the resources to track my progress while searching.'

'Why?' asked Eoghan. 'Does the Fae queen, the... was she the Fane or the Fand?'

'My mother is the Fand.'

'Well, why does the Fand not provide the same resources as the Fane? Why has your mother no presence here? Why this imbalance?'

Rhíona's head shook slightly. 'The question of balance. The Fane over-extends, the Fand advances. The Fand shows weakness, the Fane seeks to exploit it. It has been this way throughout the ages. As we experience the might of the Fane's influence here, his grip in the Fae world lessens where my mother is pressing there with all her might. It falls to me to do this thing for two reasons. Firstly, as a measure of spite from my mother to upset my father in any way she can.

Whether I succeed in this is not as important to her as it is to me. Through his efforts at conquest here, he is sure to make significant losses there, and that will appease my mother without end. She does not see the future as I do, however. There is much we do not know about how strong he will become with this world at his feet.

'Secondly, and more importantly than that, this world deserves to be free from conquest at the hands of such hostility. The Fane represents an evil that you would not recognise. He wishes not to rule here in peace. He wants to take this place and all that it may offer him. There would be no mercy shown, only suffering and death until extinction.

'The Fand, though capable of ambition, and even conquest at times, represents purity. That desire to intertwine all the worlds into one. The multiverse existing in harmony. With her as the head.'

'Your father. He sounds like a real charmer. Did he tell you stories as you sat on his lap when you were young?' Rúadhan's face was a picture of sincerity.

Laoise swung a fist at his arm, which he dodged with a smirk.

'It is always a question of balance,' said Rhíona. 'For him to concentrate so much away from our world, represents something that has not happened before. A gamble, it most certainly is, but a gamble where the stakes are not clear. Nothing is clear anymore.'

'So, we make our decision based on what we know and what we need to do next,' said Laoise.

'And do our best to keep them guessing. Even if they are playing us for fools.' Eoghan was determined.

'Well, they expect us to keep searching do they not?' asked Laoise.

No one disagreed.

'Then let us go somewhere decent, find somewhere comfortable to sleep and pick up provisions, weapons and whatever else we might need next. We can even steal horses if you still feel strongly about it, Eoghan.'

'Probably best if we forget the horses. Rúadhan is afraid of them.'

Rúadhan grimaced. 'I told you before, you blithering wretch, I am not afraid of them. I just never had a chance to learn. You want horses? I will steal them myself and I can learn how to ride in the saddle. How about that then?'

'Good idea,' said Eoghan. 'Let's do exactly what Rúadhan said.'

'Grand. Let's do that so,' responded Rúadhan.

'All we need do is find this comfortable, well-stocked place, with easily stealable horses who are patient instructors,' Laoise said calmly.

There was another, longer pause.

One by one, they started to laugh. They were sitting around a miserable fire in a miserable thicket on a miserable evening, and there was nothing else to do.

'That does sound nice from where we're sitting,' Rhíona admitted.

'With some nice leg of lamb and mushrooms,' said Eoghan.

'And a bath,' Laoise added.

'And not a horse to be found for two days journey in any direction,' Rúadhan said. They all laughed.

'Let's go towards *Uí Failge Túath*. Hopefully, Laoise can guide us? It will take us a few days to get there so we can find somewhere to settle briefly on the path. If we don't stay there too long, we can have a night or two of proper rest, and arrive useful,' Eoghan said and all agreed.

There followed an awkward conversation where all four agreed that sleeping huddled in a group would keep everyone as warm as possible without decent shelter. The boys both made a case for sleeping on the outside of the group, followed by a deal of to-ing and fro-ing, so that Rúadhan would be next to Laoise and Rhíona would be next to Eoghan. When they eventually settled down, the girls had huddled close together, and the boys had awkwardly arranged themselves an arm's length from either.

The four of them were cold and grumpy in the morning. Their cloaks were wet through, the discomfort substantial. They decided to spend the morning apart to water, wash, and dry their clothes in the fresh breeze.

When they reunited and started their journey towards *Uí Failge,* their spirits were higher, despite the realisation that, except for Eoghan's knife and Laoise's three darts, they were unarmed; not a good situation if they met Uad's warriors. They travelled quickly, nervously, each husbanding their memory of the warriors and their brutality.

The Fae prince Aill'en wore a sleek cloak of greens and browns, which shrouded him so that only his head could be seen. His chestnut brown skin was flawless and smooth. His face had been painted in streaks of bright colour, though under it, he looked as young as a child. When combined with the hatred flowing from him, the combination of his characteristics was deeply unsettling. The tall spear, *Birga,* seemed short beside him. He looked down upon the two with utter disdain.

'Your flapping lips, *File Cú*, have a flowing stream passing through. Twas only a mere matter of ensuring your presence before the queen,' his own painted yellow lips spat the word, 'and await the snippet with which I may spoil your efforts further.'

Éine tried to cast his mind back. He had become too bothered about Cassius. He agreed with the Fae creature.

A pox on my flapping lips indeed.

He could not see what information he might have given that Aill'en could use to his advantage.

Caoilte was on guard and started to move closer to the Fae prince.

The prince's yellow eyes spotted the movement.

'The sot advances. You wonder can you make it up here? You wonder is there strength in your sword arm to best me?' Aill'en asked as his hand swept one half of his cloak aside to reveal a curved sword in scabbard. 'And yet the threat you once represented has long since waned, even if *draíocht* still dances around you,' he said as his other hand swept his cloak aside and he threw something down at Caoilte's feet.

Éine looked down to see a wineskin.

He glanced at Caoilte, who was looking impassively at the bag, and said, 'Alas, had I known you would serve us something to wet our lips, I would have asked for it in a mug.'

The Fae's eyes did not leave Caoilte's.

'You talk lots,' whispered Caoilte. 'Come down'.

Aill'en tilted his head to one side, giggling musically.

'Weakness left to fester becomes chain links to bind. Your weakness is obvious. Your greatness is no more...' Aill'en paused in thought. 'I have long wondered what might have happened if we had crossed blades. A display of most beautiful violence would have been ensured. The *Draoí* themselves would have wished it. Time, as it stands, does not grace us, I fear. For you, lingering, squalid, tragic violence is all you have left. A battle between you and the wineskin. An end is what you secretly desire Mac Rónán. Cast away notions of a grander conclusion. I will not come down there. Just in case you land a lucky blow and slow our progress.'

'It would be in keeping,' said Éine, 'that you turn tail and flee from your superiors. We have come to expect nothing less from you.'

The Fae's expression darkened.

'Expect what you wish. Those times where I lacked direction have passed into history. A course has now been laid. A journey has begun. Your rabble of would-be protectors are no more. Your master is but a memory. Now is the time of the Fae. The Fane has a mind to ensure victory. Your potential for action is no more in his estimations.

'That said, I must go. I suspect that it is long past time that I renew my acquaintance with the High King at Tara. That is your hope for aid, is it not? Your catalogue of allies is concise indeed. Those that are known to us have been dealt with. The High King represents the last aid that could yet be sought. I will ensure that no such aid will come.'

Éine's heart sank. Aill'en, the dark Fae prince, was headed back to his old haunt. To do as he had done in the past: destroy Tara. Aill'en went to turn, and then paused, turning back to address them.

'These halls require the services of a *scealaí* Mac Éine. A court fool will ease the suffering ahead of you all. When the great warrior falls back to his frailty, you should prove fitting for such a task.'

Before lifting his hood, Aill'en fixed them both with a look of unbridled hatred. Then he was gone. Caoilte and Éine looked at each other as they considered what had happened, and how their already shaky plans looked to be falling to ruin.

A LIFE MORE ORDINARY

***

When the opportunity arises for Eoghan, Rhíona, Rúadhan and Laoise to relax and feel half normal again, they jump at it. Whether it is the right decision or not remains to be seen.

Maireann croí éadrom i bhfad

A light heart lives longer.

***

They found a suitable hamlet of welcoming huts on the way towards *Uí Failge*. It was a sleepy little place. Their hunters had gone off for the day; the farmers were in their fields. A little old woman beckoned them as they passed. She needed a few extra hands to help finish a hut, which had sat incomplete for too long. The woman had grown tired of listening to excuses. She was happy to provide lodging to the four in exchange. When Laoise enquired, the woman suggested that there was a blacksmith who lived on a hill nearby who should be able to service Laoise's need for new darts.

The offer was too good to refuse. They were mindful of overstaying their welcome and putting the picturesque little community at risk, and so they said that they would stay until no later than the coming dawn.

'Name's Pegg,' the old woman said. 'You get started and I'll prepare some scram.'

Laoise and Rhíona took to the wattling. They worked well together from the outset. Laoise was a skilled weaver, and Rhíona took to it like a *sciortáin* to a cow's udder. The girls clearly found common points of interest; their chatting was incessant.

The boys knew the process of making up daub well enough. Before going to make food, Pegg showed them a mound of crushed stones in a shed nearby and they used hay and local soil. Rúadhan went off with a barrow and arrived back before long with a fine mound of old cow dung to add to the mixture.

'The roof will have to be left for the inhabitants,' Rúadhan said as he started to mix some daub. 'Thatching is not a job to be rushed.'

Eoghan snorted at the weak attempt at humour.

They worked hard, stopping only to eat. During the day, Laoise went to find the blacksmith. When she returned, she was shown to the shed where the others were already sleeping. She curled up in a ball next to Rúadhan and was quick to join them.

Eoghan awoke with a start to find Rhíona's finger over his lips. It was still dark. He sat up quickly and looked around searching for danger. Rhíona's smile signalled no threat.

'What is it, Rhíona?' he whispered.

'Come with me,' she said softly.

Eoghan looked at the others. They had somehow found their way towards each other in their sleep and were lying close, Rúadhan's long arm draped over Laoise's shoulder.

Eoghan felt a pang of jealousy over their blooming intimacy, but it was quickly replaced by keen curiosity. Taking his hand, Rhíona led him outside to where the night was bright under a watchful moon.

'What is it?' he asked again, even though distracted and enjoying the warmth of her hand.

'Will you come for a walk with me?' she asked. Eoghan gazed at her, but it was hard to make out her expression in the darkness.

'Now?'

'Yes. This very moment.'

He could hear humour in her voice; and something else. Although perplexed, his head started nodding before he could speak.

'Lead on, my lady,' he said. 'And try not to walk me into a tree or a large hole.'

Dropping his hand, Rhíona led him away from the shed.

He watched her back as she walked. He could just make out the shape of her hips through her dress, her buttocks at the top of her long legs, her delicate shoulders, and his chest ached. He closed his eyes for a moment as he walked.

A perfect back. Perfect everything. She is just so beautiful.

'Tell me about you, Eoghan,' she said as they walked.

He made a face in the darkness. 'About me?' he asked. 'Well. There isn't a whole lot to tell, Rhíona. Not to someone like you.'

'I am like you are, Eoghan. In so many ways.'

'Tell me about you then,' he said. 'Convince me that you are, and I'll feel less of a donkey talking about my quiet world.'

She laughed a little; the rich musical sound soothed him.

'Follow me up here,' she said, moving into the trees at the edge of the hamlet. They had to slow their pace but a well-worn path allowed them to continue walking.

'Where are we going?' asked Eoghan.

'Here.'

They walked into a little natural clearing among the ancient trees; like a wooded amphitheatre for the moon to observe this beautiful patch of woodland floor.

'What is this place?' Eoghan asked.

'It called to me earlier when I walked,' said Rhíona. 'Then whispered to me while I was here. There is *draíocht* here. It's easy to forget that the beauty of the world can attract powerful *draíocht*, just as much as the inhabitants.'

Her faced looked alien in the moonlight; alive. There was something about this place, but he could not see how the *draíocht* would be interested in anything but her.

'Rhíona. What is happening? Why are we here?' he asked urgently.

She took his other hand and leaned in to kiss him. A sense of disbelief passed through him until it struck him that his mouth was against hers. Then he kissed her back.

Her tongue slowly moved with his: her kiss, gentle and open; her arms wrapping around his shoulders and her hips suddenly pressing against him. Eoghan's head swam trying to collect every moment as if they were precious stones. She stopped to gaze into his eyes.

'What do you want?' she whispered.

'You.' *And to kiss again as soon as possible.*

'You can now… if you wish. I want you too.'

He frowned. Did she mean… Does she mean…

'Do you mean… us being together? Now?' he stammered.

'If that is what you want.'

'Rhíona,' he whispered louder than he meant to. 'I've never… done that. I don't really know what to do.' He suddenly felt like he should run away but stayed to search her moonlit eyes for a reaction.

They narrowed for a second and then she smiled comfortingly. They remained open as she kissed him again. Not for long enough. How long is forever?

Her hands moved to her long dresses, and she started to pull at them. Eoghan's eyes and mouth opened wide. He knew he was not dreaming but also knew this couldn't be real.

Could it?

Her clothes seemed to fall away, and she stood before him, her skin pale with the lustre of moonlight. He stared at her, this exquisite creature before him. Gazing at her neck and shoulders; drinking them in; her breasts, her waist. His gaze travelled down to her little hair. Looking at her then was something from a dream.

It made him almost afraid. When he looked back at her face, she was smiling.

'I would like to look at you too, you know.'

'Oh,' he said, eyes opening wide. 'Oh, yes. Sorry.'

Eoghan tore at his clothes until they were off him, strewn on the soft grassy clearing. His heart skipped when she stopped smiling, still looking him up and down, but beat ever faster as she came close and kissed him again, her tongue meeting his, driving him to wild thoughts.

Her scent was intoxicating. It was like she had been untouched by the travel and firepits, the dirt and the sweat. Her body was wrapped in a fragrance, which urged him on, heightening his senses.

Wrapping his arms around her, he drew her in; trying to press as much of himself on her as he could. His hands trembled as he moved them slowly down her soft back.

She stood before him for a moment; a perfect silhouette framed by the expansive starry sky; a gentle breeze moving her hair. If he had had the words of a poet, he would have spoken them. Instead, he reached out and took her hand, encouraging her to lie in the grass.

Eoghan could not see the blue of her eyes, but he imagined her black pupils were enormous. Like two magical portals, through which he wanted to pass and disappear into her world forever.

Morning brought torrential rain and a decent breeze. From inside the shelter of the shed it looked particularly unpleasant.

‘It is not the weather for walking,’ Rhíona said, looking out the door.

‘Eh, what?’ Eoghan mumbled.

‘Staying put suits me,’ Laoise said from her place beside Rúadhan. ‘As it so happens, the smith will need more time to finish my darts. We should probably stay around this morning. Finish the parts of the house we didn’t get to.’

She yawned and stretched half-heartedly. ‘I’m going back to sleep.’

‘Hold on a moment,’ said Rúadhan, in wonder. ‘You went to a smith and asked him for how many throwing darts?’

‘As many as he could make before this afternoon.’

‘I can’t imagine he will have too many done in such a short space of time, to be fair to the poor man,’ ventured Eoghan.

Laoise nestled into the hay under her cloak with a smile. A half-sigh, half-growl escaped her, and she laughed.

‘He and his apprentice worked through the night.’

Rúadhan’s eyes narrowed. ‘What exactly would possess them to do that?’

‘A gold ring will generally resolve many of life’s people-problems.’

‘How many gold rings do you people have exactly?’ asked Eoghan.

‘Lots. Would you like some?’

‘Yes,’ said Eoghan, nodding. He wasn’t sure what he could spend it on. *Maybe if I get enough, I can be a prince. Worthy of her.*

‘Me too,’ said Rúadhan.

'I will give you all the gold I possess to shut your incessant chatter so I can rest for the first time in too long.'

Rhíona laughed and Eoghan shrugged.

'That'll do me,' said Rúadhan, shrugging too.

'Definitely,' agreed Eoghan, just as Pegg threw open the shed door to let in the grey light of dawn.

'Well would ya look at the state of ye. Ye do one decent day's work and spend half the following day napping. What is happening to the young people in the world? In my day we would have been beaten out the door with a lathe or worse. Up, let ye.'

Laoise groaned.

'Up ya scut. I have the breakfast done for ye and a fire going. In ye come and ye'll be warmed and fed before ye go and finish the work that needs doing.'

Breakfast and a warming fire sounded like just the thing to Eoghan, who got a little wink from Rhíona, and thought his head might fall off.

The rain looked worse than it was when they got out in it. It was still a miserable morning, and they pulled their hoods over their heads as they worked. More time meant the house was turning out to be grand. They talked and laughed. Even Rhíona started to come out of herself, both making jokes and accepting being the butt of one or two. Eoghan found her trailing close behind him more than once; his questioning looks met with sly smiles, which caused his heart to thump loudly.

To forget about recent worries for a little while was a blessing. Once it came to the time for Laoise to leave, they decided they would say their farewells to Peggy and travel to the smith to collect her darts on the way to meet the others.

Pegg expressed her delight with their work. She had prepared provisions for the road, which were generous. She gave the boys stout *shillelaghs* to travel with and "help mind against bad things."

'I am fond of old Pegg,' Eoghan said as they were preparing to depart.

'As are we all,' Rúadhan said. 'But staying will only put her in harm's way.' The others nodded their agreement.

So, it was with regret that they left Pegg admiring the work on the house. Despite the regrets, they left with full bellies and warm smiles. Walking in the rain did little to dampen those smiles until, as they crested a long lazy hill before reaching the blacksmith's, Rhíona threw herself to the ground and urgently hissed, 'Get down.'

The others followed her, before rising slightly to look for the threat. Rhíona pointed across the valley to a parallel hill some distance away. Ten riders were moving away from them over the crest of the hill. Four pairs of eyes watched the riders until they disappeared.

Shaken, the companions did not rise for a long time. They had ridden their luck long enough and had almost allowed a warm night's sleep, fine breakfast, and a little old lady to be the cause of their capture, or worse.

When they finally stood, they ran, in the mindset of prey once again. Stopping briefly to pick up Laoise's darts, they did not let that mindset slip until they arrived at the wooden ringfort at *Uí Failge*.

Escape

***

Caoilte and Éine face capture and have to find a way out of harm's way before it is too late.

Is fearr rith maith ná drochsheasamh

A good run is better than a bad stand.

***

As Éine thought about escape, he noted that Caoilte could not take his eyes off the wineskin that had landed amid the bodies and limbs in front of him.

Éine stood for a moment in disbelief.

'Oh, by all means, pop it open and drink it back. A fabulous idea really. It's a shame we didn't think of that before we arrived. Surely none of this would have happened, and we would be having the time of our lives.'

He picked up a bloody sword and slashed the skin open. The liquid inside was clear. *Fuische.* A flash of anger crossed Caoilte's face, as he leaned forward to watch the liquid spill out and dilute the blood.

Éine was already moving. He picked up a severed arm still leaking blood, walked to his friend and began to cover him in blood: face, hands, and clothing.

'Go and sit over there,' he said pointing to one side of the door. 'And hide the sword,' he added.

Caoilte did as he was told, back to his usual impassive self. When he was seated and had *Lus an Chrom Cinn* wrapped in his cloak, Éine opened the doors and roared loudly.

'Hai, Hai. The queen has been attacked. Caoilte Mac Rónán is to blame. Find him. Find the giant and capture him.'

Éine felt confusion would lend towards a successful *geis* on those around him. Few enough people ever believed that Caoilte was Caoilte anyway so it would just be a question of supporting their disbeliefs.

He roared and shouted the place into a frenzy. When more warriors arrived, he started directing them to go to the queen's aid, and check for survivors. He directed one of them to organise search parties to find the giant Fianna, Caoilte Mac Rónán whose sunlight blade would surely still be alight. The scene in the hall was so shocking that those arriving did not suspect two old men. Especially since one of them appeared to be in bad shape.

Happy that the confusion was rife, Éine walked over to his friend and made a show of helping him up. They walked slowly from the hall, back down through the gate, and off towards the slave dock.

Long *currachs*, hookers, and *gleotógs* were dotted around the almost still, shimmering bay. The sails of autumnal red, brown, and copper hoisted over the blackened hide hulls were beautiful to behold, if somewhat tarnished by noisy seagulls and brash traders.

Éine's eye scanned the docks. His underhand scheme at the fort would only give them a small amount of time to escape. He saw what he was looking for approaching him along the track.

A cart load of slaves rolled by. The driver was a burly woman accompanied by an even burlier protector. Her thick red curls and round red freckled face, and his thick red curls and round freckled face marked them as brother and sister. He held his arm aloft to hail them. The woman considering whether to stop was clear on her face. Dropping his hand, Éine grinned knowingly, shrugged his shoulders, and looked past the cart for the next. Immediately, she pulled hard on the reins to stop the old grey mare.

'Make it quick,' she snapped, her southern accent a twanging assault on Éine's ears.

'I am pleased, in truth, that you made the considered decision to stop today and may I bid you and your brother a good day at that.'

The man's eyes narrowed sharply, and he leaned out of the cart and growled, 'She is my wife, not my sister.'

'Ahh, indeed she is. Forgive my bumbling tongue, I pray you. Old age has affected me severely, and I am prone to loose-minded outbursts, as my friend will testify most animatedly.'

All three looked at Caoilte. His eyes were closed, and he seemed to be sleeping where he stood.

'Or not, as seems to be the case. Now, onto business, so that ye may be off upon your own most swiftly. I am sure you are both eager to procreate and populate for such is the world we live in.'

'What are you babbling about?' asked the woman, face vacant.

'I have a wish to buy seats upon your cart.'

The husband-and-wife twins looked at each other and made an unspoken decision to leave without further nonsense.

'I would say, a gold ring to purchase two of your slaves so we may take their seats. Another for you to take us west. I suspect that you have plans to go south before long, so I suspect you will require another gold ring to take us to a ferry across the river or midlakes. Three it is then. Shall I pick the slaves, or do you wish to do so?'

The two appeared astounded by the offer, which showed on their faces like a single cloud in an otherwise blue sky. The man's eyes narrowed again in a most irritating way.

'Five,' he said, and his wife's eye's narrowed with greed and glee at the thought.

'Ah, I see you are persons who operate in the highest echelons of trade and exchange. I would never dream of such a ridiculous suggestion after my own ridiculously generous offer was so coldly swept aside. I think I will wait for this next fellow here. And actually, I think I will offer him two gold rings instead. I am too wounded for any more.'

'Fine, three,' said the man now a little sullen.

‘Oh, my poor man, I seem to have been somewhat unclear. I offered you three an age ago. The offer has changed to two now as it will be for the cart coming along behind you. As it so happens, I think I see another cart coming. It seems as though I am spoiled for choice. I wonder should I drop my offer further. Perhaps...’

‘Two it is, you conniving old crab,’ barked the woman. ‘What exactly do you plan to do with the slaves?’

‘Business that I can attend to myself I assure you. Open the chains.’

The red man opened the chains and Éine picked the two nearest. He did not want to enter into a philosophical decision-making process. The two women, both of mid years, were confounded.

He took them aside.

‘I can do no more for you than this. Your wit must defend you henceforth. Be clever with how you proceed, and be careful who you talk to. Take the gold ring they missed out on and go free. Keep the sharpest side facing out.’

Caoilte and he climbed aboard the cart and off it went at a frustratingly slow speed. The two slaves stood in utter shock, holding a fortune, and surely wondering what had happened to their lives.

As soon as the muddier tracks were behind them, the cart picked up pace. It would serve them better than walking would. Over the course of the day, they were passed by Uad’s warriors from both directions. Éine, though pretending to doze, listened in on the husband and wife’s conversation when he could hear it. More than once the two talked about the warriors and of Uad’s army growing large. There were other stranger rumours too. Rumours of monster and Fae walking once again on the darkest nights. They talked. Éine listened.

When the cart stopped for the slaves to eat, a group of the warriors seemed to slow as if to inspect them but thought better of it at the last moment and continued past. It appeared that Éine's stratagem had worked. The only issue now was when would the married twins attempt to murder them and steal their rings. Éine felt sure they would not try until after dark, but it would be wise to be wary.

After the slaves and passengers finished eating, the couple had a heated conversation in whispers. Strong feelings seemed to be voiced before they quietened for a while. When Éine noticed another quiet word passing between them, the cart ground to a halt. The man arrived at the back of the cart, his hand over his mouth as if yawning.

'I want no soil nor piss on my cart, so you'll all get off for water or movings. Anyone acting up will lose a finger and that's for a start. You should do the same,' he suggested to his passengers. 'You are both old and I don't want any accidents.'

Despite his words, the man made no move to open the slaves' chains. Éine's gaze caught Caoilte's as he started to get off the cart awkwardly without actually getting off.

'You are correct indeed. A man of remarkable wisdom.'

Éine's words seemed to prompt a knife flashing from behind the large man's back, intent on stabbing him, but a boot slammed the man's arm against the cart's floor. Caoilte stood over him, slowly drawing the

Daffodil Blade. The man's face contorted into a mask of fear just before the sword slashed across it. The woman shrieked and, leaping from the cart, ran around to her husband's twitching body.

In the meantime, Caoilte used his sword to cut the chains from the slaves.

'You are free. She has rings if you want them,' Caoilte rasped as he climbed to the front of the cart, took the reins, and clicked the horse forward.

One by one, the eight slaves pushed past Éine and leapt from the cart. Making himself as comfortable as he could on the cart's floor, Éine half listened to the sound of the newly freed slaves killing the slaver becoming, fainter with distance.

They arrived in *Uí Failge* after waiting several days for a ferry. Because of the delay, the others were there to meet them. There was little talk and less rejoicing. A grim reuniting of an unlikely band. The most unusual event was when Caoilte embraced his granddaughter and held her close for a long while. Éine felt a wave of sadness as he watched. Laoise wept in Caoilte's arms.

When someone asked where the cart had come from, Éine said they had miraculously found it in a field after finding out what they needed to know from their old friend Neala. He needed all his will to stop from weeping when he thought about her grumpy old face.

MAXIMS OF THE FIANNA

***

Éine tells of the maxims of the Fianna, and the reasoning behind their creation.

Tar éis a thuigtear gach beart

All is clear in hindsight.

***

Éine stood before them that night and they welcomed his voice.

'The maxims of the Fianna were as light in the darkness to guide those who may have strayed otherwise. Without them the Fianna could never have become such a force. Because of them, the playing field was level for all who entered those ranks. In the beginning only the mottos were needed.' As he spoke, Caoilte's voice joined his.

Glaine ár gcroí
Neart ár ngéag
Beart de réir ár mbriathar

Pureness of our hearts
Strength of our limbs
Deeds to match our words

'Over time Fionn found it increasingly more difficult to keep some of those under his command in check. And so, the maxims were born, and he told them to Mac Luga:

If armed service be thy design, in a great man's household be quiet, be surly in the narrow pass.

Without a fault of his beat not thy hound; until thou hast ascertained her guilt, bring not a charge against thy wife.

In battle meddle not with a buffoon, for he is but a fool.

Censure not any if he be of grave repute; stand not up to take part in a brawl; have naught to do with a madman or a wicked one.

Two-thirds of thy gentleness be shown to women and to those who creep on the floor and to poets, and be not violent to the common people.

Utter not swaggering speech, nor say thou wilt not yield that which is right; it is a shameful thing to speak too stiffly unless that it be feasible to carry out thy words.

So long as though shalt live, thy lord forsake not; neither for gold nor reward in the world abandon one whom thou art pledged to protect.

To a chief do not abuse his people, for that is no work for a man of gentle blood.

Be no tale-bearer, nor utterer of falsehoods; be not talkative nor rashly censorious. Stir not up strife against thee, however good a man thou be.

Be no frequenter of the drinking-house, nor given to carping at the old; meddle not with a man of mean estate.

Dispense thy meat freely; have no niggard for thy familiar.

Force not thyself upon a chief, nor give him cause to speak ill of thee.

Stick to thy gear; hold fast to thy arms till the stern fight with its weapon-glitter be ended.

Be more apt to give than to deny, and follow after gentleness.'

Éine paused. 'A strong heartbeat in Fionn's chest. A good heart. Perhaps it was naivety that caused him to miss the actions of those who betrayed him. Perhaps it was the hope that somehow, they would choose the right path over the dark one.

'Over time, the maxims became less and less well heeded. Drinking houses and the swaggering talk of such men who frequent them, became the norm for many of the Fianna. Some offered their services to those in need, but the prices for said tasks grew, while commitment to the undertaking waned.

'The numbers of the band were never allowed to swell to huge numbers. The tests ensured that. What they could not ensure was that the most talented warriors of the land would hold the same values as those listed by Fionn to Mac Luga. And so, time and human nature had already started to rot the Fianna from the inside out. The battle of *Gamhra* was the death knell.'

‘What of the battle?’ asked Rúadhan with the embers of the fire reflected in his eyes.

Éine looked over at Caoilte and then at the youngster.

‘It was the day he was presented with the Adopted Blades. The Mac Mornas had had the swords made by Handell in the Lowest Lands in Europe. They were crafted over many months and were bathed in *draíocht* from the outset. He never drew them in anger. Only to admire the incredible craftsmanship.

‘The battle was the worst day there has ever been. A king driven by greed and power ensured that we would lose by way of treachery. Goll Mac Morna and his twin brothers, Fachtaí and Fathartaí, worked with King Conn to lead the forces of the *Féinnid* into a terrible trap, ensuring their demise. Such betrayal.’ Éine’s voice almost cracked. ‘Then with Goll attempting to end Fionn’s life as he had Fionn’s father Cumhal… It illuminated the darkest reality: there is no force of good that will stand in the way of people and their black hearts. I will not talk of it further.’

His bowed his head for a while.

With that, the storyteller finished for the evening. It was a long time before the first of them went to sleep, as they thought of some of the black deeds they had witnessed over the days behind them.

ON A SEARCH FOR A GUIDE

***

The group find the waterfall. They look for the chest, seeking further clues to the whereabouts of the guide.

An té nach gcuirfidh san earrach, ní bhainfidh sé san fhómhar

He who does not sow in spring, will not reap in the autumn.

***

The waterfall was beautiful as the witch foretold, framed by the spring forest, blossoms, green leaves and the cloudless morning sky. Ribbons of icy water blurred the rock face and noisily entered a darkened pool, deep and ageless. The metallic smell of silt and minerals invaded their nostrils, trying to mask the thick and heavy scent of blooming flowers, coloured foliage, and thick growth around the valley floor. The busy sounds of flourishing wildlife were washed away by the constant watery chorus, which was equally soothing and overawing. The waterfall raged amid unblemished natural serenity, utterly one with its surroundings.

Poetic words could do this place no justice. It felt almost alien, unspoiled by the presence of men, the perfect place; reaching inside those who looked upon the setting.

Rúadhan felt sure it would be impossible for Éine to look upon such a picturesque corner of the world without marking the occasion with a verbose and dramatic delivery. The poet might describe every detail of the valley before them. He sighed and shook his head slightly. And of course, Éine stepped forward, clearing his throat, blood and hand rising…

'Look,' cried Laoise. The companions' gazes followed her outstretched finger. Their eyes landed on her intended target at the same time. There was a tiny expression of hisses, and sharp intakes of breath.

There, nestled at the foot of the rock face and the bank of the pond, stood a small ornate cottage. Unthatched, it was a mixture of wood and rock, with tiles of slate stone overlapping to create the roof. The rock and wood had been intricately engraved, making the building look foreign. Cascading water veiled some of the cottage from view, and the mist billowing around, gave it the lustre of a Fae dwelling from legends old.

Rhíona froze and started to scan the brush around them. 'I do not like the way this looks. We should be gone or get hidden.'

Her unease was infectious, quickly shared by more than one of the group. As beautiful as the background was, the sight of such an unusual building seemingly rising from the stone was unsettling.

Caoilte's gaze bore into the small abode with an unusual intensity. Rúadhan found his manner more alert. Combined with the surroundings and the situation, already unnerved, Rúadhan was made more so when Caoilte's voice rasped from cracked lips, 'Cover would be wise. Our presence here may be noted.'

He walked towards the nearest tree line dragging his granddaughter with him.

'We'll need to get a good gander up close at some stage, though,' Rúadhan said to no-one in particular.

Éine clapped him gently on the back. 'You are a brave one indeed, young master. Like the legendary Finbarr Rúa Ó Caighin when he stood fearless before the might of the *Wyrm of Cnoc an Fhathaigh*. Your courage gives strength to us all. When you get inside, make sure to capture the detail in your minds-eye so as to make your report most useful. We will be hiding nearby but will make ourselves known to you when you return.'

As Éine issued the last details, he was already moving towards the thick copse nearby.

Rúadhan felt everyone looking at him. Even Caoilte had stopped short of cover to turn and stare. Laoise wore a look he had never seen before. Was she… impressed? He was sure if he told them, that it had never been his intention to even dream of going to such a scary-looking place all by himself, that look would disappear forever.

'I'll go, too, I suppose,' mumbled Eoghan. 'Two is better than one. We can surround the place. Maybe even lay a brief but song-worthy siege.'

‘Bad idea,’ Rúadhan said, with a calmness that belied his thumping chest, surprisingly. ‘You may not be a Fomorian Warrior king, but you’re the only one who might help Laoise provide a moments protection for the men should things go awry. Stay. I’ll have a look and come back.’

Turning, he looked for ways to approach the structure without attracting too much notice. The black winding path clung to the bank of the pond. It was shouldered by a steep rock wall, which narrowed closer to the cottage. Any watching eyes taking refuge in the place would see him the moment he walked out from the safety of the woods. There was nothing to do but go. He didn’t bother turning towards them again. They would surely see his heart beating wildly through his thick cloak, exposing his deception.

‘I’ll go with you.’

The intrusion of Laoise’s soft voice blocked out all other sound. The roar of the waterfall became a whisper, and his thumping heart calmed. He turned to face her, confident that whether he liked it or not, his face would betray his ever-growing feelings for the girl. He cared not a jot.

‘Will you not be distracted by my magnificent arse reflected in the pond?’ he said.

‘A pond you say? I was looking at your arse so much I didn’t even notice there was a pond,’ she replied, looking at him in a strange way. They stood looking into each other’s eyes for a moment.

Clearing his throat, Eoghan said, ‘As lovely day as it is for a ramble through the woods, and a blossoming romance by the waterfall. Can you go if ye’re going?’

Though they both reddened, Laoise's glare at Eoghan made him redden in response. Rhíona, eyes shooting toward the cloudless morning sky, exasperated, took Eoghan's arm, and led him after Éine and the relative safety of the nearby trees. 'Come Fomorian warrior, I fear for my safety, and long for your masculine protection.'

Caoilte watched the volunteers wordlessly for a moment, then turned and disappeared.

Rúadhan smiled at Laoise briefly and started for the path. As they got closer it became clear that the path, a thick layer of crushed slate, had long since fallen into disrepair. Full grown flowering weeds and shooting usurpers dotted the once grand way.

As they approached, the cottage looked increasingly foreign and intimidating. The carvings covering every inch of the building's exterior, were strange and frightening. Neither of them had the faintest idea what the carvings meant. The slick dampness all over caused the walls to shine dully. The two windows were crowned by jutting angled smoothed stone. They looked like furrowed eyebrows over black rectangular eyes, keeping the bulk of the water from the roof from falling into the tiny house.

As they neared the cottage, they both pictured the door opening and a giant warrior of the Fianna, or worse, racing towards them with weapon raised. No such warrior came.

What a suitable abode for such a mysterious figure, thought Rúadhan. *Who is this guide we're looking for? Why could he not just live in a nice little cottage in a bustling village with beer and smoked trout? Who lives in a place like this?*

Then a chilling thought crossed his mind. Who *would* live in a place like this? And why were they walking towards such a character? What would they say at the door? This had not been a good idea. He wished he had never suggested it. *Hold on*, he thought, *I didn't think of this. Why am I the one going?* His stomach started to knot.

Laoise stumbled slightly and put a hand to his back to right herself. It was only the briefest contact, but it acted like *draíocht*.

Ah yes. He thought. *Her.*

From where they stood, the small porch blocked what had become quite a steady drizzle from the waterfall, which had been starting to seep into their cloaks. Laoise shivered visibly. From the wetting or the worry of what might happen next, Rúadhan did not know.

His hand reached out slowly. He knocked gently; hand hovering by the door; he listened so hard his eyes almost bulged. He wished he had told Laoise to stay behind.

I won't be able to run away now that she's here, he thought, and gripped his *shillelagh* tighter.

Again, he knocked. This time, with a little more backbone. The knocks were greeted by as much silence as the valley could provide. They were going to have to look inside.

Rúadhan reached through the bolt handle hole to find that the handle had become rusty. It took several attempts and thirteen curses before the lock started to budge. In the end, he had to wedge a stone under the door to raise it slightly, before it would open. He pushed it wide and stood in the doorway.

The cottage's interior was not at all in keeping with the impressive exterior. The two entered the single, very damp room, and waited for their eyes to adjust to the darkness.

There was not much furniture. Something that might be a long chest sat under an oilskin in the centre of the room with a bench behind it. The rest was featureless. The two houseguests shivered at the same time, obviously on edge and finding it more difficult to hide it.

'If anyone ever lived here, they did so ages and ages ago,' whispered Laoise. Rúadhan walked to the chest and pulled off the oilskin.

'Well, at least there's the chest she spoke of. I'd hate if we found out she was a liar along with everything else.'

Rúadhan was wary of opening the suspicious box but was eager to find whatever was of worth here and to be gone as quickly as possible. 'Maybe we should wait for them,' whispered Laoise as Rúadhan reached out, giving him cause to hesitate.

'Why?'

'I don't know. Just maybe it might be a better thing to do. We don't know what's in there.' Her eyes narrowed. 'What if it's something… evil?'

Rúadhan straightened. *She makes a deal of sense, so she does.*

'Have a look up above and see what's keeping them', he said.

Laoise made a panicked noise in her throat as she looked out one of the tiny windows. Rúadhan quickly joined her to look out. The group had obviously started towards the cottage but were partially surrounded by nine warriors in black armour holding weapons that looked particularly deadly.

A trap had been sprung.

SKIRMISH

***

The group become ensnared in a trap. Cruel warriors of Uad move in for the kill.

An té a bhíonn thíos buailtear cos air

They kick the ones who are down.

***

Eoghan watched as the men came out of the trees behind them, armoured and armed, eyes promising ill-intent. Another was disappearing into the thicket, probably off to find more warriors.

They had ensured no escape back up the path, and the only other way led to the cottage. Éine leapt in a most unmanly fashion, making a more unmanly noise and positioned himself behind Eoghan. Eoghan, in turn, pulled Rhíona behind him and held out his *shillelagh* as a challenge.

The men spread out. Eoghan counted nine.

'Greetings,' said a warrior in a foreign accent. 'We were hoping you could tell us the story of how a fine group such as yourselves would be found wandering like tinkers gone astray?'

The warrior had a shaggy mop of brown hair and a savage scar that disfigured the right side of his face. His longsword gleamed in the afternoon light. Eoghan considered calling for Rúadhan. They were in trouble.

Neither Eoghan nor his companions spoke. His trembling knuckles were white, gripping his *shillelagh*. He noticed someone was standing at his side. Caoilte. His shining sword was drawn; scabbard discarded. The warriors, who had clearly discounted him as a threat, glanced at each other and slowed their approach, continuing to spread out.

One spoke, 'Come on, let ye. I'm positive we can enjoy the pleasures of each other's company without so much bloody posturing. Let down ye're pretty walking sticks, and let us all enjoy the beautiful setting around us with talk. The girl must come with us. It will be much better for you if you let her do so.'

Eoghan's heart was thumping. He nearly fell over when Caoilte rasped quietly. 'Go first. Charge at the one on your far left. Don't let them get around you.'

He angled his mouth backwards and spoke no more loudly, 'Poet, when you run, take the girl. Go to the house. Wait until I tell you.'

Éine, who may or may not have heard the entire instruction, took off at speed down the path.

'Come girl,' he shouted over his shoulder.

Rhíona did not follow. She walked between Eoghan and Caoilte.

'What are you doing?' hissed Eoghan.

'Too late,' said Caoilte for all to hear

'What do we do?' asked Laoise, with a strangely flat voice.

'Wait,' said Rúadhan. He scanned the empty room. His *shillelagh* was a glorified walking stick, and he would not last seconds against armed and armoured men.

'We have to go to them,' she said again, a dart in each hand.

'Wait,' barked Rúadhan. He felt compelled not to leave; something was holding him back. The chest sat cold and still as it must have done for some considerable time, yet there was something about it, making him feel like a curious child. More than that, he felt the box was compelling him to look inside.

'Maybe something in there,' he murmured as he stalked towards it. He cast his *shillelagh* aside and threw back the lid of the chest. A bound oilskin lay inside. He tore off the bindings and unwrapped the bundle. As he did so, a clink of metal aroused the curiosity of his fellow explorer.

'Quickly, Rúadhan.'

Rúadhan's eyes opened wide as he uncovered two of the strangest-looking weapons he had ever seen. They were short swords with matching hounds' heads at the base of each hilt lying on an ornate scabbard. Longer handled than a traditional short sword, one was a blade topped with a wicked-looking curve; the other blade was waved metal topped with a spike for stabbing. Even with a basic knowledge of weapons, Rúadhan could tell the blades were crafted from superior metal by skilled hands. They emanated a faint glow.

The large leather scabbard underneath was in the shape of a harp. It had straps for shoulders to be carried on the wielder's back. It was also an incredible piece of craftsmanship, where both blades would fit snug inside but could be drawn quickly despite the odd shape. Only the hound heads appeared over the top of the case when sheathed. At the base of the blades were two names etched in ogham. Bran and Sceolan.

'Hurry,' urged Laoise.

Rúadhan shouldered the straps of the harp scabbard, and lifted the weapons. They felt marvellously light, and a wave of euphoria passed through him. Holding the swords, his hands appeared different: the hands of a warrior. Moving to the window, he felt changed. He felt stronger.

As Laoise and he looked out the warriors started to fan out to cut off escape attempts. Rúadhan knew it was time to act. He took a breath to steady himself and went towards the door.

'Wait here,' he said, before kicking open the door and running up the path. She followed.

Éine and Rúadhan did not acknowledge each other as they passed on the pathway.

Eoghan was hoping the violence might not happen. That somehow this would all just stop. The men would turn and leave. But as they closed around them brandishing weapons, he realised the truth.

He sprang forward suddenly, stabbing out with the butt of his *shillelagh* to catch the oncoming warrior unprepared. There was a sickening crunch of bone, closely followed by a spray of teeth and bloody spit. The warrior crashed heavily to the ground with a gurgling moan.

Eoghan was aware of another warrior's attack and turned just quickly enough to block a sword whistling through the air towards him. The *shillelagh* snapped but deflected the blow. However, an elbow struck his temple, and he fell back, senses reeling. Eoghan held out the stub of his stick to block the killing blow as he tried to clear his head. Scrambling backwards, ears ringing, he shook his head and tried to stand, but no killing blow came. Instead, he thought he could hear the sound of metal on metal; he wasn't sure because the only member of the group with a sword was Caoilte.

Is Caoilte using his sword?

As Eoghan began to refocus, he took stock as best he could. The fighting had stopped, a tense standoff was taking place. Caoilte stood in front of Eoghan with his sword unsheathed; causing the warriors to hesitate. Eoghan thought Caoilte unlikely to pose much threat to young warriors. Caoilte cocked his head to one side as if he heard something before standing back.

The attackers were organising themselves; shepherding their prey; isolating them expertly. All but one had passed Eoghan as if discounting him as a threat against the need to neutralise the others. They were correct. As hard as he tried, he could not stand. A few grunts and words were exchanged by the warriors as they positioned themselves for the assault.

Still trying to gain his feet, Eoghan could just make Rúadhan out as he charged wildly into the warriors. Even with his head ringing, Eoghan could see there was something different about his friend.

Where did he find those strange swords?

The blades were spinning and curving around him, creating a beautiful shield of silvery metal and freshly spilt blood. He cut the warriors standing before him into pieces, hacking and severing with the sharpened edges, dragging them towards him with the sickle and skewering them with the deadly spike. Those who lashed out at him found their weapons blocked and him gone from where they thought him to be. It was like a strange dream.

Caoilte just stood and watched.

An echo of Rúadhan's hurling skill rang out; he used many of his hurling moves to slaughter battle-hardened veterans. It was different, though, as though his movements were slower than those of the men he fought; concise and direct; as if he had more time to think, leaving the men panicked. It seemed to Eoghan that Rúadhan had fought a thousand warriors and bested them all.

The warriors attempted to regroup, but Laoise sprang into action as they did. Her darts flew with incomparable speed and accuracy. The next attacker reeled from an impact to his helm before he managed to complete a single sword swing. As he fell, Laoise kicked his knee joint, which snapped sharply as he barrelled backwards into two of his comrades. Laoise's body whirled once more and she used a dart as a dagger to puncture one of the warrior's upraised arms at the elbow. She lashed at him with the spike three more times until he stopped moving. Suddenly wary, the other warriors began to back away.

One, standing apart from his fellows, was trapped facing Rhíona. His eyes narrowed as he moved. He swung his sword in a deadly arc but met only air. Momentum carried him off balance and before he could right himself, Rhíona grabbed his wrist and pulled sharply. As he stepped forward, she vaulted onto his back. Her arms wrapped around his neck and her legs around his midriff. Her arm caught his as he tried to angle his sword backwards to stab at her. Drawing a thin blade from her sleeve, she stabbed his neck three times. He collapsed underneath her. Looking up calmly, she found the men from both sides gaping at her, open mouthed. Laoise was watching with an approving countenance.

Rhíona walked back and joined the line between Caoilte and Rúadhan. Eoghan looked at Caoilte. The old man stood with his sword out but not fighting. Eoghan tried to figure out who had saved him from the killing stroke. Caoilte would have had to move like the wind. But who else could it be?

Only three attackers remained standing, only one of whom was unscathed. Clearly seasoned warriors, they must have witnessed many strange sights on many fields of combat, but were unnerved. They retreated back up the path slowly, only breaking into a run as they neared the relative safety of the tree line.

'We can't let them go so easily,' said Rúadhan, as he sheathed his newfound weaponry and went to assist Eoghan off the ground. 'Another has gone for help. We could be surrounded any second.'

'We must forget the house and be gone', said Eoghan rubbing his temple where an egg-shaped bruise had risen. He turned and beckoned to Éine in the cottage. The sudden movement made his head spin, and he would have pitched forwards if Rúadhan had not been there to catch him.

'Take a weapon if you want one, and purses if they have them,' Eoghan said to anyone listening as he freed himself from Rúadhan's grasp and gingerly picked up a sword. Rhíona unbuckled a plain scabbard belt from one of the warriors and gave it to him with a look of concern in her eyes.

The warrior Eoghan had hit at the start groaned and moved slightly, alive but badly injured, one of Laoise's darts sticking up from his leather armour. She, it seemed, was the one who had saved Eoghan's life. *But she was so far away…* She appeared beside him, saying nothing.

'How many of you are there close-by?' Eoghan asked the injured warrior, attempting to conceal his trembling voice with a menacing growl and bared teeth.

'Piss off and die, boy,' came a menacing growl through bared teeth in reply.

Eoghan winced at how much more believable the injured warrior was. He went about binding the man's hands and feet with his own belts. 'Rhíona, go get Éine and follow us. Rúadhan and I will try and see which direction they went. We'll meet you back at the trees in the length of time it takes everyone to get there. Be quick.'

Rúadhan and he headed towards where they last saw the warriors. Eoghan was still unsteady on his feet but had no time to worry about it.

'These were the only two things in the cottage, Eoghan. It was for naught,' Rúadhan said as they walked. 'Eoghan, what are we doing? Why are we following the warriors?'

‘We can go back and search the cottage again,’ said Eoghan groggily. His head was pounding.

‘You’re not listening. The swords were the only thing in there. There’s no guide here. Eoghan, you’re hurt badly. Where are we going?’

Eoghan didn’t hear his friend. He was trying to clear his blurring vision by blinking.

They cautiously walked into the trees, raising their newly acquired swords in front of them. The way ahead was eerily quiet, as if some person, place or thing ahead was expecting their arrival.

After walking a few paces, they stopped abruptly, mouths dropping open. Sitting on a mossy rock beneath the bough and branches of a towering horse chestnut, sat a grizzled-looking woodsman with a long, bloodied sword. His single eye regarded the two boys with sneering hostility. An ancient leather patch covered the other eye. A jagged scar from above his eyebrow down to his cheek told that eye’s story well enough. The warriors who ran lay dead at his feet. The one who had been sent for help earlier had died ten paces to his right.

A silence hung in the air.

When the seated man spoke, his gravelly voice was slow and matter of fact. His fingers gently tapped the hilt of his sword as he did so.

‘You are alive for only one reason. Because that boy,’ he nodded slightly towards Rúadhan, ‘is carrying those weapons. Explain to me how it has come to pass, boy, before I kill you and return them to their rightful place.’

The sword he held was a wonder to behold. It was heavily embellished with tiny emeralds, green blue turquoise stones and other glass-like green gems.

Ornate work along the blade made it seem like the sword must belong to the Fae *Rí*. Beautiful waves in the steel made it look almost liquid and the metal itself shone with a green tinge. The stones and the blade combined to create a sword that seemed to blend into the green of the woods.

He was far less of a wonder to behold. Greasy strands of hair had been positioned over his bald head, a vain ritual for a man whose foul body odour was already assaulting their nostrils across the clearing.

Though he was in no position to offer any assistance, Eoghan felt buoyed after their rout of the warriors. This man was but one, and Caoilte and Rhíona were bound to appear at any moment.

'Perhaps,' he said, 'or indeed you should put down the pretty sword before you get yourself injured. There are more of us on the way, and you will find us most difficult to kill.'

The man, of indeterminate age, looked down slightly and shook his head slowly. A hand came up to push the few greasy hairs back over his baldness. Once, twice, three times. The hand was coarse and weather-beaten, ridged with scars, and missing a finger.

'I have had a bird's eye view of some of the more recent goings on. I think my suggestion still applies. I grow weary of today's events, and I have only just arrived. How did you open the chest, boy?'

A commotion from behind, followed by a loud silence, suggested the other party members had arrived as promised. The woodsman's relaxed posture remained the same. As he surveyed the others, however, a look of amazement crossed his face, and he stood slowly.

‘Caoilte? Caoilte. Is it really you?’

Caoilte went rigid. His hand trembled as it clenched tightly around his sword. Éine seemed to be in shock.

When he spoke, his voice was filled with uncharacteristic anger. ‘Mac Morna! You black hearted bastard. You treacherous dog.’

Caoilte’s voice betrayed no emotion. ‘Put up your weapons’. His voice rasped slowly. ‘He would kill you all with little effort.’

‘Caoilte.’ Mac Morna’s voice seemed to plead. ‘It is… good to know that you were not amongst… the fallen. I would speak of such things if you would hear it from me.’

Caoilte walked towards him, stopping a hairsbreadth from the man’s weathered face. ‘You may speak all you wish while I rest, Cónán. In the morning you and I will cross. One of us will die, and I hope with all my heart it is you.’

The Traitor

***

The group have to deal with the infamous Cónán Mac Morna.

Fear na bó faoína heireaball

The cow's owner must go under her tail.

***

Everyone was on their guard, raw tension keen. They moved far enough away from the waterfall to a place where they might be discovered less easily, all wary of another encounter with the warriors in black. Cónán Maol Mac Morna sitting in their midst only augmented the tension. More so than Éine or Caoilte, the presence of such a living legend both exciting and worried the youngsters. His presence was not easily missed. The odour that surrounded him was so foul that more than one member of the group was retching.

For the most part, he sat alone; one good eye looking regularly towards the ash tree where Caoilte had removed himself earlier. His shoulders were slumped, and he picked at the skin around his filthy fingers. Laoise knew about such men from her trading visits to towns, forts and villages.

Quick to speak of honour and right, quicker to violence, bloodshed and anger. Loosely bound by airs of loyalty, of conscience, driven by the practical actualities of greed, self-promotion, and the search for glory. His pained expression made her feel more ill than his foul odour ever could. Her grandfather had told her about the brothers Mac Morna. Their treacherous and scurrilous ways were infamous. The list of their cruel deeds was long indeed. The brothers would have painted their acts as cunning or honour-bound necessity. There was no honour in such a man as this. Not a lick of it.

Had he cared to notice, the man may have felt her cold stare of hatred boring into him. She knew the truth about his brother's final act of treachery. The betrayal of Fionn by the Mac Morna clan led to the destruction of the Fianna and the deep sadness that threatened to wash her grandfather away more and more with each passing day. Cónán's part in the betrayal had never been clear. In her mind, he was guilty by association. Guilty as his cur brothers. And now here he sat, with the look of a scorned child.

She could not stop her rage from forming words in her mouth.

'You are a lying pig, and you should be dead.'

The man did not look at her.

'You can hear me when I speak, pig. I thought your feigned honour would not allow such talk to go unchallenged. Have you now become a meek and simple-minded old fool as well as a liar?'

The one pale blue eye narrowed, though his broad shoulders slumped slightly.

'Girl,' he growled. 'You think you are the only one who hates me? You think that I have not done all of this before today? You bore me with your words, and this will be my one and only response to them. Be silent, yapping bitchlet. I have no interest in your feelings and will not any time soon... unless you feel like those three darts you have hidden in your jerkin can fell me before I chop one side of your body from the other?' The cycloptic stare landed on her very briefly and she was filled with sudden fear. As quick, it was gone again.

'Do not speak to me. I will not be listening,' he finished before standing and ambling away.

Laoise saw that Rúadhan held his breath as the man passed and made a disgusted face. A soft boy indeed to be around such a man as Mac Morna. Still, seeing him making a face took the edge off her anger. He caught sight of her looking and waved his hand in front of his face as if to waft the smell away. His crinkling nose made her smile in spite of herself, and she went to sit with him.

Eoghan lay nearby with his eyes closed. His head was still ringing, and he was sure the lump was going to continue rising. He heard someone approaching from behind. An accompanying odour ruined the mystery. He did not open his eyes.

'What do you want?'

'I need to talk to someone about what it is this group of people are doing together, and how it is that the boy over there is carrying those weapons... You, my young man, are going to tell me what I need to know. Let's start by you getting to your feet and having some respect when you talk to me, boy.'

Feeling nauseous, Eoghan neither stood nor opened his eyes. 'Firstly… no, secondly, I don't have to tell you a thing, and I do not give a hoot who you are. Leave me alone and find someone else to talk to. You stink of shit or worse.'

'There is no one else. Caoilte will not look upon me. Éine's talk would drive me to killing him. Caoilte's girl and the lad with the swords fawning over her are not disposed towards my company, and the other girl... she may not be whoever she told you she is.'

Eoghan opened his eyes. He came up onto one elbow to look at the old warrior. It was as much as he could manage for now.

'What exactly do you mean by that?' he asked, suddenly wondering if he should call the others.

'I mean she is not what she seems. You think her to be a normal girl. She is not that. I will tell you more about her, but first you will answer my questions.'

'I said no. That will not change.'

'Perhaps I will make it change by pulling off one of your fingers.'

'Perhaps. But then I am quite sure that Caoilte might find that difficult to stand, or the lad with the new swords. And if you go pulling parts of my body off, I think I might like you even less and would probably not speak to you at all.'

Cónán chuckled quietly. It was both an unnerving sight and sound. Eoghan wished this over.

'I am Cónán Mac Morna. There have been many lads with many swords, and they are all dead. I am not. Caoilte and I will fight at any rate, so perhaps it does not bother me when. And I am beginning to like the idea of pulling off your fingers because you are becoming quite a source of irritation, little puppy.'

Eoghan lay back down as dizziness swept over him. 'Ruff ruff,' he said quietly and closed his eyes. The smell of the man was going to make him throw up.

'You search for answers in the wrong places Mac Morna,' said Éine who had been listening from behind the massive warrior. 'You will find them laid out at your feet should you wish. All that is required is a nod and your attention. And of course, your word that my words will not indeed drive you to killing me. I do not enjoy being killed. I find it so desperately terminal.'

Cónán bristled. 'Be at ease, coward. My curiosity seems to be outweighing my desires for now. Keep your speak plain, as I am in no mood for flowered foolery.'

Eoghan managed to sit up propping his back against the tree. A wave of nausea accompanied his efforts. Éine continued.

'You wish to know of our quest. I will tell you, for you have played more of a part in it than any of us thus far. I speak now of the Fianna and its questionable conclusion. Alas, it seems that it remains unfinished Cónán, and it falls upon the frail shoulders of we forgathered to play a part in overseeing the end absolute.' He had raised his voice to get the group's attention. Caoilte and Laoise rejoined, keeping a respectful distance.

'Any story I tell has a beginning and a middle before it can reach its end, and so does ours. Three of us here have lived through those times, and now we carry the weight of knowing. Everyday those days become distant memories. We endure the legends and the myths that have sprouted like weeds around the black truth we witnessed.

'The days of the Fianna are over and never has there been a greater and more dire need for those brave men and women as now. From my attentive listening, I have gleaned some harrowing information. Three Fae ambassadors walk our lands. Among them, is Moghrugh. He has returned to these shores and has gathered and harvested like the farmer in the autumn.' Cónán gasped and covered his face with his hands. Rhíona's face was granite.

'They say he has amassed a warband under the banner of another; a man known as Uad. The warband is said to be camped outside Dún Ailinne and numbering in the thousands.

'There are other factions at work as well, Mac Morna. Darker, ancient enemies are poised and set against us. Aill'en is alive and the second ambassador. The third is something else. Something darker.'

One or two heads turned towards Rhíona.

'The truths of their plotting will not be told to you any day soon, for you have lost the trust that we had so grudgingly given you. But the end of our story is not so clearcut as we have all been thinking over these last long years. We may yet have a part to play in the protection of the land. Perhaps there could have been a way for you to insert yourself into our final story. However, it is you. Perhaps it is only right that you and Caoilte do battle in the morning, for it is unlikely that trust will ever be restored. It is even less likely that you will survive a duel with him.'

Laoise caught Rúadhan's look. It made sense that he held little faith in Caoilte's abilities as a swordfighter. Especially after his part in the skirmish. Laoise knew that Caoilte had been testing the boy's mettle. She was annoyed with her grandfather for not aiding them further; though she was sure he would not have allowed them to be killed. Mostly sure anyway. She shook her head.

All of a sudden Eoghan groaned. He had slipped off into unconsciousness and was looking worse for wear. 'He needs help,' said Rúadhan. 'We will not be able to go and meet Donnacha if he is like this.'

Rhíona stood and went to him. 'Let me be with him. Do not approach nor disturb us.' She moved around behind Eoghan, and the others moved back close around the fire. Cónán watched her, his eye narrowed.

He moved towards the fire as if to speak.

'Make your own fire if you want fire. Your stink will have us all in worse condition than the boy before long,' growled Caoilte. Cónán bristled and turned to leave.

He did not turn around as he addressed his erstwhile companion. 'I have been thinking. I will not fight you. You know I will not. You will have to just kill me or get used to the smell. If I don't die in the morning, I'm coming with you. I have been watching over the chest in that house down there for long years. I knew there was something of his inside because I was drawn here. I thought it might be the horn but could not open the chest. None of the few who have ventured here could ever open it. And now the boy has. It is not so easily explained. I will be coming with you, Caoilte. You don't have to like it. Or else kill me in the morning. I won't draw my sword or curse you or anything.'

Caoilte's hard stare bore into the fire.

'I will not kill you in the morning,' he said. 'If you will not fight me, I will give you until the morning after to convince me there is a reason you should live. We were brothers once you and I, Cónán. I owe you that and no more. Do not beg me for mercy when the time comes. You will look like a fool, and it will make no odds to me.'

Cónán grunted and walked away.

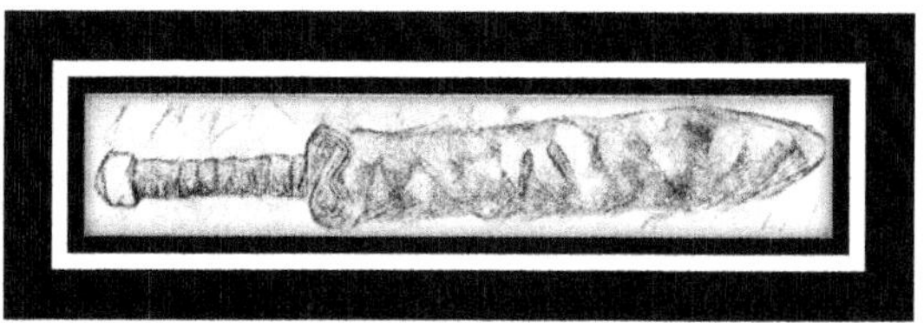

Eimear and Donnacha

***

Donnacha's quest to secure the assistance of the High King is joined by Eimear. The two travel to Tara together.

Is fearr cara sa chúirt ná punt sa sparán

Better a friend in court than a pound in the purse.

***

They sat staring at each other. Donnacha had relayed the story as best he could. He felt sure he had forgotten parts but was happy that Eimear got the idea. She had said nothing since, even though looking like she was on the verge of speaking many times. Now, he felt it best to say nothing in case he upset her, as was his way around people.

She had finished crying. Her eyes looked different to when they first met. Carefree had changed to hard-edged, burdened. It made him uncomfortable. He could do hard eyes with the best of them, but there was something about the look she had now which was genuinely disconcerting.

'Just so we are clear, I have made no decision. I would much rather stay here and forget what you have told me. You could stay with me if it pleases you,' she said in a pleading voice. 'We could forget together, Donnacha.' Sincerity trickled through her words, but neither of them believed it possible, even a little bit.

'Would that be something you might consider?'

'Well, if I was being honest about it, I'd have to say that my heart leaps high at the thought; I think I might just do that, altogether. Just as soon as I do this thing that needs doing. I have come across the warriors of Uad several times now, and I fear they mean conquest and badness and nasty business not too far down that trail. These mercenaries are everywhere and seem to be growing in number, and bald-faced... poxy, belligerence.' He felt his neck flush. 'The Fianna are no more, and the High King and the other kings seem to be ignoring the whole lot. Someone needs to stand up to them…' Donnacha's voice trailed off before he said just above a whisper, 'I am good for little, but I'll do what I can.'

Eimear straightened up a little.

'I have made no decision, as I have said. If I do decide to become involved, I would need to know exactly what is required of me. I am not sure what Éine or the others have said about me. There are some things I can no longer be involved in,' she said, studying his face carefully as if searching for something.

'I was told that if you would come, not badgering on you now or the like, yet should that be what you decide to do of your own volition, we are to go to the hill fort of the King and petition for his support. The group seem to think a warrior of the Fianna, such as yourself, will instantly glean favour in the *hillfort of the High King*. And rightly so. My telling of events will represent things as they stand. We need help, Eimear, and that's not too far from the truth of things. We need an army to fight them. Without an army we will be lost.'

Eimear reverted to silent contemplation. When she spoke again, her eyes were harder and more harrowed than before. 'I cannot get involved in violence anymore, Donnacha. I have parted from that way of life. I was younger. I was… not the same person I am today. I belong here, away from it all. So do you. We could just stay.'

'Come along to see the king with me. Help me with that undertaking, and you will have fulfilled any obligation that might be dragging at you; I'm full sure of it. You'll have no need to be lying up thinking about it and wondering and feeling bad and all that. Come and see him with me and then return to this lovely place. Maybe when I get done and thrown clear, I could come back here, too, and be away from the world. I would be thinking that would suit me the finest as long as you could stand my talk and my talking.'

Eimear smiled a sad smile. 'I could stand that, Donnacha. Who could not?' She leaned over and kissed him gently. 'Remember this place. Come back here someday,' she whispered, 'and let us never be heard of again.'

Donnacha sat wondering what she was thinking. He watched as she moved to her sleeping sack in the corner and casually swept it aside with her foot. There was a small trapdoor underneath, which she lifted clear. Kneeling, she paused, looking down into the hole. A slight crimson hue reflected off her face. When she remained like that for some time, Donnacha felt a curious urge to go and look in the hole. Eimear was breathing heavily and seemed unsettled as she stared.

Donnacha thought he might alleviate her tension.

'I know my conversation can be dull, but surely, it's better than staring into a hole in the ground?'

She did not look up. Her hands reached in, and she lifted out a battered leather scabbard holding a sword with a worn, plain handle. Donnacha looked at the hole again, waiting for her to take something else out, but there was nothing else.

'A sword?' he asked.

'It's been in there a long time. I had hoped never to see it again,' said Eimear matter-of-factly, though her eyes were still troubled.

'Could you not have thrown it away?'

'It would not have liked that,' she whispered, with her eyes closed.

'I will be at your side and do my utmost to ensure you never have to draw it,' said Donnacha resolutely.

She gazed into his eyes and his breath caught.

'You are a good man, Donnacha. I know you will do your best,' she said as she turned back to the sword. 'I used to tell them that sometimes they just needed to leap and trust that the *draíocht* would lift them. They used to find it so difficult to do. I always just leapt and the *draíocht* was always there. Even before the *Draoí…* came to me. I never had to think about it and never did. Now I am afraid to leap, Donnacha.'

'I do not understand your words, lady. I am not a man of the deepest thought, even when I do chance a bit of thinking, which is rare enough to be straight.'

She smiled a little. 'Nor am I the deepest thinker. More of a doer. We are well matched it seems.'

'What is *draíocht*, Eimear? I mean, I suppose that everyone knows what it is, but I'm asking what is it? From your understanding even.'

'The *Draoí* were here even before the Fae, as the world was born. Wild and free, they were so at one with the land that they became spirits in tune with nature to its roots. As the world came through its infancy, the *Draoí* became whimsical, playful. They sought delight in the beauty of interconnection, of alignment.'

Eimear stopped for a moment; her head tilted.

'Where they found creatures or places that showed rare beauty or gifts, the *Draoí* inhabited and extended. They exaggerated these rarities and made them otherworldly. Over time, they changed. Not for the better. Now all that is left is their legacy; for all others at least.'

Looking up at him, she seemed to realise what she was saying and stopped.

'*Draíocht*. In people, it enhances the most amazing among us: our most adventurous; most accomplished; doers of great, great deeds, Donnacha. The great deeds of those same few who truly know themselves.'

'How is it you know so much about the *Draoí*?'

Eimear went to sit, putting the sword across her lap. 'That is a story for another time.'

'And so,' posed Donnacha, 'your particular gift was leaping you say?'

Eimear snorted back a laugh and covered her smile with an apologetic fist.

'No, my wonderful new friend.' Her smile evaporated, replaced by a sad look. 'No. My gift was…

not a gift at all. It was a curse. I am very much hoping it is lost.'

Donnacha's eyes narrowed. 'You can speak to me about all things you know.'

She looked at him. 'Perhaps. Not just yet though. I love the way you look at me when I speak, Donnacha. I do not want that to change.'

'It will not change so quickly'

'Another time. For now, let us go to this place and speak with the High King of *Éire*, and do what must be done. I have not been to see a high king since your grandfather was a child.'

Donnacha shook his head. 'How old are you, Eimear *Féinnid*?'

She looked at him with a show of mock scorn.

'Surely you know that it is not in the remit of a free gentleman to question a lady of her years. Or have you been living by yourself for so long you have forgotten social requirements.'

Unrepentant, he smiled. 'How... old?'

'Extremely,' she answered.

'Exactly how extremely?'

She stood and looked around her home, reaching for items meant for impending travel. 'Leap, Donnacha,' she said. 'Leap and trust the *draíocht* to lift you.'

After two days' gentle travelling by horse without a saddle, Donnacha was just about getting the hang of the wild-spirited creature. Eimear pulled up, alert, and sat, staring forward.

'What is it?' he asked. Her hand came out to silence him. Something was amiss.

He slid his bow from his satchel, whipped a string from his pouch, and strung the bow in a heartbeat. Peering forward, he tried to identify what had Eimear on edge. They were travelling through the vast cattle pastures of Tara and had been for some time. Apart from a couple of herders in the far distance, he could not ascertain what the cause of her delay was.

'We are coming close to Tara,' she said tersely without turning around. 'There is something strange... I have a strange feeling about what's up ahead.'

She clicked the horse and rode on leaving Donnacha to wonder should he unstring the bow. Nothing grated on his nerves more than a strung bow that was not going to be used. In light of her behaviour, he decided to leave it strung.

He took the rain covering from over his quiver and rested it as best he could across his lap while trying to steer the horse with a bow in his hand, trying equally as hard not to fall off and brain himself.

He had not quite caught up with her when she slowed her horse again. Not stopping but down to a lazy walk. Donnacha grew warier. She appeared to be resting the horse in case she needed to move quickly for as long as possible. It seemed they were walking towards danger.

But in Tara? What could possibly be dangerous there?

Sliding an arrow from the quiver, Donnacha nocked it. Nudging his horse in the ribs with his heels, he clicked his tongue and drew alongside Eimear. 'I'm not putting pressure on you or trying to appear in need of minding if you get me, but I can't for the life of me see anything undue, and that's the truth of it now,' he said quietly.

'I am unsure of my feelings. It has been a long time since I have felt the like.'

She turned to him then, scrutinising, as if looking for something. 'How good are you with the bow? Ego and humility aside; I need a precise assessment.'

Donnacha was taken aback by the question. He considered his answer carefully. Eimear sat patiently waiting, watching him.

'I am without equal. There may have been someone better throughout your long life or during the days of the Fianna. Now, however, I am the best. I would say I am, anyway, at least. But because I am probably the best, it means I am the likeliest person to be able to recognise my own greatness. With the bow, of course, I mean. I am only normal in other ways.'

Eimear's head tilted slightly while she watched him, suggesting she had the answer she needed.

'There is *draíocht* up ahead, which means someone using it. Or something. If you are as good as you say you are, then there is a good chance you have been touched by *draíocht* and will be able to cause damage to—'

'*Draíocht* did not play a part, Eimear. I have worked hard. I have worked with fingers bleeding and numb from cold where no one else would. I have made myself what I am from force of will.'

She was watching him again, eyes full of fierce admiration. 'Of that, I have no doubt. However, you must remember, *draíocht* lands on the shoulders of the greatest. It comes unbeckoned to those who would never need it. It is greedy; it has no interest in anything not spectacular. As long as there is *draíocht* on this side of the worlds, it will be drawn to people like you. It will find you, Donnacha, as it did many of the Fianna in the days of old.'

'Would you not sense it, as you can sense it being used ahead?'

'No. The *draíocht* that might visit you or I is insignificant. It is almost gone on this side. Without deeds to mark it, you might never feel its presence. That is what has given me cause for concern. What I feel from ahead is as clear as stream water. We are travelling towards someone born into *draíocht*; someone who can control it here. There are Fae ahead. Have your bow ready and Donnacha...' she said seriously, 'it's time to believe the *draíocht* affects you because you will have need of it before long. If you do not have it, you may not be able to damage our enemy.'

Donnacha was both confused and a little bit hurt. He thought it was plain enough that all his hard work is what made him a great bowman.

Draíocht my bare arse, he thought.

Though he did begin to wonder what she meant by putting him in the same category as the greats of the Fianna.

They rounded a corner passing a long rolling hillock and the High King's fort at Tara came into view. Donnacha had seen it before, and it was clear Eimear had too, as she barely reacted to its grandeur. An enormous hillfort, big enough to fit the entire population of *Uisneach* inside its palisade. Four tall wooden towers stood skyward from each of the corners and the fort sat between them. A labyrinthine settlement that had grown around it, skirting the walls, was a marvel in its own right. Throughout the settlement large wooden watch platforms were placed strategically for guards to watch or cover the retreat of the inhabitants if the settlement was to come under attack. It was, simply put, a place where a lot of people lived. The smells that would normally accompany such a collection of people were strangely absent. Even more strange was the absence of people.

The track into the settlement gate, had been filled in with loose stone chippings repeatedly for fear that the ever-reappearing wagon ruts would dig their way to the underworld. The chippings had compacted and the horses' hooves clipping and clopping suddenly became the only noise the two could hear.

They stopped when Eimear's hand shot up again. She slid off her horse, threw her belongings to the side of the outer gate and buckled on her sword belt.

'There is no noise from inside,' she said. 'We need to make little ourselves. Leave the horse and bring only weapons and a mind to use them.'

Donnacha nodded and slid from the horse. As he removed his cloak and added his belongings to the pile, he watched the horses wander off towards a lush green patch. 'Are they going to be there when we get back?' he asked.

Eimear was standing looking at him with a strange gleam in her eye. 'Donnacha, my dear, if what I think is in this place, we may never see the outside of this gate again.'

ALE AND A CHAT

***

Eoghan and Cónán take an opportunity to socialise and get to know each other better.

Is fearr an t-imreas ná an t-uaigneas

Arguing is better than loneliness.

***

The next day the camp was quiet. Rhíona was in a deep sleep, and Eoghan was feeling grand altogether. He had sat up after dawn like nothing had befallen him. His head showed no sign of injury. They decided they would let Rhíona wake naturally. She was exhausted after healing Eoghan's injuries. Even the remaining marks on his face had disappeared.

The day passed slowly. The group checked and cleaned their weapons, changed and cleaned their clothes. They foraged, hunted, held hushed conversations and sat around for most of the day.

That evening, while Rhíona was still asleep, Cónán stood and said to Eoghan, 'I want a drink. You can come with me. There is a place we can go over towards the grasslands.'

Eoghan shifted uncomfortably when he found the finger pointed at him, and squeaked, 'Me? I don't have any interest in a drink, thank you.'

'Well, I can't go with Caoilte because he is going to kill me tomorrow. His girl would likely nag and drive me towards more drink; by the looks of what happened to you, the other one is Fae, and I might try and step on her. Your man with the swords has a face that annoys me, and so that leaves you. I'm not going on my own.'

'I shall join you should you ask it, Cónán. We have much to discuss of time's passed and there are many holes in life's story that sorely need to be filled,' Éine said, stiff and upright. Still, but there was an air of reconciliation in his tone.

'No.'

'Surely we—'

'I said no. If you go for a drink, I will stay here. I do not wish to catch up with you. Ever. You,' he pointed at Eoghan. 'Get up off your arse. Let's go.'

All eyes but those of the wounded Éine, were looking at Eoghan, who picked at a thorn stuck in his thumb. He knew he shouldn't entertain the idea, but also knew the tension within the group was thick. A quiet unease was gnawing at him since Cónán had joined, and he knew the others felt it too.

I can give them a break from the man at least.

He stretched his arms over his head, before slapping his hands down on his lap. 'Well, I guess I might go for a drink after all. Who can resist the possible pleasures of such charming company, and what is sure to be stiff wit and diverting convers—'

'Shut up and hurry on, boy. You're testing my patience.'

Rúadhan sat upright with a scowl creeping across his face. The movement did not go unnoticed. A gruff chuckle emerged from somewhere deep inside Cónán; deep enough that no hint of it appeared in his mean features. He turned and walked off. Eoghan put out his hands to warn Rúadhan away from silly thinking and followed after.

Though the walk was not short, not a word was spoken until after they arrived in a small drinking house in a small village. The small room was packed, but quiet as an elderly lady told a story about an enormous fish that longed to fly through a forest. It was obviously going down well because as the two sat on stools, the room erupted in uproarious laughter. The old woman sat po-faced, waiting patiently for the laughter to stop, so she could continue. This was clearly not her first telling.

Cónán asked a serving woman for four mugs of ale. When she asked him for something in exchange, he elbowed Eoghan roughly and nodded. Eoghan took his rings out of his shirt and presented one to the woman. She bit it and looked at them carefully, before smiling happily. As she made to leave, Cónán barked at her. 'Wait,' he said, and turning to Eoghan asked, 'Are you not getting a drink?'

Eoghan nodded glumly.

'Now girl, bring another four for him, and the same ring will do for the night, so no lip.'

The woman knew that to argue would be just plain ignorant. The ring was enough to keep the two swimming in ale for a week, if not more.

The two did not talk until the story had stopped and Cónán had drained six of the ales. Eoghan was still getting to know his first. The warrior sat up and cast his gaze around the room. 'Needa woman,' he muttered to no one.

'Perhaps you should stand in front of the room and tell the story of how you became the man you are today. I'm sure they will come flocking from across the land,' said Eoghan in a voice dripping sarcasm.

One eye focused on him for a moment, and Eoghan could have sworn he saw a crease around it that might have represented the beginnings of a smile. He finished a seventh mug in one go. 'Stay here,' he growled and slid off the stool. He shouldered his way through the room and disappeared out the front door.

Eoghan looked into his mug thoughtfully. He had had enough. Not just of this ridiculous set-up, but of the whole ridiculous set-up. He was fast becoming the butt of a bad joke and the thought had become unbearable. His lips drew back from his teeth in frustration as he reviewed his part since he left home with fruit on his back. The ale no longer appealed to him. It was time to go. He was as useful as tits on a bull to Rhíona and Rúadhan; the rest of them hardly knew he existed. He had dragged poor Rúadhan across the country because he didn't want to live his life. What was he now? What was he ever? What would this life bring him? Death. Probably within a week or two. Time to go home.

The night air was bracing after the overheating room, but he welcomed the feel of it. It felt like his cold resolve. He started to march back towards the shed when a strange sound in the otherwise still night air caused him to stop with his ears pricked. A muffled sound almost like a scream. It was coming from behind the ale house and his blood suddenly ran cold.

Where was Cónán? What was he doing?

The sound came again and was followed by others, sounds of distress. Eoghan was filled with fear that steered him towards flight. Anywhere but towards the sounds and what he imagined was causing them. His newly found resolve had been quickly forgotten. There was nothing he could do anyway. His head turned and he searched for a way to escape.

It was the gruff chuckle that changed his mind. He was walking before he knew it, quickly and full of seething fury. He had the scabbarded sword with him. He realised that it should not be there. He would never use it. He didn't know how.

He rounded the corner of the building to find what he had feared. Cónán had the serving woman pushed across a barrel. Her face was bloodied where she had resisted and some of her clothes were torn. He had dropped his trousers and was in the process of lifting the woman's dresses. It seemed that the chuckle's timing was impeccable.

A voice came from inside Eoghan that sounded just as full of revulsion as he felt. 'Leave her alone, old man.'

Cónán's head hardly turned. 'Get back inside and mind your business, boy.'

'Two-thirds of thy gentleness be shown to women and to those who creep on the floor and to poets, and be not violent to the common people.'

Cónán stopped.

'You are starting to grate upon my nerves, boy. That is not a good idea on your part.'

'Sneaking out of the drinking house to catch women in the dark like a whorecad. You wouldn't touch her if Fionn were here; you wouldn't even be in the drinking house, would you? It would never have crossed your mind. Why is that? Was he that much better a fighter than you, Cónán? Or was it something else. You were afraid of him, is that it?'

Cónán turned to face Eoghan. He pulled up his trousers again and buckled his sword belt. The shadows covered most of his face, and one gleaming eye was all Eoghan could make out. He was scared and unsure of how he would survive the conversation, yet he did not stop himself. He could not have if he had tried.

'Fearful and jealous because he was more of a man than you could have even imagined. *So long as thou shalt live, thy lord forsake not; neither for gold nor reward in the world abandon one whom thou art pledged to protect.* Did I get that right? Is that not one of the Maxims you swore to uphold? Neither gold, nor reward. Is that why you and your brothers plotted to betray him? Was it for gold rings? Maybe for women? Women bought and paid for obviously since you seem to have difficulty finding success with them short of rape.'

Cónán slowly walked towards him with his hand on the hilt of *Tairne Glas*.

'And now you are here, free from the shackles of those maxims that held the real you in check. The real cur that you are. The wretch that you must have worked so hard to hide from the Fianna, and from him. Do you think he knew when he would look in your eye? Did you have two back then, Cónán?'

Cónán stopped within a breath of Eoghan's face, his own breathing ragged. His stare bore into Eoghan's. His face was crimson, apparent even in the dim light.

'Are you not going to finish raping the woman or are you going to kill me first and then do it? Maybe you could do the two simultaneously. You were one of the Fianna, of whose exploits have been heard the length and breadth of the land; whose mighty deeds of heroism have become beacons in the darkened world, after which we might strive and improve ourselves. Surely stabbing the woman and I together would be no problem for such a valiant man as yourself.'

Something in Cónán's lined face seemed to soften slightly, just for a fleeting moment. 'I am no longer in the mood,' he grumbled. 'You can have her.'

He barged past Eoghan, but Eoghan was not finished yet.

'No, no, no, no you sick minded old fool. No, you worthless donkey, we need to talk, you and I. The world can change very quickly; sometimes a push towards that change is required.'

Cónán had stopped, still facing away, shoulders hunched. His hand moved to his hilt and the sword slid slowly out of its scabbard. Eoghan gulped down his nausea and pretended not to notice.

'You, girl,' said Eoghan over his shoulder. 'Go straight home and tell them what happened. Tell them what you heard and tell them that you fought him bravely. You did. You fought him off. They must not send anyone to try and reap justice or revenge because none of them will return. They will only bring harm upon themselves. Go and rest. You are safe now. I will deal with this wretch.' The woman disappeared without a sound and Eoghan continued.

'You cannot come back to my group, Cónán. You do not have my permission.' Eoghan's tone oozed finality. 'You go back to whatever hole you crawled from when we found you that day, but you will play no more part in our search, and when I do find Fionn, I will remind him of your real worth. So off with you. I'll tell the others what happened. Best of luck.'

He took a step forward towards the swordsman.

'Or. Kill me here and now and dance off with you then, because you surely won't be welcomed back without me. In fact, I suspect you might run into some most aggressive behaviour; and even if you manage to kill them all, you'll be back on your own anyway. So, do whatever you need to do but, make it quick and then be on your own again. I'm quite positive that you are the only person I've ever met who might find that company anything other than unbearable. I can't imagine how another single living soul would.'

Cónán turned. His face was still crimson but there was a new look. A strange mash of emotions. 'I need to come with ye,' said the old man whose voice was shaking slightly.

'Yes. Yes, you do,' said Eoghan as he walked closer to Cónán. Close enough to smell the ale on his fetid breath. 'And yet I am telling you no. No, because you are a wretch, a rapist, a traitor, and useless to us. Everyone there provides a service to the group. Even me, though I am no fighter or poet or hunter, nor am I brave nor clever nor wise; yet I try my best to be of service, when I can, and will prove my worth someday. I came here with you to give them relief from your presence. That was my gift to them.

'I know why you served under him, Cónán. It is because he was the great man you have never been and will never be. But maybe in days gone by, you strived, like I strive. Maybe you hoped, like I hope now. The reality of it must be a curse for you. You were the pitiful fool of a man that you are today, despite all the great men and women you surrounded yourself with. Only they managed to hold you in check, whereas all you do now is stumble around from one wretched act to another. Your sword is always at the ready, though, isn't it, Cónán? Your famous sword. Ready to cut the irritation of me annoying you out of your life, so you can get back to raping.'

The sword disappeared back into the scabbard. 'I am... I need to see him, if he still lives. I will behave myself. I swear it.' The eye was full of pleading urgency.

'Ah. I see it now. You need us. The thing is not only do we not need you, you stinking sack of shit, you are proving quite the burden, and not one of us knew of your pitiful existence until yesterday.' Now Eoghan walked past him. 'Your time is up. Do not return to the group.'

'Wait,' pleaded Cónán. 'Please. Eoghan, is it? Wait. Please. I beg you to reconsider.'

Eoghan rounded on the old man with fury pulsing through him. 'You are desperate. And you are weak; I am too kind to desperate weaklings and dogs. And so, it will happen like this: from now on you will answer to me, dog. You will be to me, as you were to him, as you were around your fellow Fianna. You will be a party to no decision making unless I ask it of you. You will cause no trouble, and give me no reason to regret your coming along, or you will be cast out to go back to whatever. Your place will be to serve our group and to aid when and where possible. I am telling you this because this is how it will be. You will answer to me and me alone so that none of this messy business need ever rear its head in daylight. More than that, you will swear it. From this moment forth, I am Fionn Mac Cumhal, until the day you meet him, or the day you draw your last breath. You are my liege man. That is your lot, or you walk away or draw your sword and strike me down.'

Cónán nodded slowly. 'You are dead wrong, boy.'

Eoghan suddenly grew cold, though he hid it well. 'What do you mean?'

'You said you weren't clever or brave. I do not agree.' The one eye gazed downward as if trying to bore a hole in the ground for Cónán to crawl into. 'I agree to your terms, boy. I will follow where you lead and will cause no trouble for anyone. I swear it to you. I will even try not to be a cantankerous prick from one day to another, but I cannot promise you a chirpy demeanour. I am... tired, boy. I am tired of the pile of shit that we walk on. I will follow where you lead, and we'll see where it takes us.'

He walked away into the darkness. When Eoghan felt sure he was gone, he unbuckled his sword belt and tossed it away. He knelt on the ground and took long deep breaths, so as not to throw up.

OISÍN AND CÓNÁN

***

Éine tells tales of two of the most famous warriors of the Fianna.

Eochair feasa foghlaim

Learning is the key to knowledge.

***

Rhíona woke up when Eoghan and Cónán were absent. She was hungry but in good spirits and pleased to hear that Eoghan had made a full recovery. She started eating and continued to do so at an alarming rate. While she ate, Éine stood to speak.

'I will tell you of Oisín. A fine warrior and poet in his own right and admired by many as having the traits of a great future leader. Fionn was prouder of his son Oisín than any of his other achievements combined and loved him fiercely.

'One day when the women and men of the Fianna stood near the hill of *Binn Éadair*, gazing over the bay where Caoilte and I cast our gazes but a few days ago, Oisín, whose eyes were the sharpest, uttered a cry and raised his hand to point into the distance.

'There they saw but a speck. And on the speck came and became a dot. And the dot became a spot. And as they looked and tracked it the spot became a shape. On it came and before any other could fathom what approached, Oisín noted that it was a rider. Streams of golden hair had she, for he could see that it was a woman. She rode no steed but the white horses of the cresting waves. No words could describe her beauty and Oisín could think of no way to sing of it neither.

'Oisín went to meet her as she set foot on the beach. A brisk breeze blew around her but neither her hair nor long white dresses were disturbed. She spoke and her voice was melodious and enchanting. None who heard it could resist her beguiling charms; none but Oisín, he himself a poet of unrivalled measure. Oisín and the lady spoke together and fell in love. Her name was Níamh, who would be called Níamh *Cinn Óir*. Some men wept as their eyes alighted upon her form.

'Her purposes for the visit on our shores were never made clear, but she begged Oisín to return with her to *Tír na nÓg* to involve himself in matters regarding the future of our land. Those present overheard talk of 'The Arrangement' with the Fae and those forfeits to be paid for meddling. None truly understood the meaning. Many did not seem to care, as they stood riveted in the company of such otherworldly and alien beauty.

'Yet Oisín trusted her, and the need seemed great. Before he left, he turned to those present and said he would one day return and rejoin the Fianna. He spoke with the breeze and promised that he would once again set things aright. But Níamh spoke to him, saying he could never again set foot in the land of *Éire* because our time is not their time, and our rules are not their rules.

'His words before leaving concerned his love for his father and for his young son, Oscar. He spoke of his countrymen and the need for future unity; a great kingdom replacing the many small ones, the great cost of ignoring the land and the animals. He spoke of a journey and how the first steps could only be taken by the few, to show the many the path.

'Then he was gone.'

Éine took a long breath in, and out, as if feeling lingering melancholy and a longing for those days long since passed.

'What of Cónán?' asked Rúadhan quietly. 'We have heard stories. Were they just stories or was there truth in them? You know... is it true about his back?'

Éine's brow furrowed.

'There are truths and trickery in any story ever told. The stories of the Fianna were never going to be told as they happened. When people tell stories about their heroes, both hero and story become larger than the facts.

'Cónán was Féinnid for many long years. His part in the great days of the band can never be disputed. More than any of his brothers, he was a believer. He was the butt of many jests, and jibes because of his rounded belly and his bald head. Cónán was a great warrior though and feared more than most. If you have heard stories about the days of the Fianna, then he was probably a part of it in some way, but since you asked me a question, I will answer.

'The stories about his back are mainly true, for it would have been difficult to concoct such a peculiar saga. There had been an exchange between him and the druid, Fergheal Seóige, from the northern mountains. Fergheal was an elder druid of great power and Cónán ended up being caught in a cottage after attempting escape. As we came to his aid, the druid rained fire down on the cottage. Fire that was blue and green, violet and red. Cónán had no way of getting out, and the cottage collapsed upon him. Some of the Fianna went to intercept Fergheal, there ending the firestorm. The rest of us went to aid Cónán, fearing the worst. The building was still burning when Fionn walked into it, knocking great piles of the wall away with his fists. There we found Cónán, badly burnt. His back was a ruin and we feared for his life. Fionn thought quickly and slaughtered a nearby sheep. He removed the fleece from the animal and put it onto Cónán, binding it onto his body with rope and dressing.

'Cónán became very ill. Some of Cónán's family blamed Fionn for him being in danger in the first place, and they were convinced that was why Fionn sat beside Cónán as he convalesced. It was not the truth. Fionn would have sat with any of us.'

Éine sighed a long sad breath.

'It took many long days for Cónán to recover, but the fleece had become a part of him in the meantime. The wool started to grow anew and does still to this day. He uses his sword to shear it when he can be bothered. Or he used to when last we were in each other's company. You might have noticed an... odour emanating from the man. The fleece is as much his now as it was the sheep's in many ways. You could ask him to see it if you wished, but I can assure you, it is no fine sight to behold.

'There are many unanswered questions when it comes to his part in the treachery of the Mac Morna brothers. He always claimed that he was not party to the plot. I always assumed we would never find out the truth. I cannot imagine he will tell us too much of it. Should he ever meet Fionn, however, I think that the truth will out then.'

The next morning Eoghan woke to find Caoilte standing over him. A gasp of shock escaped before he could stop it, and he was embarrassed.

'Excuse me,' he said. 'What can I do for you this morning?'

'I am led to believe that he is sworn to you in some way now.'

'He is.'

'How did this come about?'

'Conversation.'

'Do not think to fence words with me,' the rasping whisper warned. 'Answer the question.'

'You have your answer, Caoilte. What was discussed is between he and I.'

Eoghan felt his chin rising. Maybe that was what was called for. *Maybe it's time to tell the old men what needs doing and how.*

'I have yet to decide whether to kill him or not. I am leaning strongly in one direction,' growled Caoilte.

Eoghan stood and looked at Caoilte straight.

'You do not have my permission to kill him.'

Caoilte's eyebrows raised.

'I... do not have permission? From you?'

'I cannot make myself clearer than that. He is sworn to me. He is my man now. He has promised something, and I have promised something in return. If you kill him, you will break a promise I have made. I can only assume that you are considering my opinion on the issue because you were standing over me when I woke. You do not have my permission to kill him.'

Caoilte's face became stone and his eyes iron. Eoghan moved towards him a little.

'And… no more games. No more measuring. I know it was your sword that parried the blow by the waterfall. It must have been. You've been watching us. Testing us. You cannot talk so openly about how you plan to kill a warrior like him without possessing the means.'

Suddenly Caoilte's face softened a little.

'Clever, boy.'

'Enough of that shite too,' growled Eoghan now. 'You are not so far above the ground to speak to me like that. You were happy enough to sit on your arse, drunk, for many years. It's taken me days to get to where I can speak to you like this. It's taken me until now to realise I should have been speaking a lot more often. Afford me some respect. More importantly, afford Laoise some respect, Caoilte. Show her your pride, your love. There can be nothing gained hiding it from her. Not now.'

Caoilte stared blankly into nothing for a moment. Then his gaze locked onto Eoghan once more.

'So be it, *Canteóir*.' He nodded and promptly turned around to walk away. Eoghan frowned. Éine had said something like *Canteóir* before.

Caoilte stopped again a few paces away. Without turning around, he spoke quietly.

'I… am not what I once was. She will not understand that. Her Father let her down. Let us both down. She is looking for good in men. She thinks I can be the legend walking once again. I don't remember how. I'm not even sure I ever was.' He turned his head to look over his shoulder. 'I thought him dead. Fionn. I mourned his passing until the day you came to us. I do not know if I could look upon his face, if we were to find him. Not like this.'

He slowly walked away.

Caoilte did not speak to Cónán that morning. They barely looked in each others' direction. Eoghan felt that while he may have crossed a line with Caoilte, it was time to start speaking up for himself. Especially if there was to be another one of these strange old men in their company.

As they made preparations to leave, Cónán stood before him at one point and nodded slowly. Eoghan felt sure it was akin to a lengthy song of praise from such a man.

He had forgotten about it before too long as everyone was loaded onto the cart for the journey south. The notion of the boys going home did not arise.

THE FORT OF THE HIGH KING

***

Eimear and Donnacha come upon a slaughter at the fort of the King. Donnacha stands to face the first ambassador.

Ní bhíonn in aon rud ach seal

Nothing lasts forever.

***

It was apparent from the outset that the population of Tara was enchanted by a *draíocht*. Most of them were in a deep sleep, out of which neither Donnacha nor Eimear could revive them. The less lucky few had had their throats cut in their sleep; their fate seemingly decided by their proximity to the main thoroughfare up to the gate of the hillfort. Donnacha felt revulsion and the urge to adjust the bodies to make them more presentable for their inevitable discovery. Eimear was barely aware of them.

The hillfort loomed, silent, before them. The bodies that lined their passage made its silence conspiratorial. No flags flew, no animals sounded. Donnacha stopped his teeth from grating with a slow deep breath. The place was enchanted. He was walking into a story.

'Donnacha, have you heard the legends of Fionn Mac Cumhal and his deeds.'

'Every single one,' said Donnacha. 'I have known of the maxims since I was a little boy.'

'What of the story of the dark Fae prince Aill'en?' she asked.

Donnacha stopped dead in his tracks. 'You can't mean...'

'Every year at Samhain, Aill'en came to Tara and used his harp to cause its inhabitants to fall asleep. He would then burn the fort and town around it to the ground. Fionn came to Tara and stayed awake by cutting his own forehead with his spear *Birga*. The pain kept him awake and Fionn chased and killed Aill'en.'

Donnacha had caught up and was walking beside her but was still staggered at what seemed to be happening. 'He was not killed at all and has returned to burn the fort down once again.'

'No. If Fionn said Aill'en was killed, then surely that is what happened. He did not ever feel the need to speak lies or exaggerate for his own glory. Yet... this is Fae work to be sure. It is Aill'en's work. I am confounded. I have been asking myself why, and can only think of one reason that the Fae would seek entry to the High King's fort.'

Donnacha stopped again.

'The High King.'

'If the High King is dead, then he cannot provide assistance. He is also the only one with the power to raise an army to meet the gathered army of Uad. Without leadership, this fort is nothing more than an impressive building. It could take a season for a new king to emerge and by then I think our story might have taken a different path entirely. There is a very clever plan of action against us.'

Donnacha quickened his pace to overtake Eimear. 'We have to get up there fast. The High King must be saved and that's the height of it.'

Eimear stopped. 'He is dead already, Donnacha. I think, you go no further than here.'

Donnacha turned to face her. 'I do not understand what you mean and I'm not afraid to say that to you. And, might I add, I am not afraid to keep going so let that be said.'

'You will likely fall asleep if you go up there. I will not. I will go up there and chase whatever creature it is out. This spot here is a straight sight to the gate, where I will try to force the creature to go. I will not draw my sword today; this is not my fight, and would not be my time to do so even if it was my fight. You must shoot the thing if you can. If it comes this way. If the *draíocht* rests on your shoulders, then you might kill it. If it does not...'

'Then I am dead.'

'Well, I think I would certainly move and let the thing pass. I will try and give it good reason to move quickly. It does not know that I will not draw my sword.'

'How will you cause yourself pain enough to stay awake without it?' asked Donnacha.

'I will just use the pain that I have deep in my heart Donnacha. That has kept me awake many times before today.' She took off walking.

Turning towards him, she spoke, voice stern, 'I would stay ready were I you, bowman. You will have a very small chance, and things will happen very quickly indeed.'

He watched her pass through the gates and waited.

In his right hand he held the arrow he had chosen. The fletching was thin and fine. He stood at the end of a gently downward sloping avenue that was sided by houses and trading stalls all manner of shape and size. The wind would not be a factor. Slight adjustments would be needed, after he judged the size and speed of whatever came out the gate. The quiet around him in such a place as this, was strangely unnerving.

The Fae arrived at speed. Donnacha was stunned to see it looked little more than a child, and it made him pause before releasing. Long crimson hair and a painted face marked him alien. The Fae stopped when it noticed it had become a target. It turned quickly to check for pursuit, afraid of something ... *of Eimear? Why would this monster be running away from Eimear?*

Donnacha had no time to consider the thought further.

'Flee fool,' roared the Fae to Donnacha. 'It comes forth.'

Donnacha did not understand.

'Drop what weapons you have and stay put there,' he called.

The Fae started running again directly at Donnacha, apparently unconcerned by him, and the threat he represented.

Donnacha took aim.

The Fae let forth a furious roar as he threw a spear. Donnacha ducked from its path and the spear passed within a hand of his face. He loosed an arrow, which the Fae sidestepped. The Fae creature became a blur as he charged again. Donnacha lashed out with the end of his bow and caught the creature on the jaw. It was knocked off its feet but it sprang upright in a flash. Donnacha already had the second arrow released before the Fae could react. It travelled deep into the thing's body, and it howled. Donnacha shot again, the movement fluid and the aim accurate. The arrow pierced the thing's belly and he fell. The Fae tried to rise and looked questioningly at Donnacha with its alien eyes.

'It lives,' he gasped. 'You must warn the Fane.' Blood dribbled from his mouth. '*Sío* …' He lay back and died.

Donnacha saw Eimear emerge from the gate running impossibly fast to get to where the Fae creature lay. He walked to stand over the lifeless creature.

When he looked up at Eimear, she was looking directly at him.

'I have two pieces of news,' she said. 'Firstly, you are indeed touched by *draíocht* and have killed the powerful Fae, Aill'en, whom I thought dead. For you to have killed him, means you have attracted a level of *draíocht* akin to the mightiest Fianna. You are one of us now.' Donnacha felt like he might burst into tears as pride made his head light.

Eimear continued. 'Secondly, your High King is equally dead. I would suggest it is not something you would enjoy looking at.'

Donnacha put up his bow, head shaking, fingers numb. 'What... do we do?'

Eimear was silent for a moment.

'The first thing must come first. We need to wake these people up. In more ways than one.' She walked to pick up the spear and paused to examine it.

'*Birga*,' she whispered in awe.

'What?' Donnacha could not believe it.

'The spear Fionn lost as he battled Aill'en.'

'What? That spear?'

'Yes. Quite a weapon indeed. And we need to hide it for now. Perhaps forever.'

It took many hours for Donnacha to wake the townsfolk. The death of the Fae meant the enchantment had weakened, but the effects were still apparent. The people were left with no memory of what had happened and were in a state of bewilderment. Eimear had cleared up the scene no eyes should ever be made to witness, and then she went about finding the highest level of administrators who had not been slaughtered.

Donnacha went about organising groups to attend to the bodies of those who died, which numbered fifty-five men, women, and children. The townsfolk walked in a trancelike state and did as they were told, but nothing else. The terrible loss of life seemed not to affect them as it should. Donnacha spent much of the day crying or retching.

It was late into the night when a representative council sat in the long hall of the fort. Except for two, all of those in attendance were still bewildered and close to exhaustion. Donnacha had suggested that they might leave the gathering until midday next, but Eimear had insisted.

'We must do our business while they are still enchanted,' she said gravely. 'You must not disagree with anything I say and must help to convince them. It will require a modicum of dishonesty and trickery, but without the same, the day will surely be lost before it dawns at all. Bear in mind they are under a *geis* and will do whatever you tell them to.'

She studied him carefully as she said it. Donnacha was as bewildered as the Tara folk and so decided that nodding sagely and saying nothing might be in everyone's best interest.

A plump woman who identified herself as Cáit Tríona, the town chieftain, with grey ringlets stood to speak in the manner to which she was clearly accustomed. As she did so, Eimear stood.

'Sit, woman, and be silent.'

The chieftain was strangely obedient and did as she was told. Those nobles, landowners, cattle owners, and warriors gathered fell silent and looked up at Eimear transfixed. Donnacha found their enchanted compliance strangely enjoyable.

If only people were so agreeable all the time, he thought, *I would enjoy their company far more.*

'We have been invaded. I am Eimear and am an agent for your High King, Eochaid Mac Ennaí. I have been tracking the movement of an army at his behest over many long days. The black army of Uad of *Laighin*. The man who plans to invade Tara, kill every living man, woman, and child here, steal its cattle and become High King.'

Donnacha listened with his eyebrows raised, as enthralled as the others.

'This last night, I followed a raiding party attached to that army here to Tara. Before I could raise the alarm, they managed to murder many of our people as they slept. Among those murdered were King Eochaid and his family members. This happened just as the King concluded he was the target of Uad's malice, and he had started to make plans for the defence of Tara.

'I can tell you this, however, he was mistaken in his judgement. The armies of Uad are bent on only one thing. This island and its enslavement. This despicable act is only the beginning.'

Donnacha anticipated at least a gasp and was left disappointed. Eimear was putting on a show to rival Éine. Her audience however remained focused intently on her with little movement and no reaction of note.

'And so, his plans must go ahead, and we must follow them quickly and without fuss. We must make it difficult and confusing for Uad and do something that has never been done before. The new high king will be Niall Noígíallach's young nephew, Feradach Dathí, king of *Connachta,* and known by many as Náth Í. It will not be safe for him to come here and so Náth Í will rule from his own *túath* and not set foot in Tara until it is time for his successor in the future. Nath Í is loved by his people. The high king, Eochaid, was a fool for he did not ride out to meet this threat when it was required. He learned no wisdom warmongering in Brittany and Albion. This bold move is done from the womb of necessity and not done lightly. No high king has ever ruled away from Tara since the days of the *Tuatha De Danann* where Bres brought the Stone of Fal from the ancient city of Falias.

'The name of Eochaid will be forgotten, and record of his rule will be destroyed. His line will end now. After Nath Í, Niall's son Lóegaire will return the crown to Tara. The strength of leadership required in our land will be reborn in these two men and we will reap the rewards. Until Nath Í is crowned in *Connachta*, Cáit Tríona will rule in Tara, and see out this terrible crisis. The armies of Tara and its surrounds are depleted from raids abroad. I will lead what armies are left against Uad. We will fight him back to the sea. We must work at nothing else. I want to see the armies gathered on the plain of *Núada* in no more than two weeks. To be done in time, riders must leave tomorrow. When we wake in the morning, that will be our objective. Only after it is done, can we mourn our losses.'

She stopped and thought for a few heartbeats.

'Oh, yes. All the invaders were either killed or caused to flee by the man over there.' She pointed at Donnacha and everyone turned to look at him. He blushed furiously and squirmed slightly.

'Donnacha *Súl Seabhac* or Donnacha with the hawk's eye. Great hero, is there anything else these people need to wake up ready to do in the morning?'

Donnacha's mind raced.

'Eh,' he started. 'Remember to be very nice and kind to each other as much as you can and... and everyone should practice the thing you want to be good at if you really want to be good at it, if you were to ask me... so do... that.'

He looked expectantly at Eimear, who looked at him in return. She continued to look at him as she called a command to the others.

'Go to sleep. Tomorrow, you will feel right, and we have work to do upon dawn's arrival.'

She walked over to Donnacha and stood before him with a sad look. Donnacha misread it completely.

'I am sorry. I could not think of anything useful to say. I was overwhelmed, you see and very taken aback... but also impressed with the name you have given me, which I feel is a very nice compliment.' He took a deep breath and relaxed as the last of the people left the long hall. 'You are a remarkable person, Eimear.'

'And I wish I had met you sooner, Donnacha. I never knew that people like you existed,' said Eimear honestly.

They stared at each other for a while. His hand drifted towards hers, and she took it.

The River Gailleamh and the Great Lakes

***

Rhíona receives an unwelcome visit by a messenger, who has a questionable task for Rhíona to undertake.

An rud nach bhfuil leigheas air caithfear cur suas leis

What can't be cured must be endured.

***

As planned, they picked a suitable place to make camp by the river Gailleamh. Rhíona excused herself from the fire and went to bathe at the banks of the river, whose waters flowed from the great and ancient Lough Corrib. These banks had, in the past, watered and cleansed the aborigines, who had battled for ownership of the land; battles against the Fae folk, the *Fir Bolg*, the *Tuatha Dé Danann* and the Milesians; against floods and drought, frost and storms. Now it provided sustenance for a growing settlement situated where the river met its end and flowed out to refresh the Endless Sea.

Rhíona stood talking quietly to Laoise. They were surveying the area and Laoise pointed towards the lake. Rhíona nodded once, then twice.

Eoghan watched her moving away silently, emanating grace in each movement. The camp was quiet, and he felt now may be an opportunity to give her a chance to get to know him; for her to realise that they were similar in many ways. He stood and went to intercept her. Laoise was suddenly standing before him with the warmth of the fire still on his back.

'Rhíona wishes to bathe in the lake, Eoghan. You have no business following, and I'm shocked to my bones to think that you would think that you would.'

'I mean her no harm, Laoise,' Eoghan pleaded, looking over her shoulder at the retreating form of Rhíona. 'I'm only … I am a man of honour and seek only to provide a source of security should she wish it.'

'You are not a man, and your honour is not my concern. Her's is.'

Rúadhan appeared behind the two. 'Laoise, Éine has asked me to gather herbs and nettles for soup. I could use your knowledge. Come and walk with me, and help me search,' he said, winking at Eoghan.

Laoise's eyes, still locked on Eoghan's, narrowed.

Eoghan's face turned from a grimace to a smile. He leaned towards her and whispered, 'You go with him, and I'll go with her. I swear on the name of my ancestors, I will be nothing but a gentleman'.

Her eyes burned fire for a moment. 'Let us see where your honour leads you, young scoundrel,' she suggested quietly. Raising her voice again she said, 'It seems you boys are of a similar mind this evening. Yes, Rúadhan, I will go with you, to search for these herbs of yours.' And offering her arm they tramped off into the forest and the patches of undergrowth where they might find what they were looking for.

As Eoghan rushed away he overheard Rúadhan asking, 'What did he whisper to you just then?'

'It was not meant for your ears,' Laoise snapped 'Lead on.'

'Did he say something about me?'

'Yes. He said you were very nosey, like a puppy.'

Eoghan smiled and went to find Rhíona. He caught up to her where the forest met the reeds that bordered the lumbering river. She turned to face him as he approached. The sky behind her was a messy mix of orange, crimson, white, grey, and a deep comforting blue. It was hard to read her shadowed face.

'Can I help you, Eoghan?' she asked.

Eoghan felt himself blush furiously.

'Perhaps I can accompany you... so as...well... to perhaps provide you with... to act as a guardian from... that... those things that would wish to harm you?' Rhíona looked at him closely before smiling a strange smile tinged with sadness. She nodded slightly and continued on her way.

'You can trust me, Rhíona,' he said. *Why is she being so distant?*

She turned to face him for a moment, as if to examine him further. She turned back and was off again.

He followed behind giving himself a stern telling off for being such a muttonhead. He also felt a pang in his tummy. He wanted to be with her again. He longed for it.

Maybe by the river.

As they arrived at a place Rhíona decided suitable, where the reeds parted for a narrow stretch, and the riverbank and water were accessible, she turned to face her would-be protector. Eoghan stopped walking and stood facing her smiling happily, eyebrows raised in question. Neither spoke for a moment until Rhíona raised her eyebrows in return.

'Oh,' cried Eoghan and almost fell back retreating from the clearing. 'I'll be, eh, over here somewhere. You won't even know where I am. Not that you should be worrying though. Once you're behind the reeds I won't see a thing.' Eoghan cursed himself again.

Muttonhead. She actually needs to bathe.

'You know what I mean. You can take all your clothes off, knowing you have nothing to fear.' He sighed and walked away, ears red and burning.

He glanced back to see her turning away doubled over, almost drawing blood from biting her lip in an attempt not to laugh. He sighed and cursed himself for a fool. She moved to the river and disappeared behind the reeds on the bank.

Eoghan felt certain there was almost no real chance of danger here. He was true to his word to become her protector and scanned the area between the riverbank where his charge bathed and the thick forest copse. He picked up a fallen branch and began to remove twigs, so it was more like a sword. Maybe he shouldn't have thrown the other sword away.

It wasn't long before his mind began to wander. His imagination began to provide him with perfectly reasonable situations that would cause him to have to rush back to the aid of his helpless charge: a roving band of river pirates; an ancient river beast hungry for soft flesh; a trip and a fall causing her to be swept into powerful currents.

Anything to be with her once more.

His ears prickled attempting to forewarn him of any threat before it could manifest itself. The sudden onset of her singing made it extremely difficult for them to do so. Her voice rose over the tumbling sounds of the passing river and made the hairs on his neck stand. She sang a tale from times long past, where two young loves were caught up in a struggle between their feuding families; their running away into a bitter winter with only each other's strength to keep them strong and make them stronger. As he listened, she began to sing of the assassin her family sent to kill her young lover and return her to her rightful place. Eoghan felt sad as he listened and sadder as the singing suddenly trailed off before the end. He set himself the task of finding out what happened to the young couple.

Eoghan was unaware of the Fae creature that had appeared to face Rhíona among the reeds on the riverbank. She made no sound as the figure, no taller than three feet, moved slowly towards her with a wicked grin on his boyish face. She stood in the water making no attempt to cover her exposed body.

'I have no wish to speak to you,' said Rhíona, in a language not heard in the world for many years.

'Your wishes in the matter are forfeit, I fear, for a message from home, I was bidden to bring to you.'

'This is my home at present,' Rhíona answered. She checked behind her to make sure Eoghan had not followed.

'Say it is so, if that's what you wish, our opinions on this place are not matched.'

'Do not think to toy with me, Duillechán. Deliver your message and be gone to your shitheap.'

Duillechán's innocent features twisted into a less innocent smile. 'I do not like the way you speak to me, Lady. No matter. The Fand wishes you to know the end of your task is at hand. In assisting the men of this land, and their attempt to reignite the draíocht of old in their world, the Fane provides us with an opportunity to complete our withdrawal and destroy the links between our worlds forever.'

Rhíona was suddenly cold. A mix of emotions coursed through her body and her thoughts became a jumble of possibilities, some pleasing, some less so. She found herself thinking suddenly of Eoghan and the night in the clearing.

The Fae messenger continued. *'Stay on your course and steer clear of attention. The Fane has sent three. Caen is among them. Their presence will be the cause of great change in this place, but they will also hinder your progress in any way they can. Your new friends will offer no protection. His human slave is proving effective, and the Fane has rewarded him with a gift containing His power.'* Rhíona noted a curl in his top lip at the mention of her new-found guardians.

'I think that you are not correct there.'

'The crux of your business here is this. The last link between man and Fae folk will be found once more. You must ensure that he meets his demise, though many

others have tried and failed. He is not to come back with you. He will not be welcome. Once it is done, we will be free to close the gateways and to build our power anew, free from contamination. The Fane has spread himself thin in this ludicrous gambit, and our time to capitalise draws near. Take no chances. Kill him.'

'I do not know if I can. My view on what has been happening is changing. It is a complex situation.' Rhíona's mind was reeling. She suspected her mother had planned for Fionn to die from the outset. Rhíona would not have come had that order been given then.

'You will do as you are bid.' The innocence in his features now gone, *Duillechán*'s smile had become menacing. A long-nailed finger extended towards her. *'You have been amongst them too long. Make not a mistake; I have rejoiced in your leaving. We have been busy in your absence.'* His smile twisted his mouth.

'It is our chance to be rid of these wretches, so weak and full of insatiable greed; so vain and conceited. You will be a heroine the likes of which has never been beheld in the beautiful lands. You must do what you were born to do. You must close the gateway.'

'I can still close it by bringing him back. The draíocht will not spoil him there, like the others from here. He can join our cause.'

'Our? You and I do not share so many commonalities, I think. I have been sent here to tell you. To warn you. You know the punishment for disobedience. The Fand has spoken. You will obey.'

He turned to leave.

'There must be another way. I will not do what you ask. Do you hear me? Tell her. I will not do as she

asks.' Rhíona's voice had risen to a shriek. *Duillechán*, however, was gone.

Eoghan was admiring an incredibly clear rainbow, when he heard the shriek. Because of his daydreaming, it took him a moment to realise it was Rhíona. He sped towards the riverbank, hoping that his other companions had heard the shriek and would come to his aid.

As he burst through the reeds and saw Rhíona, she was naked and raging.

'Rhíona, what's wrong?' he asked frantically, while trying to drink deeply from the sight standing before him.

*Even more beautiful in the sunligh*t.

Rhíona suddenly seemed to notice his presence and snapped at him. 'Should a gentleman not cover his eyes?' she snapped, her manner strangely harsh.

Eoghan dropped his sword-shaped stick and his hands shot up to cover his eyes with a resounding smack. 'I didn't see anything.' he retorted. 'Well. Not this time. I mean… I did…'

'So, you now feel you have free reign to stare when it pleases you?'

Eoghan began to feel nauseous. His hands flopped down resignedly to hit his thighs. 'I'm sor—'

'Cover your eyes,' repeated Rhíona as she hastily began to dress.

Eoghan spun around in despair… just in time to see Cónán soundlessly materialise from the reeds with weapon in hand. Eoghan blinked. One moment there was nothing, then Cónán was standing there, sword glistening. It was *draíocht* happening before Eoghan's eyes. He had never seen anything like it.

Cónán quickly surveyed the scene. Taking into account the naked girl, the suddenly panicked expression on Eoghan's pale face, coupled with Eoghan's frantic gesture to begone, he clearly surmised that it would not be prudent to reveal his presence at this juncture. He dived back into cover almost impaling himself on *Tairne Glas*.

Eoghan whirled again to see if he had managed to spare the girl further embarrassment, just in time to see Caoilte soundlessly materialise from the reeds behind where Rhíona stood, *Lus an Chrom Cinn* dazzling in the light. Eoghan was baffled by how gracefully the old man could move. Caoilte scanned what was happening and assessed the danger. Rhíona would surely spot him if Eoghan didn't think quickly. He went to Rhíona, put his arms around her and kissed her before she could shriek.

Caoilte also quickly realised that his presence was unwarranted and let his legs go from under him to drop back into the reeds before he could be spotted.

Eoghan's heart leapt. Rhíona was kissing him back as she had in the moonlight. The kiss lasted only a fraction as long as Eoghan would wish, but a fine length by any standards. As he pulled away, though, still embracing, both were unsure what to do.

'I have to tell you something, Eoghan.'

It was then that Rúadhan erupted from the reeds close to them in as noisily as anyone could. He was brandishing a tree branch. As he came, he caught his foot on a protruding rock, tripped awkwardly and pitched forward into the river with a strange sound half way between a curse and a small child's yelp. He made an enormous splash and spluttered some more. As his body realised the temperature of the water, the curse vanished for a full-blown squeal, which would have had mothers rushing to check their infant children.

Eoghan released Rhíona and went to see if his friend was safe. Rúadhan stood up quickly, spitting out water. There were rips of stifled laughter from within the reeds. Eoghan erupted into laughter at the sorry state of Rúadhan. The reeds erupted too.

'A tree branch?' asked Eoghan. 'And the greatest weapons this land has ever seen strapped to your back?'

Rúadhan looked truly dejected. 'I forget I have them,' he muttered. The reeds were now producing gasping roars. Eoghan turned to see if Rhíona shared his amusement. Rhíona was gone and in her place stood a very angry looking Laoise.

TO BUILD AN ARMY

***

Eimear and Donnacha put their minds to the creation of a warband to face their poised enemies.

Ná cuir do leas ar cairde

Don’t let an opportunity slip from you.

***

Over ten days, Eimear oversaw the gathering of the warrior band that would fight Uad’s horde. Donnacha did the best he could to help. It was difficult considering his new-found hero status, and the hero worship that went with it. Eimear found it hilarious how uncomfortable he became when the admirers arrived. Each time he would struggle with the right thing to say, get frustrated and end up bright red and shaking his bald head.

The demise of the king had incensed the local population. However, the strength of incense waned the further away from Tara the messengers and summoners travelled. Each of the lesser kings and queens found reasons to send fewer and fewer warriors. They had their own *Túaths* to worry about - not to mention the cost of supplying warbands.

The band numbered just over two thousand. A fraction of what Eimear had wished for. She muttered about how things had changed and how back in her day there would have been five times the warriors gathered in half the time. Donnacha left her alone while she did it. As well as being overwhelming for him, it was frustrating to see. He too had hoped for more. For the people to rally when the land was in danger. Like in the days of the Fianna. Now, however, there was no name for them to rally behind.

Not that he cared. He had found this strange woman. Incredibly able and adept at just about everything she put her mind to. She was one of the Fianna standing before him. He loved her. The world was changing.

As the days went on it became apparent that the High King had not been idle when it came to Uad's army. Regular reports to Eimear came back from scouts and spies the High King had sent out weeks before. They began to learn more and more each day about the size and strength of the army, their whereabouts, and any signs of movement.

When Eimear heard the name of the leader of Uad's troops, she stalked off to be by herself. Donnacha could see she was upset even though the name was not familiar to him. That night he asked her outright and she brought him into her tent, sitting down on a wooden bench, and spoke to him in hushed tones.

'Moghrugh is a druid who has lived the span of many lifetimes. He is from a part of the land that is long since covered by mud and stone. He is an evil spirit in an evil body. He is cruel and brilliant in equal parts. If he is in the service of the Fae King, then we are in far more trouble than anyone ever knew. I do not know how our band can possibly best a strategist of his experience or cunning. He is more dangerous than most Fae.

'There is more. I had thought not to tell you, but as much as anything, you are a powerful warrior and ally, and you will be needed more than you can know in the days ahead.

'The Fae you killed was your friend Rhíona's brother, and one of the most powerful Fae to ever walk these lands.'

Donnacha stood up in shock, 'What? Rhíona's brother?'

'It is an incredible victory for us that he is dead,' said Eimear factually. 'He was one of the most devious and callous souls ever produced in either world, and has escaped death far too often. He did not perceive you as a threat, Donnacha, and that is why he is dead. You did what none of the Fianna ever achieved. Even Fionn himself, though he lost two of his greatest weapons in the attempt. Just remember what he did in the fort of the king. He and Moghrugh combined would have been a near unstoppable force in the days ahead.

'And there is more. I have had a report that I have kept secret from everyone until now. The spy that came to deliver it has been locked away in the cells of the fort at his own behest. He came upon Uad feeding a creature of darkness and shadow on an out of favour captain.

Uad ordered it to hunt 'her' down because too many of those hunting her had been lost in the process. Aill'en had appeared out of similar shadow and spoke with strange words to the creature and then it was gone.

'The messenger was barely able to speak from his fear, and rightly so. I do not know if it is possible, but there were stories once, whispers of a Fae creature, so evil that fear prevented most from acknowledging its existence. It was called the Unspeakable Beast and the stories of it disappeared. I do not know what it is or what it is capable of, but it is here, and it is hunting Rhíona.' Eimear trailed off.

Donnacha was pale when he spoke. 'I have a duty to try and protect them as best I can. Caoilte is useless to the world. He cannot wield his sword and they are being hounded and chased. I had felt a sense of dread for being away from them for this long. I know now that I must go to them, though I want to stay at your side.'

He had expected an argument, but none came. She sat and watched him. He sighed.

'I am learning, Eimear. Learning quickly, that those days of which I dreamed never really existed. Before the grand adventure I now found myself a part of had ever started, I had been a fervent follower of the *Féinnid* way. I had memorised all the stories and poems about the deeds of the Fianna and the way they conducted themselves. I had ached for those days to return, so I could test myself and maybe someday hear my name being spoken alongside those great men and women.

'Then I met Éine and Caoilte, and I heard the stories of what really happened back then, and my world started to crumble,' saying which, he sat beside her on the bench.

'I understand. I understand, too, that I must be a part of this in whatever way it plays out. But in a real way, where those men are as much a hindrance as they are a help.' He swallowed. His secret tried to leave his lips, so he kept talking. 'I will leave you and go to them because the need is clear.'

Donnacha felt a knot in his throat.

'I will gather as many as I can, until I hear from you. By bird or by messenger, send word of your need and we will move like the wind to be on hand and to help,' Eimear said quietly.

Donnacha's love and gratitude welled up inside him as he looked at her. But his guilt did, too. His pain stabbed at him. He felt he had to tell her the truth. He was almost overwhelmed with a sudden anxiety and had to tell her but then she would know.

What if she doesn't look at me like this anymore? Would that be just as I deserve? He drew in a long, ragged breath, before he spoke slowly and quietly.

'Eimear. I did something… terrible. Long, long before we met; when I was young and foolish.'

'Donnacha, we all have...' Eimear shifted uncomfortably in her seat.

'No please.' He rubbed his forehead roughly. 'I need you to know. It explains... being with you... I have never told anyone of it. I have tried to forget, and it has been eating me from the inside out. I understand if you do not love me after I tell you, but I must tell you and that's just that.

'I was young. I travelled around learning from anyone who would teach me. Anyone who shot a bow and arrow were teachers in my mind. I would feign ignorance like I was a novice with aspirations. I would ask them questions and watch their form until they would have no more of it. I would travel and work for whomever I was studying. I would work hard for them to make it worth their while. It was a good life. I was care-free.'

Tears tried to escape from him. He took a breath and dug his fingernails into the palm of his balled-up hand.

'I passed through a place, I can't remember the name at all, but I had been told that one of the young hunters who lived nearby was a fine shot, and because he kept sheep, he always needed help. I went there and lived with his wife and he for a time. They were a beautiful happy little family. Two children they had. Two.' His lips were turning down involuntarily.

'I was inclined to be a bit wilder than I am now. I would drink when the chance arose, and eat vision mushrooms, too, on occasion. One day I found the Faeleap mushroom, and I ate it thinking it might give me powers akin to the Fianna. I don't know how long it changed me, but that's what it did. It changed me.' Tears were streaming down his face now. His fingers worried into each other, and his knees bounced nervously.

'When I came back to myself, they were dead, Eimear. The four of them were dead and I had killed them in my madness.' He stopped for a moment and looked into the past. His head bobbed. 'They were cut into pieces.

'I had to bury them outside their home; a home they had asked the forest for. I had to set free their sheep that they had tended so well as to make them fat and happy. I ended their line and their lives, and I wanted to die.'

He looked at Eimear. 'I cannot remember doing it exactly, but every night I hear their screams and every night I listen to them to remember the man that I am.'

She stood looking at him, utterly devoid of any expression.

'And now, now I have met you, the screams have gone, and I can't remember them anymore.' His head bowed and he sobbed.

'I know about the screams,' she said, voice hollow.

'Wha… what do you mean?' asked Donnacha as he sniffled.

Eimear quickly shook her head and then put her arms around him.

'I love you. Remember my valley. Remember it and go back. No matter what happens to anyone else, stay alive and meet me there and we will forget the world together. We will bathe in nature and the land and become part of it.' There was a tear in her eye. 'We can help each other forget.'

Gazing at her, Donnacha said, 'I desire nothing more. I will drop my bow on the ground when this is over, and we will walk that path of yours and dance and make love and bore each other silly, and I'm not codding you there.' The good humour crept back into his voice as if telling his secret had released something inside him.

'But for now,' he said. 'I must go. I will send word when I can. You lead Eimear *Ceannasaí* – Eimear Captain. Let others do the fighting. It's not for you.'

'That, my sensitive, charming goat, is my exact thought. I shall ride the countryside on horseback and occasionally send people to their deaths on the battlefield.' She paused and considered. 'Tell Caoilte and Éine... tell them I hope they find what they are looking for.'

'Fionn, you mean?'

'Yes. Yes, I suppose that's what I mean.'

They kissed then and held each other until long after nightfall. At which time they decided it was too late to travel, so they made their way to Eimear's tent.

Revelations

***

Upon Donnacha's arrival back at the group, they discover the key to finding Fionn may lie closer than they thought.

Ní mar a shíltear a bhítear

Things aren't always what they seem.

***

Donnacha found them on the banks of the river on the morning of the fifteenth day. He was surprised to find they had been there for two days and was concerned it was a long time for their pursuers to gain ground.

As he began to point out his concern, he saw a lumbering monster crawl from the river, and gasped in alarm. The thing was the shape of a man but had only one eye and what seemed to be ragged wool covering its back; it was naked and foul, but slow and awkward. Donnacha took a bow string from his pouch and his bow from over his shoulder.

'Is anyone else armed?' he asked as calmly as he could manage, knowing that should the monster attack, he might not have his bow ready in time. A stench from the thing invaded his nostrils, burning tears from his eyes.

'Donnacha,' said Rhíona softly. There was a hint of amusement in her voice that left Donnacha perplexed.

'Donnacha,' she said again, and he turned his head. The rest of them were standing looking at him. The two boys were laughing behind their hands. Laoise and Éine were smiling broadly. Even Caoilte had a strange grin.

'His name is Cónán Mac Morna. He has joined our search.'

Donnacha's hands flopped by his side, and he turned again to look at the monster. The man straightened up and walked past Donnacha.

'Who's this gobshite?' he asked gruffly, as he pissed up against a tree.

Donnacha looked at the man's back. The white sheep's hair was wet after bathing and most unpleasant to look at.

'Cónán Mac Morna? I... do not understand.'

'It is a long story,' said Laoise, pity on her face.

Éine said, 'The young lady has made an astute observation; a long story it is indeed. There is need now of frank discussion, strategic planning, and a relocation. We are in danger of staying too long in one place. And I'm sure I speak for Caoilte and Cónán when I say we are eager to hear news of Eimear and how she fares.'

Cónán's head jerked around mid-stream, eye opening wide in alarm; face a mask of horror. The others did not notice. He looked from Éine to Caoilte and back again.

'I feel it is extremely important the man over there put some clothing on, as soon as he possibly can, and that's the bare truth, in fairness,' the bald one said.

Everyone nodded agreement.

Still, no one noticed Cónán standing in shock with a furrowed brow, piss down his leg, slowly whispering a name: Eimear.

'That's what happened up until Cónán gave me a bit of a start coming out of the water, so you did. I am sorry that I killed him, Rhíona. I don't really know how, but he was your brother after all. Eimear said you would not be too upset over it, and I hope that's the truth?'

The group sat, looking as stunned as Eoghan felt, as Donnacha finished his recounting.

'This little maggot killed Aill'en?' said Cónán, incredulously. 'Well dip my head in a bucket of rotten eggs and fish shite.'

'You might smell somewhat more pleasant if we did,' snapped Éine.

Eoghan put his hand up to cover the smile. Cónán looked at him and his leathery face reddened.

Rhíona spoke carefully. 'The notion of siblings and family as you see them and I see them are very different, Donnacha. Yes. He was my brother, but another will be chosen to replace him. Then he will be my brother instead. Our worlds are just so different. In ways that would cause you great confusion were I to attempt to explain. My brothers and sisters and parents alike, represent certain... forces. We are the tip of pyramids that, when bound together, become the one. The pyramids are all capable of movement, yet never really grow nor shrink. And so, the movement of each pyramid dictates the proximity to the centre of one, and the source of all power. Yet by coordinated movement of more than one pyramid, one can realign the centre to suit certain places.'

She stopped and raised her eyebrows. Eoghan wondered had anyone else the faintest idea what she had just said.

The others were looking at her, as silent as their looks were vacant.

Rúadhan broke the silence. 'Right. I think it's safe to say that our worlds are different, and we might just leave it at that.'

Rhíona's smile did not reach her eyes.

'Forgive me. I should stick to my own rules at least. Aill'en was not the only one of my family members who will aim to thwart us in the days ahead. The beast Donnacha spoke of is my brother, too. He is Caen. If he is here, then we are in the gravest danger. He is old beyond words. He is the most powerful of my brothers, and I am the least powerful of the sisters. His *draíocht* is violence and rage and mine is healing and care. We need to move.'

'Where do we move to? Four shiny swords aside, we are no closer to finding Fionn than when we began,' said Eoghan, arms and legs feeling suddenly weary. 'And now, we have strange beasts after us?'

'Moghrugh, too. A different kind of beast entirely,' said Cónán, quieter than usual.

'You know of him?' asked Rhíona.

Looking at the faces around him, Cónán grimaced. 'I was a young man, I almost served under him in a… campaign.'

'Almost?' said Rúadhan.

'I was a mercenary. I did what I needed to do to make my way in the world,' said Cónán as he turned his back to them, to gaze into the distance. 'The job seemed like a simple task and came with a handful of silver. I chose not to join them at the last moment. We had a disagreement.' He turned back to them and tapped his eye patch.

'Why did you choose not to join them?' asked Eoghan.

Cónán stretched his neck, arms folding. 'Contrary to what some of you think. I'm not a monster.' He looked around at them all. 'Not fully anyway.'

The group went quiet.

'So where do we go? How do we decide?' Eoghan asked, straightening out his shirt.

'What was it that the witch told you?' asked Rhíona, 'One of either Cónán or Eimear already knows where Fionn is.'

'Well,' said Cónán. 'It most certainly isn't me, so that leaves her. And I do not think we should be going near Eimear. Ever.' He looked at Caoilte for a few moments. 'I'm surprised anyone thought it was a good idea to disturb her.'

Caoilte looked away and took a long drink from his waterskin.

'It is my understanding that she left the ranks of the Fianna, did she not?' Rhíona asked.

Nodding, silence, and strange looks came from all three of the former Fianna.

'And so, it stands that he might not have had the foresight to tell her where he would go, should his world turn upside down. It stands more to reason that he would tell you, Cónán.' She stood and went to face Cónán.

'Well, he didn't, so that must mean you are wrong, little girl.'

'Well, perhaps you are correct, but perhaps you might let me try and jar your memory to see if, in fact, you do know something?'

'Well, why don't you try and jar my hairy throbbing co...'

'He will be pleased to answer your questions as well as he can,' said Eoghan.

Éine's grin oozed malice. 'You two boys continue to impress and amaze. I especially enjoy the manner in which you have been training your new pet, young Eoghan *Canteóir*, speaker of truths.'

Eoghan fixed him with as hard a stare as Cónán. 'I trust you will attend to your own business and allow our arrangement to remain free from external pressures, old man.'

If Éine was taken aback by Eoghan's sudden venom, it was not obvious, though his eye's narrowed. 'I can think of some external pressure I deeply long to apply my young companion…'

Eoghan's eyes narrowed. Cónán's one eye did the same. Eoghan took a breath to speak, but Rhíona spoke first.

'The last time you spoke with Fionn at any length. When was it?'

Cónán appeared irritated to be diverted so obviously but did his duty.

'I do not recall. It was a long time ago.' Rhíona asked the same question again. 'The last time you spoke. Tell me when it was.'

It felt like there was a palpable pressure on Eoghan's shoulders, as she asked the second time.

He needs to answer her.

Looking around, it seemed to Eoghan that everyone was eager for Cónán to answer the question, as if they wanted Rhíona to find out what she needed to know. It was only fair after all. The pressure on their shoulders seemed to be felt by Cónán too. His face scrunched into an ugly mask of concentration. Eoghan spotted Rhíona's fingers dancing gently.

Draíocht.

'There were a few fireside chats with others present. One or two alone, and one alone outside *Corca Dhuibhne*. They are the only ones I can remember. There were probably others.'

'What did you talk about? On any of those occasions. Consider what you discussed with him.'

'We talked about me, as we usually did. I would tell him things, and he would listen. Now that I think of it, a lot of our talking in those days concerned...' he looked around, self-consciously. 'Well... I was talking to him about me... someday raising a family.'

The way he said it caused Eoghan a moment's pity for this lonely old man; a man who surely carried his own weight of gnarled and withered memories, which would haunt him forever. Éine laughed gruffly, as if the thought it was both funny and ludicrous. Cónán started to redden, either from rage or embarrassment.

Donnacha broke into the uneasy silence, 'It is something we all think about, and talk about far too little. You were showing wisdom, and I don't mind in telling you. Feelings about family reveals a lot about a man.'

Cónán looked at Donnacha as if suddenly noticing him for the first time. Before continuing, 'Fionn was always talking to people about themselves. He was good at listening and wanted to know. Or maybe he was good at pretending he wanted to know. He would tell you anything about himself that you...' Cónán stopped as a thought struck him. His head jerked up to look at Donnacha and he said, 'Feelings about family reveals a lot.'

Eoghan watched, looking from him to Rhíona, to see if she was aware of something they were not. The pressure from her was getting stronger.

'There was another time. After the black days of *Síor Feargach* but before the end; before the battle. It was nothing then, but...

'It was as we marched on the way back from the southwest up through *Corcu Ochae* and *Déis*. He and I had been talking a week before about a family and a bit of land somewhere to raise them in peace. A piece of land to live on, die on, and be buried under. So that someday, my children and my children's children could join me, if it pleased them. It was nothing, but as we passed the plains south of the mountains and near the caves of Fintán Mac Bóchra, I passed him. He was stopped, looking across the plains and bog lands where the caves lie. He didn't turn to me as I was passing and quietly said something like "plenty of space to rest in there" or "enough for us all in there" or something like that. I... I don't remember, I was hardly even listening to him and just kept walking thinking he wasn't talking to me. But... maybe he was. Maybe he was saying that is the place his family could lie. Yes, his children and grandchildren, but the Fianna to boot.'

Everyone was standing except for Caoilte. When Eoghan looked, he saw the old man shaking his head with his eyes closed; seemingly unwilling to listen to what was being said.

'Was he talking to you, Cónán? Cast your mind back to that moment, as you walked past Fionn. Was he talking to you?' The invisible pressure made Eoghan want to sit again, but his heart was pounding.

Cónán looked at Eoghan, his unspoken message clear. *If I wasn't here, you never would have found him.*

'He is there. In the caves.'

Caoilte rubbed his agitated looking face with agitated looking hands.

'Can you bring us there?' asked Rhíona. 'Do you remember the way?'

'Yes. The plains of *Capall Liath* are rugged and lonely. Few travel that way as it is difficult to pass. If we can find it, there is a path that leads through them. An ancient pathway from days of old. It must pass close to the caves, but it is said to be a cursed place. A place to be avoided. The caves have long been said to be the fort of a Fae king. And as the saying goes "where the Fae *Rí* plays, be *draíocht*, despair, and death".'

The group exchanged glances. Eoghan felt an urgent sense of purpose filling them. The pressure was gone. Eoghan's relief was mixed with renewed urgency.

'We have a way,' he said. 'Rhíona. We have a way.' He looked at Cónán and nodded slowly. Cónán stared at him for a moment, before licking his lips.

‘So, we might meet him again,’ he said. ‘After all these years. After all that happened.’ He hawked and spat, as if he had tasted something foul.

Rhíona was shaking her head. ‘At last,’ she said. ‘An end presents itself.’

‘Where is my grandfather?’ asked Laoise.

They all looked around. No one had noticed his leaving.

Rúadhan spoke. ‘Probably pissing. We need to be moving now. As delightful as you are, Rhíona and you are wonderful and all-round good company, I do not fancy the thought of meeting your angry hairy brother.’

Rhíona’s face became very serious. ‘You most certainly do not, Rúadhan.’

‘Then let us get gone.’

They later found Caoilte near the water, as drunk as an ass. He stood looking into the lake humming a terrible song of sadness and loss. Laoise was struck dumb.

Rúadhan followed and the others were not far behind.

‘Caoilte? What are you doing? We know where he is at last. We have to go, and we need you,’ he said.

Laoise stood with her hands slumped by her sides.

Donnacha brought the wineskin Caoilte drank from on his horse. Caoilte had lifted it when no one was paying attention.

‘You are a child, you little snapping fool,’ he said to Rúadhan, his voice came as close to roaring as it could manage. ‘You are excited and self-important and a nobody.’

Caoilte stood bolt upright when he saw the others arriving.

'What are you all at? Why are you looking at me as if I'm in the wrong? Me?'

He turned to the teary-eyed Laoise.

'I love you, Laoise,' he whispered, 'with all my heart. I love you, but I am not Caoilte anymore. He… will see me and know how far I have fallen; how weak I have become. I... cannot let him see me. He knew about my doubts. He had such… faith… in me.'

Caoilte pointed at Éine, and then Cónán. 'Us. He stood behind all of us when we were nothing. Will you go to meet him now? You Éine, who ran when he needed you? You Cónán? You, who betrayed him?'

He looked up at the sky.

'Sh. I am the nobody now. Don't you see, girl? I'm not a hero hidden by the years. I was never a hero. I was always just pretending. He knew. He cannot see me like this… No, no, no, no.'

Caoilte had the daffodil blade dropped near him. Staggering over to it, he picked it up and drew it. He tossed away the scabbard and examined the sword unsteadily. 'I wish you had left it to rot, Laoise. I wished you had cared for it as little as I do. I am nothing and your time caring for this was nothing,' he screamed. He took a couple of long steps and hurled the sword into the lake with all his might.

The sword made an unremarkable splash and was gone.

He turned abruptly.

'I am going home. Do you want to come with me, Laoise?' Laoise looked at him as her heart broke into pieces. 'I am going to go. I am leaving, Laoise. I want you to come back home away from this.'

Laoise just shook her head as giant globs of tears ran down her face into her open mouth and she cried soundlessly.

Caoilte straightened up as best he could.

'So be it. Farewell, granddaughter.' He staggered away, calling over his shoulder, 'Éine get ready and let's go.'

Éine stood watching the girl's heart breaking for the second time in his life and was filled with that same self-loathing and despair faced by his oldest friend. She was the most capable and ferociously independent person Éine had ever met. All she had ever wanted was someone to stand by her as an equal. Éine and Caoilte could never have managed matching up to how she had viewed her father. Even after he left. Éine could not leave her now. Not this girl that he loved so dearly. Not even for Caoilte.

Caoilte stood looking at Éine. 'You're staying, so? Is that it?' he rasped. 'Stay. I'm going.'

He took one last look around at six faces watching impassively and one face covered with shaking hands. He turned and trudged off.

Rúadhan put his arms around Laoise. She tried to embrace him but the weapons on his back made it difficult, so he quickly shrugged them loose. They held each other quietly. Cónán spoke gruffly.

'I don't think they are meant to have an audience for times like this. It's probably difficult enough for the scrawny one to rise to the challenge, as it is,' he said.

Rúadhan looked at them from one face to another.

'So, Caoilte is marching home drunk. His sword is gone. What now?' No one spoke.

He looked at Eoghan. 'Start walking and we'll catch up.'

Eoghan turned and did as he was told, walking south towards the southernmost stretch of the great river, and the caves Cónán told them about. Rhíona, Donnacha, Éine, and Cónán followed. The older men were grim; silent as they walked. Donnacha led his horse shaking his head.

Rúadhan whispered into Laoise's ear. 'It's just as well, really. He never would have approved of us anyway.'

Laoise's face was teary, and her nose was snotty. She wiped it with the back of her sleeve, making her eye paint smear across her face.

'Tell me I'm beautiful,' she said with a broken-hearted smile.

'Certainly, most of the time, you are so beautiful you make me want to cling to you like ivy and grow strong from the light of your face.'

Her nose wrinkled at the horrific attempt at poetry.

'At the moment however, you more than slightly resemble a hedgehog that has suffered a most grievous bout of chills. That said, I also happen to think that is beautiful.'

'You find hedgehogs attractive?'

'In a certain light, most definitely.'

'I think you are quite a moonchild a lot of the time.'

'I will take care of you if you will take care of me, too.' Rúadhan's face felt serious, and his lips were dry.

'I will.'

'Settled. How should we start?'

'Kiss me.'

‘Perhaps you might just wipe your face a little bit more with your sleeve. It’s still got quite a few... wet bits on it.’

Laoise slapped his arm. Rúadhan then wiped her face with his own sleeve, which left her standing agape.

‘See? I’m minding you already,’ he said with a sly smile.

‘You are quite a scoundrel,’ she said still feigning shock.

He kissed her. She kissed him back.

‘It is just as well that I had asked you to do that, or you would be in grave danger.’

‘That’s my girl,’ he said as he held her close once more.

‘You are correct,’ she whispered, and he was.

PRACTICALITY, PROXIMITY AND PREDICAMENT

***

Wheels are in motion and an end is in sight. The group splits up again. Caoilte dies violently.

An rud a ghoilleas ar an gcroí caithfidh an t-súil é a shileas

What pains the heart must be washed away with tears.

***

When Rúadhan and Laoise caught up, the others had stopped. Cónán looked bored and disinterested. Éine fumed. The other two looked like they had been fighting. Donnacha was speaking.

'If you were to ask me, perhaps we're not going about the decision the right way. Telling people what to do can upset them, if you can see that from here.' He scratched at the back of his head.

'What is happening? Why are we not moving?'

Éine said, 'My young man. You and Eoghan have been the source of inspiration for us all throughout these last few weeks. There is, however, a need now. We need to send word to Eimear where to bring the army in case Uad manages to discover Fionn's whereabouts first. My point was merely this: where better to do it from than in the safety of one's own *Túath*? You two can attend to an urgent need, yet also to go back to safety. And now it seems, your darling friend Eoghan wishes to stay amongst us.'

'You need us,' said Eoghan.

'You have told us that already, Eoghan,' said Rhíona, standing in front of him. 'Yet you are not thinking clearly. Maybe it is time for you both to go home.'

'Are you so eager to be rid of us? Of me? Have we not proven our worth yet?'

'Can we not do this while walking?' growled Cónán. 'I am in agreement with the scrawny one's thoughts on the angry hairy brother.'

'You are not being fair to me, Eoghan,' said Rhíona. 'I am only trying to look out for you and your safety.'

'I'm not going either, if it helps to clarify the issue,' said Rúadhan. All turned to him. 'It turns out that I love Laoise. I will go where she goes.'

Laoise blushed furiously. 'Aren't I the lucky one? It is his subtle discretion that I find so irresistible.'

'Well, I am only delighted to hear of it,' said Donnacha, delighted indeed. 'As someone who has only recently discovered the joys of love, and the hardship attached with leaving her behind, I say good on the two of ye, and twice again.'

Éine gasped. 'By the raging hound of Culann, the youth of today are a confusing group indeed.'

Rhíona spoke to Eoghan. 'I cannot allow myself to be the cause of your death. Nor Rúadhan's. Nor any of yours for that matter.' She shook her head as if to clear it.

'In fact, perhaps it is time that I continue the last part of our journey alone. There are forces in play here that are larger than us all. I have involved you all in something that I should never have done. I have dragged you across the land away from your homes and your lives. I...'

'This is our life now,' said Eoghan matter-of-factly. 'No one is here against their will, Rhíona. The only one with questions has left us. Laoise and Rúadhan both agree he should stay. I don't know what I can do to help… I'll be there… for you,' he trailed off.

He turned to address Éine with a hardness around his eyes. 'We stay. The message needs to be delivered; I suggest that you go. You have no interest in violence or danger and we will be walking towards it presently. That said, the message is as crucial as Eimear's presence, so you will need protection.'

'So be it, *Canteóir*. If you wish to argue this to the end, let us do it.' He pursed his lips in thought.

'Cónán will accompany you,' said Eoghan. 'When you have delivered the message successfully, you can return to us. Neither of you will be the focus of attention I reckon. You will not need to carry on if it has gone awry.'

Eoghan did not wait for an answer, but turned to Donnacha and asked, 'Can I assume you want to continue?'

Donnacha nodded 'I am staying. I mean I am going with ye, is what I mean. So yes.'

'Then give them your horse. If you travel on horseback, you can reach *Átha Luain* before long and ensure a way that Eimear gets the message. You can be a part of this to the end, Éine, and steer clear of the worst danger. You have been involved in enough of that already. Is that acceptable to you?'

Éine nodded slowly. He said nothing looking at Eoghan with narrowed eyes.

'And you?' Eoghan asked, looking at Cónán.

'Angry. Hairy. Brother,' said Cónán.

Eoghan turned to Rhíona. 'Now is not the time to be alone. Now is the time to accept the help from your friends and get to where we need to get. And with any luck, not meet your brother.'

Rhíona was not given the chance to respond. Eoghan walked past her, followed by the couple and the bowman. The other two accepted the horse, clambered on and were gone.

Caoilte staggered. It had crossed his mind several times that he was lost. Having thrown the wineskin in a ditch hours before, his head was beginning to clear. He would need to find some other way to deal with his ferocious thirst.

A voice deep inside whispered at him to go find the sword and help his beautiful Laoise.

He scolded the voice for doubting him. It was only a question of getting a full wineskin for the journey and he would go back, find the group, and make his apologies.

It had felt good to have his sword in hand in the hall of the queen. He felt younger than he had in years. Now he was back to himself, he would take control of his drinking again. He could grow in Caoilte's boots once again.

Boots that had something in them. He found a large flat rock and sat down, dragging off a boot. He started to hiccough and grimaced. He hated hiccoughs.

The boot was empty but he thought it prudent to have a good root around to make sure.

As he brought the boot down, he found a giant shape blocking the sunlight from him. He looked up and his hiccoughing stopped.

'So, you're the Fae's brother,' he growled quietly. 'If I had my sword, I would make you...'

Caoilte's supposition became his final words.

Éine and Cónán came to an agreement early on that they would ride the unfortunate horse in silence; yet not before a few issues were addressed. Both had realised early enough that if they got another horse in *Átha Luain* and rode hard, they would likely arrive at the caves with or before the others.

Both had also realised they would be spared the company of the young folk who were becoming quite unbearable for the two cynical old men and had rejoiced at the thought. More importantly they realised no matter what happened, they would be present when Fionn's whereabouts was discovered. It was possible to probable that it represented the first peaceful and mutual agreement the two had ever reached. They celebrated by maintaining silence until they reached the rattling old wooden fort of *Átha Luain*. The fort and palisade had fallen into a state of disrepair after years of peace and prosperity. A warm and bountiful market spilled out from around the walls.

Éine knew someone who could help to deliver the message. Dióraeg was a man of trade who loved gold more than most. He would have to do. Eoghan staying on also provided Éine a chance to build on his work at the camp of the robbers.

They dismounted some way from the fort, tied the horse to a sheltered tree with green grass surrounding it and walked in. *Átha Luain* was an agricultural centre for many kingdoms and *Túaths* and the market around the fort was a wonder of the land. If one needed something, it was probably there.

Éine sent Cónán to buy a second horse and meet him at the blackberry baskets as quickly as possible. He then proceeded to walk as casually as he could manage through the market. The warriors of Uad were mingled through the crowd, wary and alert. Éine walked tall and proud as if having nothing to hide and did so until he came to a world weary looking young man selling pottery mugs and bowls. His curly black hair was tousled, and his clothes were dishevelled.

'Have your prices come down from the elevated heights at which they flew when last we met?' Éine asked loudly.

The young man responded in guarded hushed tones. 'You have been a busy old trout.'

'Are you aware of the army outside Tara?' asked Éine quietly. The man nodded.

'And the army of Uad?' Another nod.

'Have either broken camp?'

'I do not know,' came the reply.

'I need to get a message to Eimear at Tara, and I need it done extremely quickly. Three independent messengers will be required, Dióraeg.'

A gold ring flashed briefly landing in a bowl near the man's hand. Dióraeg placed another bowl on top.

'Tell Eimear she will be needed, post haste, on the Plains of *Capall Liath*. Do you know where they are?' Dióraeg nodded again as his eyes darted, scanning the crowds for any curious onlookers or worse.

'The caves of Fintán Mac Bóchra?'

A curt shake of his head signalled no.

'She will know them. Tell her there is no longer any need for secrecy. Things, it would seem, are coming to an end of some kind. And tell her to make it quick.'

Dióraeg made no move to suggest he had either heard or understood.

'The messengers will be gone by the time you have left the market,' he said.

'I am pleased to hear it. There is one more thing. Have you heard tell of Eoghan *Canteóir*?'

Dióraeg smiled slyly. 'Is that your work?' Éine nodded.

'I have heard his name mentioned in two stories. There are stories of beasts, Éine, and the Fae. Stimulating stuff entirely.'

'Good. I want the messengers to do a second thing. Once they have delivered to Eimear, I want them to reach as many ears as they can on their return journey. Tell them to speak of the Fianna and Eimear *Ceannasaí*. And tell them about the words of Eoghan *Canteóir* and how a change for the good will come from the seeds his words are planting. Make sure they speak of his rising from a common home to become the new great leader of our time. The next Fionn Mac Cumhal. The Fianna are to rise again...'

Éine turned on his heel. He made his way back towards Cónán with a distinct skip in his step. It seemed that the stories of Eoghan *Canteóir* he had concocted and told at Seán Seosamh's fire that night had grabbed hold of some imaginations.

A good story will lead the way, he thought, very pleased with himself.

There was a commotion ahead of him and he made ready to bolt. *Not Mac Morna. Not today.*

Sure enough, there was Cónán surrounded by two dozen dead bodies with an arrow in his back and another dozen bowmen aiming at him from point blank range. His one-eyed gaze caught Éine's, as he allowed his sword to be taken, and then he was led away.

Dióraeg stood in the clearing where he had arranged the meet. He scanned the tree line. Nothing. He was on edge with dry lips and shaking, sweaty hands. He was kept waiting for far longer than he would have liked. He scanned the tree line once again, this time there was a hooded figure standing there. Dióraeg almost jumped. It was as if the figure had appeared from nothing.

'Is it you?' he asked, fearful now.

'A strange question indeed, young man. I suggest that everyone is someone and therefore anyone in this place answering yes to the question would surely be telling the truth.'

Dióraeg did his best not to show a reaction.

'I have news that I know you wish to hear.'

'Why did you not come to visit me in my warm and welcoming home, instead of skulking around here in the forest.'

'I have seen the way your warband conduct themselves. They are too quick to violence for my personal taste. I find that the less of them there are around me, the more I can relax and not fear for my life.'

'So be it, young man. What news have you for me?'

'The *scealaí* came to see me.'

The hooded figure laughed. 'The old one has been busy.'

Dióraeg went on to deliver the same message that Éine had given him to the hooded figure.

'Eoghan *Canteóir*? The name is not familiar to me,' muttered the hooded figure to himself. 'Eimear, I have heard little talk of, and I have been aware of the army for a time now. The plains of *Capall Liath*. I do not know this place.'

'If I might distract you from your thoughts a moment longer,' said Dióraeg.

'What?' snapped the hooded figure.

'I am not interested in any further dealings with you. I have an interest only in the payment discussed.'

This seemed to renew the mysterious figure's interest. 'You have no interest in the lands around, young man? No concern for the welfare of those people on this island?'

'Those people mean nothing to me. To feign interest would either be a nonsense or self-indulgent. I want to improve the standing of my own children and their children thereafter. There are too many kings in this world, and too many others who wish to be one.'

'It is not long before there will be one king and no others. A king of kings.'

'It will mean nothing to me. I'll have to get off my sleeping pallet every morning anyway. My business is with my own kin. Did you bring my reward, or do you plan to kill me?' Dióraeg asked outright.

'Deliver the message as you have been paid to do.'

A purse appeared from inside the cloak and was tossed to land at Dióraeg's feet. He picked it up and walked away.

THE CAVES AHEAD

***

As the group get nearer to the caves, events ensure that not everyone makes it to meet Fionn.

Ní bhíonn an rath ach mar a mbíonn an smacht

There are no successes without discipline.

***

They reached the great river, but a ferry crossing past *Déis*, that Éine swore had been there when last he visited did not exist anymore. It took them a day and a half to find another ferry crossing. They brought the cart across the river, though they had to pay extra for the risks involved in ferrying over very choppy water.

They reached the plains between *Uaithne* and the southern slopes of the mountains. Though the mountains were by no means the tallest in the land, the range was wide enough that finding the caves might take time. In one direction, the grassy plains stretched as far as the eye could see. The other, was the beginning of bogland.

'In hindsight,' Rúadhan said to no one in particular, pulling on the reins to stop the cart. 'It might have been wiser to bring the two among us who could identify the caves' location. Sending them away was a mistake.'

'Ah now, Rúadhan, don't be like that, in fairness,' said Donnacha. 'There is a pathway through the boglands. We just have to find it. It's here somewhere.'

'We haven't even looked yet,' added Laoise.

'So, stop being such a badger's arse,' growled Eoghan. 'The mountains are tallest towards the bog. It stands to reason the path would be through the bog. It's also reasonable to consider the caves might be in the taller hills.'

Rhíona nodded. 'It stands to reason, Eoghan.'

'Then this way,' he pointed.

The cart lurched forward. Travel was painfully slow. Every time they seemed to make progress, they would come to a wall of jagged rocks rising from the swamp and have to double back. When they made camp to eat, they were unable to light a fire because the small amount of wood they found was sodden. Rúadhan suggested they break the cart up and burn that, but it was not entertained. As a sullen silence descended on the group, wolves howled in the distance.

After a day of searching, they decide to backtrack to the plains. Tempers were short. They were nearly back to where the plains met the bog when Rhíona stood, eyes narrowed.

'What? What do you see?' asked Eoghan.

'There,' she pointed. 'Those trees there. Look at them.'

All eyes followed in the direction she was pointing, and they saw a gap in the tree line that might be a path. On either side, there was sporadic brush and copse, but mainly marsh and bogland. The hills behind them were low and sullen.

'That's it,' said Eoghan.

'Let's go,' said Rhíona.

'Oh no,' said Laoise.

All eyes now turned to look and see what she was looking at. In the distance, a group of ten warriors on horseback were closing fast. The noise of the hooves reached them. As they approached, the riders looked like a black many-legged creature, wild with intent.

'Go, go, go fast,' said Donnacha and Rúadhan lashed the reins. The cart took off, groaning from the strain. There were a series of sounds of complaining wood and one of the wheels leant alarmingly to one side.

'We're too heavy for speed,' shouted Rúadhan. The wheels were wobbling badly as they headed to the path's entrance. The wagon was starting to come apart.

The warriors were also having problems with the ground and had slowed their horses down from a full gallop, judging that their current speed would cut the cart off before it could reach the path.

Rúadhan looked around and made some calculations.

'Here,' he shouted, handing the reins to Donnacha who was sitting up front with him. 'We're too heavy. Don't stop. Get her to the caves no matter what.' And with that, he slid down from the moving cart and drew his swords.

‘Rúadhan,’ Eoghan shouted. ‘What are you doing? Get back on the cart.’

Rúadhan looked at him as the cart moved away. ‘Get Rhíona to the caves, Eoghan,’ he called to his friend. He turned to look squarely at Rhíona. ‘I hope he’s there.’

Then Laoise was gone too, landing easily in the soft ground. The cart lurched forward picking up pace with two less people.

Eoghan watched her walk over to his friend. He waited for her with a huge smile, and they kissed then in the face of the danger ahead.

‘Rúadhan,’ called Eoghan and the two boys exchanged a look. It all felt so out of control. He held up a hand and his friend did the same.

‘I knew all along you were letting me win the wrestling matches, Eoghan.’

As the cart moved away, Eoghan felt useless. He could not jump down to help them because he had no way to be of help. He thought for a moment of his father’s knife. What could he do against soldiers on horseback with that? He wanted to shout something more. He could not think of what to say.

The cart rattled and creaked its way between the trees into the long grassy pathway.

Rúadhan drew away from Laoise. She looked at the fast-approaching riders.

‘I like it this way,’ she said with a smile. She loosened her bandolier, so that her darts were fully exposed.

‘I don’t know why I jumped off the cart, Laoise.’

‘You did it because you are one of the Fianna.’

'I can't say I'd be very good at running through the woods quietly and that kind of thing. I'm quite noisy.'

'I know you are. I love you.'

'I love you,' he said and held up one of the swords to signal the riders to stop.

They were becoming more and more bogged down and they had slowed to a walk, after seeing the cart disappear.

They stopped in a semi-circle around the two youngsters.

A man with dark skin spoke. 'We have no time for flitting about here. It took us long enough to get through this swamp. Put down your weapons and walk away and you will live.'

'I suspect,' started Rúadhan, 'that you have heard tell of us, and of how many of you have died trying to catch us. Being on horseback in this terrain will hardly serve you well. It is likely you will fall and if that doesn't kill you, we will. Fionn Mac Cumhal is in that cave and they're going to get him. You will die here by one way or by the other; or you can turn and begone and neither Laoise nor I will think lesser of you for it.'

The warriors seemed to disagree with his assessment of conditions underfoot. They started forward to encircle the pair.

Laoise started to cast her darts with as much speed as she could manage. She aimed for the horses and hit most of her targets. They started to kick and rear and it became chaotic. One rider fell, his skull was crushed by a stray hoof.

Rúadhan leapt forward and found himself between two of the riders ten paces away after the leap. The warriors both cried out in the face of the *draíocht* they witnessed. Rúadhan lashed out Fionn's swords, which punched through the warriors' armour and into their midriffs. Then he was gone. He had arrived behind the horsemen. A single leap brought him up to stand on a horse's rear. He beheaded the rider and then leapt to a horse nearby. His swords flashed, and the man went down.

'Rúadhan,' shrieked Laoise as a sword swung down at her. She dived and rolled away only to have to try and avoid a spear lancing towards her.

Rúadhan leapt and found himself by her side. He parried the blows aimed at her. With startling speed, he disarmed spearman and swordsman. Laoise twisted to throw a dart at a rider bearing down on them. His arms came up to block, and the dart stuck in his elbow. She cast another that bounced off his armour, but a third was already on the way. It took him in the neck, and he fell gurgling from the frantic horse.

The riders regrouped, as they realised the damage they were taking. Laoise gave them no peace. She stood and threw her missiles. The horses and the warriors started to panic.

Rúadhan leapt and was among them. He found he could block the blows as easily as if they were from children. The blades blurred in his hands and where they touched, they hewed. The last two riders left mounted, suddenly wheeled their horses, and retreated.

There were moans and cries from some of the injured warriors. Rúadhan rushed to Laoise, and she collapsed in his arms. There was blood coming from her arm. He examined her and his heart almost stopped when saw blood coming from her ribs. The spear had passed through her arm and into the side of her chest. It was impossible to know how deep. Though her breathing was ragged from exertion and pain, it did not have the sound of a weakness in her lung.

'Is there pain?' He asked.

'I am a woman. We are not so affected by pain as you men.' She spoke through gritted teeth.

'We need Rhíona to have a look at you, I daresay.' He lay her down and after checking for danger, he started binding her wounds until he could bring her to Rhíona.

Up and Down Towards Objective

***

The caves are neither easy to find nor easily traversed.

Níl íseal ná uasal ach thíos seal agus thuas seal

There is neither low nor high, but down for a while and up for a while.

***

Donnacha stopped the cart and jumped down as they left the path. He started to unhitch the failing horse.

'What are you doing?' asked Rhíona

'Ah now, I'm thinking this poor old horse needs a break, and we will not get too much further on the cart. I think it's walking for us, and a rest for the horse.'

Eoghan looked up at the stony hills before him. Lonely and bleak, they were a delicate mix of majestic and pathetic countryside. His heart was laden. Questions over his decision to leave Rúadhan and Laoise gnawed at him. That said, the path he had chosen to walk before had left little choice for anything else.

'Should just keep going this way?'

Rhíona was looking too, perfect eyes wide and alert.

'Yes. I can feel a presence up there. It is drawing me.'

Donnacha finished unhitching the horse and poured some water into a little rocky hollow for it to drink. 'Then let's go that way.'

They ventured into the hills, wary of pursuit and spurred on by urgency. Eoghan's stomach was turning.

To find the resting place of Fintán Mac Bóchra. I am indeed in the middle of a fantastical story.

The mythical character of Fintán, the Salmon of Knowledge, had carved a place in history. He was a much-debated cause of mystery and speculation. Eoghan had heard stories of him since he was tiny. Stories told that Fintán himself was a shape changer who lived since before the first foot was set on the island and could assume many forms. They said he had turned into a salmon during a great flood that threatened to submerge the land and that after it subsided, he lived in a pond at Linn Féic along the river Boyne. A man named Fionneagas tried to catch Fintán the salmon over long years. He thought that whoever ate the salmon would be imbued with great wisdom and knowledge and forever hold answers that most never would.

In the end it was Fionn who tasted the salmon and inherited his legendary wisdom, thereby adding to his own legend and the stories of Fintán Mac Bóchra.

It had been playing a bit on Eoghan's mind about such a place for Fionn to seek refuge. Surely Fionneagas and Fionn had not buried the fish after eating it? Or had he changed form after Fionn had tasted his flesh.

Eoghan's nose wrinkled. It all sounded very mysterious and a fair bit rotten. He was still strangely excited. That he might shake the hand of the man and pay him respect for his great deeds.

The foothills they trekked continued to be marshy and made for slow passage. Purple heather and yellow gorse were thick in patches and covered large areas to add to the difficulty. All three were preoccupied, lost in their own thoughts and expectations. It was only as Donnacha turned to check for pursuit that he realised they had passed by the entrance to the caves two hundred paces before.

There was little to herald the existence of the entrance. A break in the gorse and a view of flat stone on the side of a small hollow. Indeed, they were not sure until they stood facing the hole in the ground. Eoghan noticed a trickling stream from the higher hills rushing inside ahead of them, as if eager to ensure the cave was as cold and damp as possible.

Perfect for a salmon's resting place.

The cave mouth opened into a narrow dark passageway. It was damp and cold as the little trickling stream suggested it might be and nowhere near tall enough for them to stand in. If they were going to find

Fionn Mac Cumhal in the ground, they were going to do it wet.

They picked their way carefully through the passage. It quickly became dark. As it got darker, it got steeper. They came to a shelf that descended into black. Donnacha turned to the others.

'Now, I will say this without trying to sound unenthusiastic, but it would not be wise to leap forward into darkness, at this point. I think the world down here can be an unforgiving place to alight blindly.'

'We have no torches or anything we could use to make them.' Eoghan found it strange to be listening to the man, though he couldn't clearly make out his features.

'Close your eyes for a moment. Both of you. Please,' said Rhíona quietly.

'I can't really see anyway,' said Eoghan peering down into the pitch-black recess.

'My eyes are adjusting a little,' said Donnacha. 'I think I can see a rock.'

The men allowed themselves a little chuckle. Eoghan felt he had known Donnacha all his life.

'My request still stands. Please.'

They looked at each other grinning sheepishly and did as they were asked. She put her hands over their eyes.

'You must both remember not to rush into anywhere there is light. You will damage yourself if you do. You will need extra time for your eyes to adjust if there is light. Remember.'

'How long?' asked Donnacha.

Eoghan was curious. 'What are you doing to us?'

Rhíona said nothing. Her cool hands started to feel lightly warm on his eyes. More warming comfort than heating.

She removed her hands, and he opened his eyes to find her smiling at him. He blinked several times. It was as if he could see perfectly, except all of the colours had fallen out of the world. It was black, shades of grey, and white. Then it was her smile.

As Donnacha looked around the caves in wonder, Eoghan looked at Rhíona. Her smile made his insides ache. When she looked at him, it gave him a wave of warmth just as her hands had moments before. Her smile faltered a little, as he stared at her, yet she didn't look away.

'Ah. Perhaps... we should have a look,' interrupted Donnacha, who must have stopped looking around and found himself standing ignored and awkward. 'Oh. I see the way has become clear to us after all.' With his terrible attempt at moving things along he filled the passageway with further awkwardness.

Sure enough, however, the mysterious pitch-black problem had been solved. A slight drop of two naturally occurring steps led to another narrower passageway and led them into a small cavern. The bottom of the cavern was filled with a pool of chill tranquillity. The ceiling arched upward and then down to the back wall, which seemed to mark the end of their journey. The discomfort of cold, wet and awkwardness was set aside for harsh disappointment. Donnacha and Eoghan exchanged glances.

'I think we might have the wrong cave if you're with me,' mumbled Donnacha.

'No,' said Rhíona brow furrowed from concentrating. 'Something. I can feel it somewhere here.'

'Something you say?' enquired Donnacha.

'Somewhere where?' asked Eoghan.

'There is a way.'

Eoghan walked slowly into the pool and pushed his way around with his toe in case of sudden drops. His feet were numb with the cold after a very short submerging. He shuddered at the thought of losing his footing and falling in.

As he came towards the back wall of the cavern, the water levels had risen to his knees and his teeth were chattering. The cold was starting to move up through him. His head was the only part of him that wasn't affected.

My head is strangely warm.

Looking up, he smiled, despite the cold.

'Here we are,' he said with as much excitement in his voice as he could muster. 'You will both have to get your legs wet. We'll have to help each other up as well.'

Splashing behind him and more teeth chattering marked the arrival of his two friends.

'A salmon's leap would get you up there, young Eoghan,' said Donnacha mustering far more excitement.

'I fear that if I put my mind to it, I would leap too high and shake the foundations of the cave with my mighty skull.'

Rhíona, who was standing below the opening in the cavern ceiling suddenly leapt. Though it was just under the height of two tall men she disappeared over the lip and managed not to do damage to the cave or her skull.

The two had become somewhat accustomed to her alien actions yet both found themselves in awe.

Donnacha and Eoghan looked at each other. The white teeth of their smiles were particularly striking in the colourless world where they now existed.

'Are you two planning on joining me up here?' She was looking down at them, the white of her teeth on show.

Eoghan joined his hands and leaned forward. Donnacha placed his foot on and leaped as Eoghan lifted. Once up Donnacha leaned down and extended his hand. A leap from Eoghan with a hand to help him reunited the three.

Another long tunnel lay ahead of them sloping downwards. Misshapen jaws with stalagmites and stalactites, like sharpened fangs, were a gaping maw ready to swallow them. It was as Eoghan looked past the teeth, that he noticed a tiny show of colour at the edge of his range of vision. His hand shot up to alert the others.

It took them a moment of adjustment until they were staring at the little corner of colour, eyes narrowed.

'What is it?' whispered Donnacha.

'Fire,' Rhíona whispered back. 'Somewhere up ahead.'

A shiver of excitement passed through them, and they moved forward in a crouch, slowly, and without sound. The colour spread as they neared, welcoming them forward. It was a source of heat and light. Donnacha and Eoghan started to blink as their eyes adjusted.

Eoghan found he could see less as they neared the light. Tears started to well up in his eyes. He was tempted to ask them to stop, but his curiosity got the better of him. Half blind and blinking would have to do.

When the passageway opened into a large cavern, he had no choice but to stop. The colours were making his head swim, and his eyes close. He felt a hand grasping his arm. Donnacha. Rhíona's *draíocht* was wearing off in the presence of a source of light. 'Will we be like this for long?'

The voice that answered was not Rhíona's.

'You may not have that long to live. Your eyes are not the problem.' The deep voice was halting as if the words were heavy and unfamiliar. The voice was filled with uncertainty. 'One of you tell me fast, why you have come here and invaded my home?'

Eoghan never wanted to be able to see clearly more in his whole life.

The Plains of Capall Liath

***

Cónán and Éine are brought before the second ambassador and his horde. A number of unlikely turns greet them there.

Is fearr go mall ná go brách

It's better late than never.

***

Moghrugh's band followed the oxen-led chariot across the plains of *Capall Liath*. They had been marching at pace for hours and even a cruel taskmaster such as their ambassador general knew that respite was required. His menacing voice carried over the din caused by the band and its passing. 'Eat. Rest. Quickly.'

He found himself irritated by the hint of shrillness in his orders; a reminder of age threatening to undermine his command. For centuries he had been wreaking havoc across many lands. Laying siege to great cities and sacking tiny villages; bringing about the rise and fall of nations; masterminding bloody battles and executing multitudes.

He had proffered his services to many masters in innumerable campaigns, with varying degrees of success. He had outlived them all and now he was in the employ of a great master; indeed, a master who had sacrificed much. Perhaps too much to ever recover? The Fae *Rí* was just that: a king like the many others who had been cast aside by their actions.

Moghrugh's cracked lips twitched slightly. One road or another, the day drew near where he could claim his prize. He did not doubt that the Fae had more *draíocht* but once this world was conquered, the Fane would surely come to survey his new domain. Moghrugh would then have his chance, to create a new kingdom, standing over the corpse of his master.

The din soon became a raucous cacophony as preparations were made and orders followed. The mercenary horde busied themselves with resting and eating. Few among his followers were ignorant of their responsibilities. Those who were, were made aware by their peers with alarming brutality. They were heavy-handed war makers. Sell-swords mainly, who had witnessed their fair share of the horrors of war and violence: hard men, and harder women. Moghrugh felt at home among them; at home with their wicked tongues, moral ambiguity, and sickening smells.

Moghrugh drove the chariot onto a rise near the bottom slopes of the adjoining foothills and dismounted. Here lay huge misshapen rocks, strewn over the lush grassland, deposited in the days when the Fae *Cailleach* Sélath had frozen the world. It looked as if the plains had been the setting for a great game played by the gods, with the ancient boulders as their pieces. The army occupying the plains brought the game of the gods to life - his gods would be pleased.

And like a child who saves his honeyed apple until no longer distracted by the goings on of the world, so the general called upon his guards to bring up the alleged warrior of the Fianna.

The captive was brought through the ranks, the scene arousing the curiosity of many. Moghrugh resisted feelings welling in his rankled bowels. One of the *Féinnid*? Alive? Could it be true? He drew his sword, the grey blade that had beheaded John the Baptist, Pope Sixtus II, and so many others. The sword that had seen him rise from a solider to the great general he had become. A great sword for a great general. He had never thought to name the blade. It was an extension of his own power. It was his arm sharpened into a deadly point. A grim smile at the thought of treating the blade to another execution. It would be an enjoyable diversion.

Éine had been waiting in the long grass behind one of the huge rocks, as close as he dared to the army. He marvelled and was afraid as he looked out upon the sea of men. Armour and sharpened weapons gave the lustre of a wealth of precious silver to the gathered host. Black and brown shades hinted at the malice they represented. The band, weary from the chase and thirsty for blood, numbering close to five thousand, turned from their hurried meal to face their giant general.

Moghrugh stood before them, weapon free, his sightless eyes turned towards the prisoner, long dirty hair draped over his face like a tattered and ancient veil.

A sharp gesture from Moghrugh caused him to refocus on events, and the guards cast Cónán down onto the muddied grass.

Moghrugh's sword danced as if searching; prying until it came to rest upon a shoulder that belonged to the prostrate Cónán. Cónán's head suddenly snapping up to face his captor, suggested the sword had not alighted gently.

'Have a care you shrivelled up, blind old stinking goat raper. Or by my word, I will take that sword and impale you in such a manner that farmers will use you to scare away crows,' he growled, spittle spraying from his bloodied mouth.

A long silence followed.

'Are you struck dumb now as well as being blind, decaying and as useless as a sodden faggot, or would you like me to come back at another time so you can consider your responses?' queried Cónán.

'Guard, release me.' He ordered loudly. 'Your General seems to be uninterested in conversing with me and would rather reflect on the day's happening thus far.'

Éine cringed. Maybe once Cónán could have kept his mouth shut. Just once.

Someday Cónán's inability to do so will land us in trouble, he thought bitterly.

'Mac Morna?' whispered the old druid incredulously. 'Surely it cannot be. How… why would…' Looking visibly shaken, cracked lips pursed, Moghrugh descended into thoughtful silence.

Éine heard Cónán speak louder in a harsh rasping voice. 'What say you now, druid? With only one working eye between the two of us, we would make some fine show, were we to duel before your band of milksops.'

Silence.

Unease amongst the observing troops was growing. They were used to an interminable confidence and certitude from their master, and such a public display of apparent shock was jarring to many.

Their shock ended when Moghrugh threw back his head and laughed, his hawk feathered armour rattling loudly, as if irritated by this intrusion of humour. Many of his followers had never heard the general's laughter before and found it more unsettling than if he had been in one of his usual bouts of foul humour.

'Perhaps the question would be best put before those milksops of whom you speak,' said Moghrugh, amusement causing his cracked eyelids to hike slightly, as if threatening to reveal some untold horror beneath. His voice lifted into the evening wind, 'What say ye my fine men, ye men of honour and good standing? By my word, do express your notions and innermost thoughts. Wish ye to see a duel between cripples, or would ye prefer, perhaps, a swift and brutal execution to stay this cur's wagging tongue?'

The silent response left little doubt. The warband had no patience for a duel between cripples. Many returned to their impromptu meal, knowing it would be over as soon as the scene before them concluded.

Moghrugh spoke next for Cónán's benefit alone.

'It seems you are yet to make a decision as to where your loyalties truly lie,' he whispered, voice now like acid. 'Yet unfailingly, you have again chosen to side with the losers, you witless prick. And so, bound and trussed, I will strike you down like the conniving pig you are. I will leave you for the foxes and maggots and worms. I can only imagine the terrible ache they will feel in their stomachs after digesting such an ass.'

Éine was torn between action and retreat knowing neither course could save the life of his ally; knowing too, that only one of those courses could save his own. Yet the logic of the unfolding situation could not be ignored, were he as blind as Moghrugh himself or as dull witted as the oxen that led the druid's chariot. He had missed his chance to extricate himself from the ever-increasing complexity of the situation back at *Uisneach*. His life was now surely forfeit. In the stories he told, a saviour army would appear on the plains behind them. This was not one of his stories. The army was surely countless leagues away. He surveyed the scene with a rising sense of despair. *Tairne Glas* leaned against a small rock close to the captor and captive. It looked beautiful.

The question then arose of how Éine File Cú Mac Éine would face his impending death; and it was answered by a most unexpected choice.

And so, it came to be that on the plains of *Capall Liath*, Éine the cowardly poet, leapt from his place of hiding, and in nine great strides, went to stand before an army. He scooped up *Tairne Glas* as he went. Behind him, the sun began to retreat, red and angered, in the grim realisation that it had again been flanked by its melancholy nemesis that crept slowly across the sky. Éine drew his borrowed sword and moved quickly. He needed to reach up on balancing toes to touch the tip of his weapon against Moghrugh's filthy neck.

He cast out his great voice so that all around could hear.

‘You will free us both or your general will suffer the terrible wrath of my sword *Tairne Glas*.’ The weight of Cónán’s blade caused his wrists to tremble with exertion. Not for the first time Éine wished he had spent more time with practice blades; sweating and striking for long hours with his comrades.

Silence again.

‘You,’ he roared at a stunned looking nearby guard. ‘Release my man from his bindings and make it fast. And, let me tell you, should any of you move for more than a pulse or a breath, or should any of you make a sound more than that of a starling’s whispering wings in distant fog, I will shower myself in the black blood of your master.’

The words had not yet finished escaping Éine’s lips when, with incredible speed Moghrugh’s blade swept from Cónán’s shoulder to catch *Tairne Glas* above the rain guard and dislodge it from its trembling wielder’s grasp. The sword tumbled away from the place where it was needed the most, with no empathy for the plight of its erstwhile master or more recent handler.

The watching army laughed heartily at the miserable rescue attempt, and Cónán seemed to bury his face into the earth while muttering something. Éine surmised he was being cursed by his companion, but only the worms in the ground below Cónán’s face would ever know the crude details of such.

Not one witness, participant in the fracas or worms below them could have anticipated what happened next.

As the guards drew their own weapons and made for the poet, he threw himself at *Tairne Glas*, rolled his body as he picked it up and hurled it with all the might he could muster, in the direction of Moghrugh.

Moghrugh was probably the most startled of all when he realised that the *Draoí* sword had passed through his neck just above the armour, and through the thick protective torc. Blood - more crimson than black, flowed from the wound onto his chest and the lush grass below. He tried to express his sudden onset of rage and amazement but died before a word left his lips.

'Now,' shouted Éine. 'Now.'

His voice rang out in the most commanding tone he could muster while trying to put a *geis* on those watching. 'I am your general, now. You will follow me, and I will treat you well. Your master was cruel, where you will find me fair. Your cause was evil, where you will find mine to the benefit of the land. I am your general now, and you will do as you are told. And the grandchildren of those who love you will speak of you in reverent tones for the great deeds ahead of us. The guilt of your nefarious past deeds will no longer haunt you as you sleep, as we carve out a place in history that will rival that of the Fianna themselves. Join me.'

Once again, the plain was silent. Many of those watching, were still trying to make sense of what had happened. Others seemed to be considering his argument. Éine's voice was having its desired effect. Maybe, just maybe, there would be a way out of this for the two Fianna. Éine would have to consider his next words very carefully, as even the slightest distraction or rogue word could render his *draíocht* useless.

It was Cónán's laughter that broke the strange silence; and oh, how Mac Morna laughed.

Éine stood with his hands slumped by his sides looking at Cónán, who had begun to change colour and continued to laugh helplessly. The guards stood slack jawed.

'I thought… you… were… supposed to… be a… coward,' managed the strange man with the sheep's fleece back between racks of hysterical cackling. 'That was magnificent.' He looked over to see the lifeless body of Moghrugh. 'And you,' he howled. 'You killed him. You.'

Éine watched his attempts at heroism fall asunder. He wondered what had led him to leave the safety of the perfectly fine rock. His legs began to shake from exertion, and he dropped to his knees.

Some of the observers began to laugh, as did the guards. Éine, perplexed by what had happened in the last two minutes of his life, realised he was laughing too.

The guards drew their swords and walked towards the pair who were now shaking with laughter, teary eyed and resigned. And that was the time that Cónán Maol Mac Morna and Éine File Cú Mac Éine died laughing, as the men who killed them laughed too.

The Path of Backward Glances

***

Rúadhan and Laoise find themselves standing before the ferocious advance of the third ambassador.

Is fearr súil romhat ná dhá shúil i do dhiaidh

Better one look before you than two behind.

***

And so Laoise and Rúadhan came to be walking on the path of Righteous Reflection, which was called the path of backward glances and known by some as De Faoites' way.

The path of backward glances. How strange a name for such a place, thought Rúadhan as he walked.

The path was in fact an incredibly straight and very long grassy trail, bordered and enclosed by tall overhanging trees with thicket and hedge between. The pathway cut through the boggy mire that featured on either side. The improbability of such a pathway was one thing on its own but combined with how it had lasted in such good condition spoke volumes about the effort that must have been involved in its construction. It was an incredible thing. The grasses were wild, reaching their knees in places and making for slow going. It was an eerily quiet corridor unlike anything either he or Laoise had ever seen.

The tall grass showed evidence of the passing of the cart before them. The others were long since gone. Laoise and Rúadhan had fallen far behind and Rúadhan's mind reeled. He had no answers to the ever-growing number of questions about what may yet befall him and his love. Laoise's pain was obvious, and though she struggled to move as fast as she could, Rúadhan could see they would never catch up at this rate.

He checked back to gauge how far they had travelled. Slow, slow going.

Rúadhan thought of carrying her but knew that he now represented the rearguard of this insane quest and may require his strength to defend both his love and his friends from following foes. Their enemies would certainly be making ground quicker than Laoise and he.

He looked back but could see no sign of pursuit. He hoped that, should they decide to follow, they would have the decency to come in staggered waves of one or fewer; or preferably unarmed, drunk as piss, and perhaps even crippled. Though his new-found talent in the use of Fionn Mac Cumhal's famed weapons had come easily, and made him powerful, he was desperately afraid. The weapons were just that and he was just himself. Rúadhan smiled ruefully as he glanced backwards again.

Maybe it's not such a strange name after all.

Laoise saw him smile and mistook it for a gesture of support. She visibly straightened and smiled back. She smoothed her hair from her face and attempted to pick up the pace. There was blood flowing from her bound arm and ribs.

Rúadhan loved her. The cool breeze against his skin felt different than it had. The long grass bending underfoot was lush and the trees were brilliant green and brown. He felt a terrible urgency to have her wounds seen to. He was sure she would be well. She was so strong.

His first goal, however, would have to be to get them both to safety, and help the others if he could. Warm and longed-for homecomings, he knew, were not going to take place in the nearest future. He needed focus.

Rúadhan felt a strange feeling in his stomach reminding him of everything he wasn't. He pushed the feelings away quickly. He was what he was, and as his Grandmother Jillín used to say, "head down to milk the cow you're next to and bring the stool with you when you're done." He shook his head slightly. In truth, he had never been sure what it meant. Indeed, Grandmother Jillín's head was probably touched by the Fae.

With his next backward glance, however, Rúadhan spied his death at the entrance to the Path of Righteous Reflection. In the distance, standing at the entrance to the concealed track, stood the third ambassador sent to thwart Fionn's would-be saviours.

The Unspeakable Beast had found them.

The huge figure, of wicked points and deadly potency, effused a chilling shadow that filled Rúadhan's weary heart with dread. Squatting patiently, the thing observed the path before it with calm intent. Its features were an amalgam of all things ferocious and cruel. Taloned hands rested on the ground before it. Its face, though blurred resembled a hound. Yellow protruding fangs and a crown of jagged horns labelled it like no hound before. It's rippling muscular torso was set upon huge legs like that of a prize bull.

Rúadhan knew that they could not both outrun such a creature, nor would he be its match in battle. His mind raced. They were dead. His hand moved imperceptibly upwards towards one of the swords over his shoulder. If they died together, then they would be together with the gods and his people now gone. All he had to do was plunge a blade into her neck and his after, and it would save her the horror of what was sure to come. Any of the Fianna would surely do the same for it was right and the alternative seemed beyond imagining.

He was not of the *Féinnid.* He cursed himself and everything he wasn't.

As it began to stride forward with a speed that belied its hulking size, the Unspeakable Beast let fourth a victorious bellowing howl that caused Laoise to spin suddenly. 'Gods, what is it? What is that, Rúadhan?' she whispered, her weakened form shaking.

'Listen to me now, Laoise,' he replied instinctively, standing between her and the thing, trying to steady his voice and offer wisdom. 'Get up and go as fast as you can after the others. I can't go with you. By my hand must our flank remain shielded, and I can protect you as you go. I'll catch up when I can.' A cold shiver ran through him as the stark realisation of his lie attempted to overwhelm him.

'Up Laoise,' he roared urgently. 'Up and off with you now. The darts won't hurt him enough. Don't look back, just go.'

He turned back to find the path was not as long as he had imagined.

The Unspeakable Beast bore down upon them with vile and cruel intentions. A malevolent mind behind menacing black orbs focused solely on the pathetic beings before it; a blotch of frenzied darkness that covered the distance between them with alarming swiftness.

'I'll stay with you,' said Laoise. He turned and her eyes bore into his. Time seemed to slow and halt around them. All the barriers that can exist between a man and a woman were gone. In those seconds, they adored each other and knew love like few others had known or will know until the passing of time ends. Poetic words of promise, or flowered descriptions of devotion would mean little to them. They were two and there was one. They shared and understood. They gave and accepted, and for those brief moments, their paralyzing fear was forgotten for exultation.

Rúadhan held her as far away as his arms allowed.

I'll kill it. That's what I'll do. I'll cut it into pieces, he thought, as he stared at his strength and his weakness standing before him.

'You watch. Watch me so. I'll kill it,' he said as his hands reached over his shoulders in a way that was becoming familiar. Bran and Sceolan, the Adopted Blades of Fionn Mac Cumhal leapt into his hands.

Laoise's eyes were still locked on to his and she murmured, 'Hold me and let him send us away.'

A tear trickled down her smooth cheek and her brow was furrowed. She knew the truth.

He noticed a freckle amongst the perfect depressions and wondered how he had never come to notice it before. He wanted to tell her. He wanted to tell her so many things he hadn't thought of.

'Stand behind me,' he ordered. She moved alongside him and drew two darts.

Rúadhan walked out to meet the ancient beast of evil, and the beast was given reason to pause. Its touch was death and its legacy far reaching and heinous, yet this man now stood in its path where to do so was to face certain doom.

Rúadhan's newly begotten blades seemed to want to go to the beast. They hummed in his hands and responded to the slightest movement as if alive and a part of his own flesh.

'Stop. Stop there,' said Rúadhan with a level voice and a clear gaze. 'Best that you head off quickly you ugly… black hound thing. I am no Fianna warrior, but I will chop your head off, if you come closer.' Rage bubbled under the surface of his seemingly composed exterior. Anger, in knowing that now he had found rapture, this creature could steal it away from him so quickly.

The beast began to move forward again, slower; the shadow around it seemed darker as it approached. Black eyes flicked towards the blades and a sneering lip curled further. The lush grass grew cold and faded against its cloven hooves. The cool breeze chilled Rúadhan to the core.

Laoise's heart was filled with adoration and fear. Her whole being sang with pride as her love stepped between her and their certain death. Rúadhan seemed to grow in stature before her eyes. He had changed from the boy she met to the man before her; tall and strong; his blades shone cold. The beast approaching looked less ferocious and her fear became diluted by streams of hate. And the streams became rivers. And where another may have felt helpless in her stead, in that instant Laoise knew what to do.

She opened her mouth and lungs and from deep inside her came a terrible cry, borne of her love, and of her pride, of her fear and her hatred. A sound of fury that caused the beast to hesitate once more, unused to such embittered defiance in place of the usual dread. It told the story of their love and the power that bound them together. It told of towering heights and plummeting depths, vast distances and intimate closeness. Lifting her darts to her mouth, she poured her hatred into them, and prepared to throw.

Rúadhan heard the sound and knew pure joy. His breath caught as the cry caused his heart to swell, sending *draíocht* coursing through his body and soul. He raised his swords, crossing them once in salute.

The beast roared a demon wail. A wail that had paralysed countless brave warriors with fear. A wail that had left stronger and weaker men alike weeping and calling out for their mothers.

Rúadhan, instead, strode forward boldly, and at the last, as Laoise's scream echoed through his own swelling heart, he thrust himself towards the black heart of his enemy.

Eimear Ceannasí

***

Eimear leads a warband onto the field of battle against a superior force. A change happens to her.

Is treise dúchas ná oiliúint

Nature is stronger than training.

***

As Eimear arrived on the plains of *Capall Liath* with her horde behind her, she looked before her and was afraid. It was not the same fear; however, faced by those gathered for war. The army of Moghrugh was there and their colours were of blacks and of browns and their presence was as a blight on the land itself. The evening's fading light added ominous shadow. Something stirred within her.

Her breath became ragged, though she tried to hide it, to appear strong in front of her lieutenants. She had known all through the years that she might see battle once more, yet she had hoped against hope that she could run away or surrender or fall upon her own sword. Anything so as not to have to draw it again.

She had gathered mainly light infantry *Ceithearn* and two sections of horse riding *Marcaigh*. Her men and women numbered somewhere in the region of two and a half thousand. Her outriders reported that they would be outnumbered by almost two to one. She clicked her horse forward and it trotted confidently onwards. She was grateful.

No scouts from her enemy had been sighted and both she and her advisors were perplexed. Indeed, as they made their way onto the plains, the army of Moghrugh did not seem to be aware of their arrival. There was something distracting them to a man. The *Ceithearn* were divided into two sections with the *Marcaigh* into two sections on either side.

There would be no call for champions to fight in the fore and no time for subtle military tactics. She would send the two *Ceithearn* sections on a mild arching march to attack the front from two converging angles and use the *Marcaigh* to disrupt the larger cavalry of the enemy and protect the flanks. She and two hundred *Marcaigh* would remain behind and remain vigilant and prepared to provide offensive or defensive support quickly.

The apparent ill preparedness of Moghrugh seemed to give Eimear unexpected initiative, as unnerving as it was for its unlikelihood. She did not dwell on the matter and took to the business at hand.

Eimear had assigned the command of the two sections to the most obvious leaders she could. Her left was commanded by a mercenary named Mac Ulladh. He was a weedy, sickly looking fellow, with a razor-sharp wit and keen eye. While these traits alone may not have marked him a leader amongst many; combined with his obvious knowledge of battle and the fact that his lover was an enormously intimidating bullock of a man who only answered to the name Pan had led him to stand out from his peers.

The other flank would be led by an old farmer named Ó Roinn. He was a practical man who ironically leaned at times towards hyperbole. He had a raucous humour that appealed to his soldiers, however, and they respected his voice. He had an aura about him that marked him for future greatness. Eimear had no notion of a more rigorous selection process. He stood out as the leader and that was that.

Some looked at her for words. Her mouth was bone dry, and her lips were sitting upon her teeth as if belonging to someone else. She was bursting to make water and was unsure if she could hold it. She had no words. Yet still, silence seemed to fall now before her, and more and more faces turned in her direction.

Moghrugh's army were aware of them but had been caught off guard. As a result, they were in a state of near-panicked preparations.

She stood in her stirrups and searched for something to say that would spur these brave people towards great deeds. She desperately searched through her memories for heroic speeches or timely wit, for an idea or ideal. She had heard and seen many great orations in her time. Fionn had always been able to pick words from the sky that would lift those in his command. In those days, however, Eimear would not have needed motivation.

Those watching her on the plains of *Capall Liath*, saw the warrior woman, Eimear, standing quietly astride her mount in the face of impending chaos, waiting for utter silence and the attention of those under her command. Admiration rose at the thought of this woman being so calm, without fear and apparently immune to the gut-wrenching terror most of them now faced. Her icy gaze passed across the face of each man and woman as if searching for strength.

When she finally spoke, her voice was louder than she expected.

'If you have come here for flowered words of glory to stir you, then you have come to the wrong place. I have not one. We passed an inn at Ó Dúlraigh's *Túath*. Go back there and they might have a storyteller if you feel cheated. But let me first remind you, in case you have forgotten. An army of black hearted whoresons over there want to kill you and everyone you know. I am not here to talk. I am here to kill them.' She spurred her horse on a few steps.

'Don't stand there looking at me. Kill them all and we'll go back to our families and know that they will be safe once our work here is done.'

Two and a half thousand voices erupted in a blood curdling roar. Faces turned almost in unison towards the enemy. As the roar abated, the roars of the captains took their place and they continued to raise fire in bellies as commands were issued.

Eimear *Ceannasaí* watched as the army, her army, took to the field and so began the Battle of *Capall Liath*.

Let them have this victory because it is right. Let them do it without me.

Moghrugh's army was still in considerable disarray and again Eimear found herself confused. This was not what she expected of his command. That, or something had gone awry for them, which was giving Eimear a huge advantage. Either way, the battle was upon them and it was time to see who would win. She moved her horse along as close as she could while still able to get a view of all that might happen.

Her newly accumulated advisors rode behind her but not too close. They had learned not to advise unbidden. One of them still bore a large blackness around his eye from when she had taught them that lesson.

'Split and watch both flanks carefully. I want regular reports whether there is anything to report or not. Find something to relay to me. If I join the battle, find me anyway. I want to know everything as it happens or before. Actually, before is better. Go. Now.'

She did not look behind as they split themselves and galloped off to take staggered positions behind the quickly moving army.

Eimear could hear the roaring of her captains and a strange yet wholly familiar feeling of calm came over her, like seeing the face of an old friend. There was nothing else she could do for now. She looked around and saw a great rock protruding from the ground off to her left. She turned to Fáinne Buí, the round-faced girl who was in command of her floating *Marcaigh* section. 'Stay here and be more than ready. You're going in very soon. One way or the other.' It had been a long, long time since she had felt these feelings. Her hand moved slightly closer to the hilt of her battered old sword. She looked down. The sword moved a little towards her fingers.

Clicking her horse forward towards the rock, she stood on the saddle and leapt onto the least steep side and then sprightly up on top. She could see the armies approaching each other, surprisingly close to where she stood. Her calm was replaced with euphoria, and she had to stop herself from cheering and shouting support.

The two fronts met on the plains. The mercenaries were just about organised, and gaps started appearing in Eimear's lines. The problem of number becoming clear. Twice as many bodies is hard to see a way around, and Uad's mercenaries were doing what they were paid to do. The battle was becoming fierce. Aggression alone, Eimear knew, would only go so far. She had seen the use of an arching march towards the front many years before and had learned that the angle a *Ceithearn* created by their approach served a twin purpose. Firstly, it meant that the mercenaries' front was forced to stretch slightly, with luck, opening gaps in the ranks. She had long since realised that soldiers like to engage in warfare at the same time as their peers and may rush forwards to get to the fighting at the same time. Secondly, the two sections slowly started to funnel the mercenaries together pushing them in on each other and making it difficult for them to disengage. The whole notion of positioning and angled approaches made sense to her as a fighter; use of position and angle was how she won fights. Not using the same for her army would be anathema. Position and angle; then all that was left was to control one's fear and anger, which had never been an issue for her.

This battle would be less jab, parry and thrust; more bludgeon, beat and bash.

Reports started coming in from her advisors. Mostly just testing their voices and reporting for the sake of it. Eimear gave her head an imperceptible shake. They were spouting nonsense, and it galled her how useless these men and women were compared to those at the front. She had seen many battles, however, and was aware how important they would become should the battle draw out. Rivers of blood had washed past her in countless conflicts. She gave her head a second shake. She could hear something else too. The music was calling her.

Mac Ulladh was mounted slightly behind his section on the left. There was no sign of Pan, but Eimear figured he was covered in blood by now. Indeed, as she thought it, she spotted his huge frame at the front line. He had a long spear and small round shield and was using one to skewer and one to pummel. What he lacked in skill, he made up for in blunt aggression. As she watched he was trying to un-skewer a writhing blood-spraying mercenary from halfway down the shaft of the spear using his shield to push as well as defend himself from a hacking axe.

A burning desire pushed her to get to Pan; to stand beside the great lug of a man and carve future stories from the mercenary ranks. She closed her eyes and stilled her mind. The longing had always been there. As she had sat in the long grasses of her valley, watching the creatures she adored; swam in the brown, silty lakes; gorged on the delicious honey of the valley bees. The longing had whispered then. Now it roared. It screamed. The prevailing sound of those battles long since passed had always been screams. The screams had made the music that she most adored. Her eyes stayed closed. The music of the dying.

'*Ceannasaí*,' came a panicked voice from below. Eimear shook herself out of her digressing thoughts. 'Ó Roinn is down from a stray arrow and the section is showing signs of collapse.' The advisor had a long cut across his forehead and dripping blood was making one of his eyes close. He held a sword and it too was dripping dark crimson.

A grim smile creased her lips. This was more like the battles of old. Blood covering the plains, and there was always more. She looked down to find her hand wrapped tightly around the hilt of her sword. *Sciobtha*; it had come to be known, but that was not what she had called it.

Her gaze drifted to the right and she could see a clearing forming in the centre front where the *Ceithearn* were lacking in leadership and the mercenaries were regrouping as if sensing the advantage.

A giant strode from their side swinging a long sword hacking at those who had not stood clear in time. He cut men and women into pieces, screaming guttural screams as he did to add fear to the minds of his increasingly uncertain enemy. The music… but missing something… something only she could produce: truest despair; purest suffering

A grim smile as she watched him scream his curses. The giant was cunning in this way. He was a veteran and understood how such fear at such a critical time could cloud minds and begin routs. Eimear started to hum quietly. The sad tune that her father had sung.

Her arm rose and she signalled the riders behind her to make ready. They would never make it in time. It had happened too quickly, and the right was now surely lost. The giant, as if sensing this, started to march forward, swinging and roaring. A chant came from the mercenaries as they continued to regroup behind him and prepare offence. Eimear's stomach dropped and she felt the urge to vomit. This was the beginning of the end and it had happened in a flash.

Then she froze. There was sudden movement from the *Ceithearn* front. In the face of her comrades backing away and turning to run, a lone soldier detached and ran towards the giant. Eimear stood very tall as she watched. The soldier had a spear and threw it at less than twenty paces from the mark. The spear passed through the upper leg of the giant, who roared in anger. The soldier drew a sword and leapt into a spinning attack. Long flowing hair marked her as a woman. Her sword became a blur and the giant only just managed to block it. The woman spun again, and her sword slashed at the giant's midsection, which the giant's armour deflected. The giant swung a broad stroke in return, but the woman dropped and spun again, kicking the giant's lead leg, causing him to stagger forward a step. She swung her sword downwards and the giant's head was removed from his shoulders. Eimear's heart was thumping in her chest at what she was witnessing.

The soldier dragged off a helmet and turned to face the *Ceithearn*. Eimear watched the woman call out to her allies. Eimear could make out the long tawny hair of the woman as she turned to her comrades now. Two sliver streaks that ran from her temples were caught by the dim sunlight, as she held her sword tall and appeared to be shouting. A silver torc gleamed around her neck. Attackers from the mercenary line ran towards her as she continued to implore the *Ceithearn* to follow her. Eimear's eyes started filling with tears, that she wiped away quickly. She longed beyond reason to hear what words the woman was saying.

Eimear opened her mouth and she found herself making an unfamiliar sound, as the female warrior turned towards the oncoming ranks of the enemy, alone, sword raised. She blocked a sword swing and cut an attacker down. Then in two bounding steps she leapt up onto another attacker's shoulder, then onto the tip of the now vertical spear that had passed through the giant's leg and soared above to descend into the seething mass of warriors with her sword swinging.

The *Ceithearn* suddenly surged too, in an effort to support the heroic warrior woman. The mercenaries attacked simultaneously, and it became like a scene from the darkened lands of the Fae. Eimear's teary eyes searched for the tawny hair with the silver streaks but never saw them again. The battle became a faceless thing once more. The brave actions of that one lone warrior had turned it around, however. She had certainly saved the *Ceithearn* for now.

For now.

The reality of the field was increasingly obvious to her. Her side was losing. The numbers were too great, and a rout was imminent.

It has been too long, whispered Sword.

It has.

Will you let me free?

I will.

Eimear felt herself smiling as she hummed the sad tune. Her heart soared; knowing that the music was to come. She thought of Donnacha for a moment and wondered if he could love the music as she did. He had heard the screams. He had heard the music when he slaughtered that family. Maybe he loves it too.

In one lithe movement, she leapt from the rock onto the back of her mount that stood almost thirty paces away. Many of the riders behind her gasped openly.

When *Síor Feargach* turned to them her eyes had gone entirely white and become cold and deadly like a hungry pike. The rest of her face, though deathly pale and smoother than it had been a moment prior, was devoid of emotion. *Síor Feargach* surveyed the battle before her. It was time for her opus. They had forgotten her. She would kill them by the hundreds. I will make such glorious music so the gods themselves will listen and despair.

'Follow me,' she said. Turning back to look into the ranks of the mercenaries attacking her people, *Síor Feargach* drew Sword, *Sciobtha*, for its intended purpose for the first time in many decades. A spray of fresh blood of the deepest crimson arced before her as she drew. It dribbled down the blade, dripping from the tip onto the grass below.

'Or not,' she added, voice flat.

Síor Feargach rode into battle then. Terror rode before her and death beside her. And the music she made was deafening.

THE FINAL DECISION OF FIONN

***

After a strange meeting with the man, Fionn is presented with the realities of the world outside.

Má tá tú ag lorg cara gan locht, beidh tú gan cara go deo

If you are looking for a friend without a fault, you will be without a friend forever.

***

As the recounting of events took place, all three interjecting in parts in an attempt to identify crucial information that Fionn should know, his gaze bore into the rocky walls of the cave. Eoghan and Donnacha had spent the last while blinking frantically to catch a glimpse of the man they had searched for, but they could only make out basic detail.

Fionn was tall and fair.

The sound of three voices became too much to bear. Fionn held his hands out. 'I... I am unaccustomed to this. To so much... talking. I was thinking of something. I must finish.' He turned to move back down the cavern towards where the torches burned the brightest.

'Wait,' cried Rhíona. 'You do not grasp the urgent need that has accompanied us.'

Fionn's head shook without turning back to them. 'There is a *sceach*, a patch of briar, near enough to here. Each Autumn, I harvest its blackberries when they are presented...' There was a long pause. Eoghan wondered if that had been his point or had he more to add.

'Over long years the bush and I had a share of... disagreements. It would scrape at me, and its thorns would lance my skin. At times I would tire, not relieving it of all its worthy fruits. Over time I began to ask it for aid so that it would not cut me so that I would not tire as quickly. It learned to allow the breeze to bend its branches towards me and I learned to be patient until it was free of its ready fruits. Over time I would arrive at the *sceach* and the picking of fruits would be painless and swift. I would spread some of those seeds around the *sceach* and tend them as they grew and spread. We have become friends. I must finish being... thankful.'

He walked over to where a small fire was lazily burning embers, knelt before it and bowed his head. Rhíona made to move closer, and his voice sounded once again. 'Do not move from that spot.'

After what seemed like a half a day's passing, he stood once again.

'The Fae girl presents what would be quite the dilemma.' His voice was coming back to itself though he seemed disinterested in looking at the invaders. 'My name was burden enough, yet alas, not enough.'

His eyebrows rose as if he was trying to convince… someone… but his gaze never fully focused on anything.

'I could not choose if I had to. There is no right way or wrong way; just two endings.'

He shook his head sadly. 'It's the end.

'For countless years I watched and protected the people of this land, until I was rejected like a thorn from the *sceach* too long in my thumb. I have sat in here for many long years, feeling the *draíocht* leaving. I knew too that it could not leave fully with me here. But I never meant to leave.' He pointed to a corner of the cave. There was a dusty hunting horn sitting by the wall. *Dord Fionn*.

He looked at Rhíona. An unblinking, hawk-like gaze. She stood, steely eyed, and stared back.

'You know of what I'm talking about,' he said. 'What would you have me do? You know the decision I must make. Stay and fight for the people once again or leave them to whatever fate awaits. You must have an answer to have navigated through such perils. What would you have me do, child? Why have you come if you do not know what is required of me?'

Rhíona turned away.

'Ah,' he said. 'You have a mind to take the decision out of my hands entirely.' He threw his head back and laughed. 'I admire your resolve for contemplating such a course of action, young Fae princess. I suspect that you would have a difficulty in killing me, but it might be interesting to see your reaction after failure.'

Eoghan and Donnacha looked over at Rhíona. Were the *draíocht* still over their eyes, the heat and colour of her face would have had them blinking once again.

She spoke quietly but with a more assured tone than she should have. 'I am aware of your plight. I'm afraid I have neither an answer nor words of wisdom from which you could take comfort. I know only this: the time has come for you to choose or have the choice be taken from you. Both my people and Uad's seek to remove it. I thought that, perhaps, I could have helped you in some way. I felt ashamed that one who had given so much would be left alone. I was asked to kill you. I never really...'

'…had any idea what you were being asked to do,' smirked Fionn. 'I am no ordinary man now. I am more. You are a child. No more. There is much to consider. I think it is time that you leave. I wish to...'

Eoghan stood forward. 'We have endured much to find you. And find you we did, before any of the others. So perhaps it is time for you to decide. Perhaps not so much this monumental choice which you dread, but a more reasonable one in its place. Decide. Do you wish our aid, for our part, or would you prefer us to leave you alone until the others find you, which they will, Fionn Mac Cumhal. We may not be the Fianna, or warriors from some old legend but we are here, and we are in as much danger as you. If we leave now, it is likely we leave to meet our death outside these chambers.'

The cave went very still when Fionn Mac Cumhal laid eyes on Eoghan. Eoghan suddenly felt ice in his stomach as if a hand of frost had grabbed his guts. Fionn walked slowly toward Eoghan until they stood almost nose to nose.

'You must have courage indeed to speak to me in such discourteous tones, boy. Was I not preoccupied in such a manner, then I might dash your brains all over my wall with a flick of my hand.'

It was Donnacha's turn to stand forward, arms unfolding slowly. His face was dark. 'I think… I think that you might find such a thing more difficult than you first imagined, no matter who you are… or were once. I think perhaps it is you who might need to mind their tone if you…'

'Stop it,' shouted Rhíona. 'Fionn, they are close, and you know it. You must act and as Eoghan rightly said, we're the only aid you will have. Caoilte, Rúadhan, Laoise, Éine and the others have fought and bled to get us here. Even Cónán Mac Morna. I see your problem, but it is a problem that must be solved now.'

'You see nothing,' roared Fionn, rounding on her. 'If I stay, then our land will be covered by Uad and his Fae co-conspirators. *Éire* will one day become the greatest nation of them all but its people will suffer for many long years under a mad man and his sons and their sons after. For generations the land will be raped.

'If I die or even go to the land of your people and close the gate behind me, then *Éire* will fade and will no longer have the strength to stop the coming darkness from the east. Do you understand me? Our country will die forever. A slow and tortured end. A tormented demise that will leave it vacant and insipid forever more. Which would you have me choose? Torture or death? I could risk trying to fight Uad or trying to raise an army and wipe him and his people off the earth but the Fae folk would find me and take me or worse. I managed to come back once because it was allowed. You are aware of the chances of my return should they not see fit to grant it to me.' His eyes were darting around as if considering once more. 'Maybe to kill him alone might be enough before they found me. But his rot has taken hold in some parts. And who would wield *draíocht* enough to stop his horrors?'

Eoghan shifted uncomfortably. This talk that he was hearing made him sick with worry. His legs felt like water. His stomach still a ball of ice.

'You are Fionn Mac Cumhal.' He hated himself for his near whine. 'Just about everybody thinks you dead. We are here because we believed... believe in you. If there's a decision to be made, then so it is. We cannot help you with it, but we can help to see it done.'

'And what would you do, boy?'

'I... like you say, I am a boy. Not a great hero. I have seen little in my time compared to you. How could I have, coming from a tiny village in the middle of nowhere? For me to give you an answer would be wicked because I would be speaking words without wisdom.'

'None of us understand,' said Donnacha quietly. 'But you do. You know what must be done, don't you?'

'And deep down inside you, you have your mind made up,' Rhíona said. 'You are too great a man not to have. The decision has been thrust upon you as many were before. You will do what you think is best as you have many times before.'

Fionn broke into laughter. An echoing chuckle, cold as the rocky walls. 'Do you know what the real problem is? The real reason I do not seek the company of Éire's men and women any longer? You spoke of it yourself. Belief. The *draíocht* is all but dead in their minds even though it could be as strong as it ever was. They don't believe. Nor do they believe in themselves.' He cast a gaze over his three young companions. 'You said that your belief got you here. You see how powerful it is; to know that you can and will succeed. The *draíocht* must die. But to ensure its death will steal the soul of our people. What we once were will be gone.'

Fionn looked up at something behind them. There was a small sound of movement. Eoghan, Donnacha and Rhíona spun around to find a tall, pale skinned man with streaks of silver through his shoulder length slick black hair. He was dressed in unremarkable clothing except for a pendant that hung from around his neck that was glowing green. Behind him was a large black opening in the cave wall that had not been there a moment before.

Fionn spoke quietly. 'Maybe you don't sound like such a bad option after all.'

An End

***

The end of this.

Go n-éirí an bóthar leat is do chosán cóngair

May your journey, long or short be a success.

***

Eoghan pulled Rhíona behind him and Donnacha's bow leapt into his hand without making a sound.

'Put away your bow you fool.' hissed Fionn, but Donnacha started notching an arrow. His face broke into a huge smile.

'Uad, I presume. Well met, good sir. I envy your hair, and your jewellery must be the talk of the town's ladyfolk, mustn't it indeed? I must say, however, I thought you would look grumpier, so I did.'

Uad's cold gaze turned on Donnacha. His head tilted slightly.

‘Put away the bow, lad.’ barked Fionn with more force.

Rhíona rushed to Donnacha’s side.

‘Put it down, Donnacha. Now. Put it down or he’ll kill you’

Donnacha took a step towards Uad. His bow string pulled taut and came to rest against pursed lips.

‘What do you think? Aill’en didn’t manage it. Will you kill me?’

Suddenly, the only sound in the darkened space was the almost imperceptible hum of a tightly drawn bow string.

Uad’s sigh and glance at Fionn gave the impression of utter boredom. When he spoke, his voice had changed. ‘No farmhand. Kill yourself.’

Fionn moved to close the distance between Donnacha in a single stride. He spoke quickly. ‘It’s you who’s in control. Put his words from you. Wash your hands of them. Listen to my voice and your own.’

Donnacha released the tension on the bow. He dropped it and held onto the arrow. ‘Rhíona?’ He asked quietly.

His eyes looked desperately confused as he tried to plunge it into his own throat. Fionn’s hand became a blur and intercepted Donnacha’s wrist.

Rhíona shrieked and rushed to his side, desperately trying to pry the arrow out Donnacha’s hand. Fionn whirled to face Uad; face dark and furious. Eoghan could not believe what was happening. The world was falling apart in front of him, and he was completely helpless. Like a child in the world of adults.

‘Attend to my words, boy,’ Fionn implored. ‘This thing you do is not your work. It is a choice like all the others you will face or have faced before. Trust yourself to make the right choice but then follow the path you choose. Do not think the thing, do the thing. Put your hand down and drop the arrow, son.'

'I cannot control my own arm,' whispered Donnacha, a tear fell from one eye.

Fionn's free hand raised and swung. Donnacha was knocked senseless to land ten paces away. His eyes rolled in his head, and the arrow fell from his grip.

Fionn walked towards Uad, his steps heavy. His knuckles were white, his eyes, cold as ice. He raised his mallet-like fist and brought it crashing down onto Uad's face, where it bounced harmlessly off, as if an invisible helm was sitting atop the man's head. More and more blows rained down but had no effect. Fionn stood back, gasping.

Uad smirked, his hands grasping the pendant around his neck. 'You know as well as I do, I cannot be harmed by you or that whore witch, Mac Cumhal. My warmly received gift ensures this. So please, spare me your anger. It will do no good and you do not wish to irritate me further. I assure you that I am irritated enough as it is.' Uad's fist lashed out. Fionn flew backward to land beside Donnacha.

'The fact is that now I have true *draíocht*. *Draíocht* that you could only dream of. You have become soft and weak. These two,' he gestured, 'and many others will live or die by your hand. You will come with me, and we will hammer out a new arrangement and our land will become strong again. We will knock down the barriers that have kept us separate and let the *draíocht* spill back onto our plains; into our lakes and streams; into the towns and villages. There will be no land greater, no rulers more powerful. Do you not long for this as I do? Has this not been your dream more than all others over the long years with which you have guarded the coasts? Pain upon you.' His hand shot out again and this time Rhíona screamed loudly, hands clutching her head. She fell forward to her knees and vomited. Blood spilled out of her mouth and covered the stone beneath her. Eoghan cried out and went to her.

Fionn stood and walked slowly towards Uad. The two men stood before each other.

'Nevertheless. You will do it Fionn. You will. Else, I swear, I will raise a new army and sweep through the land like a pestilence. I will knock anything standing and light the world ablaze. I will make them all pay, and it will be because you did not stop me the only way you can. Do as I say...'

Eoghan spoke suddenly. His tone was strange, ill-fitting for such a moment. He seemed almost relieved, as if something had been resolved in his mind. 'I feel like for the first time in a long time, I know what to do.' Rhíona's retching stopped and she looked up.

'Silence dog,' roared Uad. He cast out a manicured finger towards Eoghan and screamed. 'Take another arrow and stick it in your eye and it will teach you not to inter—'

'—rupt you?' interrupted Eoghan with a smile. Fionn and Rhianna openly stared at their companion. *No one knows what's happening. No one, except me.*

He ran a hand over Rhíona's soft hair, then he gently kissed her brow, stood and turned to Uad.

'You are a horrible man. But you are like any bully; any weakling who walks this land. You are afraid and you wear armour you have received from cupping someone's balls and being their pet piglet. And funnily enough, not one of you knows what to do next. With all your *draíocht* necklaces or legendary deeds or *draíocht* king and queen of all the Fae parents and pyramids the what-have-you like it. It's me.'

'Do as you are told. Pick up an arrow and kill yourself with it,' ordered Uad, once again.

'It's like Fionn said, my good fellow. I am in control. I choose not to do as you wish. You can shove your *geis* in your arse if you'll excuse my crude language. I know what to do.' He paused, closing his eyes and taking a deep breath. 'But what do I do then?' he murmured.

His right hand slipped unnoticed behind his back.

'Let's consider this in a practical manner. Fionn. It's time for you to go. Go and find your son. It is a chance for you to be at peace, not discussing things with blackberry bushes. Rhíona, you're going to go because you have to. I am very much in love with you and that is something sad I think, but the world does not really worry about one sided love stories. As for you Uad, I think you probably have several large armed men somewhere but came in here alone because you are a smug prick and perhaps have a liking for being dramatic.' He walked towards his increasingly bothered looking enemy.

'...and they, like you think your necklace can protect you because it gives you *draíocht*. I think they do not have what I have though. Like Fionn said: belief. The *draíocht* is leaving our world which shows that it is not as powerful as you all would think. I think that they believe the necklace will protect you. I think if they did not, then they would be here to protect you. But I think, no I believe, that neither they nor the necklace will be able to do much about this.'

Eoghan's father's non *Draoí*, very ordinary, knife entered Uad's neck at an upward angle and caused the man to be carried backward a step or two from the force behind it.

Uad was still standing, blood streaming from the puncture, face cast in a look of utter horror and disbelief, as Eoghan turned to face the two behind him.

They watched Uad fall backwards and die twitching as Eoghan spoke.

'You've done enough, Fionn. You've served this land as much as the land serves any. You have watched as we have come from the forests and have tried to steer us as best you can. You cannot do this forever. The land will be here for the rest of time, even when the wind wipes our dust away from it, the land will be here. You, living here, like this. It's no way for you to be living. Not you. The people of this land owe you nothing but love and respect. They will talk about your past deeds forever. There will be people to lead and take charge in your absence. I know that now because I know I could be one of them. Maybe. Or someone like me. Someone who is only part of their own story. Your future, Fionn, and your future deeds are not here. Your story is over here. It finished on that battlefield whether you died or not. Most of us will only be involved in one great story though we might try to involve ourselves in others. You have had many great stories and will have many more where you're going. All you have to do is go. There is *draíocht* in you to help you there. Go to Oisín.'

Rhíona was looking from one to the other. Fionn's eyes had glazed over as he thought deeply and drank in the young man's words. He moved slowly towards the walls that had come to protect him and his fingers moved out to them, touching, almost caressing them.

Eoghan spoke to Rhíona. 'I love you, Rhíona. I cannot help that it's the truth. Since the second I put that cloak around you under the tree. I love you and want the world to be a simpler place where I could take your hand and we could dance together or walk by a stream. It will not be like that for us in this world. Now,' he took a long breath, 'go back to your home and bring him with you. There'll be more of them in a very short while.' He reached out and wiped the bloody spit from her chin.

'I love you, Eoghan,' she said, voice thick, as if the tears she held back were trying to mute her. 'I want you to come with me but the *draíocht* in my world would make you mad or worse. And I cannot stay.' The tears that trickled down her exquisite face, glistened in the firelight.

'My beautiful land will be lost,' whispered Fionn, 'never to be found again.'

Both his hands were on the walls of the cave. His eyes closed as if he was trying to commune with the land itself; to relate his pain and struggle to it.

'If that is the case then so be it. Everything changes, Fionn. But you cannot still affect those changes without releasing the unnatural; blighting the world, making all those wonderful things you did, and sacrifices you made be in vain. Those stories of your deeds that will be told around the fire until the world ends would be forgotten. It is time, Fionn Mac Cumhal, for you to go. Finish this story so another can truly begin.'

He looked at Rhíona. 'Do it. They're coming. Go.'

She wept and shook as she reached out for him to hold her.

'There is no time. Do not forget me,' he said.

Her weeping became painful anguished cries, but she moved back from him and put her hands together raising them over her. She looked towards them hindered by tears streaming out her eyes.

The hands came down in a broad circle and up again. She started to speak quietly between miserable sniffles. Eoghan could not make out her words. She made the circle again slower and more deliberately. Then again, even more slowly.

Without fuss, flashing lightning nor peals of thunder a large hole appeared in front of her causing Eoghan to gasp and fall backwards landing on top of Uad's body. It was a hole. It would be hard to describe it otherwise. An oval of jet black like Uad had just stepped out of. It was like the black of the darkest night that allowed no light to enter; gave it no way to leave.

Eoghan could see Rhíona's legs from under it and could still hear her. This was Fae *draíocht* of a different sort. Every hair he had was standing on end as if craning to glimpse the spectacle.

'I cannot stay, Eoghan,' she said, as she came around from behind the doorway of nothing. 'And my heart is broken because all I want is here. All I want is you.'

Eoghan heard a noise from back in the cave and his heart filled with dread. 'Fionn, take her and go, fast.' He urged in as hushed a tone as he could manage. 'They won't be bothered with us once you are both gone.'

Fionn smiled grimly at Eoghan and looked over at Rhíona. 'You first girl,' he said, calm now. 'I don't want anyone on the other side to think that I am invading.'

'Eoghan... they are coming,' she said looking at him wretched and heartbroken. She reached out to him and pressed her lips to his. He could taste the salt of blood and tears. She pulled back and looked at Fionn, eyes welling up. Then she stepped into the blackness that opened up to receive her.

Fionn went to follow, then paused for a moment and extending a hand to Eoghan before crossing through.

'You are some man, indeed, Eoghan. A great man of times to come. It was an honour to meet you.' He paused for a moment to listen to the distant sounds of pursuers. Fionn frowned in the darkness. His ears seemed to perk up to some sound or other. Even in the poor light, Eoghan noticed his face turn pale.

'It is almost like Eimear's music,' he whispered. He looked into the black portal for a moment and then disappeared into the realm of Fae folk.

Eoghan heard the noises again. He looked but could not see those approaching. It sounded like there was fighting going on in the caves. Surveying the area around him, he spied the amulet that adorned his fallen enemy. He looked at it and then towards the *Draoí* portal, which was starting to get smaller now.

A thought struck him and caused him to make quite a rash decision, which was neither based on sense nor sound thinking. Whether he made the right or wrong decision or lived to regret it or died righteously; he took the weighty pendant then and hung it around his neck. He pulled his father's knife from Uad's neck and wiped it on the man's fine clothing before putting back into its sheath. He went to stand in front of the doorway, which was back to its original size and shrinking slowly.

He felt no different wearing the new jewellery. He felt no *draíocht* coursing through his veins. There were only questions racing through his mind.

Would the *draíocht* work for him or even against? What would it do to him if it did work? Where did the door lead and would the *draíocht* of the amulet let him pass? What would become of him if it didn't? Would the land of the Fae drive him to madness? What of the world he left behind? His mother had no knowledge of the world anymore. She would not know any different. His sisters would be left never knowing what became of him. They would manage well enough.

Rúadhan would know what to do to keep them all right. He would be happy with Laoise, and they would have a great life together. She was a good woman and made him a better lad. A better man. Eoghan knew Rúadhan would take care of his family.

He looked over at Donnacha; the strange, wonderful man who had wanted the world to be something it isn't. He was starting to move, reaching for a handhold with which to pull himself up. Maybe this world wasn't what anyone wanted it to be.

'Farewell, Donnacha.'

He had never said anything so earnestly before.

His hand passed into the black space, and it quickly grew large again enough to allow him passage.

Eoghan smiled, took a slow deep breath and stepped into the black.

A New Beginning

Síor Feargach came to that place then, as the portal disappeared. She watched Donnacha regain consciousness and as she did the rage lessened and Eimear took control of herself once again. The *draíocht* left her then, to follow Fionn as the gate closed.

She took Donnacha in her arms and the two swore their love for each other. Their work had been done and a long happy life awaited them in the valley at *Uí Garrchon*.

They walked hand in hand from the caves and the end of Fionn Mac Cumhal's time in this world.

They walked away at the end of the time of *draíocht* in this world.

They walked through the scores of her dead enemies, and were never heard from again.

PERCHEDCROWPRESS

Dear reader, thank you for choosing to read *The Last Five Swords*. We hope you enjoyed the ride. PerchedCrowPress are a small Indie publisher who pride ourselves in giving a voice to the underrepresented writers of Ireland.

PerchedCrowPress is an imprint of Philip Hughes Publishing

To find more information about PerchedCrowPress, you can visit our website at:

www.philhughespublishing.com

Contact us at: info@philhughespublishing.com

OUR HISTORICAL BOOKS

Conaire

During his reign, Conaire Mór was known as the Peaceful King. Reaving was forbidden and the five kingdoms were at peace. However, not all the people favoured peace - amid them, the warrior caste and it was only a matter of time before they once more took to reaving, reaving that would lead to the Peaceful King's destruction.

Cladáin takes the story of Da Derga's hostel and removes the faeries and the Sidh and leaves what might be the history of the event.

He builds believable characters that are a joy to read. I would recommend Conaire to any who enjoy historical fiction and Celtic mythology.

Amazon Customer

Available: https://www.amazon.co.uk/dp/B075X33W6F

Berserker

Conor Mac Nessa, king of Ulster, rapes queen Medb of Connacht on the banks of the river Boyne, which causes an inexorable sequence of events. The outcome of those events is war between Connacht and Ulster. As the tension builds, a hero of Ulster gets caught up in a love triangle which ends in tragedy and forces him to adorn the mantle of Berserker!

I really enjoyed this, though I stupidly realised just too late that this was the second in a series and must now go back and read the first one! Still, that hasn't spoiled anything. It takes a great deal of courage to pick up something so well-loved as the Irish sagas of the Red Branch and the Milesian Kings and dust them off. But the author has managed to do this very well. As he says in the closing notes, there are frequently inconsistencies and confusions in the versions that have come down to us, so here is a well-written attempt to fill some of the gaps, to take some of the more fantastical segments and translate them into a world that we can more readily understand - in the great tradition of writers like Rosemary Sutcliff and Henry Treece. Highly recommended!

David Ebsworth, Author of Historical Fiction

Available: https://www.amazon.co.uk/dp/B079V6Q2FR

Milesian Son of Light

I am dying tied to a rock! Connacht's finest are watching, waiting for my end. Too afraid of me to kill me, and too afraid of her to leave!

The hero is tied to a rock. He is dying, but slowly. The warriors of Connacht are sitting around their campfires, swords across their knees, watching, waiting. All can hear the flapping of The Raven of Death's wings. It is only a question of time. The hero will not stand against his rock and wait in silence. He knows it is his fearsome reputation holding back the warriors. He tells his tale. The true tale and they must listen, because to leave would be to invite the wrath of their warrior queen. And so it is that they hear the true story of the Milesian Son of Light!

Available: https://www.amazon.co.uk/dp/B07QH1JY48

I enjoy Irish myths and legends and what I liked about this was it was the familiar story of Cú Chulainn but told in a completely original way. All the politics and the action is very realistic, not at all magical. It's the grim and dirty version, as if Cú Chulainn was an historical person. Thoroughly enjoyable.

Conor Kostick, bestselling author of Epic

Milesian Daughter of War

Warrior Queen or Witch? Enemy of Ériu or Saviour?

The Five Kingdoms are about to discover!

Medb has been unsuccessful in her attempts to punish King Conor for raping her beside the banks of the River Bóand. Burdened by a weak husband and a weaker army, she pressures the kings of Leinster and Munster to bring war to Ulster; her professed target, Don Cuailnge, The Brown Bull of Cooley; her actual target, the head of Conor Mac Nessa, king of the Ulster.

In sight of her goal, Medb encounters the greatest hero Ireland has ever known. The hero's successes in holding her armies at bay, force the queen to ever more desperate measures until the boundaries between the Good she professes to represent and the Evil she is attempting to thwart are blurred to the point of nonexistence.

Available: https://www.amazon.co.uk/dp/B08GM7YGP8

After Gairech

Imagine a world where the Romans are in ascendancy; a world where Christ is soon to be born. A world where the Battle of Gáirech has ripped the heart out of Ireland.

Medb's armies have been destroyed! Survivors are ravaging the Five Kingdoms in search of the riches they were promised!

While working to repair the damage, Cathbadh is murdered and dies beside his son. Genonn vows to avenge his father. But, with the culprits locked away in their fastnesses, to break them out, he needs Elder Council approval, and they will not provide it without proof.

Genonn needs Conall to help get the proof, but Conall is gone, searching for the head of Cú Chulainn. So Genonn sets out to find him, aided by the beautiful Fedelm, the capricious Lee Flaith, and the stalwart Bradán.

Bernard Cornwell meets Ellis Peters in this historical murder mystery.

"I thought this novel was amazing!" – I Got Lost in a Book – Internet Book Blogger

Available: https://www.amazon.co.uk/dp/B093TF86Z4

Historical Short Stories

Genonn Rising

Taught by the druid, Cathbadh, Genonn goes to Ráth Droma as adviser to the chieftain. Young and idealistic, his moral compass is put to the test when the chieftain falls for the daughter of one of his land workers.

The girl is betrothed to a young woodsman. They are in love. The chieftain, Mathaman, wants her for himself but she refuses.

To get his way, Mathaman accuses the woodsman of stealing a sheep. He will be strangled with the knotted hide if Genonn cannot prevent a miscarriage of justice.

Available: https://www.amazon.co.uk/dp/B08BDML5WK

Genonn in Shadow

Genonn has seen the injustice of his father's world, the world of the Elder Council. He has decided he does not want to belong in it. Overhearing some warriors talking of their exploits in a hostel just north of Átha Clíath, he heads for the Smithy of Cullen to have a sword made and go to The Shadowy Isle to learn how to use it. Despite ten years training to become a druid, Genonn's naiveté is no preparation for the brutality of his chosen path.

Available: https://www.amazon.co.uk/dp/B08GZGP814

OUR CRIME NOIRE

Archie's Problem

Bald Archie Moses has been the butt of peer jokes all his short life. Abandoned by his mother when only a few days old, maltreated in the orphanage where he grew up and discharged by the army he loved as family, Archie takes pride in a role as a bodyguard to celebrities. While defending his client, Archie is arrested and then sent by his lawyer in search of a wayward son. What should have been a simple job turned into an Odyssey. An Odyssey during which Archie falls in with his antithesis, and together they pit their combined wits and muscle to the detriment of a vicious Camorra clan.

Archie's Problem is a fantastic book. It's well written, well thought out, and if you like twists and mysteries, this is the book for you. [...] The characters are well rounded, the settings come to life in Hughes['s] capable hands, and I certainly wasn't expecting the ending. I believe this is part of a series of books and though this one stands alone in its own right, I wouldn't mind reading the other two as well.

Gloria (Amazon Customer)

Available: https://www.amazon.co.uk/dp/B06WRV5BH3

Gigi's Cause

Released from prison after sixteen years, Gigi felt that he had something worth fighting for. It was not something that would have the masses scrambling to donate money they did not have to celebrities they did not like, but it was his, and he was proud to have it. Better a worthless something than nothing at all, that was Gigi's mantra. He was not to know that it would lead to love and ultimately to death, but it was Gigi's Cause!

Excellent read. Love the slightly dark comedy which [brings] the characters to life. Great descriptions of life in southern Italy. I have enjoyed all of the writer's novels to date. Looking forward to the next one!!

Amazon Customer

Available: https://www.amazon.co.uk/dp/B07451NJKX

Izzo's Solution

Pietro Izzo has been returned to his position as Senior Investigator for the Pozzuoli region of Italy's Antimafia squad, the DIA. High Command has finally realised that Sub-Lieutenant Cipolle was out of his depth and have busted him back to the role of Investigating Sergeant under Izzo.

Shortly after the inspector's reinstatement an American sailor is executed in the middle of the day outside the village bar in Lucrino, and Cipolle is killed by a sniper later that same day. Izzo must work with a Senior Field Agent of the NCIS to discover the killer. This becomes a major problem for the Italian, because not only is the investigator a foreigner, she is also a feminist.

A chauvinist and a feminist are a bad combination, but to be successful, they must learn to work together.

Eventually that comes to pass and together they achieve Izzo's Solution!

I loved this book. It took me into the heart of Neapolitan life, as well as through a story of burgeoning romance. It has all the elements of a great read: love, intrigue, crime and blood. I highly recommend!

Amazon Customer

Available: https://www.amazon.co.uk/dp/B07B2YRPQH

The Hidden Syndicate

The Hidden Syndicate is the omnibus edition, which combines the trilogy Problem, Cause and Solution. As well as combining the three, it includes changes to the original stories to make them more enjoyable.

Available: https://www.amazon.co.uk/dp/B0862GX8W6

The Reticent Detective

'We are all outside the law, just some of us are further out than others.'

The words uttered by Laconto's stepfather, echo through the detective's mind as he tries to come to terms with his reality as a police inspector with a past, he does not want to discuss. He'd graduated the academy with ideals buoyed by innocence, only to have them crushed by policing a quasi-dystopian state, ruled by Mafiosi. 'Just some are further out than others,' bouncing about his cranium, a bat trapped in his one-room apartment.

Following his dream of crushing organized crime, Laconto encounters a transvestite mugger and his lover being hunted by two bent cops, all being manipulated by an unscrupulous Secret Service Agent.

His success or failure in the balance, he resorts to some questionable methods to achieve his goal.

Available: https://www.amazon.co.uk/dp/B07YGPGCBG

The Alcoholic Mercenary

They said, "See Naples and then die!"

Rachel had thought it was to do with the place's natural beauty. A misconception she soon lost after climbing down from the C130 troop carrier. Her predecessor's suspicious death, the murder of a sailor, and an enforced liaison with a chauvinistic and probably corrupt cop saw to that.

“See Naples and then die!”

Some said the saying was anonymous. Some attributed it to Goethe. Still, others said it was Lord Byron or maybe Keats. When the young brother of a mercenary hitman became her main suspect, Rachel leant toward Keats. Didn’t the poet die here? Somewhere near, for sure. He probably coined the phrase on his deathbed.

And then, the cherry on the top of her ice cream soda, she could smell grappa on the breath of the mercenary when she interviewed him—the only thing worse than a violent man: a violent man who drinks.

The only thing worse than a violent man who drinks is a violent man who drinks and considers himself Rachel’s enemy.

Printed in Great Britain
by Amazon

32681780R00260